THE BURN OF A THOUSAND SUNS

THE FORGOTTEN ONES
BOOK 2

JILLIAN WEBSTER

ALSO BY JILLIAN WEBSTER

Scared to Life: A Memoir

The Weight of a Thousand Oceans: The Forgotten Ones - Book One

The Echo of a Thousand Voices: The Forgotten Ones - Book Three

AUTHOR'S NOTE

This is a work of fiction. This story takes place along the western coast of North America, but it is not as we know it today. The oceans have risen hundreds of feet, and the coastline and climate have changed. Some geography and places have been altered, while others have been invented entirely.

For Lizzie.

PROLOGUE

A cloud of dust billows from Maia's feet.

Like everything else around these parts, the gravel has shriveled up. Caved in. Crumbled to dust like hollow bones of the earth.

A mirage of water hovers along the horizon in a tsunami-like, metallic wave. The hot air blowing across them is like the inside of a furnace, the heat so intense it nears suffocating. Every step is a struggle. It's as if Maia's legs have been wrapped in lead, weighing each foot down to the ground the moment she lifts it.

A scorpion scurries across the road.

The endless desert highway they now roam has been swallowed in oscillating mounds of sand, the scorched earth cracked open like a gaping spider's web. Any cement left exposed to the elements has been ruptured by the crooked arms of barren shrubs, desperately clawing from beneath the rubble.

Maia casts a glance at Lucas. A red cloth is wrapped across his nose and mouth like a mask, a thin layer of sand glued to the areas wet with condensation. His tired eyes squint against the early evening sun, suspended like a demonic orb in the hazy brown sky.

Another gust of sand hurls across them. Maia motions her hand to catch Lucas's attention. He nods, and he hands her a small rag, and she tosses him her staff. They've been switching the two items every few miles. The staff doubles nicely as a walking stick, and with just a flick of the wrist, the rag can swat away the relentless black flies, frantic for the moisture of their skin and eyes.

Maia's face is also wrapped with a bandana, now matted and drenched across her nose. Her auburn hair has been tied into a thick bun on top of her head, not only keeping her cooler but also protecting her scalp from the harsh rays of the sun.

A black shadow flickers across them as another circling vulture curls on a wing. The birds have been tracking them for miles, ready to swoop should one of them crumble to the ground.

Maia reaches for her steel canister, secured with a rope against the side of her pack. She brings the hot metal to her lips, delicately sipping the warm water and swirling it around the taut skin of her mouth. She crunches on a piece of sand before swallowing it down.

The vulture circles around again.

This Californian desert road has felt endless, but the wide-open expanse—albeit harsh—has been a blessing. It takes a tremendous amount of energy to constantly be on guard, and out here, they've got none to spare.

But the harsh terrain also filters out the crazies, so they don't have to worry as much about malicious bandits taking something they hold dear. There are no half-breeds—*bounders*—hiding behind seemingly innocent, rotted-out vehicles abandoned on the side of the road.

Like that one car in particular, with the juvenile cottonwood exploding from the hood.

With every skeleton of a vehicle they approach, they each take a side, splitting around it with a wide and cautious stance. So far, there has only been one body found out here, and he was far from alive. The only threats on this road seem to be the scorpions and the rattlesnakes—and even they want nothing to do with the lethargic, shuffling humans.

A rusted sign on the side of the road lies crooked and covered in layers of sand. Lucas swats the dust from the faded green metal.

Seattle 994 Miles.

Nine hundred and ninety-four miles. Maia's heart sinks. Having grown up with kilometers, she's not as familiar with the unit of distance, but she knows the number isn't good. They've been in America for over two months, and they haven't even traveled a hundred miles.

Of course, most of that time was spent hiding within the treacherous streets of Los Angeles, preparing for their four-thousand-mile journey up the new North American West Coast. Every day, they scavenged the crumbling, deserted homes and eerie, waterlogged streets in search of the right supplies. They planned for every possible danger, packed for every harsh and foreboding terrain. They knew they were using precious time staying in LA, but every minute was desperately needed.

Even still, after all that, she feels like nothing could have prepared her for any of this. Sitting around a fire in a deserted home *talking* about what to expect doesn't shield one from the numbing pain of swollen feet, open blisters, and a merciless desert sun. Or the bee stings, the slithering things, and the icy-cold evenings.

But, one foot in front of the other—they've discussed this. They've made a pact. There's no room for negative thinking, which, especially when out in the elements, can prove equally as fatal.

Just keep moving.

Lucas turns from the sign and his face drops. Maia's seen this face before, back when they were stuck on a collapsing raft of garbage in the middle of the Pacific Ocean and a storm was heading their way. Her heart plummets as Lucas slowly pulls the bandana from his gaping mouth, his eyes wide in horror as he scans the horizon behind her. He mouths something. She can't hear him, but she knows exactly what he said. She reluctantly follows his gaze and her rag drops to the dust.

"*Meu Deus*," she echoes as Lucas steps beside her.

They stand frozen before the swiftly approaching mammoth wall of sand.

Lucas turns toward her and yells through the barrage of dust suddenly pelting his sun-scorched cheeks, but she can no longer hear him.

Every possible danger.

Every imaginable terrain.

The billowing cloud mushrooms from the horizon, quickly choking out the last remnants of the sun. They should be running for their lives, but Maia is paralyzed by her thoughts.

What she wouldn't give to be back in the hellish streets of LA.

ONE

The once stagnant layers of grime now swirl along the surface of the murky waters. Maia nudges a floating teddy bear with the tip of her finger. Drowned face down, its fur is matted with thick layers of dust. Lucas is ahead of her, slowly wading through the flooded mall's thigh-high waters.

They crane their necks as they scour the massive lobby for a map. Heavy layers of black mold sprawl across the cathedral ceiling windows, interrupted only by the occasional beam of light streaming through its broken glass. Rows of suspicious murmuring pigeons perched along the ceiling's high ledges glare down at them as they carefully maneuver around another rusted grocery cart tipped on its side.

"Careful around these escalators." Lucas's whispers echo across the lobby. "Lots of broken glass around the railings."

"Escalators?" Maia whispers back.

"Yes, the stairs here." He points toward the steps

leading down from the floor above. "They're called escalators. They used to move so people didn't have to walk down them."

Maia studies the corrugated metal steps. "Move ... And go where?"

Lucas smiles, shaking his head. "I'll explain later. We need to keep moving."

They quietly shuffle past a row of submerged benches engulfed in weeds. Maia's foot slips beneath the black water. She sinks to her chin and her hands slide along the gritty tiles below.

"You okay?" Lucas wades back toward her.

She gains her footing and lifts herself out of the muck, nervously scanning her palms.

Lucas grabs her hands, flipping them front to back. "*Nada?*" he whispers.

"Nothing."

"Good. A cut is the last thing we need." He looks around. "Okay, back on the ship, Mario told me there would be maps in open areas like this. Look for some sort of framed glass, something that would have information on it."

Maia glances around. They're in the middle of something called a mall, in a lobby of some sort. Dark halls extend in every direction while four different escalators descend from the floor above, circling them with tarnished metal railings. In the middle of the room, a Romanesque statue of a man is emerging from the water. His marble fingers reach to the ceiling as if in a desperate plea for help.

Nestled against one of the back walls is a large glass frame supported by a stand.

"Lucas," Maia whispers.

He stops in a beam of light and turns toward her. His long curls are tied off his face, half-hidden once again under a thick beard. He looks at her with that same serious Lucas face, the face she has probably seen far too much of these last few weeks living in LA. Always worried. Always on guard.

She tilts her head, smiling at him, and his features soften.

"You okay?" he whispers.

She nods toward the sign. "Could that be what we're looking for?"

He twists in the water, following her gaze. "Could be."

They carefully wade toward the sign. Slowly. Methodically. Their feet search beneath the black waters for sure footing before taking each step.

Maia tears the vines from the glass while Lucas scoops water between his cupped hands, splashing it against the cracked pane. The water rolls down in tiny balls across the layers of dust. Lucas wipes the sign with the back of his fist, revealing a diagram of multicolored boxes. He sighs in relief.

"Okay, Mario said that our best hope to find supplies would be from places most out of reach. Difficult places." He glances at Maia from the corner of his eye. "Dangerous places."

She nods.

He looks back at the map. "There should be a shop here that used to sell hunting equipment. Mario mentioned it will be at the end of one of the dark corridors and will have many floors. The most coveted supplies will be underwater on the lowest levels."

He continues to wipe the frame. Along the far edge is an index. He drags his finger along the glass. "Here, I think this is it." He looks up, scanning the massive space for the correct entryway. "There." He points. "It will be down there."

They both look in the direction he points—a gaping black hole leading down a corridor. A curtain of vines hangs from the opening with a green *Emergency Exit* sign dangling half-unhinged from its post, slowly being pulled from its grip by a vine's leafy tendrils.

Lucas looks at Maia, his eyes plagued with doubt.

She grabs his hand. "We have to do this. We need more supplies before we try to find your brother, and this city is *tragically* picked over."

"Yes, okay," he says with a sigh. "Let's get this over with."

Together, they wade across the expansive foyer to the corridor and push through the vines. Lucas reaches into his pack and pulls out a small flashlight. Flicking it on, a white beam cuts through the blackness.

The ceiling appears to be pulsing. He flicks his light upwards, revealing hundreds of sleeping bats.

"Oh, *God*," Maia whispers.

"It's okay. They won't bother us if we don't bother them."

"I guess that would explain the smell," she says with a grimace. "No wonder this water is so dark."

"Try not to think about it."

Lucas sweeps the torch back and forth across the flooded corridor, guiding their path in bursts of light as they navigate their way deeper and deeper down the dark passageway. There are much smaller shops down here, their busted-out storefronts tattooed with graffiti, thick weeds, and a lacework of vines. He shines his light inside each but only briefly. One by one, they are all the same, their insides long gutted from years of looting.

"That torch is amazing," Maia whispers. "I can't believe Jake would ever part with it."

Lucas is quiet. "Yes, well," he finally says without looking at her. "They had a few. They were very kind to me with their supplies."

Maia's foot rams into something beneath the water. "Lucas?" she whispers.

"What is it?" He shines the torch into the murky water, but the light only reflects back at him.

"I don't know, but it's not completely solid. Do I step over it?" she asks.

"Go around."

She nudges the mound with the tip of her foot, slowly inching toward Lucas. A metal shelf sticking out from the water slides off the submerged bulk, sending small waves in every direction. Lucas shines his light where Maia now stands. A few air bubbles break the water's surface, and a bloated body of a man emerges.

Maia recoils, her hand at her mouth. The back of his matted head has been gravely injured, his skull caving in at the site of his wound.

"He's not very decomposed, Lucas. People have been down here."

"Let's keep moving."

Lucas continues to sweep the torch's light across the corridor, stopping every so often to listen for noise. It is eerily quiet, save for the occasional flutter above. His light pauses on a row of vending machines looming before them, a perfect place to hide. He holds up his hand, telling Maia without words to *stop*. Pulling his knife from its sheath, he takes a wide angle around the machines, searching the surroundings with his torch. He stops and glances back at Maia. "All clear."

Finally reaching the end of the corridor, they are met with a large wall of busted glass doors. Lucas's flashlight skims the rusted letters sprawled above them.

Outdoor World.

"This is it."

They carefully step through the doorways of broken glass. Once inside, they wade past lane after lane of small black screens, the drawers below them open and emptied. It's a scene Maia has come across her entire life. Those drawers used to hold papers and coins inside that held all the power in the world—a power now as useless as the papers. She wades past the closest lane. Its empty drawer sits on the countertop, untouched and covered in dust. A few paper bills still float beneath it.

They reach the railings of another set of escalator stairs peeking out from the water, leading down into a gaping black hole.

"I think this is it," Lucas says.

They stare down into the murky depths. Maia unzips her pack and pulls out a bundled rope.

"Let me go first," Lucas whispers.

"But I'm the stronger swimmer."

He takes the rope from her hands. "Maia, this is a fight you will never win."

She sighs, and snatches the torch from his hand, shining the light on him as he unravels the bundle. He ties it around his waist and knots it a few times, then hooks the rest of the rope around his shoulder. Fumbling below the water, he unties his shoes, then hands the dripping sneakers to Maia. She sets them on the counter behind her, then turns to grab his shoulders.

"Okay, start packing your lungs like we've practiced. We'll do the first round together." She holds up her pack, and he loops his arms through the straps. "As soon as you dive, I'll start counting," she continues. "After thirty seconds, I'll tug the rope, and unless you give three sharp tugs back, I'll start pulling to help you get up as fast as possible. If you need me to pull at any time, just tug the rope once."

She holds up one finger. In unison, they take a deep breath and hold it. She uncurls a second finger, and they fill their puffed cheeks with more oxygen and push it down into their lungs. Lucas nods and turns toward the escalators. Without hesitating, he dives into the black hole leading to the lower level.

Maia exhales, and Lucas's tiny beam of light disappears beneath the murk, leaving her blanketed in darkness. She grips the end of the rope as the water sloshes against the shelving.

One one-thousand, two one-thousand, three one-thousand.

After thirty seconds, she tugs the rope. No response. She pulls hard, one hand over the other, grunting from the weight as her feet slide beneath her. She props them against the bottom of the escalator railings for leverage.

Just when she's about to panic, the light of the torch cuts through the blackness, and Lucas breaks the surface with a desperate gasp. She holds the escalator railing and pulls him to shallow water.

"Are you okay?" she whispers. She takes the torch from his hand and surveys his body for cuts.

He looks at her, but can only respond in gasps.

She lifts the pack from his back and he wriggles out his arms.

"What's it like down there?" she asks.

"There's not much," he says, still catching his breath, "but we'll keep diving. It's hard at first not to panic and vision is limited." He unties the knot around his waist, then hands it to Maia and takes the torch from her. As she works on tying it around herself, Lucas clears his throat. "Any chance you can use those powers of yours to hold your breath longer?"

She looks up at him, unsure. "I wouldn't know how. But I can hold my breath for a long time. I've been diving my entire life."

"I have too, Maia, but it's pretty unsettling down there."

"Where should I go? No point scouring the same area."

"Yes, dive straight to the back. There seems to be a lot more the farther back you go. Looks like hunting supplies back there."

Maia smiles.

He grabs her hand. "Be careful. Don't let your rope get caught on anything. It's a mess down there. Keep it wrapped like this." He hands her the bundle. "And let it unravel as you swim."

"Okay."

"Don't forget to keep track of time. The farther back you go, the longer I have to pull you out, and the more dangerous this becomes."

"I know, Lucas. I can do this." She puts her shoes next to his on the counter.

"Don't be stubborn! Listen to your body—"

"Lucas, *I've got this.*"

He grabs her face and kisses her. "Okay," he finally says. "Just be careful."

Maia takes the torch from his hand and wades to the end of the stairs until her toes totter on the edge. She works through packing her lungs and dives down. The water is disturbingly warm. She places the torch between her teeth, and the light cuts through the darkness in a narrow beam. She kicks farther down, gliding above the long trail of escalator stairs as the rope unravels around her arm.

Once at the bottom, her light trips over layers of toppled shelving covered in a thick blanket of sand. The mountains of rubbish seem to blend in one muted mess. She sweeps her light across the clutter until she sees the back wall.

She's only just arrived and can already feel the strain on her lungs, like a balloon about to pop. Panic sets in, but she pushes it down, kicking deeper through the chaos of half-floating boxes, shreds of clothing, and endless bits of debris.

The darkness and the wreckage seem to close in on her. Lightheaded and disorientated, Maia twists within the water. Which way are the escalators? She traces the trail of rope beneath her with her torch. Reassured, she flips toward the back wall again, scanning its contents with her light.

And that's when she sees them.

Still encased in flooded glass are what appear to be a

selection of carbon hunting bows. Made with a system of cables and pulleys, they give the hunter a power and speed unmatched by any handmade bow.

Her lungs thrash beneath her chest. She's out of time. The rope unravels around her arm, and she grabs hold as Lucas pulls from above. Kicking ferociously, she swims up the escalators, desperate to take a breath.

She gasps as she breaks the surface and swims toward Lucas's open arms. "I didn't ... get anything."

"It's okay. Take a rest. I'll try again."

"Back wall. *Go*..."

"Yes, I've got it." He unties the knot from her waist and winds the rope around his arm, then dives back under.

Maia stands gasping in the dark, starting her count-down again.

When Lucas comes back up, it's sooner than before. "I'm out of practice," he says, coughing. "I had to turn around before I reached the back wall."

Maia is more determined than ever. She can do this. She has held her breath many times diving for food. But then again, there was an endless ocean above her. And light. And she wasn't in a flooded mall in the middle of Los Angeles with danger lurking around every corner.

That back wall. That back wall has everything they need. She must get to that back wall.

Plunging beneath the water, Maia follows the same path as before. Her tired lungs begin to ache, but she keeps kicking, gliding over the mountains of refuse and bins and shelving. Her light sweeps over the back wall as she tries to ignore her panicked lungs.

Reaching the bows, she bangs the glass with the back

of the torch. Air bubbles escape her pressed lips. She hammers again—nothing. She scans her light around for something sharp to break it.

Breathe. Need to breathe. Can't breathe.

More air bubbles escape.

She's waited too long. She tugs the rope and holds on tight as it drags her along. Grimacing, she covers her nose and mouth. The pressure from her burning lungs feels like it's ripping her from the inside out.

Can't ... breathe...

She's on the verge of passing out. The rope tightens around her waist, and Lucas tears her from the water.

"*Maia*!" he screams. "That was too long!"

Wheezing and coughing, she falls into Lucas's arms. "I ... made it ... to the ... back wall. There are bows down there."

He sighs, holding her until her breathing calms. "Maia, what good is a bow if you're not here to shoot it?"

She pushes away from him. "I have to go back down."

"No."

She laughs. "*No*?"

"It's too dangerous, Maia." He gazes down at her. Then shaking his head, he adds, "I don't trust you."

"I can hold my breath longer than you. I'm the only one between the two of us that can make it that far." She coughs again. "Those bows ... just *one* of those bows will make all the difference in the world for our journey. It will allow us to hunt and protect ourselves in a way that far exceeds any homemade bow. And they're *right there*. I just need to break the glass. Give me your knife."

Lucas reluctantly hands her his knife, and she tucks it into a zipper on the outside of her pack. He glares at her as he winds up the rope, then lassos it around her arm and hooks it over her shoulder. "This is the last time, Maia. I won't lose you over a bow," he says dryly.

"You won't. I'll get it this time." She doesn't wait for a response. She fills her lungs and dives back down. Gliding through the water, she is focused. Resolute. Her lungs begin to panic but she's already at the glass. She keeps her flashlight between her teeth and pulls the knife from her pack, driving it hard into the case. Nothing. She stabs again. And again.

Fractures splinter across the glass. Her lungs burn. Panicked, she continues to bang. Hard, *harder*. Desperate for air, her chest feels like it'll burst.

This is all in her mind. She needs to calm her mind. There's plenty of oxygen in her blood. She'll be okay— she knows this.

The glass has fractured, but it won't break. The pressure from the water must be holding it in place. This is her last shot; she can't come down here again. She closes her eyes and focuses on the energy of the water surrounding her. Hovering her hand just outside the case, she pushes the weight of the ocean against it. She opens her eyes, watching in awe as the glass splinters further.

She rips her hand back, and the glass shatters across the gloom.

Maia's rope tugs hard and without a second's notice, begins to pull her from the bows. She reaches for the wall, but Lucas has already pulled her too far. She twists within the water and grabs the rope, tugging back three times. The rope slacks, and she kicks back through the floating layers of shattered glass.

Grasping the bow with both hands, she places her feet against the wall and rips the contraption from its mount. She swims farther down and grabs a container of arrows. The rope around her waist tightens once again. She wraps her arms around the glorious carbon as Lucas drags her across the ceiling of the enormous warehouse and up the escalator stairs.

Breaking the surface, she thrashes as Lucas shouts. Grabbing her pack, he yanks her from the flooded stairwell and holds her until she finds her footing.

Embracing her brand-new bow, she catches her breath, peering up at an unimpressed-looking Lucas with a smile.

TWO

Endless rows of dust-covered cars line the deserted streets of LA. Lucas and Maia walk side by side down the middle of the crumbling road, stepping around small patches of bushes flourishing between the cracks.

Constantly scanning their surroundings, their pace is hurried. Quiet. Their time is limited. With the light around them already beginning to fade, they must get back to their home base before dark.

Maia's beloved new bow is strapped across her chest. Their mission in the flooded mall was dangerous but necessary. The streets of LA have been completely destroyed and scavenged over the years, but there are still treasures to be found. They just have to know where to look. It's been a process, but with thousands of miles ahead of them, they must take full advantage of their current location to find what's left.

A stray dog growls from the shadows. A few more

wander alongside them, curious and sniffing with their noses in the air.

Maia smiles at Lucas with his dripping sack of new supplies, but she does not say a word. It is imperative that they travel as quietly as possible. Do not attract attention; no speaking allowed. Maia waves her hand to grab Lucas's attention. When he glances at her, she points to her eye. He smiles and points to his heart. She points back at him, and he nods with a grin.

The sun disappears behind the hill, and they pick up their pace. Fireflies flicker in small clusters, and right on time, the endless hordes of crickets begin their nightly symphony. Maia has never heard so many crickets in her entire life; the sound is nothing short of magnificent. If it weren't for the looming and near-constant threat of danger from walking the city streets, she might actually enjoy being here.

There's beauty to be found in the simplicity of nature slowly devouring the ugliness left behind. Green weeds and brush are swallowing up the roads. Dust and dirt are tackling the slow and steady transition from man-made rot back into earth. It will take a long time, but it will be just as Grandpa said: it will be like humans were never here.

Maia and Lucas approach an intersection with an enormous yellow traffic light smashed in the middle. They quickly skirt around it and continue across. A decaying car on the other side catches Maia's eye. The tires have been stripped and the windows broken, but this car has a small tree bursting from its hollowed-out hood. She wonders what sort of tree it is. A cottonwood, maybe? Do those grow here?

Something moves from behind the car, and Maia's heart skips a beat. Another stray dog? They're everywhere.

No—not right. Something isn't right.

The hairs on the back of her neck stand on end. The tranquil beauty of their surroundings fades, and Maia's world becomes eerily quiet. She slows her pace, holding up her hand. *Stop.* Lucas glances in her direction.

She listens for movement, her heart pounding. Lucas waves his hand, trying to steal her attention.

A dark figure pops up from behind the rusted car, and Lucas and Maia stop in the middle of the intersection. A man steps out into the street. Shuffling his feet along the sandy cement, torn strips of his baggy pants drag behind him. He smiles a haggardly black grin, and his crusted skin wrinkles into folds around his eyes.

Another figure wanders out just a little farther behind him. He's also smiling. A little younger than the first man, he wears thick leather boots, and his bony hands tremble at his side.

Maia can't help wondering how old these men actually are—it's impossible to say. They are cloaked in the harshness of their surroundings. Small scabs cover their faces, and their long hair grows sparsely around clusters of scaly, blood-crusted bald patches.

Bounders. Despite being mostly deserted, this city is overrun with them, making Maia and Lucas's short time here a living hell. The smiles slide from the men's faces as they slowly approach.

"Stop right there," Lucas says.

The older man cocks his head to the side, never once

taking his eyes off Maia. A smile curves from his cracked lips. "What is that you have there?" he sneers.

She slides the bow behind her, as if her petite frame could possibly shield the large weapon from view.

The man steps closer.

Lucas lifts his hand. "I said—"

Glaring at Lucas, the man pulls out his gun and points it at Maia. "I heard ya."

"What do you want?" she asks. Her words are clipped as she clutches her bow. She knows exactly what he wants.

"That's an intriguing question you ask," the man says, turning toward her. His cheek twitches as he looks her up and down. "Is that—" His face tics again and he stops, picking at a scab on his cheek. He flicks the crust at her.

Refusing to react, she lifts her chin.

He smiles. "Is that a *bowgun* you got there?"

"We were just passing through," Lucas says, keeping his hand lifted. "We'll be on our way."

The man looks at Lucas in annoyance and pivots his gun toward him. "I said, I *heard* ya." Keeping his weapon pointed at Lucas, he walks toward Maia.

She steps back.

"*Ah*-ah. Don't move a muscle," he warns.

The younger man behind him approaches, laughing and covering his mouth. "Boss, she's a demon! Look! She got one blue eye and one green! *Demon!*"

The older man tilts his head. "*Nah*, she's not a demon. She's just a *freak*."

She glares at him.

"I think..." He pauses, rubbing his chin with his other hand. "Yes, I think you should hand that bow over to me."

She tightens her grip. He veers his gun toward her, pressing the cool metal against her forehead.

He's bluffing. Surely. There are a lot of crazies around here, a lot of old guns. Never ammunition.

At least not yet.

"Lady! He's going to *shoot* you!" the young man yells, jumping up and down.

"I'll shoot the both of ya if you don't hand over that bow."

He's bluffing. He would have done it by now.

"Hold him," the older man barks.

The young man marches up to Lucas, now holding his knife before him.

"Throw the knife to the ground," the older man yells. He keeps his gun against Maia's head, never once taking his eyes off hers. "Do it now, or I'll shoot her."

"Don't do it, Lucas," she says through gritted teeth. There's no ammunition in that gun. She doesn't know how, but she's sure of it.

The man lifts a brow. "You got a death wish, girl?"

"Maia?" Lucas yells, and she glances at him.

The man pummels his fist into her ribs. She doubles over, gasping, and something metallic skids across the cement. She closes her eyes. *Lucas's knife.*

She looks up as the younger man swipes it from the ground, then punches Lucas hard across his chin. She flinches, struggling to keep a straight face as Lucas falls to the ground. The young man kicks him in the back. Repeatedly. Lucas cries out, arching against the cement.

"*Stop!*" she shrieks.

The man drags Lucas up by his hair and shoves the knife against his throat.

"This is your last chance," the older man says. He wraps his hand around the back of her neck, pressing the pistol deeper into her head. "Hand it over or die."

"Maia?!" Lucas pleads.

She glares at the man.

"No?" He releases her and steps back, keeping the gun pointed at her head. "Okay, then." He shrugs. "Better step away. This'll be messy."

"No, *please!*" Lucas yells.

He pulls the trigger. *Click.*

She knew it.

"What the—" He looks at the other man.

"Shit, boss, I *told you*—"

Maia glances at Lucas, and he nods. He reaches for the young man's hand, twisting it behind him and kicking him into a car. Maia grips her bow and arches back, swinging it around and bashing it across the older man's face. He stumbles backward, screaming and holding his cheek. Blood pours between his fingers.

"*Run*, Maia!" Lucas yells.

They race back up the street, bursting through clouds of fireflies. The younger man advances behind Maia, panting loudly as his boots hit the pavement. She keeps the bow held out before her, slowing her stride. The man lurches and clutches her shirt, ripping the lower half. She wavers but maintains her footing. Lucas is running ahead of her. Their precious pack of supplies has been left behind.

A pack of stray dogs races alongside them, barking and nipping at their heels. The young man cries out from behind and pounces on top of Maia, and they fly onto the sandy cement. The dogs surround them, barking and growling and revealing their teeth. The man straddles her, grunting as he fumbles with the bow's strap around her neck.

"No!" she screams into the dust. She flips to face him, clutching the strap. "No, *please!*"

"Just give us the ... *bow!*" he spits through his gasps. He wraps his hands around her neck and places all his weight on top.

She releases the strap, clutching at his hands and kicking her feet. Lucas runs to her side and tears the man off, throwing him to the ground and kicking him. She crawls away on all fours, gasping for air, her bow dragging against the cement.

The older man walks up with their pack on his back and grabs Maia by her hair, ripping her up from the ground. He holds her against him as she clutches her bow, and wraps his arm around her neck. "Stop. *Now*," he says to the men.

Lucas looks up and releases his grip from the younger man's shirt. The man wipes the blood from his nose, then pounds Lucas hard in the gut. Lucas doubles over and drops to his knees.

"Okay," the older man says. "So, you called our bluff —no bullets. But *here's* something new, my buddy left your knife for me." He waves the blade before Maia's face. "And I've grown *tired* of this fighting."

Lucas holds up his hands in a sign of truce.

"Such a beautiful lady," the man whispers in her ear.

She closes her eyes, fighting the rage rising within.

"Maia!" Lucas yells from the ground. "Just *give* it to him!"

The man yanks her hair, forcing her chin to the sky. "Can you feel *this*?" A sharp pain digs into her throat.

"Maia, *please!*" Lucas begs.

"Okay!" she cries out. "*Okay.*" She holds out her hands, leaving her bow hanging across her chest.

The man pushes her away, pulling the strap of her bow out from around her. He holds it in the air and howls with laughter. The dogs around them continue to bark.

"Look at this *beauty!*" he sings with wide, twitching eyes, the blood still oozing from his cheek. "We're done here," he says with a nod. "Now, don't move until you can no longer see us." He straps the bow across his chest and spits at Maia's feet. "Ya hear me? Or I'll kill the both of ya." He wags the bloody knife in her face.

The men back up slowly. Maia doesn't break her glare, her cheeks hot with indignation. A stray German shepherd barks at the older man, and he swipes at it with the bow, barely missing its head. The men continue to walk backward up the street until they are out of sight. Their cheers echo off the buildings.

Maia falls to her knees beside Lucas as he grimaces and rubs his back. They gaze at one another for a long while without speaking. Something trickles down her neck, and she swipes at it. Her fingertips are coated in blood.

Lucas leans over, scrutinizing the cut. "We need to get you home."

"How badly are you hurt?" she asks.

"Not bad," he says, opening and closing his jaw. He eyes her, shaking his head. "You are the most *stubborn* woman I have *ever*—"

"I knew they were bluffing," she whispers.

25

He stares at her neck. She covers it with her hand.

"You didn't know that," he finally responds.

"They would have shot us in the beginning, surely."

"No, not *surely*. Not if they were smart. They would have tried to hold on to their bullets unless it was an emergency. But I promise you, taking our bow would have been worth a bullet," he says, hanging his head between his knees.

She looks up the street, a small hill shadowed by a barely lit sky. A few silhouetted dogs sit at the top, another one scampering across.

"They took my bow," she whispers, her eyes unblinking.

"They took everything," Lucas mumbles.

"*Everything* can be replaced, and we have backups at home base. They *took* my *bow*." She fights back tears. "I nearly died getting that bow."

"You nearly died for keeping it too."

She hangs her head.

"Can't you just make one?" he quietly asks.

"Not like that. Not anything *near* close to that. Having a bow of that caliber could mean the difference between life and death for us."

"Well..." Lucas shakes his head. "It's gone now."

A fiery anger burns inside her. After everything they've been through. All that risk. All that time diving and endangering their lives for that bow, and just like that ... *it's gone*.

"This can't happen again," she mutters.

"What are you thinking?" he asks.

"Combat training," she says definitively. "At home

base. We don't leave LA until we can seriously fight and defend ourselves."

He looks at her for a long while before answering.

"I know what you're thinking, Lucas. But it has to be done."

"I could never fight you."

"You can. And you will." Her voice breaks. "You *must*."

He sighs, staring at the small cut on her neck. He lifts a single finger to his eye. Then his heart.

A muggy darkness falls over them.

"I love you too," Maia whispers.

THREE

S unlight pours through the expansive windows lining the bedroom wall, the curtains swaying with the autumn breeze. Outside, countless birds flood the early morning sky with the symphony of their song.

Maia reaches above her head as she stretches, knocking a succession of pillows to the floor. She's engulfed in a plush featherbed, the down nearly swallowing her whole. This bed. She'd stay in LA forever just for this bed—bounders and all.

The curtains cast away from the wall, revealing the green foliage surrounding them. This house reminds her of her favorite childhood home back in New Zealand ... before those heartless apes tore it apart. It was her reprieve, the one place she could escape to as a child, with her pretend friends and the ornate gate, and the magnets plastering the fridge. She's never found a place quite like it. Until now.

It took so long to find a decent home. At least that's

how it felt. After a few terrifying nights sleeping locked in the back office of an abandoned pharmacy, Maia and Lucas left the streets of LA to explore the sprawling neighborhoods outside the city.

It took days, in and out of home after home. No speaking. Peeking through broken glass. Prying open boarded windows. It could have been easier, but they had a few non-negotiables. The house had to be secure—no missing windows or walls or caved-in roofs. Preferably unlived in recently, even better if it was still stocked with kitchen supplies and sheets. Any houses with doors busted open were a pass. Leftover bodies or skeletons inside were a *definite* pass. It must be out of sight and earshot from any trails or roads. And close to a water source—this was key and discounted most homes immediately.

This house is a real haven, although it's not completely secure. Even with the tall iron gates lining the front of the property, the backyard is open, snuggled against the woods with a small creek about a five-minute walk away. The lack of security is a bit of a risk, but the house ticked the rest of the boxes, and beggars can't be choosers.

Once settled, Lucas and Maia spent two days securing the rest of the house by setting up traps of noisemakers—strings that clanked when tripped, hidden across trails and doorways. Anyone with a set of eyes could spot them during the day, but these are for when darkness falls. When Maia and Lucas are the most vulnerable. When the few crazies left behind come out from the shadows after hiding from the sweltering heat of the sun.

After all this time, they haven't seen a soul up in these

parts, but security is an illusion. One can never be too careful. All they need is a little warning.

Maia sinks into her bounty of pillows, yawning. She tenderly sweeps her fingers across the bandage on her neck. Last night—what a nightmare. They've been in LA for weeks, scavenging and foraging for supplies. Considering the city's population before The End, the seemingly endless cement jungle has been mostly deserted during the day. They've passed a few suspicious-looking souls who clearly weren't bounders, but no one said a word. They take a wide circumference around one another, Maia and Lucas on one side of the street and the strangers on the other, glaring from the corner of their eyes as they slowly walk past. For the life of her, Maia can't figure out why these people are still here, but so far, they've been harmless.

It's the *bounders* that are the problem. Lucas warned her about them on their first night in LA.

"Why are they called bounders?" Maia whispered from a dark corner of the office.

"I learned it on the ship. It seems to be a widely accepted term for people like them."

"People like them? What happened to them?"

He shrugged. "There are a few theories, but no one really knows for sure. Some say it's from homemade drugs they've manufactured from old chemicals left behind. Others say it's just the harsh reality of life, people living in poor conditions with poor sanitation and little nutrients. Others have the opinion that they are half-breeds."

"Half-breeds?"

"The virus released from the Great Permafrost Melt ended up wiping out most of humanity, which, if you think about it, is not very smart of the virus. It needs a host in order to live. So, it mutated. At least, this is the theory. Most of us who are still around today have only survived because the small portion of the population strong enough to fight the deadly effects of the virus—our parents—have passed that gene onto us. But some haven't been so lucky. Maybe that gene bypassed them ... We don't really know. But the theory is that the mutated virus has now found a way to survive in the host without killing it, leaving these decrepit half-breed humans slowly losing their minds."

A shiver ran down Maia's spine. *"And they're everywhere?"*

"Mostly areas that used to be densely populated, but there's no logic behind it. Our ship visited places free of them and places inundated with them—we learned to stay away from those places."

Because most of these poor souls have clearly lost touch with reality, they are loud—easy to spot. Lucas and Maia can often find a place to hide until they pass. Even when turning a corner and running into them, the bounders scare easily. With just a flicker of their knife and a stern talking to, Lucas and Maia can often send them running. They don't seem to want any trouble.

It's the bounders who *hide* who send shivers down Maia's spine. The ones who have their wits about them, although they seem to have been stripped of their humanity. *They* are the ones making this stay a living hell. You never know where they are or what they are capable of. It's enough to push anyone sane from the city.

Maia slides her feet out from the comforter and stands next to the bed, the carpet like heaven beneath her feet. The floor is still a little crusty, but definitely better than it was. After deciding this would be their base, she opened the home's windows, spending hours—*days*—sweeping and re-sweeping the carpet, beating the furniture, mopping the floors, and wiping the walls from their layers of dust. Who knows the next time they'll have a good home in which to rest. Might as well make it nice.

She steps to the windows, briefly pulling the curtain aside. The expansive yard is surrounded by a dense forest. The lawn has a few deciduous trees, now half-naked with bright orange leaves slowly drifting to the grass. An empty pool the shape of a lima bean sits off to the side with a wrought iron fence around it. Next to that, a barren firepit with benches all around. A wooden deck sprawls across the back of the house where Lucas now sits, stripping the fur from something called a raccoon.

Breakfast.

Lucas has cut his hair back into his preferred messy head of short curls, his beard trimmed into a shadow. There are new bruises across his face from last night's altercation. His lower lip is swollen, his left cheekbone purple. That's only what Maia can see—most of his abuse came as kicks to his back and punches to his gut. Guilt clenches her chest.

This isn't the first time Lucas has sustained injuries because of her.

Somehow, she *knew* that gun was empty. But how? Something about its energy just seemed ... *lacking.* Missing.

Like her bow. *Missing.* It should be sitting on the chair

in the corner of the room. That's where she would have placed it so when she awoke this morning, she could admire it again from the down heaven of her bed. What is it about someone taking something from you that brings out the most archaic of anger? It burns deep within her chest. She would give anything to fight them again right now. *Anything.* Besides her koru jade necklace, that bow would have been the most prized possession of her entire life.

And she owned it for a grand total of thirty minutes.

She tiptoes down the long staircase leading to the front foyer, its glass windows now boarded for extra protection. She turns toward the back of the home, walking through the massive living room, then through the dining room and into the kitchen. With its white cabinets and intricate tiles—nearly all of them still intact—lining the walls, this is easily her favorite room in the house. The island in the middle is adorned with a rustic wooden crate suspended by chains from the ceiling. Pots and pans used to hang from it, but now it's covered in avocado and mint leaves, drying for Maia's tea.

The massive stove along the back wall works off gas bottles, which were still stockpiled in a small, locked room in the basement. It was the biggest selling point of the house. Once they discovered the bottles, they were happy to overlook the lack of fencing along the back edge of the yard. And they were quick to agree to use the gas without reservation. They won't be here for long, and they won't be back. After a long day in hell, there's nothing like coming home to a hot meal cooked over a stove.

Maia boils water in the kettle for her tea, then turns to

the kitchen table piled high with an assortment of supplies. She wanders to the heap, tracing her hand along its contents. They're down to one solar-powered flashlight, the other one—the waterproof one—was taken last night. They have an old compass, a flint and steel fire starter, a handful of knives, a scarf, a few rags, and a poncho. They've only found one poncho so far, so unless they find another, they'll have to separate their packs into one that can get wet and one that needs to stay dry. There's a collection of small pots. A mylar blanket. Rope. A few first aid kits that they'll have to condense into one. A small sewing kit. A stack of sleeping bags piled next to the table, still needing to be laid out to compare comfort and weight. Hats, gloves, coats. Not everything will come with them, but at this point, it's *collect now—decide later*.

There are still a few things they should try to find before leaving. Maia desperately needs boots. They've come across a few—none that fit. Her small feet have always been a blessing and a curse. Most closets have been picked over many times, leaving behind an assortment of different-sized shoes, some too small and others way too big. But kids are less common in these parts, so they've managed to find Maia a pair of worn children's shoes. They won't last the journey, but for now, they're all she has.

Hiking boots would have been the first to go after The End, although Lucas hit the jackpot. He found a pair in a log cabin down the road, hiding behind an inconspicuous door in the hallway's ceiling. They've spent most of their scavenges trying to look in places others haven't. Most times, there's nothing. But sometimes, like when

Lucas found his perfect, unworn hiking boots with paper tags still attached? Well, sometimes the gods give them a win.

And other times, they take it all away in one horrific night on the streets of LA.

Duct tape would be another amazing find. Well, any sort of tape, but duct tape seems to have the power to mend nearly everything, and most of it is still surprisingly adhesive. Maia and Lucas have come across rolls with tiny slivers left behind, which they've taken, but nothing substantial so far. They now have three nearly empty rolls on the table, save a small sliver left on each.

Their journey to the city of Leucothea in the Old Arctic Circle will take around a year. It's presumably late autumn in California, evident by the changing leaves and the diminishing daytime hours. Since they're so far south, it's still boiling hot during the day. The farther north they go, and with winter approaching, the cooler it will become. The desert will be along the first leg of their journey, so it will most likely be scorching hot during the day but freezing cold at night. Maia needs to find warm boots—more than anything.

Lucas slides open the door from the deck holding his bloody hands before him. He steps to the sink, washing them in the bucket with brown water, then quickly dipping them in the bucket with clear water.

"How are you feeling?" she asks, leaning on the counter beside him.

"I'm okay. Nothing I haven't endured before." He dries his hands, then places them against the counter on either side of her. "I got us breakfast," he says.

She touches his swollen lip with the tip of her finger. "I see that."

"We'll need all the strength we can get if we're going to combat train."

"*When*, Lucas. *When* we combat train."

"I'll get this all set up and will bring your tea out to you." He nods toward the backyard.

She rolls her eyes. "I've been out there every day for *weeks*. Nothing is happening. I can't force it, Lucas."

"No, but the more time you spend with your powers, the faster you'll figure them out. Life is quiet right now; we may not get this opportunity again. Off you go." He ushers her toward the door.

She opens the glass sliding door and steps onto the deck. The early morning sun sieves in streams through the trees. She walks along the choppy grass, laboriously cut by Lucas after oiling up some old, rusted garden shears. This yard is the perfect, wide-open space to test out their tents. Practice combat training. Practice her "magic." She keeps telling Lucas she doesn't have magic. It's more like influence, or power—*sometimes*. Most of the time, however, it eludes her.

She wanders to the yard's edge, as far away from the house as possible, and flops to the ground. It's the most frustrating part of her day. She lies in the butchered shards of grass, running her hands along their jagged white tips, and sighs. Gazing into the hazy blue sky, a few birds soar across her vision.

What happened under the water yesterday? Maia could use the weight of the water to crack the glass and then smash it completely. Breaking that case is clearly something people have been trying to do, what with the piles of metal bars and wooden slats stacked at the bottom of the protective glass. She did it without touching it.

She sits up, studying the line of trees before her. Taking a deep breath, she lifts her hand and spreads her fingers wide. *Please, trees ... listen to me. Why won't you listen to me?*

She swipes her hand across the foliage. The trees are motionless, save for a few birds squabbling on a branch. She drops her hand in her lap. Okay, start smaller. She lies on her side, the grass nearly overtaking her vision, and hovers her palm above the blades, *pleading* with them to bend.

Nothing.

The kitchen door slides open behind her. She keeps her head on the ground, peering back as Lucas brings out a steaming cup of tea. He leaves it for her on the last step of the deck and then walks back into the kitchen.

What did her mother say? Maia holds exquisite power but needs time yet to harness it. She's spent weeks out in this yard, her frustration growing with each passing day. She could've used her powers to fight those derelict demons last night, all scabbed over and hair left in clumps. But instead, that disgusting excuse for a man pulled her hair while holding a knife to her throat. She is *so sick* of feeling defenseless. That man was the last. It won't happen again—it can't.

Today, they will start combat training. Maia studied it back in New Zealand. Grandpa was adamant about her learning self-defense, and she was happy to oblige. She pored over their books' images, scrutinizing every move and practicing them on repeat when preparing for the elders of the Northern Tribe, but she never had anyone to train with. Now that she hasn't thought about the moves in months, she's having a hard time remembering.

Focus. Magic. No—not magic. *Power.* She sits up, glancing around the yard for some sort of sign. How can she influence the elements? If she's the soul of the Earth, shouldn't it come naturally? She stares at the blades of grass around her. What else did her mother say? She keeps racking her brain to remember everything her mum told her, but she's missing something. Something important.

She holds her head in her hands and falls back onto the grass. Stretching her arms to the side, she opens her palms to the sky. *Stop thinking.* She closes her eyes, inhaling and focusing on her breath. She exhales. In ... out. *In ... out.*

A flutter of wings breaks Maia's trance. She opens her eyes to a small black and white bird landing beside her outstretched hand. It's another male. She has no idea how she knows this—it's a newer revelation since arriving on the shores of LA. It was the same with the adolescent tiger who followed her and Lucas on the trails; she was immediately aware it was a male. Maybe it's her strengthening connection to the Earth, but some things she just ... *knows.*

The bird sits in the grass and hops toward her.

She gazes at him fondly. "Hi," she whispers with a smile. "You look like an old friend of mine from New Zealand."

He hops closer, his movements quick. His facial markings are so similar to her beloved pīwakawaka back home, yet uniquely different. He tilts his head to the side, watching her in silence. The feathers covering his body are a dusty gray, his face white. But the top of his head is black, as well as around his eyes and below his beak.

He's exquisite.

He hops closer. There's something about this bird ... something in his eyes. It's like he recognizes her. The outline of his body blurs for a moment, and a bright blue spark flickers from his back. Something is happening.

Maia doesn't move.

Another bird joins him, surprising Maia. Both birds remain silent, taking her in. Another bird lands behind them. And then another. Yet another, until there are a dozen identical birds gathered before her.

Maia sits up, and the birds lift in flight. She reaches to the sky as they circle around the yard, and they land before her again. She slowly leans toward them, holding out her hand. More birds join in behind them. There are now twenty—no, thirty identical birds standing in the grass, all completely silent.

They are watching her.

Maia leaves her hand outstretched, and a single bird breaks away from the flock, hopping toward her. *Hop. Hop. Hop.* He hesitates, looking up at her. She waits. A few minutes pass while neither Maia nor the flock moves.

Finally, the little bird lifts in flight and lands on Maia's outstretched hand, his delicate black feet wrapping around her finger. More birds move forward. Closer. *Hop. Hop. Hop.* Until, one by one, they line her hands, her arms, and the top of her head.

More birds land on the ground before her. They tilt their heads, but not a single one looks away. Not a single one makes a sound. Maia gazes at the birds, their presence like a warm embrace, and a childlike smile stretches across her face.

The kitchen sliding door opens, and Lucas steps out, covering his mouth in disbelief. The lawn is blanketed in a sea of silent birds surrounding Maia, seemingly in awe. Like children in adoration of their sweet mother.

FOUR

That did not go as planned.

Lucas and Maia lie on their backs in the middle of the road, panting and catching their breath. A horde of seagulls surrounds them as trails of seawater from their soaked clothing snake down the street and disappear into the advancing urban shore.

Another seagull swoops in, landing next to Maia. It pecks at her shoe, but she does not react. Transfixed by the ocean, she listens as it laps against the canals of corroded buildings around them.

She closes her eyes, fighting the visions in her head. The signs. They should have known better. There were so many signs.

Two hours earlier...

Lucas and Maia stand in silence along the shore, gazing into the flood zone. They've been scoping out this high-rise since the day they arrived in Los Angeles. So tall. So pristine. It seems untouched, like a sculpture of glass emerging from the sea. After all these weeks, never once have they seen a single sign of life around it. No boats docked at its base. No faces peeking from its windows. No clothing hanging from rope, drying in the sun. Even at night, not a single light has burned inside its windows.

The building is surrounded by a cemetery of drowned buildings, their antennas popping like barbed wire from the sea. It'll be dangerous to get to without a boat, making it an ideal place to look for boots for Maia. Or duct tape. Supplies. It just *has* to be loaded with supplies.

They've decided to swim to the structure during the day—easier to watch out for bounders and jellyfish. They'll each hold onto an old buoy they've found around town, just in case. The building is far into the flood zone. It'll be at least a twenty-minute swim, but it's hard to gauge from shore.

"Ready?" Lucas asks.

"As I'll ever be," Maia says.

Together, they wade into the shore, a band of ghostly buildings towering alongside them. The submerged cement beneath their feet is slippery, blanketed in moss, so as soon as the water reaches her thighs, Maia lowers to her stomach, holding her large buoy in front of her as she swims. Lucas splashes behind her, quickly catching up.

They zigzag between LA's sunken skyscrapers. Some of the buildings are completely submerged, while the taller structures still cling to life half above the sea, their windows broken and consumed by brush.

Lucas ducks his head below the water and scans the

scenery beneath them. He comes up for air. "There are jellyfish to our left, but they're pretty far down. Swim to your right."

Maia kicks to the right, sinking her head beneath the sea to investigate. The weather has been calm this past week, keeping the murk of the waters subdued and therefore widening their visibility—another reason they couldn't wait any longer to make this trip. They can never be sure of when their stint of peace may end.

Maia comes up for air. "Antenna ahead," she breathes, wiping the water from her eyes.

"Where?"

"It's just below the surface. I can't tell if we'll clear it. Best to go around."

Lucas drops his head below the water, then back up again. "I see it. Let's swim to the left."

Maia is grateful they each have a buoy. This crossing is taking a lot longer than anticipated, and despite the fact that they're good swimmers, it takes a lot of concentration to constantly scan the waters for debris and jellyfish. They can't just swim straight there. There is constant stopping and checking and maneuvering around possible risks and looming dangers.

As they approach the tower, they find the glass and metal along its base covered in a black slime that was camouflaged from shore. They stop, holding their buoys while treading the water. There doesn't seem to be any way in.

Lucas whistles, grabbing Maia's attention. He nods to the left and starts to swim. Maia follows.

They paddle around the building, looking for something stable enough to work their way in. There are doors and windows along the skyscraper's base, but they are all half-submerged, covered in grime, and locked. The doors above the water have small decks extending from them, but none are close enough to reach. It seems the entryways near the water have had their patios destroyed.

"Let's keep swimming around," Lucas whispers. "We'll figure something out."

They kick around the circumference, scanning along the water's edge for any weakness in the building's barrier. Maia tries prying her fingers between the slimy layers of black moss coating the glass. There's got to be *something*.

Lucas swims in front of her. "There." He points around the corner.

Maia swims to him. A small iron balcony extends from the building, just a few feet above. It's odd, this one deck so close to the water. The rest of the building's balconies start at least ten feet up.

Lucas holds his buoy for leverage and pushes himself above the water, just barely grabbing the balcony's base with his hand. He swings his other hand around, grunting as he hangs out of the ocean. He repositions his grip. "Okay, climb up."

Maia climbs up his back. With a knee on each shoulder, she clutches the top of the railing and climbs over. Lucas shifts his grip once again, still dangling from the deck, and throws his leg onto its base. Maia reaches over and helps him slide his hands up the rungs until he stands on the other side. He climbs over. The rusted metal groans from their weight.

The balcony's windows are boarded up, the wood molded and warped. A single door leads into the building, its glass protected by plywood. Maia twists the door-knob. Locked. They stand across from one another on the deck, dripping wet and debating in whispers. A bolted door could mean there's life inside. *Or* it could mean no one has ventured this far yet to bust it down.

After all that effort, they agree there's no way they're turning back. Lucas pulls a small crowbar from his bag and works the door while Maia keeps watch. She leans over the railing. Another door similar to this one is beneath them, half submerged in the water. It's covered in slime, but its hinges appear clean. The door groans open behind her.

"Maia," Lucas whispers.

The entryway leads into a damp, barren apartment. The smell of ammonia is overwhelming—*rat urine*. They pull out their knives. Steak knives today—something they can part with if things don't go as planned. Maia has a small switchblade tucked inside a hidden pocket of her pants for backup—but only in an absolute emergency. Such debates they've had about what to take with them on these excursions and what to leave safe at home. They don't want to take their best supplies, but they also can't be left empty-handed in a confrontation with a bounder.

They make their way across the apartment, the carpet crusted and littered with rat feces. The dead bolt on the front door is rusted and sticky, but eventually, Lucas manages to open it. The apartment is located at the end of a dark hallway. Across from them is an emergency exit stairwell. They agree to start a few floors up—if anything but to get away from the smell.

The first floor they explore is empty. Same with the next. And the next. Every floor they wind up leaves Maia feeling more and more discouraged. Ten stories up and the apartments are all the same: unlocked and cleaned out, the doors left open, illuminating the musty hallways in a dim but manageable light. But Maia and Lucas forge ahead, holding their hope like their knives before them—as if their lives depend on it.

Tiptoeing through another gutted apartment, Maia finds herself alone in the dining room. The floor-to-ceiling windows overlooking the decaying city have been shattered, the ocean breeze a welcome relief to the smell of rot burning her nose. Sporadic bushes and clumps of weeds have taken root within the carpet. Maia picks up an old frame lying face down on a hutch, only noticeable under the thick layers of dust by its outline.

It's a wedding photo, the bride and groom walking along the shores of a beach. The bride's lacy dress is flowing in the wind behind her. They look so happy. Maia wonders if she'll ever get married. Is that something people still do?

The floor above her head creaks, and she freezes. It groans again, ever so slightly. She snaps her fingers, and Lucas peers around the corner from the living room. She points at the ceiling. They wait, gazing up at the crumbling plaster. Nothing. They nod at one another and keep moving.

At the top of the next floor, Maia slowly opens the door leading into the hallway, flooding the pitch-black stairwell in a dim light. It doesn't smell as musty up here. The floors aren't coated in decades of dust. She peers into the hallway.

A small boy, maybe the age of ten, is sitting halfway down the corridor on a stool. He looks up at her, and she flinches into the stairwell. Lucas taps her shoulder. She leaves the door cracked for light and turns toward him, pointing in the direction of the boy. She holds up one finger. Lucas's shoulders slump.

"It's a child," she whispers.

His brow furrows.

"What do we do?" she asks.

Lucas points behind him. *We leave.*

"We can't just leave him, Lucas."

"That boy won't be alone," he whispers.

The door pushes open. The boy stands on the other side, holding his hand against it. He gazes up at them with wide eyes, and they freeze, unsure of what to do.

"Hey, buddy—" Lucas reaches out.

The boy grabs the whistle hanging around his neck, and he turns and runs, repeatedly blowing the whistle as he sprints down the hall.

Maia slams the door closed, and they race back down the dark stairs as men's voices echo above. More shouting from below, and beams from flashlights flicker across the darkness. Maia grips the railings as she runs down the steps, catching herself repeatedly as she loses her footing. Lucas is in front of her, counting in Portuguese.

"Where's our exit?!" she screams. "I've lost track of the floors!"

"Here!" Lucas stops, and Maia slams into him.

The door swings open, and they shield their eyes from the blinding lights of the men's flashlights.

"Throw down your knives!" a man behind a light shouts.

More men pound down the steps, surrounding them.

"NOW!" the same man shouts, and Maia places her knife on the ground. Lucas reluctantly follows.

"Keep your hands where I can see them. Search them," the man barks. A set of hands grabs Maia from behind, groping her arms and her chest and her thighs.

Her switchblade.

"Are there any more of you?" the man asks.

"Just us," Lucas says.

The man behind Maia stops on her pocket, and he shoves her against the wall.

"Get your hands off her!" Lucas shouts, another man holding him back.

"What is this?" the man behind Maia asks. More of the group join in, holding her against the cement wall as he works at her pocket. He pulls the knife from her pants.

"Switchblade," he says. He passes the knife to another and continues searching.

"That's it!" Maia yells into the wall. "That's all I've got!"

"Back up the stairs, you two," the first man says. "Keep your hands where we can see them."

Lucas and Maia follow the group back up the stairs until they have returned to the level where they first discovered the boy. When they enter the hallway, at least a dozen men await. They each hold a weapon: a club or a gun or a bat, some of which are stacked with nails.

Maia keeps her hands in the air. "Please, we don't mean—"

"Shut up." The leader circles from behind, his nail-laden bat stained with blood. "You saw the signs, and you ignored them. You are trespassing."

"*Please*, we did not see any signs!" Lucas shouts.

"Bullshit!" another man yells, pushing him into Maia.

The group leads them into an empty apartment with floor-to-ceiling windows that have been knocked out, the drowned city of Los Angeles sprawling for miles in every direction.

The tip of a man's bat rams into Maia's back, pushing her toward the windows. She turns toward the man with her hands in the air, the back of her heel tottering on the window ledge. "Please don't do this. We were just looking for boots."

The man shoves his bat against her chest. "You saw the signs."

"There were no signs!" Lucas screams, another man pushing him toward Maia.

A strong breeze swirls between the angry crowd of men, and Maia glances over her shoulder. The drowned valley of antennas sticking out of the ocean stretches at least fifteen stories below. One building has toppled into another, leaving a large mast crossing the water directly beneath them.

Lucas is nudged again, and he wobbles along the ledge. His arm slams into Maia. Her foot slips from the window, and she drops to her chest, her legs dangling from the building.

"*Maia!*" Lucas screams, and he crouches down to help her.

The man standing before Lucas doesn't waste a second. He steps forward and kicks Lucas from the building.

"*Lucas!*" Maia's horrified screams echo across the waters, and the men step to the ledge to watch. She peers over her shoulder as Lucas plunges into the sea, just missing the toppled building's antenna.

She slides from the window, her entire body now hanging from the building. She's losing her grip. Panicked, she scans the sea below. She'll have to jump, but to miss the metal of the antenna, she'll need to simultaneously push herself away from the building as she does.

A sharp pain resonates from her fingers, and she cries out. A man is staring down at her with the tip of his bat pressing into her nails. She jerks her hand away, then clutches the ledge again.

The man leans closer. "Don't come back here. You hear? Or I'll kill you, *bounder*."

He slides his boot against her fingertips, watching with pleasure as her fingers buckle against the thick rubber sole. She places both feet against the building and jumps. She falls story after story, her world twisting into a muted blur until she plunges into the water below.

She misses the building's antenna by inches.

FIVE

Giant puffs of cloud hover in the deep blue dome of the sky. Their swirling white edges reach out and fade in. Maia watches, mesmerized, as the seagull next to her pecks at her shoe.

"Maia, we shouldn't just lie here," Lucas says beside her.

The seagull pecks again.

The clouds ... Look how they change, how they move —so effortless. What once *was* now fades into nothing. Just like that, the sky changes. Over and over again. Sort of like life.

"Maia?"

Back in New Zealand, some winter mornings would get cold enough for Maia to see her breath. The clouds sort of look like that—only the process has slowed right down. That's the funny thing about time. How relative it is. How sometimes, the moments pass by in the blink of an eye, while others seem to last a lifetime.

Like how less than an hour ago, Maia was clinging for

her life from a window ledge, surrounded by a sea of glass and metal. Time moved very quickly then. And now? Now, she's lying on the shore while a seagull pecks at her shoe. Every breath feels like a lifetime.

I miss Grandpa.

The bird taps again. This time it is hard, aggressive. Maia sits up with her fist ready to swing and the bird lifts in flight, squawking and raising a great fuss. She tilts back her head, inhaling deeply. She holds her breath for a moment, then releases it back out, glaring at that glass skyscraper in the flood zone sparkling in the sun.

Without missing a beat, that same bird lands beside her and pecks at her shoe.

That building looks pristine. *What a lie.* So many risks she and Lucas have taken. So many homes and buildings and flooded malls they've scavenged. Every day they spend in this city, they risk their lives. In the end, they've found a few treasures invaluable for their journey, but at what cost?

After all that effort today, and they still haven't found Maia a pair of boots that fit. There is nothing more disheartening than walking away from a mission empty-handed.

Lucas rubs her back. "We need to keep moving."

She glares at the building. "I am *so tired.*"

He slides closer to her and puts his arm around her shoulder. "I know you are. I am too. We're nearly done for the day."

She lays her head against him, and they gaze out at the flood zone. "No, Lucas, of *Los Angeles.* I'm exhausted with this city. I think it's time to move on."

"We will. I promise we will. We just have a few more places to check."

She turns toward him. "There's *nothing* left, Lucas. It's surprising we've found as much as we have, but at what cost? We nearly died out there—*again*."

"I know that," Lucas says, his voice stern. "My heart stopped beating the moment you fell from that ledge. But Maia, you can't start a journey of thousands of miles in old children's shoes. We won't make it out of California. And then what?"

"If we stay here much longer, we may not start a journey *at all*."

He sighs and rubs his forehead.

"Let's just go home," she says, defeated.

"We will. We just have that one stop—"

"*Lucas*! No! No more stops."

"But it's on our way! We've been scoping it out for weeks."

"Like we've scoped out that high-rise?"

"This is different. We are stopping by a gated house on our way *back* to base. We know the area. It's not the same as being trapped in a skyscraper in the middle of the flood zone."

She sits in silence, shaking her head.

"After all that ... We can't just go home with nothing," Lucas says softly.

"I don't think I can handle any more today."

He pulls her back into him. "It's nearly a full moon, and the skies are clear. We *have* to take advantage."

She sighs. "We don't even have knives."

"I do." He pulls off his shoe. Peeling back the inner

sole, he digs out a switchblade, much smaller than the one Maia just lost.

She shakes her head, smiling despite herself. "I forgot about that one."

"Never would have helped us in that situation, but at least we have it now."

She covers her face with her hands. "Lucas—"

"Just one house?" he pleads.

She looks back at the flood zone. The glass tower, once a shining beacon of hope, now stands in smug mockery of her naïvety.

"Those men called me a bounder. A *bounder*, Lucas."

"So?"

"So, that's what we call *them*." She points behind her to the streets. "Those soulless humans. We're not *them*. Those men called us thieves."

"But we *are* thieves."

"We're not stealing from people, Lucas. Not any that are still alive, at least. We would never do that."

"They don't know that. *Us vs. them*, remember? It's human nature's most basic tribal mentality. It's been ingrained in our DNA for thousands of years. You and I? We are *them* and will always be treated that way."

Maia kicks at the seagull pecking at her shoe. "We should have known better."

"Don't, Maia."

"There were so many signs. Those floors were cleaned out."

"Yes, a lot of places are. We still find things."

"The rats, Lucas. There's no way that place could be infested the way it was without something for those rats to eat."

"Maia, there's no point doing this. What's done is done."

She sighs and wrings the water from her dripping hair, then twists it into a bun on top of her head. "Just one stop?"

"Just one. And then we'll go home, and I'll make you a cup of tea." He looks behind them, scanning the streets, then climbs to his feet and helps Maia up. He lifts her chin and kisses her. "Okay," he says. "*Vamos*—let's go. No more talking."

She nods, and they begin their long journey to the other side of town.

Their shoes squishing and water-logged, they leave trails side by side through the layers of sand. Despite being late in the afternoon, the sun weighs heavy on Maia's shoulders. Lucas waves his hand to grab her attention, then twirls his finger in a circle. They need to pick up the pace.

Nightfall is coming.

They stick to the new shoreline. Maia can't figure out why, but the sound of the waves lapping against the buildings brings her so much comfort. Relief. Maybe it's just the gentle reminder that the ocean is still here. It may be empty. It may be warm. But it holds within it the breath of the Earth.

And the Earth ... the Earth is still breathing.

The Hollywood sign sits off in the distance on a hill. Maia has always dreamed of seeing it—never once had she imagined she actually would. But there it is. It's not exactly the same as the one she's seen in magazines. It's missing an *L*, an *O* has slipped from its stand, and the *D* is tipped on its side. But it's still standing.

They wander past large portions of the city ravaged by fire. It's difficult to imagine what this place once was. All that remains are rows of blackened skeletons, hollowed shells of brick and metal. The scorched roads are lined with charred vehicles. It looks like an old black-and-white scene from the newspapers Maia would burn back in New Zealand.

Palm trees taller than skyscrapers line the streets, their thick layers of dead leaves clumped like scarves around their necks. Lucas and Maia quietly shuffle past a man and a young boy. It's the usual encounter they've come across when the humans are normal and not being eaten away from the inside out. Not a single word is spoken. A wide girth is taken. Glares all around. The boy instinctively steps behind the man, eyeing them as they pass.

Just as Lucas and Maia pass the sprawling quarantine camp on the outskirts of the city, they turn inward to a gated community they've been exploring from the beginning. A rusted gate lies across the road, broken from its hinges long ago. As they cross the dusty street, a stray dog trails closely behind them.

They are constantly being followed. When they are in the hills around their home base, there's a presence around them that Maia can't pinpoint. Something timid and shy, always watching her from behind the trees. She believes it to be the tiger. She hasn't seen him since the day they arrived in LA. When Lucas came out of the little shack, the tiger ran. Maia has looked for him every day since, but so far, like her powers, he eludes her.

And then there's Charlie, the German shepherd happily trotting behind them now. Maia has secretly named him despite Lucas's pleadings to not get attached. The dog waits for them in town whenever they come back and follows them everywhere they go. She sneaks quick pats to his furry head, and he looks up at her, his mouth curving like a smile—just like her beloved Huck. She thinks he's the stray the bounder tried to hit with her bow. Lucas told her there would be hundreds of dogs in the area that look the same, but she can tell it's the same dog. Charlie has been with them from the beginning.

But he never follows them home. He slows his stride, stopping around the same part of the street as Lucas and Maia head into the hills. He'll often sit in the middle of the road, sometimes whimpering. Something is keeping him from following. Is it the tiger? Maia can't be sure. There is something in the woods behind their house. Something alive, something watching her. Whatever it is, Charlie seems to want nothing to do with it. She keeps these thoughts to herself.

Lucas leads the way down a narrow driveway to the house. He lifts his hand, his fingers wide. *Stop.* Unmoving, they listen for life. Undistracted for the first time since they left the shore, Maia feels the raw pain of a blister forming on her heel from her small, wet shoes. Lucas waves his hand and points twice to the side of the house. *This way.*

They've scoped out a few of these hidden gems. They're rare in the massive metropolis, but they still exist. The two no longer waste their time on unlocked homes, most of which have been emptied long ago. It's the *locked* houses they want.

To ensure the places aren't occupied, they scope out the property multiple times—at least once at night. This is the best giveaway as noticeable slivers of light peek between the boarded-up or blacked-out windows. Or they'll crouch outside the doors, listening for the quiet clanking of dishes. The murmurings of voices. A single cough or a sneeze.

This house is dead quiet.

As dusk falls around them, they must be quick. They slink into the backyard. As Lucas works the lock, Maia keeps her back against his, scanning the yard and fence line. The decking behind them hems in a large empty pool filled with stagnant black water. Fireflies float in the distance.

Lucas opens the door to a large kitchen. They step inside, careful to avoid the children's shoes stacked near the entrance. This does not look like the rest of the homes they've been in. Dishes are stacked next to the sink. The scraps of food on the top plate have not been confiscated by rats or consumed by mold. A doll lies at the foot of the table.

This home is lived in.

Lucas glances at her and grimaces. He shrugs his shoulders. *What do we do?*

She shakes her head. *No.*

He nods and points toward the door.

She agrees, and he quickly steps out.

She looks around. There's no doubt there are children living here. She plucks the old rag doll from the faded linoleum floor. One eye has been rubbed clean into a white plastic disc. This doll is loved. She scans the room, listening for movement. Whoever lives here is clearly not home—at least not yet.

She turns to leave and that's when she sees it, sitting

innocently on the countertop: a roll of duct tape, halfway gone. They have searched and scavenged. Risked their lives. Rummaged through shop after home after dusty, cobweb-filled attic, desperate to find something like this. It would make all the difference in the world for their trip.

She glances back at the open door, the outside light quickly fading, then back at the duct tape, her heart thudding beneath her chest.

SIX

"**R**emember the pressure points. The throat, here." Lucas presses the tip of his finger into the concavity of Maia's neck, just above her collarbones. "The chest, here." He slides his finger down to the middle of her sternum.

She looks up at him, a seductive smile tugging her lip.

His eyes flicker to hers. He shakes his head and looks away. "Always find stability by grabbing them back and using their body against them," he continues. "Take control. Hold them like we've practiced and work their joints against them. Use your elbow, the back of your hand—hard, strong parts of your body. Work their joints backward."

Lucas and Maia stand across from one another in their home base's backyard. The midday cloud covers the sky in a blanket of gray, a welcomed relief after a long string of sunny days.

"Ready?" He crouches with his hands on his knees.

"I was born ready." She holds her hands before her, bracing one leg in front of the other. "What's the scenario?"

"Nope. No more scenarios. We've gone through every scenario at least a hundred times. Now, *wild card*. I'm not going to tell you."

"Really?" She lights up. "*Okay*." She smiles and holds her stance.

He approaches, and they slowly circle one another. He grabs a stick from the ground. "I have a knife—you don't." He stabs the air.

Using the back of her arm against his, she blocks him, then mimics a strike with the back of her hand to his jaw.

"Very good." He drops his stick. Walking behind her, he grabs the top of her ponytail. "What about this?"

She clutches his hand and twists her body beneath his arm. She inches behind him, gripping his hand and twisting his arm behind him until he lets go.

"Good," he says, shaking out his hand.

Maia paces the backyard. Back and forth and back again. "I know you're going for the element of surprise," she yells as she closes her eyes. "But I know you're com—"

Lucas jumps behind her, wrapping his arm around her neck.

She holds his arm with both hands. Twisting her hips to the side, she fakes a chop to his groin. He releases her and leans forward with a moan, and she turns and grabs his shoulders, mimicking repeated knees to his face and chest.

Rolling around in the grass, Lucas and Maia are a

grunting jumble of legs and arms. He pins her, holding his hands around her neck. She smirks.

"Maia!" He fights a smile. "I'm a dangerous bounder, and I'm going to take off your pants."

"*Okay*."

"Maia!" He lifts off her and grins despite himself, wiping the sweat from his brow. "You have to take this seriously. *Please*. I'm very nervous about this journey."

"Okay, I'm sorry. Go." She lies on her back with her hands above her head.

He straddles her and lightly wraps his hands around her neck. She suppresses a smile.

"*Don't*, Maia."

She sighs. "Fine." She hugs his arms and grabs her opposite elbows, then throws her heels on his shoulders and lifts her hips, arching off the ground and bending his elbows backward.

"Okay!" he yells, and they release their lock and roll away from one another. "*Excelente*," he says, bending his elbows. "That was good—very swift."

She catches her breath, retying her messy hair on top of her head. "I think we're ready."

The smile fades from his face. "Yes. The combat's good. We have as many supplies as we can hope to get for now..." He scratches his head. "How's the ... magic coming along?"

"Please stop calling it that."

"I'm sorry. I agree that we're nearly ready to go, but I don't think you've had enough time with your powers. I don't want to rush it. It could..." He hesitates. "It could really come in handy when we're in trouble."

"Don't you think I know that?" she snaps. "I feel the

pressure every day to do this ... *thing* that I know nothing about."

"I don't mean it like that. That's why I don't want to leave just yet. You need more time. Do you think you're resisting it somehow? What happened the other day with the birds? How did that happen?"

She holds her head. "I have no idea," she grumbles.

He crawls toward her across the grass. "You're conflicted. I can see it." He grabs her hand. "Isn't this what you wanted?"

"What I *wanted*?" She pulls away her hand. "You mean, to be in Los Angeles, battling for our lives every single day? You think I *wanted* this? My life has become a series of events, one after the next, of things I *don't* want."

Lucas bristles. "I see."

"Don't do that," she says. "You know I love you. I wouldn't want to be anywhere else if I couldn't be with you. But obviously, I would prefer to be up in Leucothea than here, with this massive journey ahead of us."

The two sit in the long grass for a while without speaking. Maia stares unblinking at a small cloud of gnats hovering above a pile of dead leaves. Lucas is right —they're ready, but she's the one holding them back.

"Maia." A smile spreads across Lucas's face.

She eyes him. "What."

"I have something for you. Come." He stands and holds out his hand. She takes it, and he lifts her to her feet. Together, they walk back into the house.

Lucas locks the sliding glass doors and closes the curtains. He steps into the kitchen, doing the same with the large open window above the sink, sliding the blinds down to the ledge.

She watches him, her arms crossed. "What are you up to?"

"*Por favor,* go upstairs and make sure every window is closed and every curtain drawn."

"Really?" Her nerves prickle.

"Just do it. It's okay—nothing's wrong."

Maia heads upstairs, her feet pattering against the lush carpet. She wanders into their bathroom, closing the window and drawing the curtains. She shakes her head. It's going to get really hot in this house. She latches all the windows in their bedroom and the two front-facing rooms, securing the curtains before heading downstairs.

Lucas is sitting in the great room with a small black box the size of a brick on the carpet before him.

She approaches. "What is this?"

"Come." He pats the carpet beside him. "Sit."

She kneels, unsure.

He holds the small box in his hands, staring at it for a while, then looks up at her and smiles.

"You're really starting to freak me out," she says.

"Have you ever heard electronic music before?" Lucas asks.

"Music? Like with instruments? I've come across a few of them but could never play—"

"No, like through electronic devices. Through something like this."

"I haven't." She shrugs. "I've seen those devices before, but they've never worked. The only music I know is a song my grandfather and I would sing."

"'You Are My Sunshine,'" Lucas says, and he shudders. "I know. I hear you humming it and then I can't get it out of my head."

She smacks his arm.

He smiles. "No, this box plays actual *music*, Maia. Like what our ancestors would listen to. And it still works."

Her mouth drops open. "*What*?"

He nods, his grin childlike. "You know how we've come across different devices made to fit those 'hundred-year batteries,' but the batteries are always missing?"

She nods.

"Well." His brow lifts. "Not this one."

"So, you can just ... make it play music?" Maia asks. "How?"

"This button here. I've tested it. It only plays one song. The rest are all ... how do you say ... *glitchy*. Or something. There's something wrong with it. But not this song. It has the instruments I've read about. Drums ... a guitar, I think, and other sounds I'm not sure about."

"Oh my God, and you're going to play it? *Now*? We're going to hear actual *music*?"

"Yes. Are you ready?"

Maia nods, her heart pounding.

Lucas sets the box between them and touches a button in the corner. Various symbols across the top light up. There's a square, an equal sign tipped on its side, and arrows pointing to the left and to the right. Between them, there's a large sideways triangle. Lucas presses the triangle.

A strange noise escapes the box, scaring Maia. She slides away as the box emits an assortment of strange sounds she has never heard before. "Is this it?"

"Just wait."

A repetitive bang starts, and she covers her mouth.

"Drums," Lucas says.

The sound of additional instruments begins to play, and Lucas bobs his head. Maia watches him, smiling, her tension easing with every beat of the drum.

A man's voice booms from the box, and Maia jumps, looking at the front door.

"No, Maia, it's coming from the box."

Her eyes widen, and she looks at Lucas. "Is that—"

"Our ancestors—*singing*."

She grabs the device, smiling as it vibrates her fingers. "What's he saying?"

"He's talking about walking down an avenue. *There*, that's my favorite part. He says he never thought he'd meet a girl like you. I know the feeling." He winks.

"Oh yeah?" She laughs. "And is that a good thing?"

"Most days." He flashes her a cheeky grin.

"Lucas, this is *amazing*. This is what our ancestors would listen to? This is what they would *dance* to?"

"Do you want to try?"

Her smile fades. "What, *dancing*?"

Lucas taps the top of the box and the music amplifies. Maia recoils, fighting the urge to cover her ears.

He laughs. "It's overwhelming at first, I know. It's okay —just go with it." He stands and reaches out his hand, helping Maia to her feet.

"What do I do?" she shouts over the music, watching him.

He starts clapping his hands. "Just let the music move you!" he yells.

"I don't know what that means!"

"Start by clapping your hands! Listen to the drums. See how they keep a regular beat?" They listen to the repetitive bang, and Maia tries to time it, clapping along.

"Then just do what makes you feel good!" Lucas yells, laughing. "Kick your feet! Jump around! Wave your hands in the air!"

She doubles over laughing. "You should see you!" she yells between gasps. "You look like an *idiot*!"

"This is how you do it!" he yells. He rips off his shirt, using it to wipe his brow. "I've seen it in my village. Come on, Maia. Try it!"

Sunlight breaks through the cracks of the curtains, highlighting flickering specks of dust. Lucas grabs Maia's hand, spinning her in a circle. She breaks away and starts kicking around the living room. She throws her hands above her head and claps, laughing the entire time.

"There you go!" Lucas shouts. "You got it!"

"Lucas!" She stops. "This guy is saying he can't get away! This song makes you think of *me*?!"

He laughs. "No way! Well, not most days, anyway." He grabs her by the waist and spins her around.

She wriggles free from his grasp and glances at him over her shoulder. She sticks out her tongue.

He puts his hand on his chest. "Oh, *meu amor*."

She smiles. *My love.*

The two jump up and down, kicking their feet as they dance in circles around the room. This is so *exhilarating*. The sounds. The beat. No wonder her books would talk about her ancestors dancing all night. It is nothing short of intoxicating.

The music slows and stops. Maia flips around, confused. "Did it break?"

"No, the song just finished. Would you like me to play it again?"

She smiles wide, nodding.

So, this is music.

Lucas taps the sideways triangle and the song starts again, like magic. They listen to it on repeat until they know every word and every beat of the drum, dancing around the stifling hot living room like lunatics and laughing so hard they can't breathe.

SEVEN

An assortment of clothing is scattered across the living room floor, along with two empty soup bowls stacked by the hearth. Lost in a daze, Maia listens to the comforting roar of the fire with her head on Lucas's chest.

This moment. If only it could last forever.

Well, this moment ... and the moment before. And the moment before that one too. She runs her fingertip along her lower lip, smiling as she relives the events of the afternoon.

It all started with her making soup in the kitchen while Lucas built her a fire. She had to beg him to use this barren fireplace. The heat of this land is unlike anything she's ever known, but she misses the nightly fires she and Grandpa used to have back in New Zealand. She and Lucas are nearly ready to hit the road, and then who knows how long it will be before they're in another home.

"Just one fire," she pleaded, pouting.

"Maia, it's hot."

"Please? For me?"

So, despite the heat, Lucas made her a fire, and then he kissed her on the cheek. He held her face in his hands and he kissed the tip of her nose. Long. Delicate. And then his lips slowly made their way down her neck. He peeled away her top, and they tumbled to the pile of blankets and pillows on the floor. He kissed her entire body over and over again until she was quivering in bliss.

And then the rains came. After over a month of nothing but a harsh and relentless sun, the clouds finally unleashed a nurturing blanket of water. The delicious smell of wet, hot earth wafted in from the window screens while Lucas and Maia made love to a chorus of rain. A crackling fire. Moaning. Kissing. Mind-tingling pleasure.

She lifts her head from his chest, pulling down his lower lip with her finger.

His eyes flutter open, and he cracks a groggy smile. "It's so hot," he mumbles.

"It's not actually that hot."

"It is, *actually*."

She wipes the beads of sweat from his brow. "Thank you for making me a fire."

He smiles tenderly. "You're crazy. But I love you."

Moments like these. Why can't these moments last forever? This home is so gorgeous. It would be so easy to stay ... But then, they would be just like the others.

"I keep thinking about that man and his child," Maia says, wrapping one of Lucas's curls around her finger. "The ones we passed the other day. They seemed normal. How is it, do you think, that they're still here? What *sane* human would live in this city? And with a child ... I don't understand."

"*Hmm*, life is complicated. *Humans* are complicated." Lucas sweeps a strand of hair from Maia's face. "You never know the stories people belong to, the battles they've faced, the scars they carry. Besides, they were probably wondering the same about us."

Maia rarely notices Lucas's accent anymore, but tonight it makes her smile. "And what about us? What story do we belong to?"

"Our story?" His brow lifts. "Oh, our story is a good one."

"Tell it to me." She looks up at him, resting her chin on his chest.

"Well," he says. "Against all odds, a pirate from Brazil and a beautiful stowaway from New Zealand were brought together on a dangerous ship. After escaping the hands of death, they found themselves stranded on a deserted island in the middle of the Pacific Ocean, and they fell in love."

She smiles. "This *is* a good story."

"It gets better. They built a ship."

"A ship?!" Maia gasps.

"Yes, a *grand* ship."

She bites her lip, trying to hold back her laugh. "Wow."

"And they escaped the island. But then a treacherous storm destroyed their boat, and they nearly died. *Again*! But then they were rescued. And the pirate discovered the beautiful stowaway was a powerful ... *mmm*, goddess. Yes, she was a goddess who somehow managed to become more and more beautiful with each passing day."

"You're sweet."

"They are now living in a dazzling mansion in Los Angeles."

"*Dazzling*. Your adjectives are on point."

"Okay, not living ... *staying*, until they are ready to be reunited with the pirate's long-lost brother. And then the three of them will travel up the coast of North America in a grand adventure to live out the rest of their days in one of the last remaining human civilizations on Earth."

"Wow," Maia whispers. "That's a pretty great story."

"I'd say so."

"A goddess, hey? I don't know about being a goddess."

"Well, you're definitely *something*."

"Yeah." She lies on her back. "But I think goddess might be a stretch."

"Do you know what I keep thinking about?" Lucas asks.

"What?"

"That it could have been anyone in charge of that basement. There were dozens of men on that ship, but Davies chose *me*. How different my life could have been."

She looks at him. "Are you happy Davies chose you? Your life is so much more complicated now."

"Complicated?" He sits up, and Maia joins him.

"Yes, Lucas. Complicated."

He runs his fingers through her hair. "Yes, okay, my life is a *little* more complicated. But at this moment, I'm sitting by the fire in this gorgeous home with the woman I love. We're about to find Miguel, God willing. And then we will travel up to Leucothea, where we can live out the rest of our days in peace. None of this would have happened if it weren't for you, Maia."

She smiles.

He looks at her with his head tipped, and his eyes narrow. "You've changed. You're different from the woman I met on the ship."

"What do you mean?"

"I can't pinpoint it. You're definitely more stubborn."

She smacks his arm.

He laughs. "Okay, you're tougher, I'll give you that. But something about your looks have changed too," he continues.

"Really?" She balks. "How so?"

"I don't really know," he says quietly. "Not in a bad way! You're beautiful."

"You've changed too," she says. "Softened."

He bows his head. "You get 'tough,' and I get 'soft'?"

"Yeah." She bites her lip.

She glances over her shoulder. The rain has stopped, and she can hear him out there—the tiger—sitting alone in the dark woods. She looks at the blackened glass doors in the kitchen.

"Do you hear something?" Lucas grabs his boxers. "Is there someone out there?"

"No, don't worry about it. It's nothing."

He pulls up his shorts and wanders to the kitchen, stopping in front of the open window. Bathing in the cooler air from the rains, no doubt. Without turning around, he says, "You're always staring into the woods. Why is that?"

She lies back on the pillows. "You'll never believe me."

"*Ha.*" He walks back to the living room. "Back on the

ship, maybe you are right. But now? Try me." He lies down next to her with his hands under his head.

"I think it's a tiger," she says.

He stares at her. "A ... *tiger*."

"Yes."

"As in, the large striped cat that's extinct."

"I've seen one here in LA. When we first arrived."

Lucas props himself on his elbow. "You've seen a tiger. When? Where was I?"

"You were in a shed. In the hills after we got off our raft. He was following us, cowering in the bushes. When you came out, he ran off. I think he's been following us."

"Are you serious?"

"One hundred percent. It makes sense with everything that's been happening. I've seen one in my dreams my entire life."

"You've dreamed about tigers your entire life?"

She sighs. "Among other things."

"What do you dream about now?"

"Nothing really."

That's not true. She *has* been dreaming again, different dreams—*new* dreams. Nothing has happened in them yet, just Maia standing alone in the woods, but the fact that they've started again makes her incredibly nervous. Her dreams throughout her life have generally not been kind.

The rain has returned, and large drops splatter through the screens.

"Maia?" Lucas says. "Do you believe in karma?"

She thinks about it for a minute. "I think so."

He sits up. "Okay, then I need to tell you something, and you're not going to like it."

She sits up beside him and wraps a sheet around herself. "Okay."

"Okay," he says. "When we first arrived in LA, I had two knives. I handed one to you. Do you remember?"

"Of course."

"I stole that knife. From Jake."

"You stole it. Lucas—"

"I also stole the waterproof torch."

She sighs. "You *took* that stuff?"

"I felt justified because it was Jake, and he was such an asshole. But it was wrong of me to steal."

She stares into the fire.

"You're judging me," he says quietly.

She hesitates. Runs a hand through her hair. "Why are you telling me this?"

"Because I believe in karma. I stole that knife and that torch, and then we used that torch to get your bow. And then those bounders stole your bow. We could have died —many times. That torch has brought us nothing but disaster."

"Lucas, none of that was your fault."

"It was, actually."

"No, I don't believe it. You're a good man. You have a good soul."

"Maia, what I am, the things I've done ... Someone with a 'good soul' doesn't ditch their family in the middle of the night. They don't fight people and drink too much, and become a pirate—"

"Okay. You want to do this?" she says. "We wouldn't even *be* here if it weren't for me. You wouldn't have been in the position to steal from Jake. You wouldn't have fought on your ship with what's-his-name—"

"Bode."

"We wouldn't be spending every day of our lives facing death in these dangerous streets, prepping for a journey that we may or may not live through."

"Maia."

"Shit happens, Lucas. You didn't *make* it happen. Everything we have on that table we've stolen."

"Not from actual people."

"But what if we did? What if I stole something and then something bad happened? Would you blame it on me?"

"Look, I'm not proud of what I've done, but I needed you to know. No secrets, remember?"

She tugs the bottom of his beard. "You're due for another trim."

"Don't change the subject."

"Yes, Lucas. *No secrets.*"

"Come here." He leans back on a mountain of pillows, and Maia curls beside him, laying her head on his chest.

"You're going to get too hot," she mumbles.

"I'll be fine. How's your practice with your powers coming along? Have you been able to figure them out?"

"No," she says. "I'm missing something, but I don't know what."

"Do you have a clue?"

"Not really. There's a resistance inside me, but I don't know why. I keep racking my brain trying to figure it out, but I'm exhausted."

"Maybe that's it," he says.

"What?"

"You're thinking too much." He rubs her arm. "Stop. Be still and listen."

"*Hmm.*"

He closes his eyes as raindrops patter against the windows, and she sighs. She promised him no secrets, but that isn't true either. She knows she's resisting. And she knows why.

Eventually, Lucas's breathing slows, and she rests her chin on his chest. She looks up at him. "Lucas?"

He's fast asleep, his soft breath barely escaping his gently parted lips.

"I know there's good within me," she whispers as he sleeps. "But I'm afraid. I know there's more—there's something else." She swallows, hesitating to say the words aloud. "There's an anger within. A power that is ... *dark.*"

The rain morphs into a torrent, slamming in waves into the side of the house, and the fire smolders to embers. Suddenly chilled, Maia pulls the sheet to her shoulders.

"I'm so afraid," she whispers, and she lays her head on Lucas's chest, listening to the drumming of his heart. She closes her eyes and keeps them shut until she slips into a deep sleep.

EIGHT

Maia stands once again in the forest of her dreams, surrounded by ancient, towering pines. Their tips are like daggers, impaling an inky black sky filled with an array of glistening stars. Her breath hangs in the air before dissipating into the deathly cold night.

She knew when she closed her eyes tonight that this dream would greet her. But what she still can't figure out, is why. An owl hoots in the distance, and she glances around, her breath suspended in clouds. It hoots again. It's a different call than her ruru owl back home—its sound more baritone.

She steps forward, and her bare foot disappears into the untouched snow. She reaches down, sinking her hand into the crisp blanket of white.

So, this is snow.

She pulls her hand out and back in again, watching in wonder as it vanishes into the fresh layer of powder. It's cold—she knows it's cold, but she doesn't feel a thing.

The owl flies above her, his enormous wings casting her in shadow from the light of the moon, and he lands on a branch above. His bright yellow eyes glare at her, his ears like horns on his swiveling head. Maia stands in awe of the majestic bird. He drops from the branch and soars between the trees.

She gathers her white gown into her hands and steps forward, the snow burying her legs to her shins. A new light burns deep within the woods, its orange glow wavering like a fire. Captivated, she weaves between the trees, her shoulders brushing against the frosty bark.

Every step she takes is a struggle as her feet sink deep into the crystalline layers of untouched snow, but she presses on. There is something there—something pulling her. She can hear crackling, like the sound of burning wood, coming from an opening beyond the dense forest of trees. She picks up her pace, drawn to the blaze by some great, unknowable force.

Stepping from the tree line, Maia covers her mouth.

What is *she* doing here?

This can't be happening again.

The mirror image of herself is similar to her old dreams, but instead of standing in the middle of a vast ocean, she now greets her in a wooded clearing. Her long white gown is the same as before, only now it disappears into flames at her feet, and her long red hair flows around her head as if it were ablaze. Her eyes still faintly glimmer, but her face, instead of being blank, now appears angry.

"No," Maia whispers, backing up.

She hits something hard behind her and falls into the snow. She flips onto her elbow to find a wall of pines like a fortress. She climbs to her feet, the snow suddenly so cold it stabs her skin. Stumbling along the wall, she falls again and again, reaching between the colossal trunks to squeeze through, but the space is too tight. There is no escape.

The light behind her grows, and Maia turns to face her reflection, who lowers her chin, looking callously at Maia. The fire laps up her dress, but she does not burn. Her lips separate as if to speak.

Maia covers her ears. "*No!*"

The image tilts her head to the side as a child's hand reaches from behind and slowly stretches across her stomach.

Maia sits up gasping on the living room floor. Lucas is sleeping peacefully on his side with his back to her. She wipes her brow and throws off the sheet, then quietly pads across the living room to the kitchen's glass sliding door. She scans the yard before stepping out.

It is peaceful outside. The rainclouds have swept away, revealing a waning moon sitting low in the sky. Maia sighs, pulling her thick hair off her back, and she wanders to the edge of the deck. She didn't think it was possible, but her nightmares have somehow become even more terrifying than those of her past.

It's no surprise her dreams now pull her to the Arctic. That burning version of herself is her worst fear. Her mother warned her that she holds exquisite power, both nurturing and destructive. She's been holding back, afraid that along with the good might come an ocean of bad. But she can't keep running from herself. The night-mares have begun, and they will not stop until she faces herself once and for all.

This leaf is life.

Maia can hear her grandfather's voice as she sits in the backyard's long grass, shaded from the sun beneath a line of trees. And she can also feel her resistance inside, fuming like a stubborn child. What is fueling this?

Fear.

She breathes deep and holds the feeling as it tumbles in circles inside her gut. Lucas said to be still and listen. The birds lining the branches above continue chirping. She focuses on the silence between their chirps.

I'm listening.

The gentle breeze kisses her cheek, and a woodpecker knocks against a tree in the distance. The tall blades of grass shift around her, tickling her skin. A black fly hovers before her face then flies high into the sky.

This leaf is life. Don't think. *Feel* the fear. She has been battling with this her entire life. Step beyond it and what lies beneath?

Life.

She reaches toward the leaves, and they flutter against her fingers. They feel waxy, tough. The woodpecker drills again. Although her eyes are closed, she can now see the bird perched high on the side of a tree. Streaks of black and white adorn its face, just like the hundreds of tiny birds from the other day, but this one is much larger, with a bright red mohawk fanning the top of its head.

The woodpecker's razor-sharp beak strikes the side of the tree. It slams into it with a force beyond its size, hammering into the bark. Shreds fly into the air, nearly crashing into a bumblebee flying past with legs coated in bright yellow pollen.

Maia smiles.

The furry bee lands on a red flower, the sharp daggers of its feet gripping the petal's soft flesh. Bands of striated veins streak down the petal, nourishing it with life. As the woodpecker drills, blood flows through its veins into its heart. Its beating heart. Its beating beak. Maia's beating heart. Their beating hearts.

With eyes still closed, Maia watches as the Earth's energy flows through every creature, every tree, every vein of every leaf—in and out like a beating heart. The bees and birds and trees shimmer before her closed eyes, their outlines visible from the life pulsing within.

The breath pouring from Maia's mouth swirls into the air like mist, and the bushes before her draw it in through their leaves. They exhale oxygen. It dances across the space and between Maia's lips, the exchange like lungs breathing back and forth, in and out. Her breath becomes their breath. Their breath becomes her breath. In. Out. Back. Forth. Again and again and again.

Maia opens her eyes. The bushes' branches have stretched toward her, reaching for her face, and deep red curls have fallen across her shoulders. She breathes out slowly, and the branches continue to bend, each of their leaves turning toward her. Breathing in her breath. Breathing out her breath.

She delicately touches a single finger to a leaf and immediately feels safe. *Home.* She smiles. The green tip melts into her, the barriers of her skin and the leaf fading between them. She moves her finger back, and the branches stretch toward her. She tips her finger forward and the branches move back. Forward. Back.

She spreads her fingers wide and swipes her hand to the left. The bushes and the trees before her follow her command, bending to the left. She moves her hand to the right and the foliage follows her. Lucas watches in awe from the kitchen window. She doesn't need to turn around; she knows he's there.

But it's not just him who is watching her. There is another heartbeat nearby.

A new one.

Maia stands and wanders to the opposite edge of the yard. The tiger is back, observing her from the woods. Drawn by a deep maternal instinct, she steps into the trees.

"Maia?" Lucas calls from the window.

Walking through the forest, she listens for the tiger. She lifts her hand, and the birds hush. The woods become eerily silent. To the left—wander to the left.

As she slowly steps across the thick layers of pine needles and broken branches, she spots the tiger standing in the distance, his striking orange coat bright against the forest of brown. He crouches with his ears pinned back as she approaches.

"It's okay," Maia whispers. "I'm not going to hurt you."

His ears flip forward, and his white whiskers flicker as he sniffs in her direction. He lifts an enormous paw, hesitating before stepping down. He lands on a twig, snapping it in two, and flinches.

"It's okay." Maia smiles, and she crouches down, offering her hand for him to smell.

He lengthens his neck, sniffing, and he takes another step closer. His size is intimidating, and Maia's heart begins to race. The tiger pauses, sensing her fear, and he backs up, his eyes searching hers.

She's scaring him. She quickly closes her eyes and lowers her hand, listening to his movement.

The forest floor rustles before her, and a cold nose touches hers. The tiger sniffs around her face, whiskers tickling her cheeks, his breath escaping in short bursts. She wants to open her eyes, but she doesn't want to scare him. She waits.

After a few moments, she braces herself to face the magnificent feline before her. But then her world becomes painfully quiet.

Hollow.

She opens her eyes to an empty forest, and she sighs, reaching across the vacant space. Her hand falls into a large pawprint in the dirt, and she bows her head.

Indifferent to her grief, the birds fill the void with their song.

NINE

A pile of flower petals covers Maia's bedside table, the glass vase now filled with a collection of twigs.

"Your flowers are dead." Lucas swipes the petals aside to set down Maia's tea.

She stretches beneath the sheets. "I know. I wasn't ready to part with them." She rubs her eyes with the back of her hand.

"Well, I think it's time to say goodbye." He kisses her forehead before heading downstairs.

She sits up and carefully lifts her cup. She taps a wildflower as she sips, and the last of its petals fall to the table.

The end of an era.

Lucas picked these flowers for her over a week ago, came home with them the same day he shot three squirrels in a row with Maia's newly constructed handmade bow. Despite being a bit flimsy, it was better than nothing, and Lucas didn't seem to mind. He was all smiles.

She sips her tea, glancing around their empty bedroom. The few things they own have been taken downstairs, ready to be packed. The room feels different now. The entire house feels different. Like the changing of the seasons, something has clicked over. It's time to move on.

They've prepped, planned, trained, and collected as much as they could hope to find. Besides the boots that Maia still desperately needs, they couldn't be more prepared.

She wonders what sort of world awaits them? It's hard to imagine. The only taste of America they've had so far has been the endless nightmare of LA. Will it be worse out there? She can't imagine it being any worse. Although, she never could have imagined the horrors of the bounders either.

Maia steps to the open windows beside the bed. Lucas is in the backyard, pacing between their rows of supplies with a furrowed brow—his pondering face. Maia watches him, taking another sip of her tea. He picks out a jacket from the pile and tries it on, then shakes his head and throws it back to the ground.

The trees have finally lost the last of their leaves. The daytime temperatures are still warm, yet something about the heat feels weakened, stripped of its edge. This will make for some frigid nights ahead of them in the desert. But it also means that hopefully, by the time they reach the Old Arctic Circle, the worst of the winter will be behind them. It certainly won't be the white wonderland it used to be, but it will still be cold. And dark. It will still be a nightmare to travel in the winter.

She heads down to the kitchen. The sliding glass door

has been left open. She steps onto the large deck and wanders to the edge.

Lucas peers up at her from the lawn. "I've separated our supplies."

"I see that."

"This side here are things that should come," he says, pointing. "Over there are things I think should stay. And in between the two piles are things I'm not sure about." He scratches his head. "We won't have much room left in either of our packs, and I don't want to add too much weight. I'd love to talk to you about all of this."

She heads down to the yard and walks among the supplies. Most of the items on the "to-be-packed" side are nonnegotiable and have been sitting on the kitchen table for weeks. The middle section has the "extras," things that would be nice to bring but not completely necessary. Extra blankets. Another shovel. More clothing.

She makes her way to the pile of things that will stay. Most of it is duplicate items: pots and pans, an assortment of buckets, and extra-large blankets. She spots a small black box half-hidden under a pillow and nudges the cushion aside with the tip of her toe. She picks up the music player and looks back at Lucas.

His shoulders slump. "Maia, we can't."

"I know," she says quietly.

"Anything not completely necessary must stay." He walks over to her and rests his hand on her back.

She gazes at the box through the haze of her tears. "Of course. I just..." She looks up at him. "What if I never hear music again?"

"You will."

"How do you know that?" she asks. "You don't know that."

"You will. I promise you will," he says. "You may not hear that particular song, but you'll hear music again. Different songs in different lands—beautiful songs."

She sets the box in the grass. The long blades nearly swallow it whole. She knows he's probably right ... But what if he's not? She could die never hearing music again, never dancing again. She can't bear the thought of it, living the rest of her life in silence.

"They'll have music in Leucothea," Lucas says. "Mario told me the life they live up there is very similar to the life of our ancestors."

She casts him a look from the corner of her eye.

"What?"

"I'm not so sure that's a good thing," she says.

"Let's just focus on getting there, okay? We'll worry about politics later."

She sighs and scans their piles of stuff.

"Hey," Lucas says, and he grabs her hand. "I could sing for you."

She grimaces. "I'd rather you didn't."

"*What*? Why?"

She laughs. "You're a terrible singer."

He begins to hum.

"Lucas—"

He lifts her hand and slowly twirls her between their rows of stolen things. He sings a lyric in Portuguese, his voice soft and low.

Maia smiles. Her Brazilian pirate.

He pulls her into him and they embrace, slowly swaying back and forth as he sings softly in her ear.

The sun is low in the sky, its dim light splitting through the trees in beams. The same little black and white birds dance along their branches and a wood-pecker sounds from the distance, its soft hammering echoing across the woods.

Maia rests her head on Lucas's shoulder. The morning hymns of the Earth may be loud, but in this moment, she can only hear Lucas.

Maia sips every last drop of her tea and then shoves the cup between the empty plates on the table, knocking a small rabbit bone to the floor.

It is their final feast.

She glances at the backyard, now drowned in the encroaching morning light. Stepping to the glass door, she slowly slides it open. The air outside is crisp, cool, the dew on the grass highlighted in the patches of sun.

Lucas calls for her from the front of the house, and she closes the slider. *Goodbye backyard.* She grabs a pile of rope and rusted cans from the floor and joins Lucas in the front foyer. He's hauled their loaded packs to the front door, now left wide open.

"I've collected the last of our noisemakers from the forest out back," she says.

"*Excelente.* Just shove them in my pack." He walks into the living room, checking for anything left behind.

"We've got it all, Lucas," she says, and she zips his pack closed.

He meets her gaze. "Yes, I think you're right."

She walks into the living room. "So, the plan."

"We'll take the open freeways, less chance of an ambush," he says, walking toward her.

"No talking," she says. "Whispers and signing only."

"We stick to our planned route no matter what." He grabs her hands. "Don't think about the journey ahead. Just focus on getting to *House A*. And then tomorrow, we'll wake before dawn and make our way to *House B*, whatever that ends up being. Since we've never ventured that far from town, we'll need to start scoping out a home within two hours of sundown. If Mario's map is correct, we should hopefully arrive at Miguel's by the third afternoon."

"Knives in holsters, always ready," Maia says.

"And stop paying attention to that dog," Lucas says. "*Please*."

She rolls her eyes. "What's the big deal? Charlie isn't hurting anyone by tagging along when he chooses."

"You've *named* him?"

"I'm not breaking any rules," she says with her hands in the air.

He tilts his head in disapproval. "Just don't feed him."

"Never."

Lucas and Maia stand side by side outside the front door of their beloved home base. A light breeze scatters brown leaves across the dusty wooden porch.

"It feels wrong not locking it," Lucas says after a while. "Just walking away ... It feels strange."

Maia can't move. This is it. All she's wanted day after day was to leave this place, despite loving it. Now, she's terrified to move. "Maybe we should lock it?" she says, not taking her eyes off the front door.

"No point," Lucas says. "We won't ever come back here again."

Maia turns to the broken path leading away from the house. The weeds have nearly swallowed it whole. Her pack is strapped to her back and clipped tight around her hips, and her new wooden bow is tied to the outside. The water bottles secured to their bags are filled to the brim.

Lucas turns and joins her. "Okay, then. *Vamos*."

Quietly walking the streets of LA, Maia and Lucas focus on the unfolding scenery before them. They've walked this street at least a dozen times, but today feels different. There's no turning back, no safe zone to rest at the end of the day. They've been planning this route from the beginning, sorting out the home where they would sleep on their first night traveling to Miguel's. They've spent weeks looking for a place that wasn't burned out or smashed up, all while quietly rummaging through the crumbling dregs of whatever has been left behind.

The arid cement city is eerily quiet today—more so than usual. There's not a single breath of wind. The sky is saturated in a deadened, milky haze. They know what that means. There'll be fires burning somewhere. There's *always* fires burning somewhere.

A stranger shuffles down the road toward them. Both Lucas and Maia rest their hands on their knives, and the stranger does the same. Their eyes bore into each other as they pass under a menacing midday sun. Lucas walks backward to keep an eye on him, and Maia steals a brief glance behind her, catching the stranger doing the same.

A creature runs out from between two blackened houses ravaged by fire. Maia and Lucas both swivel on their heels and swipe their knives from their holsters.

It's Charlie.

Maia smiles, and Lucas tips back his head in a grand display of annoyance. The large German shepherd potters up to them, his tail wagging. Maia pats the top of his head, refusing to look at Lucas. She knows he's glaring at her, but she doesn't care. It's always better to have a dog by your side.

The three of them wander for hours down the empty city streets until finally reaching the neighborhood with the familiar van, its doors wide open. The bench seats have been cleared out, the driver's seat dragged up the sidewalk about half a block up. They pass the empty rubbish bin tipped on its side, then the dust-covered teddy, face down next to a skeleton of what appears to be a small child. That's their cue to take a left.

They step down another small street, this one narrower than the first, and then quickly take the driveway to a boarded-up, half-scorched mansion. Clearly unlivable, it's the perfect place to hide. There's a small guesthouse at the very back of the property: Maia and Lucas's *House A.*

Charlie is momentarily sidetracked as another dog runs up to him. They touch noses for a moment before circling around one another, sniffing each other with their tails high in the air. Lucas raises his hand, pointing toward the back of the house. Maia nods.

They circle around the back through a lawn of waist-high grasses. Lucas closes the gate behind them while Maia unravels the noisemaker they left tied to the side. It's low to the ground, perpendicular to the metal of the gate. Should anyone enter at night, the vine will hopefully trip them and set off a bell. She places the few broken glass bottles they'd dropped off on their last visit along the fall zone.

Lucas sneaks into the back of the house while Maia waits by the locked door. He opens it, and she scans the yard before stepping inside. Charlie waits on the other side of the closed gate, looking at her with his head cocked to the side. Maia closes the door, then peeks between the curtains of a small window. The dog is mid-spin before curling up against the gate.

The light is fading quickly. She uncurls another noisemaker and attaches it to the doorknob, then sneaks to the back of the house to the long walk-in closet with only a few empty hangers left on its rods. Lucas is already laying out their sleeping bags. She sets up the final alarm: another fishing line with smashed aluminum cans placed across the closet's sliding pocket door.

She lies down next to Lucas and places her knife beside her head. She can barely make out his features, but she can tell he's looking at her. A few dogs next door begin fighting. They snarl at one another, barking loudly.

Maia tenses, and she looks at Lucas. He squeezes her hand.

Dear God, please get us out of this city in one piece.

The dogs continue to bark while both Lucas and Maia lie wide-eyed and hidden away. They haven't spoken a word to each other all day. He turns to her and places her finger beside his eye. She smiles. He traces it down his cheek and presses it against his chest. Then he flips it to her.

A cat cries out below their small escape window, its bellow sending shivers down Maia's spine. Another cat responds with a shriek and a hiss.

She takes Lucas's hand and places his finger beside her eye, then over her chest, and they lean in, forehead against forehead, bracing themselves against the night-time chorus of LA.

TEN

Something isn't right.

Moonlight spills through the small bathroom window of Maia and Lucas's *House B*. Maia lies on the floor, listening to every creak, every bump, and every possible movement around them. The winds are high tonight, howling through the trees in a blur of swooshing air, making it nearly impossible to listen for intruders.

A metal can tumbles down the street—or is it one of their noisemakers? She sits up. Did she just hear something? She just heard something. *Did* she? So many sounds. Are those footsteps in the alleyway outside their window?

Her exhaustion blankets her like a fog, and she lies back on her side, facing Lucas. He's awake as well. He searches her eyes, and his eyebrows lift in question. She shakes her head. *Nothing.*

They've spent the entire day on high alert. Hiking the open expressways has been a blessing compared to the cramped city streets, but their time on the road has taken a toll. Maia's eyes close, forcing sleep upon her.

She opens them again. No—something isn't right.

They spent hours before sundown scoping out a place to sleep. Since they were unfamiliar with the area, it took much longer than they anticipated. Wandering off the expansive highway, they found themselves in what appeared to be an endless sprawl of slums—apparent refugee housing according to the signs—most of which had not survived the fires that had swept through the area. It was slim pickings. With darkness quickly falling, they had no choice but to settle in this house.

It was better than most, although not wholly intact. A large portion of the dining room wall has caved in, leaving a gaping hole open to the streets. Maia set a few noisemakers across the broken wall, but having no bedrooms with both a door that locks and a decent escape window, they've had to settle for a bathroom. At this time of night, that's all that matters.

Charlie has continued to follow them, even though they're far from the area he used to call home. He's now sleeping curled up outside the tiny home's front door. Lucas tried scaring him away, worried that a sleeping dog at the entry could alert others that there are people inside, but Charlie wouldn't budge—much to Maia's delight. Lucas has gotten on her last nerve about that dog. She knows Lucas means well, but sometimes he can seem a little ... controlling.

Maia sits up again. Something isn't right. She can feel it; there's danger lurking. Charlie barks from the front of the house, and Lucas sits up beside her. Charlie never barks. The dog growls, followed by more barking and a high-pitched yelp. A rumbling of voices reverberates through the walls.

"Lucas?" Maia whispers.

He shoots her a look of panic.

Charlie's barking is louder now—he's inside the house. The aluminum cans from the kitchen clank together, and the ground shakes with a *thud*. A man cries out a chorus of curse words.

Maia and Lucas jump to their feet. She swipes her knife from the ground and presses her body against the door, listening for movement on the other side. Lucas unlatches the bathroom window and cranks it open. Grabbing the small mirror from his pack, he inches it outside the very top of the window. He snaps his fingers once, then gives a thumbs-up. She slides her knife into its holster and throws her bag at his feet. She helps him out the window as Charlie's barking moves closer to their door.

The knob jiggles. Lucas drops to the ground outside, and Maia slings their packs out to him. The door shakes violently.

"In here!" a voice yells from the other side.

Maia climbs over the window ledge.

Lucas is below with open arms. "Jump, Maia!"

The door is rammed open and a man rolls across the floor. Maia throws herself from the window into Lucas's arms, and they tumble to the ground.

The man sticks his head from the window. "They're outside! It's the ones we saw earlier! I knew it!" His laughter is maniacal—*psychotic*.

Maia and Lucas run down the alleyway with the

man's shrill laugh echoing behind them. Lucas slows, holding up his hand with his fingers spread wide. *Stop.*

They listen to footsteps against the pavement on the other side of the house.

Lucas twirls his finger. *Turn around.*

Maia pivots and runs smack into the crazy man.

His sour stench slams into her as he grabs her by the shoulders. Like a wind-up toy, he continues laughing, gasping for breath between his high-pitched squeals. She knees him in the groin, and he smiles at her, unfazed. His face has been tragically picked at with open craters in his skin. *Maggots.* There are maggots inside his wounds.

She tries to reach for her knife, but her arms are trapped. Grunting, Lucas and another man start fighting behind her.

The lunatic pulls her closer to him. "You're pretty," he says with a smile.

She grabs his forearms. Confused, he looks at her hands and then at her, and she butts her head against his. They drop to the ground. White glitter blurs her vision and she rolls to the side, stumbling back to her feet. She frantically wipes the man's blood from her face and pulls her knife from its sheath. Lucas leaves the other man gasping on the ground and joins her.

"She's got a *knife!*" the lunatic yells, rocking and holding his head. Fresh blood pours from an open wound on his face.

A new man approaches from the alleyway before them, while another two close in from behind. They all have knives.

"We were just leaving," Lucas says, panting. "Let us pass, or there'll be trouble."

The man standing before them laughs, then peers at the men behind them. "Get 'em."

Lucas and Maia turn with their knives held out as the men help the lunatic from the ground. All three approach with smiles on their faces.

The lunatic jabs his knife in the air. "I want the pretty one."

As Maia grips her knife before her, a fiery temper burns within. She and Lucas haven't even left the city limits of LA. They haven't found Miguel. They've been on their journey north less than forty-eight hours. *Why* can't they just be left *alone*?

She closes her eyes. *Come,* she inwardly whispers.

The men approach. "Drop the knives," one of them says.

Maia opens her eyes, and a smile spreads across her face. Tilting her head to the side, she lifts her knife before her and drops it to the ground. It clatters against the cement.

"Maia?" Lucas whispers. "Your *hair*."

The men standing before her watch, horrified, as Maia's auburn waves transform into scarlet curls.

That's when the growling begins. A single dog approaches from the alleyway behind her.

Charlie.

And then another joins in. And another. *Another.* The men peer behind her, their wide eyes darting between Maia and the dogs, and they slowly back away.

"What are you assholes doing?!" the leader behind Maia yells. "I told you to get them, she dropped her—"

There's silence, and then, "Nice dogs," the leader says, his voice quivering. "*Good* dogs."

Maia smiles. "Get 'em."

The leader behind her screams and the other men race down the alley as the pack of dogs chases after them.

"Please! Help me!" the man behind her screams. "Get this thing off me!"

Maia turns to find the leader on the ground with Charlie's teeth clamped onto his arm. Lucas is backed up to the fence behind them.

She steps beside the man, glaring down at him and shaking her head. "You were going to kill us," she says coolly.

"No!" he shouts. "No, we just wanted your packs!"

"Same thing."

She snaps her fingers and Charlie lunges. The man's feet kick against the cement, his screams muffled as the large dog tears into his neck. Choking. Gasping. *Gurgling*. Maia stands above him with her arms crossed, watching as the life drains from his eyes. Blood sputters from his mouth, and his legs flop to the pavement.

Maia leans down, running her fingers through Charlie's bloody fur. The leader lies unmoving, his eyes wide at the sky as the thick blood pools around his mutilated neck. Charlie releases the man and tenderly licks Maia's hand.

That's when she realizes she's smiling.

"*Meu Deus*," Lucas gasps from the fence.

ELEVEN

A thick layer of clouds has swallowed the moon from the sky, leaving Lucas and Maia stumbling through an endless world of darkness.

"That was our light," Lucas says beside her. "I can't see a thing, and I don't want to waste our flashlight's battery. We should stop and have a rest."

The wind howls around them, shoving them down the blackened highway. Maia can barely see a foot in front of her, but she's insisted they keep moving. Another gust of wind slams into their backs.

"Maia?" Lucas yells.

That man's terrified voice echoes inside her mind. *"Please! Help me!" Gurgle. Sputter. Cough.*

She shakes her head and picks up her pace. It will be light soon, and then they can rest. And this nightmare will be over. And she can pretend that she didn't just hold a man's life in her hands.

And end it without hesitating.

Her foot rams into something in the street, and she

stumbles. Lucas briefly switches on his flashlight. Whatever it is, it's so covered in sand it's unrecognizable.

He scans the road with his light, and then his torch lands on her. "Oh, *Maia*," he softly says.

She looks down at her hands, covered in layers of blood. Horrified, she wipes them on her clothes, but it's caked on. She searches the darkness for Lucas's face, but all she can see is the beam from his torch. She taps on the front of her wrist for the time. Lucas puts his hand before the light and holds out four fingers. He totters his hand from side to side. *Maybe.*

She continues walking. Only a few hours left until dawn, and then they'll rest. They just need to wait for daylight, and then this heavy cloak of darkness will be over.

They continue to tread the expansive expressway in silence. Every so often, Lucas flips on his flashlight to scan the terrain. They need to watch for bridges, especially the ones that crisscross in layers, towering high into the sky. Mario said those are the ones most likely to have residents. Lucas keeps checking, briefly turning on his flashlight, but most often, they are met with sand and cement.

When the sweet relief of dawn settles across them, they find the sky drowning in a layer of black clouds. A few drops of rain spatter against Maia's head, and she holds out her bloody hands. Another drop breaks against her skin.

She waves her arm to catch Lucas's attention, and he looks up at her. She tugs on her poncho, lifting her brow. Confused, he shakes his head. She sighs and stops in the middle of the road, and she holds out her bloody hands, her eyes stinging with tears. He looks at them, then at her, and he nods. It begins to pour.

He drops his pack, and Maia does the same, and they quickly switch bags. He covers himself and the bag with the poncho, and Maia stands under the rain, tilting back her head and holding out her hands. She closes her eyes, and the tears begin to fall.

She ordered those dogs on those men. That man died while she stood over him and ... *smiled*. Charlie did that. No, *she* did that. Maia has taken a human life. She could have called Charlie off. She could have let that man live.

It never even occurred to her to stop.

Gurgle. Sputter. Cough.

The rain falls even harder now, blurring the sharp lines of the world in a haze, and Maia loses herself to the deluge. Silently sobbing, she drops to her knees, scooping handfuls of wet sand into her hands and rubbing them together. The blood comes off in rusted layers. She scrubs until her skin is raw.

Lucas steps before her, the downpour dripping off his hood, and he pulls her to her feet. He lifts her chin, and her eyes flutter against the rain. He pulls out a small rag and holds it out until it soaks, then swipes it across her forehead. She pulls down the cloth before her, shaking her head at the blood. She hit that man's face with her own. His blood must be all over her. Lucas drops the rag to the ground and clasps her hands in his, holding her in his saddened gaze.

Charlie walks up to them, his fur still matted in blood. Maia can't look at him. It's not his fault—he was only doing as he was told. But still, she can't look at him.

"Maia," Lucas says through the rain. "Those dogs saved us. *You* saved us. Those men would have killed us."

She looks down, and Lucas lifts her chin. "You understand that, don't you?" he says.

She nods.

They stand across from one another as the wind and the rain whirl around them, and Charlie sits at Maia's feet. Lucas picks up her pack from the ground and Maia turns away, letting him slip the straps over her shoulders. The weight is heavy, but not nearly as heavy as the deluge of guilt already pouring down upon her.

After the rain comes the sun, and just in time, as they have finally reached the protective wooden trails Mario said would lead to Miguel.

Lucas pulls the map from his pocket and opens the paper, now bleeding with splotches from the rain. "Shit," he whispers.

"Is it okay?"

He shakes his head as he looks at it, flipping it over and then flipping it again. "Not really, but I remember what the rain has erased."

As they begin the slow incline up the trail, a soft whimpering sounds from behind. Maia turns to see Charlie stopped in the middle of the path. He backs up, his enormous ears pinned to his head.

"Come on, bud," she whispers, patting her thigh.

"Maia—" Lucas grabs her arm.

She glares at him. He releases his grip and shakes his head, continuing up the trail without her.

"Charlie, let's go!" Maia whispers loudly, but he still doesn't move.

After a few whimpers, he runs back toward the city with his tail between his legs.

It's so strange that he never goes into the woods. Maia stands alone on the trail, listening for movement. There is certainly no tiger around, but she swears she can hear a soft whisper.

There. There it is again.

She turns in place, peeking between the tangled trees, but the whisper is soft—she can't make out what it's saying. She glances around, straining to hear, but whatever it was is gone. She searches the trail for Lucas, but he's disappeared from view.

She runs to join him. He peers behind her, looking for Charlie, then keeps walking without saying a word. The trail is overgrown, making it difficult to be sure they're headed in the right direction, but they have no other option but to keep moving forward.

After a few hours of silence, they stop for some water and rest.

Lucas puts his hand on her thigh, snapping her out of her daze. "Do you want to talk about it?" he whispers.

She takes another swig of water. "I don't know what came over me," she says. Her eyes unblinking, she glares at the ground.

"What happened? You did that ... *right*?"

She nods. "I did. I called those dogs. I didn't think. I just called them, and I knew they would come. I knew Charlie would protect us," she whispers. Then she looks up at him, her heart aching. "I ordered him to kill that man."

Lucas stares at her for a long while without speaking. Then he stands, offering his hand. "Let's keep moving."

She crosses her arms. "Why aren't you *saying* anything? You were horrified. I could see it on your face."

He retracts his hand. "It needed to be done, Maia." He starts walking.

"It didn't, actually." She stands. Breaking their number one rule, she yells at his back, "I could have let him go! You and I both know that!"

Lucas faces her, exasperated. "Maia, they were *bounders*. They would have killed us. You were magnificent back there—albeit a little scary." He chuckles, waiting for her to smile, but she's like ice.

The smile slips from his face and he continues up the trail. "What's done is done," he says over his shoulder. "Has it ever occurred to you that I may be dealing with my *own* battles right now?"

Her heart plummets. *Miguel.*

The last time Lucas saw his little brother, he was abandoning him. They were teenagers. He left Miguel all alone, the grave of their mother still fresh in the yard. It could have been a death sentence, deserting his brother like that, but Lucas left anyway.

After everything Maia and Lucas have sacrificed, they might find that Miguel may not even be there anymore. Or he may have died waiting. Or he may not want anything to do with Lucas. They could be safe in Leucothea right now, but instead, they are risking their lives every minute, and it could all be for nothing.

Maia catches up behind him and follows in his wake, her eyes locked on the back of his head. The silence between them is deafening. His shoulders are slumped, his focus on the ground, and he leaves a trail of grief littered behind him.

They follow the path until they come across a narrow road surrounded by pines. Maia is the first to step from the tree line, her shoes crunching layers of pine needles. An abandoned semitruck sits along the side of the road, now a skeleton of metal hollowed out by fire. Lucas snaps his fingers. He points to the semi, then holds up his map and nods to the other side of the road. *Keep going.* They cross the street and continue into the woods.

A large sign is nailed to a tree. *STAY OUT! Traps ahead! Enter at your own risk!*

Lucas shoves Maia behind him, and she scans the wooded floor. *Traps?* He grabs a large branch from the ground and begins sweeping it back and forth and stabbing it into the dirt, then cautiously steps forward.

She grabs his arm. "What about the sign?" she whispers.

He shakes his head. "Mario said there'd be signs," he whispers over his shoulder. "It should be fine."

"*Should* be?"

He shrugs. "Something may have changed. Just stay behind me."

They wander down the narrow path, swollen with weeds and overgrown trees. A corpse with his leg clamped in the metal claws of a trap is strewn across the trail. They step over it and carry on, passing sign after sign warning them to turn back. Lucas swings the branch and taps the ground, attempting to catch any possible hidden wire or unstable ground.

They turn another bend and are met with bodies hanging from nooses, rotted down to near skeletons and rags. They litter the path as far as the eye can see. There are at least a dozen of them.

"Oh, *God*," Maia whispers.

Lucas uses his branch to swipe aside the first one like a curtain, and Maia warily passes through. As they quietly weave their way around the bodies, she can't help wondering if the whole thing was set up—like the bodies were hung after they died. The ropes around their necks are clean. Had they died up there, the noose would be stained from slowly cutting through flesh. She knows this better than anyone, having come across more than her fair share of hanged bodies. Humans left alone with nothing to live for. Eventually, they become a pile of bones on the ground, but this takes time.

After a while, the signs and the bodies become fewer and fewer. More than once, Lucas stops and pulls his tattered and stained map from his pocket for reassurance that they haven't missed a turn somewhere. It's hard to know when your only indications on a hand-drawn map are manmade ones—a corpse or a truck or some sort of structure. They are surrounded by nothing but forest.

Eventually, the light of the trail brightens, and they step out onto a large open field with a log cabin in the middle. Lucas steps forward and drops his pack, blowing out a long breath. They've arrived.

He wanders over to a chopping block under a large oak tree. The rusted ax lodged into the block is covered in cobwebs. He swipes the wood clippings into his hand and looks at Maia, shaking his head. Nothing fresh.

They slowly sweep the yard, searching for any signs of life. To the side of the house, there's a large vegetable garden covered in weeds. It doesn't appear to have been tended to in a while.

Maia walks to the other side of the house. The overgrown lawn is expansive and surrounded by woods, but there are no signs of life. She meets Lucas again in front. A clothing line is tied between two trees with a single shirt hanging from one shoulder. It looks like someone was here but has left. A long time ago.

She waits for Lucas to look in her direction, but he won't. She leans forward, waving her hands, but he won't take his eyes off the house. He clenches his hair between his fists.

After it becomes clear he's not going to look at her, she says aloud, "Is this it? For sure?"

"For sure," Lucas says.

"Should we check inside?" she says. "Just in case?"

He looks at her with weary eyes. "Can you? *Por favor*? I don't think I can."

She nods and slowly walks up to the old cabin, her heart pounding. What if this is it, and they are too late? What if Miguel died waiting for him? It would kill Lucas. He gives the appearance of a stubborn and tough man, but inwardly, he's deeply sensitive. He would blame himself, and there would be nothing she could say to fix that.

The cabin's wraparound porch is littered with dead leaves and sticks. She inhales, preparing herself, then quickly walks up the four wooden steps to the front door.

"Hello?" she yells. "Anyone here?"

She turns toward Lucas. The color has drained from his face.

"Miguel?" she calls out, still staring at Lucas. She

turns toward the door. Wincing, she knocks, then quickly steps back.

It is silent.

After a moment, she walks to the window beside the door and wipes the grime from the glass. The home appears lived in, with blankets on the couch and dishes stacked in the kitchen, but there doesn't seem to be anyone here. She jiggles the doorknob—*locked*.

"Let's just go," Lucas says from the yard. "It's clear he's not here anymore. This stuff hasn't been touched in ages." He grabs Maia's pack from the ground.

The porch creaks, and a dark figure steps around the corner of the house. Maia turns to face him, and Mario's words slice through the air. *He's the oldest young man you'll ever meet.*

The man's dark beard is long and ratted. The top half of his thick hair is a mop of curls, descending into dreadlocks. Intricately designed tribal tattoos cover his left arm down to his wrist; the tattoos on his right arm stop just below his elbow. Despite his downtrodden appearance, his shoulders are broad, his arms muscular.

Maia holds her hand against her chest, breathless. She's never seen this man before, she knows this. Yet ... something about him seems overwhelmingly familiar.

He glares at her for a moment, his brow deeply creased. "What do you want?" he croaks with a thick accent, and he gazes across the lawn at Lucas. There are a few gray hairs in his dark mane, but there are no wrinkles around his eyes. "Just take what you want and leave me be," he says, and he turns away.

Maia looks at Lucas. He's squinting at the man in disbelief.

"Miguel?" he says, and he steps forward.

The man stops and looks at Lucas over his shoulder.

"Miguel?" Lucas says again.

The man shakes his head. "Can't be," he says. "*Impossível.*"

"Brother?" Lucas's voice cracks.

Maia's hand flies to her mouth.

"Can't be." Miguel stumbles to the railing, staring at the bracelet around Lucas's wrist.

Lucas walks across the yard as Miguel shuffles along the railing, hand over hand toward the stairs. Maia steps out of his way and backs into the house.

Lucas breaks into a run. "*Brother!*"

Miguel staggers down the stairs, and the two men run toward each other across the yard.

"*Ahhh!*"

"Is it really you?!"

They hold each other's faces in disbelief. Lucas pulls at the tangled mess on Miguel's head, speaking to him in Portuguese and laughing through his tears.

Miguel says something back, gripping Lucas's shoulders and shaking him.

"I came," Lucas says in English. "I'm here. I'm so sorry. I'll never leave you again, my brother."

The two men embrace, and Lucas closes his eyes. Maia stands watching from the porch with her hand over her mouth, a tear gliding down her cheek.

TWELVE

"Why ... won't ... you ... *budge!*" Maia wrestles with the large living room window. She pushes against the glass, grimacing as she grips the wooden ledge and shaking the old frame back and forth. The window seal cracks and it slides open, sending her tumbling across the floor. She lies on her back, catching her breath.

Water sloshes in the bathtub down the hallway. Miguel is in there. He insisted Lucas and Maia take their time cleaning up first. *Por favor, you are my guests*, he said.

Maia was grateful at the time, but is even more so considering how long he's been in there. He hums the same song Lucas sang for her in the backyard of their LA home. She smiles, softly humming along with him.

"Our mother used to sing us that song," Lucas says. He reaches out and helps her to her feet. "She'd sing it to lull us to sleep."

"One of my favorite songs," Maia says. "Although I

don't know many songs, so take that how you will." She wipes the dust from her pants.

"You don't know that many songs *yet*," Lucas corrects her, softly singing the lyrics while Miguel hums from the other room. He kisses the tip of her nose, then grabs the cushions by the door and heads outside.

One after the next, every window and door of the cabin has been opened. Lucas is outside, beating the sagging and broken couch cushions back to life. Clouds of dust billow with every whack of the broom. The fire in the backyard has been going all day, heating countless pots of water. Maia pours another bucket into a tub of steaming water, a pile of clothing at her feet.

The heat of the day is sweltering. Lucas takes off his shirt and walks inside with a cushion in each hand, the contours of his muscles highlighted in glistening sweat. Maia whistles at him from the kitchen, and he smiles at her over his shoulder.

She tilts her head. There's something different about him today. He sets the cushions on the couch and wipes his forehead with the back of his hand. He scours the living room.

"Hey," she says, rolling her wet cloth into a ball.

He opens his hands and she chucks him the rag. He smiles at her, and that's when it hits her ... Why he seems so different. He can finally breathe. Miguel is alive and has accepted him back into his life. They have a safe haven to rest before the next huge leg of their journey. She breathes a sigh of relief. Things are going to be better from now on.

Lucas wipes the layers of dust from the tables, the bookshelves, and the windowsills. He comes back to the kitchen again and again, wringing out his blackened rag and stealing kisses from Maia. They've spent hours cleaning the layers of filth from the home while Miguel remains hidden in the bath, doing the same to himself. They may not stay here for long, but there's nothing like eating and sleeping in a clean home after being surrounded by decay for so long. And besides, it's the least they can do to help Lucas's long-lost brother.

Finally, Miguel comes out. His long beard is gone, revealing a freshly shaven face. Maia is taken aback, and she clutches her chest.

He catches her reaction. "What is it?" he asks sheepishly.

"Oh," she says with an awkward smile. "It's just ... you men look so similar."

But it's not that. Sure, it's unmistakable that Miguel and Lucas are brothers. They both have darker features, curly hair, accents ... but that's pretty much where it ends. Lucas's frame is more petite than Miguel's, although Maia would never call Lucas petite. His curls are kept relatively short. Whereas Miguel is taller, more chiseled, and broad, with long dreadlocks and tattoos.

Maia watches Miguel as he jokes with Lucas in Portuguese, and he playfully punches Lucas's arm. There's something familiar about him, but she can't figure out what. Now that he's shaven his face, it's unmistakable. Somehow, Maia knows this man, despite the fact that they've never met.

"Miguel was just saying he's better looking than me," Lucas says to Maia. "I told him you would disagree with that."

"Only because she wouldn't want to hurt your precious little feelings," Miguel says.

She shakes her head. "You men are like children."

"I can't believe you think we look similar," Miguel says to her.

"Except I'm not growing a mop on my head," Lucas says, shoving him.

Miguel pats his crazy hair. "I know, I can't bring myself to cut it. But I can't do the dreads in the back."

"I can," Maia says, and she drops her rag on the counter. "I wore my hair in dreads as a teenager."

Lucas looks at her. "You? I can't picture it."

She smiles. "Used to drive my grandfather crazy, which is pretty much the only reason I did it."

Maia and Miguel walk to the bathroom, and Lucas brings in a chair, setting it in front of the mirror. "You might need this."

Miguel sits down, and Maia starts on the farthest back dreads. She looks at him, now gazing at her through the mirror.

"You make Lucas really happy, you know?" he says in his thick accent. "I can see it."

She smiles. "So do you."

"Yes, but there is much to talk about," he says.

Her smile fades. "There is."

"After all those years, I never gave up hope. I don't know how, but I just knew I would see him again."

"You've been here a long time?"

"Too long, I think. I was about ready to give up."

She puts her hand on his shoulder. "I'm really glad you didn't."

He looks at her through the mirror with those same big brown eyes as Lucas. "Me too," he says after a while.

"Okay." She ties his dreads back with a thick piece of twine. "All finished. You're like a new man now."

He looks at himself in the mirror. "Wow." He nods in approval. "Thank you."

"My pleasure." She rubs her aching eyes. "Would you mind if I took a nap? It's been a really long day."

"No, of course. *Por favor*, take the room upstairs. I just put fresh sheets on the bed, and the breeze through those windows is the best in the house."

"Thanks."

Maia grips the railing as she walks up the stairs, exhaustion setting in. She crawls on top of the bed, too tired to climb under the sheets, and closes her stinging eyes to a soft breeze and the sound of birds.

When she opens them again, dusk has fallen over the land. The chorus of crickets and tree frogs surrounds the cabin, and the echoes of laughter trail on the wafts of smoke. Maia yawns wide and stretches her arms above her head, feeling rested for the first time in days.

She follows the scent of smoke downstairs, through the living room, and down a long hallway leading to the back of the cabin. There's a large bonfire blazing in the middle of the backyard with flickers of fireflies dancing near the tree line.

Miguel and Lucas are sitting side by side on large wooden stumps beside the fire. Miguel puts his hand on Lucas's shoulder and they are all grins. Miguel leans in and says something, and Lucas tips his head back, laughing at the sky.

Maia's heart is so full. She leans against the doorframe, watching the men together. She's never seen Lucas so happy. She tries to listen to their conversation, but they are speaking Portuguese. There's something about having them both near that makes her feel safe. Complete.

She wanders out to the fire.

"There's my girl!" Lucas says as she approaches. He hands her a plate of food. "We made you dinner."

She happily takes it. "Are these mushrooms?" she asks.

"I love to forage," Miguel says. "These woods have some good mushrooms if you know where to look."

"I love mushrooms. I haven't had them in *so* long." She sinks her teeth into the large brown disc.

"Help yourself, please. I have baskets full." Miguel gestures to the house. Then, shaking his head, he says, "I can't tell you how good it is to have you both here. Please, tell me, what is your plan?"

"We are going to the Old Arctic Circle," Maia says as she tears into her grilled venison.

"Leucothea?" Miguel asks.

"You will ... come with us?" Lucas's words are choppy. Hesitant. He looks uneasy, twisting the fabric around his wrist.

"Yes, of course!" Miguel says. "Of course, I will come!"

Lucas sighs in relief, and they all grin at one another.

And then, there were three.

"Maybe we could recoup here for a few weeks?" Lucas asks Miguel. "It's so peaceful, and Maia and I have had some hellish nights back in LA."

"Oh, of course," Miguel says. "*No problema.* Tomorrow we'll go over our supplies. I have many things here."

"That would be wonderful, thank you," Maia says.

"You are most welcome," Miguel says. He smiles at her, and she can tell they are going to be good friends. "So, I have many questions," he says. "Please, tell me, how did you meet? How did you come here? How did you find me?"

"Wow." Lucas swipes the curls from his face, and he smiles tenderly at Maia. "There's so much to catch up on."

"It's okay," Miguel says. "We have nothing but time."

The last of the sky's light fades with the fireflies, and the three stay up all hours of the night as Maia tells Miguel about New Zealand, her grandfather, and Huck. Lucas tells him about the loss of his wife and son from an earthquake back in South America. He tells him about becoming a pirate and how he and Maia met. Miguel stares wide-eyed as they tell him about being stranded on an island made of plastic in the middle of the Pacific Ocean. They tell him about the raft and the storm and the ship from Leucothea that dropped them in the flood zone of LA. They tell him everything.

Well ... *nearly* everything.

The following day, Maia searches her bag for her tea. Lucas was adamant about not packing anything that wasn't "completely necessary," but tea *is* necessary. She finds her little bag of dried leaves and sets it on the bed, then opens the closet doors and tries to stuff her over-sized pack inside. This thing will be like an extension of her body soon, it would be nice to forget about it for a few weeks. She just needs to move some things aside to make room.

Under a few folded blankets, her fingers trip over a box. She slides it out from beneath the fabric and lifts it before her. It's a shoebox.

It's a … *woman's* … shoebox.

She glances over her shoulder. She knows better than to snoop around living people's things, but … *what if*? Her curiosity overtakes her, and she opens the lid.

She gasps. Women's hiking boots—hardly worn. Wide-eyed, she lifts a boot from the box, its laces dangling beneath the thick rubber soles. She loosens the laces and pulls back the tongue. *Can't be.* She slides her foot in. It's a little snug, but much better than what she's been wearing. She stands in disbelief.

"Good morning," Lucas says as he walks past the room. He backs up to the doorway. "What do you have there?"

She looks up at him, speechless. She tries on the other boot, then walks in a circle. It feels like she's walking on clouds.

"Where did you find those?" Lucas asks.

Maia paces between the bed and the closet. "In the closet." She points. "There."

Lucas's face drops. "Oh, Maia—"

Miguel walks into the room, and Lucas grimaces.

Maia stops in her tracks, looking between the brothers. "What?"

Miguel's smile fades as he looks at the boots. That isn't a good look.

"I'm sorry," she says. "I wasn't trying to snoop. I was just looking—"

"It's okay." He holds up his hand as he stares at the boots. "They look like they are a good fit," he says after a while.

"Is this okay? I mean..." Her voice trails, and a long silence ensues. "No," she says, and she bends over and unties the laces. "I'll take them off. I've overstepped ... I shouldn't have."

"No, really," Miguel says. "Good boots like those are hard to come by. But they are a good fit, yes?"

Maia doesn't speak, glancing between Lucas and Miguel. They both look uncomfortable—Lucas more so than Miguel.

She slides off the boots and places them back in the box. "I'm sorry. They go right back where I found them." She shakes her head, shoving the box back under the blankets.

Miguel walks to the closet and pulls it back out. He hands it to her. "*Por favor*, take them."

Maia looks at Lucas. He closes his eyes and nods.

"Please," Miguel says. "I would have offered them myself, but I forgot they were up here." He opens the lid and holds up a boot, dwarfed in his large hand. "You both have really small feet, no?"

Both?

Mario's words come back to her. *He was with his family. They were attacked by a mountain mob ... Pretty gruesome...*

"They were my wife's," Miguel says, reading her face.

"Oh, Miguel," Maia says. "I could never—"

"Please." He hands the boots to her. "There is no one better in this world to use these boots than you, my brother's new wife."

"Oh, we're not—" Maia stumbles on her words.

"We aren't married yet," Lucas says.

"*Yet*?" Maia looks at him.

The color drains from his face.

Miguel crosses his arms with a huge smile on his face. "Well!" he says, and he smacks Lucas hard on the back. "That was fun." He chuckles as he leaves the room.

Lucas flashes Maia an awkward smile.

Miguel pokes his head back in the doorway. "Maia. Take the boots." He disappears again, his footsteps pounding down the stairs.

THIRTEEN

Over a week has passed and Lucas, Maia, and Miguel get on like they've known each other a lifetime. There is something about Miguel that makes Maia feel like she's been united with an old friend, and the way he jokes with her, it seems the feeling is mutual.

The three head out every morning in the early hours to hunt. They work well together—effortless. Lucas has smiled more in this past week than in all the months Maia has known him combined. Miguel teaches them the lay of the land, and they spend their days cooking delicious food and talking around a roaring, outdoor fire. It seems the three of them are happy to forget the immense journey that lies ahead—if even just for a while.

Every evening, Lucas is generally the first to fall asleep, so Maia and Miguel stay up for hours talking. Miguel is happy to discuss anything and everything under the stars—everything except the events that led to him being stuck in these hills for so long. Maia, too, finds it easy to open up, although she still hasn't found the courage to tell him *everything*.

She tries to listen in when the two men are talking. Despite the fact that they are speaking Portuguese, she can tell by their tone that they never discuss anything serious. For all she knows, they are talking about the weather. She's tried asking Lucas about when he and Miguel will discuss what happened when he left his brother so long ago, but she is often met with annoyance. It seems the men would rather forget it even happened.

There are secrets lingering in the silence between them.

As they sit around the fire, sparks drift into a velvety black sky.

"I have a surprise for you," Miguel says to them with a smile. "Stay here."

As he heads into the house, Lucas grabs Maia's hand. "Do you..." He glances over his shoulder, then inches closer. "Do you think you should tell Miguel about, you know ... *everything*?"

She bites her lip. She feels safe around Miguel, she doesn't think he'd judge her. But still, she feels hesitant. "What if he doesn't accept me?"

Lucas tilts his gaze. "Maia, don't worry about him not accepting you. *You* accept you."

She looks down at her hands. "I do."

"*Do* you?"

"I just, I don't have it harnessed yet."

Lucas nods, thinking about his words. "Do you need to have it ... harnessed ... before you say anything?"

"I just need more time," she whispers. "Alone. Do you think you could go with Miguel when he goes hunting tomorrow?"

"Sure."

Miguel comes back with a bundle in his hands.

"What are you up to?" Maia laughs.

He drops the bounty onto the ground.

Lucas leans forward. "Is that—"

"Sweet corn," Miguel replies.

Maia grabs a papery husk. "I've always wanted to try these!"

"Do they not have corn in New Zealand?" Miguel asks.

"I'm sure we did. I just couldn't find the seeds."

"Well, here, it grows everywhere. Not like it used to, but you can still find some pushing its way through the layers of rot, like some sort of demon." He shakes his head. "It's practically indestructible. It was specifically engineered—even the *dirt* was manipulated so that farmers didn't need to care for the crops. Before The End, it fed billions, fed livestock ... was put into everything they ate."

"How do you know this?" Lucas asks, flipping a husk in his hands. "Last time I saw you, you wanted nothing to do with reading or books."

"Yes, well," Miguel says. "That was a long time ago."

Suddenly, the crackling of the fire seems so loud. Maia watches the two men, the silence between them like a demon of its own accord.

Miguel sighs. "After you left, I tried to learn everything you knew. I thought maybe it would help me figure out where you went."

Lucas nods, his face flooded with shame. "Well, your English is impeccable." He forces a smile, but Miguel only looks at him.

"So! What do we do with this 'demon' corn?" Maia asks. Her voice is jittery and awkward, and she bites her lip. Why is she changing the subject? It's clear these men need to talk.

"I've already soaked them." Miguel is quick to respond. "It's a bit of a process cooking them over the fire and making sure the husks don't burn." He holds out his hand, and they give him their husks. "You just sit back and keep telling me more of those beautiful stories of New Zealand."

"How about you, Brother?" Lucas says. "I'd love to hear more about your story. How you got here?"

Clearly haven't talked about anything serious.

Miguel stabs the logs in the fire, flattening them into manageable embers. "Yes, I will tell you ... someday. Today is not that day."

"Okay," Maia says. "Then at least tell us about the *bodies*." She rubs her hands together.

Miguel looks confused, and then it registers. "*Ah!* Yes. The *bodies*." He shakes his head. "Those are not my bodies."

"I knew it." She leans against a stump.

"Well, the one in the trap, that one was mine. He was on my land, but I didn't know until I found him dead. He had dragged himself a long way with his leg stuck between those steel claws. It would have been a terrible way to die. I didn't feel okay about my traps after that.

Maybe this man did not see the signs. Maybe it was dark. So, I got rid of the traps, but not the signs. I found the other bodies while foraging the land and the homes around here. I hung them as I found them. That generally did the trick, and then I didn't have to be responsible for any more deaths."

Maia swallows, thinking about the blood on her hands. "Well," she says, tucking her hair behind her ear. "They were sufficiently creepy."

"And yet, they did not stop you," Miguel says with a wink.

"Nothing would stop me, Brother," Lucas chimes in, his face serious.

Miguel glances at him for a moment, then looks back at the fire.

"So, Lucas and I have been working on combat training," Maia says to Miguel. "It'd be really nice to have someone new step in. Lucas's moves are becoming predictable."

Lucas scoffs.

"Combat?" Miguel asks. "I'd love to learn more combat." He lines a row of corn on an old metal grate he's placed over the flames. "But, if I am honest, I prefer my staff."

Maia sits up. "You're a *bo* fighter? Why am I only now just learning this?"

Miguel laughs, lifting a brow. "You want to fight with a bo?"

"Please!" she says. "Anytime I've used a stick in fighting—"

"Which was only once," Lucas interjects.

"He just grabbed it to pull me into him," Maia says, eyeing him.

"Too easy." Lucas smiles.

"I could really use some guidance. I'm so intrigued," Maia says.

Miguel nods. "Okay, training starts tomorrow. I have a few good staves, but finding the right one is very personal. I might need to whittle one down for you."

Maia sits back and grins.

Perfect. This moment is perfect.

After a while, the corn is ready.

"Okay, I think it has cooled off enough," Miguel says, and he hands both Lucas and Maia a cob. He peels back the layers of the husk, exposing the steaming, bright-yellow rows of corn. Maia's eyes widen, following him step by step. He smiles.

Then, there is silence as they crunch into their corn.

"Oh, right!" Miguel reaches into his shirt pocket and pulls out a small glass jar filled with what appears to be white sand mixed with rice.

"You have *salt*," Lucas says. "You legend."

"Is there rice in there?" Maia asks, holding out her cob with feathery stubs of missing corn.

Miguel grabs her hand. "Twist it around."

She turns her cob as Miguel salts it, and he does the same for Lucas. "Yes, the rice keeps the salt from sticking," he says before taking another bite.

Maia chomps off a mouthful, the salty kernels exploding on her tongue. She and her grandfather only used salt for special occasions. Although, toward the end of his life—like his whisky—he became more lenient on the matter.

A few hours later, they lie in the grass, listening to the crackling fire and the crickets and the frogs.

"I just can't believe you two are here," Miguel says, looking up at the stars. "This feels like a dream."

Another sharp pain digs into Maia's gut, followed by an intense rumbling. She turns away and rubs her stomach. These pains have been happening with greater frequency over the last hour. She's been struggling to let each wave pass without being noticed. Another stab from within, and she sits upright, grimacing from the pain.

"Are you okay?" Lucas sits up beside her.

She wraps her arms around herself. "Yes, I'm okay." She leans forward, stifling a moan. "Just having a bit of a stomachache." Her stomach twists again, and she stumbles to her feet. She's going to vomit.

"Maia, you don't look good," Miguel says with concern.

"I just need—" She gags, then covers her mouth, embarrassed. She looks at the men, both staring up at her. "I need to lie down," she says, turning toward the cabin.

"I'll come with." Lucas stands.

"*No!*" she shouts. "Stay there. I'll be right back." She races toward the house.

Something strange is happening.

The pain is like a knife repeatedly stabbing her stomach. She doubles over as she stumbles to the side of the cabin, finding solace in the blanket of darkness. She falls to her knees at the base of a tree and vomits.

It's the corn. There is something in that corn. She crouches on the ground, heaving until she dry-retches, coughing and gasping until every last kernel comes up.

Bracing against the tree, she climbs to her feet and looks around. The nighttime chorus she has fallen in love with is ... *warped*. The crickets are so loud. They are *screeching* —like metal against metal. She covers her ears as she stumbles forward, the world around her pulsating from the shrill grinding of countless wings.

Must get into the house. Just get into the house and close all the windows. She'll sleep this off.

As she staggers to the front of the house, the earth seesaws back and forth. Grabbing the railing of the front steps, her hand sinks into the wood. She lifts it away, the rail like goo hanging in strings from her fingers. She steps back, wiping the sticky mess on her shirt. The entire house seems to be buckling. Caving in.

This isn't real.

The screeching of the crickets intensifies. Maia covers her ears and stumbles into the woods. The trees sway as if underwater, their green leaves dripping to the ground. Tree frogs scream at her from every angle and their eyeballs glow, mirroring a light that isn't there. The blaze of their eyes grows until they pop from their skulls, hanging like reflective beads in the air. The forest is covered with them.

What is happening?

This isn't real.

The trees whisper as she passes. They are constant, the whispers, but she can't distinguish between them. She wanders through the woods until she enters the alley of hanging bodies. She stops. They hang lifeless from the trees—she knows they're dead—but ... she can hear them breathing. She turns to go back, but the forest behind her is melting, obliterating the path.

She turns toward the first corpse and cautiously pushes it aside. A low grumble escapes the man's mouth and he reaches for her, pulling at her hair. She screams, backing into the second body. The woman's rotting fingers wrap around Maia's face and dig into her mouth, muffling her screams. Maia pulls at them. The fingers snap like twigs in her grasp.

The hanging bodies are moaning, reaching, ripping her clothing, pulling her hair. She slinks to the ground and crawls on her elbows beneath the bodies, inching beneath their kicking feet. Their toes scrape along her back.

A spider crawls across her outstretched hand. She shakes it free, only to find a black centipede snaking across her arm. The ground begins heaving with creeping, slithering things, slowly covering her body. She lunges to her feet and pushes through the bodies until she finally breaks free outside of the trees.

She looks around. She's back on the road with the semi. The hollowed-out rig, once ravaged by fire, now appears normal. It sits on the side of the road with its headlights on, a young man sleeping in the driver's seat. Smoke begins to pour from the hood. She screams, running toward the truck as the flames quickly engulf it. The man inside turns to glare at her. She backs away with her hands on her mouth as his skin blackens and his lips melt from his face.

She cries out, covering her eyes. The fire's roar silences, and her screams echo against the trees. She opens her eyes to find the semi once again an old, rusted skeleton of metal.

She runs down the deserted street until she finds

herself in a neighborhood. Ghoulish figures of the dead slowly shuffle past, their spirits wafting like smoke from their bodies. They see her too, their eyes heavy with sadness. They plead with her, but like the trees, she cannot understand what they're saying.

A phantom child with blonde hair perches on a tricycle in the middle of a yard. An apparition of a man pushing a rusted mower across his yard turns toward her, his mouth open as if midscream. A young woman with bouncing curls, a floral dress, and a decaying face passes by, holding a bag of groceries. She stops in the street, staring at Maia as if *she* were the ghost. The woman drops her groceries to the ground, and the tomatoes splatter against the pavement.

Maia reaches out and the ghostly woman mirrors her. As their fingertips touch, the woman crumbles to dust and is carried away by the wind. The little girl on the tricycle shrieks with a blood-curdling scream, and Maia sprints back down the middle of the street as honking cars filled with ghoulish men swerve past.

She runs back into the forest, smashing through tree branches and stumbling over bushes. What is happening to her?

The trees whisper in response. *Poison.*

She swings around, bracing herself against the relentless chanting from the bark.

Poison. Poison. Poison.

With heavy eyes, she pushes forward, clutching a tree branch. It tenderly wraps around her hand. Another limb sweeps across the path, gently laying her to the cool earth. She lies in the dark, the visions and the whispers fading until she can only hear the beating of her heart. No, it's another heartbeat—that of an animal.

"Huck?" she mumbles, reaching into the dark. "Are you there?"

A cold nose touches her fingers, then nudges into them. Maia squints but cannot see through the blackness. She pats Huck's large head as he curls up beside her.

Strange. He doesn't carry the scent of a dog.

"You smell funny, Huck." She wraps her arms around his thick fur and lays her head on his chest, the sound of his beating heart lulling her to sleep.

FOURTEEN

When Maia awakens, an early morning light has seeped back into the world. It is quiet—not even the birds make a sound, and a dense fog has swallowed up the woods. Maia relishes the stillness. All seems right again. The trees are no longer whispering, and the darkness has been relieved of its ghosts. For the moment, it's just the sweet silence of Maia and the trees.

She rolls onto her back, snapping twigs beneath her. A dull ache throbs within her hollow gut, and her head is pounding. So *thirsty*. She doesn't miss this feeling—thirst. It's enough to make any person go mad.

Rubbing her head, she peers through the fog at the branches above. This forest is strange. Wherever she is, she's never been here before. Last night, she wandered off in the darkness, high out of her mind—*poisoned*—and now she is lost. She flips her head to the side, feeling the ground beside her. It's still warm.

She sits up. "Huck?!"

She shakes her head. No, of course not. What *happened* last night? Her boots are lying on the ground beside her; she must've kicked them off in her sleep. Wiping the crusted dirt from her top, she flips her hand to strands of coarse orange hair stuck to her palm. *Orange?*

Who *were* those people? She holds her head in her hands, rocking back and forth. She knows the answer. She stares into the woods, her hair in her fists. They were the dead of this land. But unlike her dreams where she would wander the streets of her ancestors completely unnoticed, these people could see her.

And this time, she wasn't dreaming.

There was something in that corn ... something that made her deathly ill, and her *fever* made her hallucinate. Yes, she was just hallucinating.

Except she wasn't. It was *real*. She rubs her throbbing temples. Those people were horrified, as if Maia was the ghost. As if *she* was the one who didn't belong. They looked her straight in the eye and without saying a word, they told her what happened.

It was the perfect storm of disasters that had been clawing at the edges for centuries, building beneath the masses of human feet and brick and glass. While humanity thrived, the Earth was only gathering steam— and lots of it. Before The End, there were so many things that haunted humans, but it was Mother Nature who ended them.

It was *Maia* who caused their undoing.

She is not one of them. She is not one of them. This whole time, all she wanted was to be one of them.

She is not one of them.

She looks down at her trembling hands. The tip of her finger has a small gash from a stone. She rubs her fingertips together, and the blood smears between them.

Yet, she is still human.

A wave of giggles echoes across the breeze. Maia freezes. More giggling—from a child. She knows this sound. She twists from the ground. The sun has broken through the fog, highlighting swarms of gnats. Searching between the trees, she spots red curls from behind a pine tree in the distance. The hand of a child is wrapped around its trunk.

A little girl peers out, just a single eye peeking from behind the tree. It's the same little girl Maia has chased down the drowned city streets in her dreams, but she's never seen her face. The child's gorgeous red curls fall beside her blue eye. Her chubby hand is over her mouth, and her eye is squinting from her smile. Freckles scatter across her rounded cheeks. Such innocence in her face.

"Hey," Maia says, reaching out.

The little girl runs.

"No, wait!" Maia grabs her boots and chases after her.

Specks of red flicker through the forest, but the little girl is fast. Maia pushes her way against the mess of trunks and twisted branches, but she can't keep up. She's going to lose her.

Eventually, Maia stumbles into a clearing. The little girl is standing on the other side of a large pond with her back toward her. And then Maia watches in disbelief as the child slowly turns, facing her for the first time.

After a lifetime of dreams, Maia has never seen the child's face. The little girl smiles, her chubby cheeks rounded beneath her one blue and one green eye.

It's Maia. The little girl is *Maia*.

Maia walks around the pond, praying the child doesn't run. The little girl watches her, her giggles traveling in hushed waves across the water. A heron takes flight. His curled feet drag across the surface of the pond, leaving two small wakes trailing behind him.

Maia rounds the bend and approaches the girl, now gazing up at her, and she drops to her knees before her. The child tilts her head as Maia strokes her hair. She forgot she had curly red hair as a girl. She touches a crimson spiral and the little girl mirrors her. They both flinch, and the child looks at her in surprise. Her tender young face melts into sorrow.

Her mother's voice whispers from her memory. *Your entire life, you've been afraid to acknowledge who you truly are.*

The girl grabs Maia's hand and leads her to the edge of the pond. When Maia peers into the water, early childhood memories play out across the pond. Maia is seven years old again, playing in the backyard of their cabin high up in the mountains of New Zealand. It's a hot summer day, and the sun is high in the sky. The door of her grandfather's woodshed has been left open. He is inside, crouching on the ground beside a broken kitchen chair.

Maia is sitting in the middle of the yard, bathed in sunlight despite her grandfather's strict warnings. *Be careful.* He would say. *It will burn you.* She doesn't care; she loves the heat. Hovering her hand above the grass, she moves the blades without touching them. Then she climbs to her feet and lifts her hands to the sky, giggling that same giggle she's heard her entire life in her dreams, and she harnesses the wind.

Symphony. She used to call it "playing symphony."

Her grandfather comes out of the small shed as Maia twirls on her toes. Sticks and grass and pine cones swirl around her as she laughs from the middle of the protected vortex. Her grandfather braces himself against the wind, calling out for her to *stop*! And then a large branch slams into him, knocking him off his feet. He huddles on the ground, rocking back and forth while holding his head. Maia drops her hands, and the debris falls back to the earth.

Infuriated, her grandfather marches up to her and grabs her arm. She squints at him, but the sun behind him is so bright. He keeps yelling at her to *look at him*, but she can't. He berates her, over and over and over again.

What have I told you?!

Stop doing that.

It's not safe.

You could get hurt.

It's one of Maia's first memories of feeling the profound scorn of shame. She made a resolve in her young heart to never feel that way again, but its embers never died. She's carried it with her every day of her life, burning inside her like a thousand suns.

Another memory flashes across the pond. Maia's mother is lying in a bed. Alive. Young. Maia has just been born. Her mother and father are gazing down at her, cradled in her mother's arms. They are crying with smiles on their faces. Another woman Maia doesn't recognize is also in the room, wiping her mother's brow with a damp cloth.

Her mother's eyes roll back in her head. The woman grabs Maia, placing her in a basket as her father screams with tears streaming down his face. The woman pushes against her mother's chest, but her mother remains motionless with her hand flopped to the side. The woman looks up at Maia's father, shaking her head. His bellow fills the room.

Every single one of Maia's tears falling into the pond reflects a different scene from her life, and moments of shame, one after the next, reflect back to her. Another tear falls into the pond, and the images disappear, leaving Maia staring down at her reflection. Her mother appears beside her. Maia turns to face her, but she's not there. She looks back at her reflection, and her mother smiles at her.

"Things are not as they seem, Maia. I know it appears as if you have done these things to other people … hurt them, disappointed them. But this is your destiny. Every single one of us has agreed to be here in this life to guide you. The lives we live are so much more complex than what we see before us. The gravity of who you are stretches across many lifetimes, woven throughout countless stories. You have a *right* to be here."

Another tear drips from Maia's chin, and she looks away.

"Maia? Be who you are with all that you are."

She looks back at her mother, still smiling at her from the reflection of the pond.

"It is time to let this shame go. You have been carrying it for far too long, and it has dictated your entire life." Her mother begins to disappear, and for the first time, Maia does not resist. "This world is only a reflection of what lies within, Maia. Once you realize this, you will be truly *free*."

Maia reaches to her mother with a smile, her fingertips leaving ripples along the water.

"I am always with you," her mother says, and then she is gone.

Maia stands alone before the large pond. She peers into the murky depths. Schools of tiny fish cluster beneath a lily, and a dragonfly rests on top of its leaf, fanning its glittering wings. She takes a breath and lifts her foot above the water, then closes her eyes and steps down. She lands against something hard. The jolt takes her breath away. She opens her eyes to see a mound has risen from the pond to meet her. She places all her weight against it, and the cool mud squishes between her toes. Spiraling red hair falls across her face.

She places her other foot before her, hovering it above the water, and leans forward once again. She lands on another mound. With every step she takes, the soil rises out of the water to greet her. The glimmering energy of the Earth appears, surrounding her in the water and the trees and the sky, and her head falls back as the spirit of the Earth swells up from the depths and into her veins.

For the first time in her life, it no longer burns.

She crouches along the pond, hovering her hand above its surface. Lifting her palm, she pulls the water up as if it were a stringed puppet. She pushes it down, and the shape of a hand indents the surface. She raises it farther this time, delighted as a wall of water comes up to her waist. She releases it, ducking as it splashes back down. With both hands lifted to the sky, she guides the water into a wall around her.

Symphony.

Maia spins with her hands to the sky, giggling like a child as the pond swirls around her. Small fish jump from the water below and birds twirl on a wing above. All the while, Maia dances across the pond's surface, the muddy soil catching her every step.

A woman whispers, "*Maia.*"

She releases the pond, and it falls back to the earth like rain. A new wall of water rises before her, and she gazes into it like a mirror. She is met with the reflection of herself standing as a powerful queen. She is the soul of the Earth. She is proud. Her red hair cascades across her shoulders, and her white gown flows behind her. There's a new strength behind her eyes—a power unlike anything Maia has ever known. She reaches out her hand, and her reflection does the same. They meet on either side of the water.

Something moves behind her reflection, and Maia's smile fades. She pulls back her hand, and the reflection mirrors her. Another version of herself appears, stepping behind her. Maia turns around, but there's nothing but a field of swaying reeds. She faces the wall of water, watching as the woman from her nightmares stands behind her. She's nearly identical to Maia, but she carries an unmistakable anger behind her eyes. She places her hand on the other side of the wall. Maia lifts her hand to meet it.

A new vision appears. No longer at the pond, Maia now stands on a cliff. Gale-force winds swirl around her as she overlooks a large city burning to the ground. Hordes of terrified people are screaming below, and a tiger is standing by her side. Her hair is in scarlet curls, and her eyes are faintly glimmering. She's not wearing a white dress but a uniform, like that of a soldier or prisoner—or both.

Someone is running up to her. His hands are out, pleading with her to stop. "Maia! *NO!*"

Is it Lucas? His dark hair is much shorter, but she cannot see his face.

She is *so angry*. Her heart pounds as she holds her hands out over the city, wanting more than anything to smite the land with a single decree. She's conflicted, waging a fierce battle within herself. She screams with an otherworldly wail and the flames reach high into the sky, devouring the people crying out below. Her eyes are filled with tears, quivering with rage.

Something in her heart is completely broken.

The vision fades and Maia returns to the pond, her fingers interlaced with her reflection. But she can't decipher which one. She tries to pull back, but her image won't let go. A tear falls down Maia's cheek as she understands, they are one and the same.

She is nurturing. She is destructive. She is all of it.

The reflection releases her grip and the wall of water drops, plummeting Maia into the murky pond. When she stands in the waist-high waters, her red hair slowly unravels back into auburn waves. Dripping wet and gasping, she shivers as the choppy waves slosh around her.

FIFTEEN

Maia's boots drag against the cement as she shuffles down the misty road, the towering pines around her once again shrouded in fog. Her mind is reeling. Reeling. *Reeling.* This is a force beyond her, and it's clear the more she fights it, the more she'll suffer.

Stepping from the road, she wanders among the pines. Dragging her fingertips along the bark, she can sense the life within them. How can she feel so alone when she's surrounded by life?

She stops before a great pine piercing the sky. It is an ancient tree, living well beyond its years. It would have passed decades ago, but another tree down the road had warned it of an advancing mold. She glances at the much smaller tree alongside it. It has connected itself with the older tree's roots beneath the ground. Depends on it to stay alive.

They are all connected, this mammoth forest of trees, communicating beneath the surface with sounds inaudible to humans. She places her palm against the bark, listening to the low crackling beneath the ground. Coming and going, it is throbbing like a heart.

How easy it is to live one's life on repeat, the same cycles over and over until the lessons are learned. *If* the lessons are learned. It's only natural for Maia to feel afraid. Alone. Like the ghosts of this land, she is trapped between worlds.

She is a powerful being. She is a human being.

The visions from the pond flash through her mind. Was that *Leucothea* burning to the ground at the force of her hand? And why was her heart so broken?

She drops her head against the tree. One day this mighty giant will fall, and the small tree depending on it will also die. It seems sad for the young tree. It will be before its time, but their decaying bodies will make way for new life to thrive.

Death is so misunderstood. Maia understands a part of her must die so that she can be who she was always meant to be. But what part? Her *humanity*? Can she not be both? She is ready. She is terrified.

The men must be worried. She disappeared last night without saying a word. Stepping from the gentle giant, she glances around. Usually, she would be afraid. It's clear she's lost, but she pushes that aside and continues forward, hoping with all that she is that she can find her way back.

She comes across a field of rotting corn. This must be where Miguel got their dinner. A few stalks have pushed their way through and grow tall from the mire. *Like demons.* Maia steps across the thick layers of decay to a bright green stalk. It looks so beautiful.

Touching the long leaves, she feels nothing. This plant is a hybrid. Its natural genes have been bypassed, replaced by those of other animals trapped inside. She reaches between the rotted stalks and scoops the dirt into her hand. It crumbles in her palm. This isn't dirt, this is the decrepit remains of a Petri dish. The chemicals in this soil are meant to destroy every iota of life except that of the corn. Grandpa alluded to food like this. His quivering voice echoes in her memory.

Our technology, my God, the things we could do.

She continues on her way. Turning the bend of the road, she is once again met with the charred semi tipped on its side, and she sighs relief. Nearly there. She runs her hand along the dusty metal as visions of the melting ghost flash before her. Beyond the rusted truck is the path that will lead her back to the bodies. She lifts her chin and steps onto the dirt.

The bodies hang like they did the day she and Lucas first arrived. They are lifeless, unmoving. Maia looks down at her clothing, recalling the events of the night. Her shirt is not torn. She surveys the skeletons again. They do not breathe.

She commands the branches with a swipe of her hand, and they swing the bodies away from the path. She continues down the trail. When she enters the clearing with Miguel's cabin, she approaches the tree where she was sick the night before. Why is it the men could eat the corn and she couldn't?

She is not one of them.

She walks up the porch stairs to the front door and jiggles the knob—*locked*.

"Hello?" she calls out.

Turning the corner of the wraparound deck, she peers into the windows. The house is empty. The men would be worried sick about her, probably out searching the woods. She wanders to the firepit in the backyard and folds her arms across her chest, chilled in the cooler autumn air. The heat of the sun is sluggish, still battling its way through the fog.

She grabs some wood from the stack beside the cabin to make a fire but needs something to ignite it. Because of the morning dew, the men wouldn't have left anything out overnight. The vision of the burning city flashes in her mind. She has power over the elements of the Earth … Could she start a fire?

She collects some small twigs and dead leaves to make a bed of kindling and then kneels before the pit. How to do this? She closes her eyes, conjuring up an image of a fire. She opens one eye. Nothing.

She can do this—she *knows* she can. She closes her eyes, focusing on the crispy paper-thin anatomy of the dead leaves. She dives deep into their framework, so deep she can see a vibrating network of atoms within a massive universe of space. She focuses on them, her heart beating faster as she smashes them together. Keeping her eyes closed, she digs her fingers into the earth as the molecules collide, one after the next, exploding like fireworks.

"Maia?!" Lucas's panicked voice yells from the trees.

She opens her eyes and gasps. A wisp of smoke is curling from the dead leaves. She blows on the kindling, and a flame engulfs the brush. She sits back on her heels in shock.

"*Maia!*" Lucas drops his knife as he runs toward her.

She climbs to her feet and races toward him. They

collide. He wraps his arms around her and burrows his head in her neck.

"Where have you been?" He grabs her shoulders, looking her up and down. "Are you hurt?"

"No, I'm okay."

Miguel runs up to them. Maia reaches out, and he folds her into him. "We were so worried about you," he says as he hugs her. "We searched for you all night."

"I'm *so* sorry," she says. "That corn made me really sick."

He pulls away. "The *corn* made you sick?!"

"Why did you run?" Lucas asks, his voice strained. "Couldn't you hear us screaming for you?"

She looks at him. "Lucas, I was *really* ill. I couldn't hear anything besides the screeching crickets. It was like I was in another world."

"Screeching crickets? Were you hallucinating?" he asks.

She rubs her temples. "I don't know. I wouldn't even know how to begin explaining last night to you ... Or *today,* for that matter."

"How did you get this fire going?" Miguel asks, staring at the flames.

Lucas and Maia both look at the pit, the fire now devouring the last of the kindling. Lucas looks at Maia like he doesn't recognize her. "Did ... *you*?"

She can only look at him.

"*Meu Deus,*" he mumbles.

Miguel's eyes dart between Lucas and Maia. "Am I missing something?"

She looks at him. "Miguel, there's something I need to tell you."

"Let's go in the house," Lucas says. "We'll sit down and chat." He wraps his arm around her and leads her back toward the cabin. "You must be starving. I'll make you some food."

The three of them sit in the living room, and Lucas hands Maia some venison.

Miguel plops onto the couch opposite her. "Maia, I am so sorry my food made you ill. I will never forgive myself."

"It's okay, Miguel. Honestly."

"I've been eating that corn for years and have never had an issue. There must have been a fungus in your husk ... Although they've been engineered to withstand those things—"

"Miguel," Maia cuts him off. "I am ... *different* ... from you."

He smirks. "Clearly."

She rolls her eyes, suppressing her smile. "No. I mean, I..." She hesitates. "Have powers."

He stares at her. "*Definitely* a fungus."

She drops her head in her hands. Dusk settles upon them, and Lucas steps away to light the candles.

"Is this some sort of joke?" Miguel asks. "Because I don't get it."

"Wait," Maia says to Lucas. "Hand me that candle, please."

He gives her the glass jar filled with wax, and she places it on the table between her and Miguel.

"Be patient with me," she says. "I'm still learning." She wraps her hands around the candle and closes her eyes.

"Learning *what*—" Miguel whispers.

"*Shh*!" Lucas says.

She focuses on the charred candlewick, moving the particles like she does the blades of grass. They spin and collide in faster succession until a soft glow emits beyond her closed lids.

"*Jesus*, Maia," Lucas whispers beside her.

She opens her eyes to a lit candle, and she releases her breath.

Miguel glares at the candle. "How did you do that?" He waves his hand over the flame, then lifts the candle and looks beneath. He looks at her, his eyes widening. "And *why* did your hair do that?" He looks up at Lucas. "Why did her hair do that?"

"Miguel," Maia says. "I am the incarnation of Mother Nature."

His eyes narrow. "*Que*?"

"I am human, but I am more than that."

"So..." He hesitates, staring at the candle. "I am ... *not* dreaming."

"No," she says.

He looks at her, his gaze softening. "You are like Pachamama."

"Who?"

"She is our Earth goddess, worshiped in South America for thousands of years."

"There have been varying folklores over different lifetimes and cultures. But I am not like those myths. I am a *new* story."

"Okay," he says, nodding. "So ... you can start a fire with your mind, yes?"

"Yes."

He leans back and crosses his arms. "What else can you do?"

She sighs. "Not a lot, yet," she says. "I'm still figuring it out. I can move small things—things connected to the Earth like trees and bushes. I can communicate with animals. I can harness the wind."

Miguel shrugs, and his lips pull into a grimace. "Oh, okay ... '*not a lot*.' You can only 'harness the wind.' Is that all?"

She smiles, grateful for his sarcasm.

"Miguel, be serious," Lucas says.

"I am! But with the candle and the hair. And the *hair* —" Miguel begins ranting in Portuguese.

"She's been practicing her powers since we arrived," Lucas interrupts him. "It's a newer revelation, and it's been a process."

"*Okay*." Miguel nods, and he peers around the room. He stops and looks at her. "Is that why your eyes are two different colors?"

"You don't have to be afraid," she says. "I'm still me."

Miguel gazes at her. He has that same look in his eyes as Lucas when he's deep in thought, and Maia can't help but smile. They stare at one another in silence as the outside light continues to fade.

Finally, Miguel reaches his hand across the table. "Okay," he says.

Maia sighs, and she places her palm in his. A tiny spark surges between them, surprising them both. Miguel looks at her in awe. He smiles, and Maia notices his dimple for the first time.

SIXTEEN

The next morning, Maia awakens to the smell of venison and the *clink-tink-tink* of dishes in the kitchen. She groggily pulls herself out of bed, following the delectable aroma down the stairs, and perches on a step out of view, listening to the men in the kitchen around the corner. She doesn't know what they're saying, but there is so much laughter.

Miguel turns the corner. He tilts his head, grinning wide enough to bring out his dimple. "Hello, little bird."

She smiles.

"I was just coming to wake you," he says. "I hope you're hungry."

"I am."

He offers his hand and helps her from the step.

"Look what I found," he says as they walk into the kitchen.

"Good morning, darling," Lucas says.

She leans down and kisses him.

"I made you some tea," Miguel says, handing her a steaming cup.

"You gorgeous human." She grabs the mug and takes a seat at the table next to Lucas.

Miguel stands at the kitchen counter, cutting into an enormous hunk of steak.

"Good *God*, is that all for us?" Maia asks.

"This?" Miguel points his knife at the slab. "This is all mine. I have some corn for you out back." He winks.

She fights a smile. "You're a caveman."

"Meat good. Corn *baaaad*." He cuts into the steak, and the juices spill onto the cutting board. He brings two plates of venison to the table and sets them down. Lucas is shaking his head.

"Too soon?" Miguel asks as he heads back to the kitchen.

Maia slides her plate toward her. "This is amazing."

"I make a mean steak," Miguel says. He brings the final plate to the table and sits across from them. "Eat up! There is more. You are going to need all your strength today, Maia. I am teaching you to fight with a bo."

She straightens, elated. "*Okay*."

Miguel looks up from his steak and smiles. "Somehow I knew you would not have a problem with that."

"Miguel has shown me his basement of supplies," Lucas says, and he takes another bite. "I'm going to make a plan for what we'll bring and what will stay. Maybe swap out some things. We have a big journey ahead of us. What do you think?" He looks between the two of them. "You take the next week to train, and I'll sort a route for us and test out our supplies? Can you train Maia in a week, Miguel?"

He scoffs. "Doubtful."

She smacks him.

"Why don't you just figure out how to fight without having to touch anything?" Miguel says, and he shoves another piece of venison in his mouth. "Use your powers?"

She rolls her eyes. "I can't just *make things move*. I can harness the elements of the Earth: wind, water, fire. I can't just pick up inanimate objects and throw them across the room," she says flatly.

"Damn, that would be so convenient. There are a few crazies loitering about," Miguel says.

"You have no idea," Maia mumbles, and she takes another sip of her tea.

Both men stop. Lucas levels her a look, and Miguel goes back to cutting his meat.

"Oh, Miguel, I'm sorry," she says. "I didn't mean—"

"It's okay," he says.

In a small shed out back, Maia and Miguel stand before a wall of weapons. There are at least a dozen staves of different sizes propped against the wall.

"Wow, you weren't kidding about being a bo fighter," she says, running her hand across them.

"When I settled here, I was obsessed with making them. I trained my wife. I'm going to teach you how I taught her." He pulls a staff from the collection. "I think maybe this one will be good. It is small, like you."

She snaps the rod from him. "I'm not *that* small."

He smiles. "Okay, grip it with both hands. How does it feel? It should have a little weight to it but should feel pretty effortless to hold."

She handles the long wooden pole. "It feels good ... I think."

"You will know soon enough. Let's start with this. I will teach you the basics."

Maia and Miguel step out into the yard and stand across from one another.

"Okay, first you need to build strength in your hands and wrists," he says. "So I'll teach you how to spin. After that, you build speed. *Compreendo*?"

"I understand."

"Hold your staff before you with your left hand, palm up, like this. Twist your arm and spin the staff around. Then grab it with your other hand. Hand over hand, spin. Spin and grab, spin and grab." Miguel starts slow so Maia can mimic him, and then he builds speed until the staff is a blur, revolving before him.

Maia does as he says, rolling her arm and spinning the staff. She grabs it with her other hand and rotates the long pole. It feels good—*really* good.

Miguel grins. "You are a natural. You've done this before, yes?"

"No, I haven't." She spins the staff. "But I *really* like it."

"You are good at it. Okay, you must practice this all the time. Build strength. Build your relationship with your staff—it should feel like a part of you. I want to always see you out here, spinning."

"Yes, sir."

"What about your powers?" he says, whirling his staff

before him. "Lucas told me you still need time with them."

"I do. My sole focus this next week will be working on my connection to that power. But I also think this staff training will be good for me. It'll take the pressure off if I'm not in the right place, mentally or physically, to use my powers. Plus, I think it will build my confidence," she says as she slowly spins her staff. "Besides, I've always wanted to learn. I think I might be pretty good at it." She smiles, baiting Miguel for a compliment.

"*Hmm.*" He narrows his eyes. "We will see. I'll teach you how to block, strike, and breathe—these are all very important. And then it's up to you to practice whenever you can."

The following week passes in a blur as Miguel and Maia spend hours every day practicing in the yard. When they take breaks, they lie beside each other in the grass and look up at the sky, talking about the lives they've left behind, the books they've read, and their hopes for Leucothea. Sometimes Lucas comes out and joins them, but often he's in his own world in the basement, sorting through the piles of supplies Miguel has stockpiled for years.

Every morning after breakfast, Maia heads outside. Surrounded by the sun and the birds, she sits with nature, with *herself*. Holding out her hand, she moves the blades of grass below and the branches of the trees above. She starts the fires for the men before each meal, becoming more and more comfortable with her influence over the elements of the Earth—the elements of herself.

Then she moves to spinning. When she isn't spinning, she memorizes *the routine*: a set of moves designed to build strength with blocking and to find comfort in moving her staff. Most importantly, she needs to breathe. She's gotten pretty good at the moves—it's the breathing she hasn't conquered yet.

"You will never feel natural with your bo if you're not breathing properly," Miguel says. "Your body will be rigid, your mind distracted. You need to flood your body with oxygen."

He lifts his bo over his head and swings down on Maia. She holds her staff with both hands and blocks. He pivots and veers his staff toward her knees, and she blocks. Swing, block. Swing, block. Spin, spin, spin.

Maia can now not only comfortably twirl her staff before her, but Miguel has taught her multiple techniques. She spins hand over hand, then switches to twirling in a figure eight. She whips the spiraling staff into the air and catches it. Something about this simple rod of wood makes her feel powerful, and the more powerful she feels, the more confident she becomes.

Alone in the yard, Maia kicks high in the air, then jabs her staff before her. She whirls around and holds her bo above her head, blocking an imaginary blow. She twists in place and swipes her bo across the grass.

Miguel calls out from the cabin, "*Breathe*, Maia. You are still holding your breath!"

She tilts back her head, sighing in frustration.

He walks out of the door with his staff in hand. "The routine. Let's go."

They stand across from one another and bow.

Lucas steps out of the cabin. He crosses his arms, watching in silence. He's been nervous this entire week. Every night Maia comes to bed with bruises on her body and callouses on her hands, absolutely exhausted. Lucas doesn't say anything, but she can tell he hates it. She doesn't mind the pain. Miguel seems to trust her in a way that Lucas never has. She knows Lucas means well, but she finds the way Miguel treats her incredibly refreshing. He doesn't try to protect her or baby her.

Maia and Miguel lift their bo to the sky and cross them with a *snap*. He strikes high and she holds her staff over her head, blocking him.

"You are still holding your breath. Breathe out with a strong breath every time you move, Maia. This bo is a *part* of you."

He swings low and again, she blocks, exhaling a forceful breath. She spins with her staff and then jabs toward him. He swipes his bo across his body and thwarts her move. "*Exhale!*"

He holds his staff against hers, forcing it to the ground, then whips around and swipes his bo across her calves, knocking her off her feet. She lands on her back with a grunt.

"Maia?" Lucas rushes down the steps.

"Lucas, no!" she yells at the sky. "I've got this!"

He walks away, grumbling.

Miguel steps beside her, holding out his hand. "You okay?"

"I'm fine. Let's do it again."

He pulls her to her feet. "You sure?"

"Again, Miguel. *Again*."

SEVENTEEN

It is sunrise at the cabin.

The fresh mountain air flits in short, cool wisps through Maia's open bedroom windows. The men are downstairs packing up last-minute items. It is mostly quiet besides the odd *clank* or resounding *thud* through the walls.

Maia stands before an old mirror hanging on the back of the bedroom door. Her hair, once again tied high in a messy bun, is unusually dark. Her sun-bleached waves seem to have disappeared in the short amount of time hidden within these mountains. She steps closer to the mirror, brushing her finger against a red curl falling from her auburn bun. Her brow crinkles. *Huh.*

She backs up again, taking in her reflection. Her new boots are strapped to her feet. A blue bandana is folded and wrapped across her forehead. The fabric of her clothing is light, but she's wearing many layers, prepared for the drastic changes of heat and cold. Her pack is sitting against the wall below the open window, her beloved staff propped against it. She grasps the jade carving around her neck and blows out a breath.

This is it. Today, Maia, Lucas, and Miguel will head up the western backbone of North America to the Old Arctic Circle.

Today is a new beginning.

She lifts her pack by the strap. It's undoubtedly heavier since arriving at Miguel's. She places it on top of her thigh and kicks, hurling it onto her back with a grunt. She slides the straps over each arm and pulls them tight. The closer the pack is to her body, the less it will move around as she walks and the more comfortable it will be. She wraps the belt around her hips and clicks it together, pulling the cords tight.

She walks downstairs to the men hustling around the living room. Their two packs are leaning against the open front door. She unclips her bag, letting it slide off her shoulders to the ground.

Lucas walks up to her with a wide grin. "I have something for you."

She reflects his smile. "What is it?"

"*Ah-ah*. You must close your eyes and hold out your hands. *Por favor*, my darling."

She closes her eyes and cups her hands. A slightly sticky, hard circle is placed in her hands. She wraps her fingers around the tube and gasps, opening her eyes.

Duct tape.

"Where did you—"

"Miguel. He found this lying around some dusty warehouse in Mexico."

She stares wide-eyed at the silver tube. "Lucas," she

says, looking up at him, "I found duct tape as well. In that house in LA ... with the children."

"Why didn't you say something?"

"I didn't take it. I couldn't. And now ... *Look*." She holds the roll before her. "It always works out."

"You're a good person." He kisses her forehead, then tenderly brushes her cheek. "If I could see you smile like this every day, I would be the happiest man on Earth."

"Okay, lovebirds, you're making me sick," Miguel says as he enters the kitchen. "Are we ready?"

"More than," Maia says, and she hands Lucas the roll.

"Keep it," he says. "I'll put it in your pack." He pulls at her bag, unzipping a tiny sliver and shoving it in. "Not much room," he mumbles, but he manages to get the zip closed.

"Okay," Miguel says. "Go over it one more time, please?"

"Very little speaking in cities," Maia says. "Unless completely necessary and then only whispers. We can talk quietly wherever we set up camp for the night unless we're close to a city."

"Use the hand signals I taught you," Lucas says. "Follow me. Stay in formation. Maia must always stay in the middle, between us."

She rolls her eyes.

"We'll stick to the large, open expressways for a while, but then we'll cut in to the smaller roads," Lucas says as he pulls out a map. He lays it across the kitchen table. "There are also goat tracks from time to time that we'll take. Of course, things could change at any minute. Generally speaking, the open highways expose us, but they also expose any bounders or mobs. Mario told me the roads are pretty barren up the coast. Some have become obliterated or flooded, but there should be some goat tracks to go around them."

"This is the best time to travel this area," Miguel says. "Since it's still autumn, the daytime temperatures will be pretty hot as we go back down to sea level, but when we go through the desert, it will be freezing at night. By the time we reach the far north, it should be spring. And by the time we get to the Arctic, it'll be nearing summer."

"Here." Lucas points to a highlighted zone in the old state of Oregon. "There used to be a city here. Now there's a village outside it that Mario said would be a good place to rest and barter. They are pretty wary of strangers, but he told me to use his and Jake's names, and they should hopefully let us work for food and supplies."

"How long until we get there?" Miguel asks.

Lucas scratches his chin, sucking air through his teeth. "Six weeks? Couple months? Hard to say."

"Good enough," Miguel says.

The three head out to the front yard of the cabin.

"Wait," Miguel says.

They turn to find him walking back up to the porch. He holds the railing and hangs his head. A cicada screeches in waves behind them.

"What is he—" Lucas whispers.

"He's saying goodbye," Maia says quietly.

They give Miguel a few minutes and then quickly look away when he turns toward them.

"Okay, I'm ready," he says.

And so, their journey begins.

When they arrive back in the outskirts of LA, Maia is relieved they won't be here long. After being in the mountains, the harsh cement surroundings feel like a shock to her system. The city is eerily quiet, bar the occasional seagull calling from above and the *tink tink tink* of Maia and Miguel's staves—now being used as walking sticks—against the sandy pavement.

A dog wanders toward them down the road. It staggers to the side, then charges at the air, growling and snapping at nothing.

"Whoa, guys," Miguel says quietly. "Slow down."

Lucas looks past Maia to his brother. "Rabies?"

Miguel nods. "Looks like it," he whispers. "Let me lead." He steps before them and they slow their pace, taking a wide angle as they approach the deranged dog.

It's another German shepherd. Maia covers her mouth—it's *Charlie.*

He stumbles over his legs, and a white foam gathers in the corners of his mouth. As they approach, he bares his teeth and bites the air. Miguel holds his staff before him. Charlie charges forward, then falls back on his hind legs.

"Is that Charlie?" Lucas whispers.

Maia nods, tears surfacing.

Charlie lifts to his feet, then snaps at Miguel's bo. Miguel lifts to swing.

"No!" Maia holds up her hand, stepping between the quivering dog and Miguel.

"Maia!" Lucas whispers. "That's not Charlie anymore!"

The dog snaps at Maia, lowering his head and snarling. She grips her staff before her, and Miguel does the same. Lucas holds out his knife. The three slowly back away from the growling dog.

"Maia, we should put him out of his misery," Lucas whispers, panic growing in his voice.

"I'll shoo him away," she says, slowly swinging her staff. Charlie wobbles, barking and snapping at her bo. "It's okay, just move back," she whispers to the dog. She focuses on him, trying to communicate with her friend without words.

For a moment, he seems to settle. He whimpers as Maia guides him off the street. She smiles—*it's working*.

His head snaps up and he bares his teeth. Foam drips from his mouth, and he charges toward Lucas.

"*NO!*" Maia screams.

The dog runs past her. Lucas fumbles with his knife, and a blur of orange jumps across the road, tumbling into the crazed dog. Lucas, Maia, and Miguel brace themselves, holding out their hands and watching in shock as the large tiger clutches the dog between his jaws. Charlie tries to writhe out of his mouth, but he bores his teeth farther into his neck until he goes limp. He drops him, and Charlie falls lifeless to the cement. The tiger pants, looking up at Maia with blood lining his mouth.

She recognizes him immediately, and she steps forward.

"Maia!" Lucas yells.

"It's okay, Lucas. I've got this." She holds out her hand, slowly inching toward the nervous tiger, still hunching over the dead dog. "It's okay," she whispers. "You're okay."

The tiger backs up and Maia stops. Unsure of what to do, she kneels and lays her staff across the road. She holds out her hand. The tiger glances at the men behind Maia.

"It's okay," she repeats.

The tiger steps over the lifeless dog and sniffs in Maia's direction. She keeps her hand out as he takes another step closer, his head lowered in submission.

Miguel's staff bangs loudly against the pavement, and the tiger flinches and runs in the opposite direction. Maia hangs her head.

"Sorry!" Miguel whispers.

"*Meu Deus,* Brother," Lucas whispers.

"Oh my God," Miguel says. "My life has become so *strange* since you've come back."

EIGHTEEN

Maia, Lucas, and Miguel wander the endless desert highway in silence. Mile after mile, hour after hour, they push forward, greeted with nothing but hazy skies, cracked pavement, and the occasional rusted vehicle. At times, their freeway intersects with others, and they watch in awe as their road slowly rises above roads that rise above roads that rise above roads, like an endless maze of webbed cement. Countless billboards plaster the sides of the highways. The signs are bigger than houses, corroded and peeling with faded advertisements for things Maia cannot understand.

Not a soul. They do not see a single soul the entire day.

After the incident with the tiger, they had no choice but to pick up their packs and continue on their way. Shocked and dumbfounded, no one said a word. Miguel only shook his head, mumbling in Portuguese. Lucas remained quiet but kept a watchful eye on Maia.

And Maia, Maia was heartbroken. Charlie was dead, succumbed to a horrific virus. She slowly shuffled past his lifeless body, whispering words of remorse for her dear friend. It was for the best, what happened. It would have put him out of his misery. He could have seriously injured or even killed Lucas, and Maia would have blamed herself. She should have stopped Charlie, or at the very least, allowed Miguel to stop him, but she wasn't prepared. Rabies doesn't exist in New Zealand. It's simply not a threat she could have ever been prepared for.

In the end, it was Maia's tiger that saved them. The same tiger that has been following her from the beginning. What will happen to him? Miguel says the virus is spread through saliva, generally through a bite. Charlie didn't bite him, *did* he? There's no way of knowing. All day long, Maia glances over her shoulder, but wherever the tiger is, he's no longer following them.

Within a few hours of sundown, they stick to their plan to find a place to rest for the night. For a while, there is nothing, only their snaking road carving through scorched hills and barren land. Eventually, they come across a cluster of cars next to a tall cement divider in the middle of the expressway. With nighttime swiftly settling around them, this is the best they're going to find. They decide to set up their sleeping bags between the cars and the divider, hidden from sight, but no tent. It's too obvious in the middle of the road, and they're still too close to a city.

They each roll out their sleeping bags, laying them side by side on the sandy freeway. Exhausted, they crawl into their beds without saying a word, each clutching their sheathed knives. Miguel holds his against his chest.

Lucas turns on his side, gripping his beneath his sleeping bag. Maia keeps hers on the ground beside her head.

Lying on her back, she watches as countless bats zip across the glittering night sky. As usual, she finds comfort in the night sounds, although they seem sedated compared to the woods. A shooting star burns across the moonless sky. Lucas's breathing becomes slow and heavy. She finds comfort in this too. Miguel shifts in his sleeping bag, turning toward her.

"You still awake?" he whispers.

She shifts toward him. She can barely make out his eyes in the night. "Day one," she breathes. "We made it."

He huffs. "Only seventy-two million more days to go."

She smiles. "Only."

They gaze at one another for a long while without speaking, until Maia slips into a deep sleep.

Early the next morning, Maia awakens to a hint of light seeping into the sky. Miguel is still lying beside her, rubbing the sleep from his eyes. Lucas is up, shuffling through his pack. Maia twists within her sleeping bag and peers under the cars for any movement. Just a seagull with its head down, charging at another bird with an open beak.

Maia stretches with a yawn, then unzips her sleeping bag. Lucas glances back at her and winks. She waves, then looks at Miguel, who's turning toward her. They nod at one another with a smile. Lucas hands her a bag of leafy greens they've packed from Miguel's garden, along with some cured meat. She takes her share and hands the rest to Miguel, and the three enjoy their breakfast in silence.

Today is gray. More than gray, the skies are heavy, like any minute they may rip from their seams and unleash an ocean of rain. Maia carries the lighter supplies in her pack: two sleeping bags, clothing, and essentials that shouldn't get wet. Miguel's sleeping bag is waterproof, so it stays tied up on the outside of his pack.

Between the two men, they carry the utensils, pots, and heavier items. Lucas has the tent and the kitchen gear, while Miguel has the fishing and hunting supplies. Bucket. Axe. Shovel. Maia is still the only one with a poncho, although the men have a large tarp to huddle beneath should the rains become heavy.

After an entire day of walking an endless cement highway, the three once again fight the heat of the sun peeking from the clouds. It didn't rain. It should have, Maia could have sworn it was going to, but nothing. It hasn't so much as sprinkled since Lucas and Maia first left to find Miguel, and out here, it's likely to have been longer.

After taking an exit off one highway leading to another, they find the landscape opening to a rocky desert plain. This one is more barren than the last—if that's even possible. As far as the eye can see, there's nothing but rolling farmland turned into dust, separated by the occasional decaying fence.

Maia catches Miguel watching her from the corner of his eye. She glances up at him as they walk side by side. "What is it?"

"That necklace..." He nods at her chest. "You are always holding it."

She peers down at her jade greenstone clasped within her fist. She flashes him a smile and drops her hand to her side. "I didn't realize I was doing it."

"Yes, you do it often. While we walk, while we sit by the fire and talk. You are always reaching for it. Why is that?"

"My mother made it for me. The shape is called a koru, meant to symbolize the unfurling of a fern and new beginnings. She wore it while she was pregnant with me. Where I'm from, we believe it carries a part of you once you've worn it. My mother passed away after I was born, so this is very special to me."

"Yes, I can imagine. And what do you call this stone?"

She slows her pace. "It's a greenstone. But the proper name for it is a pounamu." The word feels foreign on her tongue, it's been so long since she's used it.

"Pounamu," Miguel says, and he smiles. "I like it. You should always tell those you meet about the story of New Zealand and its pounamu. It is a beautiful story. All we have left are stories—this is how they live on."

She gazes up at him, shaking her head. After all their conversations, she is still so surprised by this brute man with such a beautiful soul. "You're right, Miguel. I will. Thank you."

He looks down at her tenderly, and then he faces forward. "Yes, I am always right. You must know this about me by now, yes?"

She rolls her eyes, and Lucas chuckles beside her. *There it is.* She smacks his arm, and the three of them carry on along the long dusty road.

NINETEEN

After days on end, the seemingly endless spread of highway lanes narrows down to two. There's the occasional corroding car or truck along the way, half-buried in sand creeping through its broken windows as if the earth was slowly swallowing it whole. Fallen signs cross the roads but are so obscured by dust they're illegible. The seagulls have been replaced by circling vultures and cawing ravens. Snakes and scorpions and beetles seem to be the only other living creatures around these parts. Oh, and the occasional roadrunner scurrying across the sandy concrete, often with a coiling rattlesnake hanging from its beak.

Now that they've traveled away from the coast, the daytime heat has become even more brutal than before, and the evenings deathly cold. Miguel says this area is a "dead zone." These desolate landscapes have been creeping across the center of the planet for decades, replacing vital terrain with land sucked dry by the sun.

Despite the intensity of the heat, Miguel also says the

weather has been cooler than expected for this time of year. Maia could smack him with her staff for saying such a ludicrous thing, but she's pretty sure she'd start something she wouldn't be able to finish. She isn't in the mood to be clotheslined.

Miguel has wrapped Maia's bandana around his head, his long dreads tied off his shoulders with twine. Lucas's hair has once again grown long enough to pull up into a knot. And Maia has braided her hair off to one side, the thick plait now draping across her shoulder. Their extra layers of clothing have been stuffed back into their oversized packs—at least until the evening. They are now wearing the lightest and most breathable fabric they own while still keeping the sun off their skin.

Miguel has given Maia something called a baseball cap. She's only heard of baseball once back in New Zealand, although she's pretty sure she saw pictures in the papers. She knows very little about it. Sports were rarely spoken of with her grandfather, but when they were, it was always *rugby*. Grandpa said it used to be worshiped by their ancestors—a national source of pride. It all seems pretty meaningless to her. Games played with balls. Guess you had to be there.

Lucas turns around, his shoulders slumped, and stops in the middle of the road. Miguel and Maia, who have been sluggishly trailing behind him, do the same. Maia takes off her hat, enjoying the fresh air on her head.

"There's an overpass ahead," Lucas says quietly. "Let's make sure it's empty and then take a break?"

Maia and Miguel nod, wiping the sweat from their brows, and the three quicken their pace as they make their way to the bridge. Shelter. Just need to sit and find shelter—nothing else matters.

As they approach the cement structure, they find a small car and a large semi in the middle of the road, forming a *T*. They spread out. Maia holds her bo before her, and Miguel does the same. Lucas keeps one hand on his knife tucked in its holster. No one says a word.

Lucas rounds the front of the little car and checks inside while Miguel looks beneath. Lucas checks around the side of the truck as well. He lifts his hand in the air and flashes a thumbs-up. Miguel and Maia smile at one another and lower their staves.

As Maia circles around the large truck, she finds Lucas on the other side kicking away a pile of human remains spilling from the semi's open door. Clearly, another traveler had the same idea as them, only he never left.

"Oh, Lucas." She cringes, holding her nose and swatting the flies.

"I meant it was *safe*, not nice," he says, grimacing.

Miguel joins him in shoveling the decomposing corpse, and together they move it out to the field. Maia holds a cloth against her face and slams the door shut, blocking the rest of the body from sight, and plops to the ground beside the car. The men join her.

"So…" Miguel says. "We stay here tonight, yes?"

Body or no body, shelter is shelter.

Lucas and Maia respond at the same time, "Yes."

And then, there is silence.

Maia holds her knees against her chest, quivering in the passenger seat of the small car. She's come across a lot of old cars here in America, but she's never sat inside one. It's so odd to see the steering wheel on the opposite side of the dashboard.

Lucas sits next to her in the driver's seat. His head is tipped back, his eyes closed. Darkness isn't far. Miguel has been out for hours looking for water. Although sparse, there's still greenery around, short grasses and shrubs. Coming from South America, the two brothers have become adept at finding water. They've agreed to take turns, never leaving Maia alone. She's gone with them a few times to learn, as finding water in New Zealand was never much of an issue, but tonight she doesn't have the energy.

She cups her hands around her mouth and blows. The evening air has turned icy cold, the expansive sky having lost its warming blanket of cloud. They discussed sleeping in this tiny matchbox of a car, but it would be horrifically uncomfortable for everyone, especially Miguel.

"Lucas?" Maia whispers between her clattering teeth. "We haven't seen another living person in ages. What do you think about making a fire?"

He turns toward her, and his gaze drops to her trembling hands. "Oh darling, you're freezing!" He leans over and grabs her hands between his.

Miguel walks up with his bucket, still empty.

Lucas opens the car door, the metal groaning loudly against itself. "Brother, what do you say about a fire?"

Miguel doesn't hesitate to respond. "Let's do it." He sets his bucket down. "The night has just begun and the temperatures will continue to plummet. I couldn't find any water, but I made a little something to collect the night dew. Should have something by morning."

"Sounds good." Lucas glances at Maia. "Ready?"

She's the fire starter. "I'm on it." She uncurls herself from the seat.

They quickly gather shrubs and tree branches and pile them in the middle of the road between the car and the truck. Maia kneels before it and closes her eyes, holding her hands above the brush. Within seconds, the smell of smoke fills the air.

She opens her eyes and smiles.

"*Magnífico*," Miguel says quietly. "Never gets old, watching that."

Sitting around the fire, they hover as close to the flames as possible, rubbing their hands together for warmth.

"You started this one really fast," Miguel says. "You're getting really good."

"I hope so," she says. She stands with her back to the fire, inching as close as she can. "It's been a journey."

"You've been like this your entire life?" Miguel asks, looking up at her.

"I have. But as I grew up, I realized I couldn't control it, and..." She glances at Lucas.

He tilts his head, waiting for her to continue.

"I hurt people," she finally says.

"Your grandfather?" Lucas asks.

"Not on purpose, but yes. I hurt animals too. Again, not on purpose. I didn't understand what was happening. I was so young when I decided to stop using my powers. I thought if I didn't use them, they'd go away. And for the most part, that seemed to work." She turns toward the fire, holding out her hands. "But they would still appear from time to time on their own, most often when I was really happy or scared or angry. It would be such a shock. I fooled myself for so long that there were periods of my life where I completely forgot I had them." The flames nearly burn her skin, and she pulls back, studying her palms. "I was so focused on the fact that the world had abandoned me. But it wasn't the world, it was me. I had abandoned *myself*. It wasn't until Lucas and I were stranded on that raft that I finally faced who I really am."

"The jellyfish," Miguel says.

She glances at Lucas. He looks away. "Lucas told you."

Miguel nods.

"Yes, the jellyfish," she says. "It was death that opened my eyes. I don't think it could have been any other way. I'm a runner, always have been. When I get really upset or angry, I run. It's easier than confronting what's in front of me. I guess I've gotten really good at it—so good I didn't even realize I was doing it."

"Sounds familiar," Lucas says.

"Yes." Miguel nods at Lucas. "He's a mighty good runner, this one. You two are like ... two peas in a pod?"

"That's the saying." Maia looks at Lucas. "But we aren't doing that anymore."

He gazes at her. "No, we are not."

She reaches out to him, and he kisses her hand.

"You two. God, it kills me a little." Miguel shakes his head, staring into the fire. "I really miss my wife."

Maia sits on the pavement across from Miguel, watching him.

He notices, then looks away sighing. "We were on our way to Leucothea," he finally says, his eyes glassy. "It was my wife and me ... and our two daughters." He peers up at Lucas. "We had come so far. My girls, they did so well." He smiles, quickly wiping a tear from his eye. "They were so gorgeous," he says quietly. "They looked just like their mother." His voice trails into silence.

"Oh, *Miguel*," Lucas says.

"I'm sorry. I don't ... I don't think I can," Miguel says, blinking fast. He glances around, shifting uncomfortably.

"It's okay." Lucas places his hand on Miguel's shoulder. "You don't have to say a word until you're ready."

Miguel stands and steps to the far edge of the fire's light. He puts his hands on his hips, keeping his back toward Lucas and Maia, and sighs repeatedly as an owl hoots in the distance.

Later that night, as the fire smolders to cinders, the icy desert air threatens at the edges. Maia leans closer to the fire as Lucas nods off.

"We should get some sleep," she says softly.

Lucas lifts his head. "Yes," he says, rubbing his eyes. "Probably should put out the last of this fire. I don't feel comfortable having a beacon of our presence when we're not on guard."

"Agreed," Miguel says.

"Should we set up our tent?" Maia glances between the two men.

"It would be best for the cold, but we are still so exposed," Lucas says. He looks at Miguel. "Could sleep in the car?"

"I agree, no tent—not yet," Miguel says. "We'd be like sitting ducks out in the open like this. But that car is too small. I'd rather sleep in my sleeping bag."

"Okay, then. Let's do this," Maia says, standing.

The three unroll their sleeping bags. Maia and Lucas zip theirs together, forming one large bed. Miguel lays his across from them on the other side of the fire.

"Are you sure you'll be okay over there, Miguel? It's mighty cold," Lucas asks as Maia climbs into their bed.

"Oh, yes. Don't worry about me."

In the middle of the night, Maia awakens. Lucas is wrapped tightly around her, the heat of their bodies radiating under the thick down, but Miguel is restless. The nylon of his bag keeps moving, followed by short gasps. Maia peeks out from the sleeping bag. Their tiny camp is highlighted by the moon, the desert air freezing cold.

Miguel's sleeping bag shivers, violently so.

"Lucas," Maia whispers.

"*Mmm*?" He doesn't open his eyes.

"Miguel," she whispers.

Lucas pulls the sleeping bag from his head, looking at his brother across the camp. His brow creased, he looks at Maia. "Okay," he says.

Together, they quickly slide out of their bed. The cold air takes Maia's breath away.

She tiptoes over to Miguel. "Miguel?"

He unzips his bag, his face grimacing.

"Up, Brother," Lucas says. "Quickly."

Miguel unzips his bag and Maia takes his arm, helping him to his feet. His hands are like ice. She leads him to her and Lucas's bed while Lucas works on unzipping Miguel's bag. Without saying a word, a trembling Miguel crawls into their sleeping bag and curls up on his side. Maia lies down behind him, wrapping her arms around him. Lucas lays Miguel's sleeping bag on top of them before climbing inside. He inches his backside as close to Miguel as possible, enveloping him between their bodies.

Within minutes, Miguel's rigid muscles ease, his shaking now flickering in short bursts. Maia buries her head between his broad shoulders, and he sighs in relief.

A large owl lands on the car next to them, its immense claws clinking against the metal. It hoots on repeat, *who who who,* as Lucas, Miguel, and Maia huddle beneath the sleeping bags, the heat between them like a cocoon. And they fall fast asleep.

TWENTY

"*Run!*" Lucas shouts.

Miguel is beside him, slowly backing up with eyes wide as he stares at the horizon. Maia turns toward the mammoth wall of dust, now billowing high into the sky.

"*Vamos,* Maia!" Lucas screams from behind.

But she can't move. The winds pick up, blowing back her hair, and a smile slowly spreads across her face. She should feel terrified, but instead, she stands in awe before the enormous squall as if it were a grand display of beauty. A low rumble sounds from the earth as the storm barrels toward them with the speed of a freight train. Something inside her whispers *yes!* and she drops her pack to the ground.

Yes.

"Maia!" Miguel shouts. "What are you doing?!"

A blast of sand hits her and she stumbles back, giggling. Crimson curls drape across her shoulders, and she knows what she must do.

Symphony.

She drops her staff to the ground and lifts her hands before her. Closing her eyes, she breathes deeply and begins pushing against the wind. She leans into it, her hands shaking from its force. When she opens her eyes, she gasps.

The sand ... it's ... *diverting* around her.

The power of the Earth surges up through her veins, and she lifts her hands to the sky, slowly spinning in place. A tunnel of dust swirls above her head as she stands at its core, protected from the winds. There's shouting somewhere behind her, and she turns to see the men fighting against the elements.

"Get behind me!" she shouts.

"Look out!" Lucas points.

She turns to find a large sheet of metal tumbling down the highway, erratically flipping top to bottom. She throws her hands before her and it collides into a wall of wind, hurdling it high into the sky. She squeals, delighted.

"Maia!" Lucas screams.

She glances over her shoulder. Panicked, he points at Miguel racing down the street, the diverted metal now plummeting toward him.

She gasps, shattering her focus, and is immediately bowled over by the elements. She tumbles down the highway, landing on her back. Coughing, she crawls to her knees and lifts her hands before her, slamming the winds into the metal. It flies in the opposite direction.

Breathless, she fumbles with her bandana and wraps it around her mouth, then climbs to her feet and grabs her pack. She scans the road for her bo. *Gone.*

"No," she whispers.

She staggers up the street, scouring the grounds. The men shout behind her, but their words are muffled by the wind. Ignoring them, she squints through the storm. It must be here somewhere. Coughing, gasping, she can't breathe! The bandana around her mouth is suffocating. It's so hard to see, her eyes burn.

She spots her bo beneath a cluster of bushes and swipes it from the sand, then rushes back toward the men. She loses her footing and tumbles back to the ground. Miguel races up to her and grabs her pack, lifting her to her feet. Together, they run toward Lucas.

As they race along the highway, the dust swirls around them, pushing them across the road. Both Lucas and Maia have coverings for their faces, but Miguel does not. Maia peels off one of her shirts and shoves it at him, and he quickly wraps it around his head.

"Maia!" Lucas pulls the cloth from his mouth. "Can you protect us?!" he screams through the wind. "Can you do that again?"

She looks around, unsure. But she has to do something. "Get behind me!" she screams.

With the last of her strength, she holds out her hands and pushes back against the howling winds. She watches in awe as the sand once again divides before her. The men huddle behind her, their coughing echoing in the small, protected space.

With every passing minute, she can feel herself weakening. Her heart is pounding at an alarming rate, her hands shaking. So lightheaded. This is too much.

Just hold on.

The force is so strong, like the weight of the world is

pushing against her. Her knees begin to buckle and she cries out, leaning against the wall of dust as her feet slide into the men behind her. Small grains of sand break through her barrier, stinging her cheeks. She coughs, her arms aching. More sand.

"I *can't!*" she screams.

Her barrier shatters, and the winds slam into them, sending them rolling across the road. Maia curls into a ball, holding her bandana over her face, and Lucas gathers her into his arms. Miguel points to a cluster of large boulders. Lucas carries her behind the largest one and places her on the ground. He wraps himself around her, and Miguel does the same.

And that's where they stay, coughing, gasping, waiting out the storm.

———

After a while, the winds calm.

Maia, Lucas, and Miguel unwrap the barriers around their faces and shake out the dust. Miguel stands, and buckets of sand fall from his clothing.

They pass around a canister of water, each taking small swigs. Maia unties her laces and slides off her boots, dumping the sand from inside. She grimaces. The dressing on her heel has come undone, the blister beneath irritated and raw. She needs to change the bandage, now wrinkled and covered in sand, but she doesn't want to use any more precious supplies. She tries to carefully pick out the sand and rewrap it.

"I thought the boots fit?" Miguel asks.

"They did—they *do*. I guess not as well as they could, but it's fine."

He shakes his head. "That does not look *fine*."

"You're going to want to change that dressing," Lucas says. "Pour a little water on your heel to get the sand out."

He hands her the bottle and she does as he says, carefully pouring the smallest amount as she can on her ankle. With her cupped hand beneath, she collects the extra water and tips it back over her blister. She pats it dry.

"We don't have many bandages," she says, assessing her wound. "I'll go through them all at this rate. Maybe hand me some gauze and a little duct tape?"

"Sure thing." Miguel rummages through her pack.

"Maia," Lucas says. "What you did back there..." A smile tugs his mouth. "I mean..."

"Yeah," she says.

The men look at her, waiting for her to explain. Not knowing how to respond, she focuses on her dressing, ripping off a tiny sliver of tape with her teeth.

"But what was that?" Lucas asks her. "A *forcefield*?"

Satisfied with her new bandage, she slides her sock back on. "Not really."

"No, *really*," Miguel chimes in.

She puts on her boot and sighs. "It's more like I ... *diverted* the winds. I commanded them to ... I don't know, go around?"

"Go ... *around*," Miguel says dryly.

The men try to hold back their laughter, tightly pressing their lips together. Lucas snorts.

She tilts her head. "Guys."

Miguel shoves Lucas. "No, thank you. Please go around."

Lucas bursts into laughter and Miguel does the same. Despite herself, Maia can't help but smile. This is so *surreal*. Did she really just do that?

The men continue, their voices now high-pitched imitations of Maia.

"*Please go around.*"

"I don't feel like that today, *no thank you.*"

"Not now. *I'm not in the mood.*"

More laughter and Maia leans back on her hands, watching the two brothers and shaking her head. Lucas falls onto his back, laughing at the sky.

She stands. "We need to keep moving." She flips her head over and runs her fingers through her hair.

Lucas sighs, shaking his head. "Go around," he says again. "Hilarious."

Miguel wipes the tears from his eyes.

"You men are like children," Maia says, shaking out her clothes.

Miguel hands over her top. "Thanks for looking out for me," he says with a smile.

She mirrors his smile. "Always." She slides her shirt back over her tank top.

They all glance at one another for a long minute with grandiose sighs, and then they pick up their bags and heave them onto their backs with a chorus of grunts. Maia grabs Miguel's staff from the ground and hands it to him, then picks up her own.

And with that, they keep moving.

Walking down the empty road, an array of crooked bushes peeks from the layers of fresh sand. For days they've seen nothing but shrubs and powerlines. Some of the poles are still holding, while others are tipped on their sides, suspended midair by their cords.

The three hardly speak. Only the crunching sand beneath their boots and the constant clinking of wooden staves against the ground break the eerie silence. Maia remains in the middle between the two men. She was annoyed at first when Lucas asked her to stay between them, but now she prefers it. Whether they are wandering foreign roads or settling into sleep for the night, she is always nestled between her love and a man she now considers a close friend. It feels right, like it should have always been this way.

New mountains carve into the boundary where the earth meets the sky, a reassuring reminder that after walking for weeks on end through this desolate desert land, new terrain is on the horizon.

As they approach the mountains, dusk settles in.

"Shall we set up camp?" Lucas glances between Maia and Miguel.

"God, yes," Maia mumbles. "Where?"

"Let's wander in from the road. Down there," Miguel says, pointing left.

They walk along the rocky terrain to a cluster of small trees, gathering brush for a fire as they go. Maia sits on a rock and slides her foot out from her boot. New spots of blood soak through her white bandage. Lucas looks at her with concern but says nothing.

The three souls sit huddled by the fire, the tent behind them flickering in its light. Now that they're a significant distance from civilization, they've finally decided they feel comfortable enough to sleep zipped up in their little box of nylon.

Miguel sighs. "Maia, I have to say … What happened back there, with that storm? That is not nothing. You know this, yes?"

She nods. "I know."

"You must be here for a reason. This I believe for certain. You must have some sort of destiny to fulfill."

"It feels that way," she says.

"But you do not know yet what that is."

"Not yet."

He pours some steaming water from their pot on the fire into Maia's mug and hands it to her. "I mean, this," he says, spanning his hand across their camp, "is history in the making. What happened today will go down in history. Without a doubt, this is what *legends* are made of, the stories humans have grown up with from the beginning of time. You see this, *yes*?"

She smiles. "I suppose I do."

"Man, I cannot wait to see what happens next. You'll be able to cause some serious damage with powers like that, you know?"

The smile slides from her face.

Miguel empties the last of the boiling water into a steel canister. "Magnificent, Maia. Unbelievable. You are here for a reason—without a doubt. And whatever that ends up being, I *definitely* want to be around to witness it," he says with a chuckle.

Visions of the burning city flash through Maia's mind.

Scores of people crying out for their lives. Maia's quivering, tear-filled eyes. That power. That *rage*.

"Yeah ... magnificent," she says. Her eyes cut to Lucas.

He's watching her, a deep crease between his brow. He clears his throat and looks away. "Yes, well," he says, standing. "Better get some sleep. Tomorrow's another big day."

He pours their bucket of sand onto the fire, quickly smothering the ravenous flames into a fleeting cloud of smoke.

TWENTY-ONE

As time passes, the rocks and the dust and the sand slowly morph into grass. The brown transforms into green, and the barren farmlands give way to lush hills until, at last, Maia, Lucas, and Miguel arrive in a thriving metropolis of towering redwoods. The air is cool, refreshing. They swivel their heads, their breath hovering in clouds in the new winter air. Hundreds of chirping birds flitter along the branches, and the sunlight drapes from the canopy in beams.

It is like heaven.

Lucas reckons they must be bordering Oregon by now. It seems like ages since they passed the sign for San Francisco. Maia always dreamed of seeing the Golden Gate Bridge, but Lucas's response was a solemn shake of his head. It is now another landmark swallowed by the sea. Once famous for its hills, the city has been reduced to islands—the area's highways destroyed from flooding and landslides.

Lucas has spent much of his spare time studying old

maps. He told them it's too risky to travel along America's new coastline. Too much damage. They've agreed to stick to the inland roads while still remaining relatively close to the coast.

Walking along the winding road, the redwoods soar above them like skyscrapers. As the three pass smiles of relief, Maia catches Lucas's gaze lingering on her longer than usual.

She tilts her head. "What is it?"

He looks at her for a while, his eyes narrowing. "Nothing. Never mind," he says, and he looks away.

"I like it in here," Miguel declares as a matter of fact. "Let's just find a cabin and stay."

Maia smiles at him.

Some of their strict rules have eased with the change of scenery. They're much more comfortable speaking as they travel. Maia has lost count of the days that have passed since they've seen another person—it must have been in LA. Mario told Lucas that the roads between hotspots are almost completely void of people. So far, he seems to be correct.

"Hotspots?" Maia asks, twirling her staff as she walks.

"Areas where humans congregate," Lucas replies. "Which also happen to be the places where the bounders and mobs loiter. LA was a big one. The old cities along the coast tend to have hotspots. We should be pretty safe until we hit the Old Alaskan Highway."

Maia stops spinning, and she and Miguel exchange worried glances.

"Don't worry about that now," Lucas says. "Best to take this journey in bite-sized chunks."

"How much farther do you think New Portland is?" Miguel asks.

"It's hard to know," Lucas says. "Mario showed me where it is on a map, but it's hard to keep track of how many miles we've walked. Hopefully, we should be there in the next few days."

"And we can barter there?" Miguel asks.

"Apparently," Lucas says. "Mario said if we drop his and Jake's names, they might let us in to restock and rest. And hopefully, get Maia some boots."

As the men talk back and forth, Maia slows her pace. The whispers are back. She stops in the middle of the road, glancing up at the trees, her clouds of breath heavy in the cool forest air.

Lucas and Miguel turn around.

"What is it?" Miguel asks.

"Can you hear that?" she whispers.

The men look around.

"Hear what?" Miguel asks. He looks at Lucas. "Can you hear anything?"

Lucas is watching her. He shakes his head.

"Ma—" Miguel begins.

"*Shh!*" she snaps.

Walking toward a tree, she places her hand on the bark. It sounds like it's ... *breathing*. She gazes up at the massive pine. There's more whispering, not just from this tree, but from all of them at once. It's so loud, yet Maia cannot make out a single word.

She sighs, feeling relieved. She hasn't heard the trees whispering since her poisoning at Miguel's. She actually wasn't even sure it happened. She pats the bark, then walks back toward the men.

"You okay?" Miguel asks.

"I am. Sorry, let's keep moving."

"I thought we should set up camp for the night," Lucas says, grabbing her hand. "You probably want to rest your feet?"

She nods.

"Good idea," Miguel says.

Maia has kept silent about her pain. She was told there would be a "wearing-in" period with new boots and that blisters weren't uncommon. But that time has long since passed, and her feet have only become more ravaged by the day.

Stepping from the road, they begin searching for a small clearing between the trees. They have their unpacking routine down pat: find a spot far from the road, Lucas assembles the tent and then heads out to set up a few traps for small mammals like rabbits or squirrels, and Miguel gathers wood for Maia and then tries to find a water source.

Maia is the fire starter. Night after night of building fires, she's become pretty quick at it now. She scours the area for kindling—anything that will burn long enough to get the bigger sticks and logs going—and then she assembles a small, makeshift pit.

She kneels before the pile of brush, and the men behind her stop working. They are watching. She used to hate knowing she had an audience but has since gotten used to it. It's good practice, learning to drown out the distractions.

She closes her eyes, focusing on the deep structure of the twigs. As she speeds up the molecules, her heart pounds—faster and faster as the heat builds. It can be stressful feeling her heart pound the way it does when she uses her powers, but she's learning to trust the process.

She hovers her hand over the brush. After a few seconds, she opens her eyes to wafts of smoke escaping between the dead leaves. The kindling catches, and orange flames flicker between the twigs.

She places her hands in her lap, catching her breath, and glances over her shoulder at the men with a smile. Miguel and Lucas are standing behind her with their arms crossed, the same look of fondness across both their faces.

———

Sitting around the fire, the three anxiously wait for their pot of water to boil. Lucas is lost in a daze, twisting the bracelet around his wrist and staring at the fire. Maia looks at Miguel. He is already watching her. She smiles and looks down, tucking her hair behind her ear.

"I'm sorry, Maia," Miguel says, and Lucas's head snaps up. "I don't mean to stare, but you look..." He hesitates.

Feeling self-conscious, she pats her hair. "*What*? What is it?"

"Sorry, no. It's silly," Miguel says.

"You look different," Lucas says.

Surprised, Maia glances between the two men. "What do you mean?"

Miguel tips his head. "I can't figure it out. But ... you don't look like the same Maia who showed up on my doorstep back in the mountains."

She huffs a laugh. "Can you be more specific?"

"Can't really say," Lucas says.

"So you see it too?" She looks at Lucas.

He half-smiles, nodding once.

Feeling uneasy, she smooths invisible wrinkles in her shirt. Both men continue to watch her.

"Stop staring at me!" She swats the air. "You're making me nervous."

"Sorry," Miguel says with a laugh, and he looks away. Lucas does not.

She glares at him, shooting him a *What the hell?* look.

He smiles, rolling his eyes. "It's not *bad*, Maia. But your face has definitely changed."

Miguel hands her a mug of hot water. She blows away the steam and takes a sip, her brow creased.

"Yes," Miguel says. "Your hair is different too. It's darker. Maybe curlier? Your face looks more like ... a woman."

She chokes on her water. Lucas and Miguel share a laugh, mumbling back and forth in Portuguese.

"Hey!" Maia points between them. "What rule did we make about that? Either teach me or *stop* it."

"I was just telling Lucas that you looked really ... *beautiful*," Miguel says.

"Miguel!" She fights a smile, surprising herself. Her eyes widen and she peers at Lucas. "And you're *okay* with that?"

Lucas shrugs as she hands him her empty mug. "It's a loose translation," he says. "He's my brother. He doesn't mean it like that." He pours more steaming water from the pot into her cup.

"Right," Maia says.

After Lucas hands her the mug, she and Miguel lock eyes.

He quickly looks away.

TWENTY-TWO

Maia adjusts her thick woolen hat. It's itchy and tight but provides a much-needed warmth in these early morning hikes.

As they advance farther north, the temperatures only continue to plummet. But they are prepared. Their layers of clothing now include heavy sweaters and down-filled coats. Hats and gloves are donned. Every evening, they huddle around their small fire and sleep nestled together inside their tiny nylon tent.

Despite the cold, the mountains have been a reprieve. Maia feels safe within these secluded forests. The trees continue to whisper, but their words are hushed. They've become like a background melody, blending with the forest and the birds and the flickering of leaves in the canopy's high breeze. Maia doesn't try anymore to decipher what they're saying, and she also doesn't tell the men. Some things are best kept to herself. All day long, she wanders past the towering giants with a growing sense of familiarity, observing the life wafting from them the same way her breath drifts in clouds from her mouth. She finds solace in this. She is surrounded by family.

Trekking along the dense forest roads, Maia, Lucas, and Miguel spend their days bantering back and forth. Up, up, up they go, the steep hills pulling the breath from their lungs. Then downward the roadways fall, awarding them a brief respite as their feet effortlessly pound the leaf-littered pavement.

"Hey." Miguel puts his arm around Maia's shoulder, and she lays her head against him. "You should keep practicing with your bo," he says. "I don't want my wing woman to become dusty. You were only just starting to figure it out." He gazes down at her.

She pushes him away. "*Only just*? I'm really good, and you know it."

"*Eh*." He shrugs.

She smacks his arm. "I could take you."

"Oh really?" He swings his staff before him with a mischievous grin.

"You starting something?" she asks, and she drops her pack to the ground.

"*Guys!*"

Maia and Miguel stop to find Lucas stepping before a large painted sign on the side of the road. They join him.

STOP! No trespassing! Armed forces beyond.

"This is it," Lucas says, his voice hushed into a whisper.

Maia and Miguel exchange a worried glance.

"This is New Portland," Lucas says. He turns toward Maia and then peers behind her to Miguel.

"*Armed forces*, Lucas?" Maia whispers.

"We have to at least try," he says.

He has that same *worried Lucas* face. It's been a while since she's seen that face. She doesn't miss it.

"So, how do you want to do this?" Miguel asks, rounding before them.

"We need to hide our knives. They'll take them from us," Lucas says, dropping his pack to his feet.

"Good idea," Miguel says, dumping his bag to the ground.

"Hide them within your things. Maybe hide one on you? What do you think?" Lucas looks at Miguel.

"No." Miguel unzips his bag. "They'll probably pat us down. Just find a hiding spot within your things." He looks at Maia. "What about your handmade bow?"

"Just ditch it," she says bitterly. "It doesn't shoot far and we hardly use it."

"No way," Lucas says. "It's come in handy and it will again. Just tuck it between the ropes on the outside of your pack."

The three crouch in the middle of the road and hide their knives in their packs, unzipping pockets and carefully digging through their meticulously packed items. When they finish, they strap their bags to their backs and hesitantly step beyond the large sign.

It is eerily quiet. Something feels off—something is ... *missing*.

That's when it hits her: *the trees*. Maia listens for their whispers, but they are silent. The hairs on the back of her neck stand on end.

They pass another sign: *Turn back now.*

And another: *You will be shot without question.*

"Lucas?" Maia whispers, panicked. She lifts her staff before her.

"Just keep walking."

"Maia," Miguel whispers. "Use your staff as a walking stick. Don't give them a reason to think we're a threat."

She takes a deep breath and lowers her bo. They scan their surroundings, listening for movement within the trees.

After turning another bend, they are met with an imposing steel gate blockading the street. Two towering brick lookouts bookend the gate, with cement walls on either side topped with barbed wire.

"*Freeze!*" a man yells from a tower's blackened window. The long barrel of a gun slides out.

They stop in their tracks.

"Turn around!" the man yells. "Go back where you've come."

"Please, sir!" Lucas yells. "We come in peace."

"I said, *turn around!*" the man shouts. "I'll shoot!" The rifle slides out farther, and another two guns extend from the opposite tower.

"Lucas!" Maia whispers through gritted teeth. "There are guns *everywhere*."

"We do not take in strangers!" the guard yells. "You are not *welcome* here! Do you hear me? Do you *understand*?"

"If we could just speak—" Lucas begins.

A gun fires into the air and the three drop to the ground.

"Hands up! Drop your weapons!" the guard shrieks.

They look at each other confused.

"Our staves," Miguel whispers to Maia. "Drop your bo!"

"This is your only warning!" the man shouts.

Maia and Miguel throw their staves across the road. Maia stares at Lucas. His eyes cut to her.

Please, she mouths, then nods her head toward the road. *Let's go*.

"Do you hear me? I'll shoot!"

"*Lucas!*" Miguel shouts in a hushed whisper. "Let's go! This isn't worth dying over."

Lucas glares at Maia. She knows they need this. *She* needs this—her blisters are getting worse by the day. Even though her feet are wrapped in every last bandage they own, the raw pain is now bordering on excruciating. She'll never make it to Washington.

She slowly stands with her hands in the air. "*Please*," she says, and she steps forward. She looks for the guard hiding behind his post, but the windows reflect the forest. "Please let us talk to your leader. We're willing to work. We'll follow your rules. Just let us speak to whoever's in charge. If they say we must go, then we'll go."

There is silence. Maia peers over her shoulder at Lucas and Miguel. They shrug. The silence continues. She looks up at the towers' darkened windows. There are outlines of people moving in there.

A different man's voice breaks through the silence. "Who are you, and what do you want?"

She drops her hands. "We are just three travelers, sir, headed to Leucothea. We were told we might find a safe harbor at your village."

"Lies. Who told you that?"

"Their names are Jake and Mario," Lucas says, and he steps beside Maia. "They traveled through here on their way to Leucothea and stayed with you. Please, sir, we come in peace."

More silence.

After a while, a voice sounds from the towers. "Leave your belongings on the ground."

The gates begin to open with a loud, metallic screech. The three step forward.

"Stay where you are!" the man shouts from the tower.

They freeze.

"Hands in the air!"

Maia grimaces and lifts her hands above her head. The gates open to a dozen uniformed men with assault rifles. They surround them and cuff their hands behind their backs, then lead them through the massive open gates.

The soldiers drop their packs against a small cement building with bars on its windows. Maia peers up to at least a dozen men glaring down at them from the towers, the tips of their guns following their every move.

The soldiers line Miguel, Maia, and Lucas along the cement building, with two men flanking each prisoner. Another guard walks up to them, and the soldiers tighten their grips, holding them in place as he slides black bags over their heads.

"Guys?!" Maia calls out.

"We're here," Lucas says beside her.

"*Quiet*." The guard shakes her.

The soldiers push her forward and she stumbles over her feet.

A metal door creaks open, and the men lead her over a threshold. She can hear Lucas and Miguel behind her. The soldiers shove her onto a chair. Wooden legs screech along the floor as Lucas and Miguel are forced into their seats beside her.

"*Merda*," Miguel says from her left.

She learned this word from the men: *shit*.

After a while, a soldier pulls the bags from their heads. They glance around. They are in an empty cement room like a jail cell. Three small windows line the barren wall before them. The light pouring through highlights thick cobwebs along the ceiling.

"You okay?" Lucas asks Maia.

She nods.

"It's okay," he whispers. "I think this is good. This is just their initiation. Mario said they are good people."

An armed guard opens the door behind them, and a new man enters. He pulls up a chair before them and rests his elbows on his wide-set knees. A pistol hangs at his side. He clasps his hands together, slowly assessing them from head to toe. He, too, is wearing a uniform—dark blue and pressed—but he has an assortment of metal pins on the right breast pocket of his shirt.

"Okay," he says after a while. He strokes his mustache and leans back in his chair. "Talk."

Maia eyes Lucas.

He lifts his chin as he looks at the man. "We mean no harm," he says. "We've already been on a long journey and have an even longer one ahead of us—"

"Did you not see the signs? We don't want you here," the leader replies.

"We were told it might be possible to barter," Lucas says. "We can help you with jobs, or—"

"We don't need your help."

"Please, sir," Maia says. "We don't want to cause any trouble. We've only come because we were told you were good people."

The man eyes her, and he sighs. "I'm sorry, but your friends have given you the wrong impression. I'm not sure how long ago they were here, but we don't take in strangers anymore. Your kind only seems to cause us trouble."

Maia glances at Miguel. His eyes cut to her, then back to the guard. This isn't going well.

As the leader glares at her, his gaze flickers to her neck. "What is that? Around your neck."

She moves to touch it, but her hands are cuffed. "We call it a pounamu."

"We?"

"Where I'm from."

"And where is that?" He leans forward, scrutinizing her necklace.

"New Zealand."

His eyes narrow. "You come from *New Zealand*?"

She nods.

He leans back in his chair, scratching the stubble on his chin. "And these men with you. Where do they come from?"

"Brazil," Miguel says.

"How does a woman from New Zealand come to travel North America with two men from Brazil?"

"I came on a ship," Maia says. "I met Lucas there." She nods toward Lucas. "Miguel is his brother. We met him in Los Angeles and have been traveling up the coast together to get to Leucothea."

The man huffs a laugh. "*Leucothea*. All you poor souls going to the Arctic."

There is silence again. His words don't sit right with her, but she says nothing.

He leans back in his chair with his hands clasped behind his head. "A man from New Zealand once saved me from a trap set by bounders. He also wore one of those things around his neck. I owe him my life."

A long silence ensues as he stares at her. He raises his hand, and with a flick of his wrist, a guard steps to his side. He whispers to him, then stands and nods at the other soldiers, who quickly step behind them to unlock their cuffs.

"You have one week," the leader says. "Your weapons stay with us. Your bags will be searched before they are given back to you. Anything questionable will remain with us. You will get it back when we release you, *away* from our village. You will work for your housing and will be locked in your cabin every night. There will be guards assigned to watch you. If you cause *any* trouble, you will be shot dead on the spot—all three of you. Do you understand?"

They nod. He turns to leave.

"Sir?" Maia asks.

He stops without turning around.

"Can we barter for supplies?" she asks. "That's why we're here. We are willing to work, but if we are just working to sleep and eat, then with all due respect, we will be on our way."

He turns toward her. "What do you want?"

"Do you have a hunting bow?"

"No. No weapons. We will never barter weapons."

"Okay," she says. "We could really use new hiking boots. Is this an option?"

He eyes their shoes. "I'll see what I can do. We have a shoemaker, but boots are very labor-intensive. You will need to work overtime for something of that caliber."

"That's okay," Lucas says. "We'll do whatever it takes."

"Anything else? Now's the time to speak up," the leader says.

"Food," Miguel says. "Food that will last. Preserved. Dried. And if we could sharpen our knives?"

The leader tilts his head. "I don't think you have the time to work for all that."

"Let us prove our value," Lucas says. After the week is up, if you deem us worthy, we'll work longer for more supplies. We will not be a bother. You have my word."

"We'll see," the leader says, and he turns to leave. "The men will show you to your quarters. Wait here while we check your bags."

The soldiers empty the room except for two armed guards by the door, leaving Lucas, Maia, and Miguel glancing between each other with wide eyes.

"That did *not* go how I expected," Miguel says.

Maia shakes her head.

"Why not?" Lucas mumbles, rubbing the red indents on his wrists. "We are *them*." He peers up at Maia and Miguel. "*Us versus them*. It has always been the way with people."

TWENTY-THREE

It's the weeds she notices the most. Or, more appropriately, the *lack* of them. There are no patches of green exploding from the cracks in the pavement or the broken seams of manmade structures. Everything looks clean-cut ... *pristine*.

The loose gravel crunches beneath their boots as Maia, Lucas, and Miguel are led by two armed officers along a street surrounded by farmland. It takes all Maia's strength not to limp, but they have been given a chance, taken in solely to work. It wouldn't bode well for her to appear injured.

The change of scenery was quite a shock to Maia—the road seemed to suddenly burst from the dense forest into vast open fields where the trees had been cleared for crops. They pass a ranch off in the distance where a woman on its covered porch is sweeping the steps.

Maia tilts her head. The mirage in the distance is making it look like that car is moving. *Mirage?* It's not hot enough for a mirage. A car down the road seems to be gliding toward them. It's not gliding—it's just moving. On wheels. *Working*. A working, *moving* car.

Maia slows to a halt with her hand on her chest, and the car approaches. Its body is a patchwork of red, clearly rebuilt from a hodgepodge of parts. It slows as it passes. All four passengers inside look at them.

Maia glances over her shoulder at Miguel. He nods at her with a knowing smile.

"Pretty amazing, isn't it?" Lucas says quietly beside her.

"You've seen one?" Maia whispers.

"I've seen a few. Electric like that one. They're generally only in communes like this, where they have the combined resources to get them moving again." He turns and walks backward to watch it drive away. "Always amazing to see, though." He faces forward again.

The young guard leading them says over his shoulder, "We only have a few, but a town of this size doesn't need many. That one apparently used to be a Honda Civic, but now it's made up of so many different cars, we don't know what to call it anymore." He shrugs.

Their small group continues down the street. More and more houses begin to fill in the sprawling acreage on either side until they finally arrive at what appears to be the village's town center.

The guard in front points. "That's our city square. We have a few shops down there along with a café, a library, and a bar. You'll be residing pretty far from there, at the edge of town beside the armed forces barracks."

"How many people live here?" Maia asks.

"Nearly three hundred."

"*Really*?!" she says. Three *hundred* people.

He smiles. "Yup, and we don't let just *anyone* in. Well, not to stay..." His cheeks flush.

"Is it possible to see the town?" Maia asks.

He glances at her, unsure. He looks young, maybe eighteen? He glances behind them at the guard flanking the back.

"I just..." She tucks her hair behind her ear. What she wouldn't give to see it. "I've never seen an actual working city. Just small tribes or ghost towns."

The young man lifts his chin. "I suppose I don't see why not. We'll take the long way around to the barracks." He glances at the guard in back. His smile quickly fades and he faces forward.

They continue down the street. Modest homes line the road, with spacious manicured lawns and petite, white picket fences.

A small gang of children on bicycles approaches. They slowly ride past, gawking at the newcomers. One little boy scrunches his chubby face and sticks out his tongue. Maia mimics him, sticking hers out in response. He looks shocked, his front tire wavering. He hurriedly continues on without looking back. She smiles. *Punk*.

As they are led through the town, Maia has to keep reminding herself to close her mouth. It's almost too much. The shops are full of things—*nice* things. The paint isn't faded or chipped or peeling. The glass panes on the windows are intact. And *clean*. There are no cobwebs over doorways or piles of rubbish clogging the streets' drains. Are the sidewalks swept? Is that an old man on a park bench, eating *ice cream*? Maia has only ever seen photos.

Wreaths of pine hang from every lamp, filled with

colorful glass bulbs. Those same bulbs hang on vines that crisscross above the road. There are small groups of people talking on street corners. Their clothes don't look worn. There are no patched holes in their trousers. Two women walk side by side with buggies, the babies inside kicking their feet and sticking their toes in their mouths.

They pass a narrow building with the word *Bar* on the front. There are a few patrons inside, two men and a woman, having a laugh. Maia nearly trips over her feet. They are perched on stools and speaking to one another —unlike her dreams, where the people stared into space, taken over by some force beyond them.

A few children exit a library, cradling a stack of books in their hands. Maia fights the urge to run inside. So many books. So many new worlds to explore.

Bright red and white striped flags hang outside every storefront. They have a blue box in the left corner with *New Portland* sewn in white across their center. They pass a lamppost with a green sign hanging from a chain: *Main Street*. The brick building behind it is called a *Post Office*.

At the end of the street, they approach a large square. Maia stops and clutches Miguel's arm. In the center of the square is a towering Douglas fir, covered in those same colorful bulbs and a spiraling fluffy silver rope, glittering in the midday sun.

Maia gawks at the tree with tears in her eyes. "Oh ... *my God*."

"It's a Christmas tree, miss," the young guard says.

She covers her mouth. A woman and her little girl standing beside the tree watch her. As Maia approaches, the woman grabs her child and they hurriedly walk away.

Maia has read about Christmas her entire life. Her

grandfather tried to celebrate with her but thought it was wasteful to cut down a tree for nothing. Plus, no electricity. No lights. No paper. They tried to celebrate a few times when Maia was a child, but it never stuck.

She grabs a branch, running the pine needles against her palm. She's thrilled to see a real Christmas tree, but also saddened to see such a beautiful giant cut down in its prime. She pushes that thought away to savor the moment. Miguel steps beside her and peers up.

"This is like the epitome of an American city," she whispers to him, not once taking her eyes off the tree. "It's like a scene from my picture books... like we're walking around in a picture book." She grazes her fingertips along the fluffy silver rope. It's so *soft*.

"Yes, but instead of being free, we are guarded by men with assault rifles and being glared at like criminals," Miguel whispers.

Maia glances around. She was so busy admiring the tree, she didn't notice all the people stopping to stare at them. Not in a welcoming way, but in an alarming way.

"Miss," the young officer says, and he nervously looks around. "We should keep moving."

Maia and Miguel rejoin Lucas and the guards, who quickly lead them away from Main Street to the backroads behind the village. This street does not have flower boxes or children on bicycles but is lined with large factories and warehouses. One building is particularly loud.

"That's where our electricity comes from," the young guard points.

"Dude!" the soldier behind them snaps. "We aren't tour guides! Just get them to their barracks so we can continue our day. We've got a lot of shit to do and a lot of questions to answer, thanks to them."

The young guard's smile drops and he nods, facing forward. He doesn't turn around or speak another word for the rest of the walk.

After twenty minutes of trekking past factories and warehouses, their small group approaches a dozen rows of wooden military-style barracks secured behind tall metal fencing. There's a one-room cabin within the property, encased inside more fencing with a small guard post at its entry.

The young soldier unlocks the gate and leads them through.

"Are you sure this is a good idea?" Miguel mutters under his breath.

"Mario wouldn't steer us wrong," Lucas says. But with a single glance, Maia can tell he's not as sure as he sounds.

The guard opens their cabin door and stands to the side, motioning for them to enter. One by one, they pile inside.

The tiny cabin has a small wood-burning stove in the corner, and three bunk beds lining the walls. Each has a cracked plastic mattress, a small clumpy pillow, and a single folded blanket on top. There's a toilet in the corner with a dripping, rusted showerhead on the wall above it and a tattered privacy curtain bunched to the side. The small sink in the opposite corner has a used bar of soap with a long black hair wrapped around it. A cockroach scurries past and squeezes through a small hole in the wall.

There's also a small fridge. Maia's never seen a

working refrigerator before. She swings open the door, then promptly slams it shut with her hand on her mouth. Whatever's inside hasn't been refrigerated in a long, *long* time.

The young guard clears his throat. "Yeah, it's pretty basic. Don't want you getting too comfortable." He cracks an awkward smile. "Someone will be back soon with your work orders and a contract to sign." He takes off his hat, looking at Maia. "Miss?"

She steps forward.

He clears his throat again, scratching the back of his neck. "These are shoot-to-kill orders."

Miguel drops his pack on the dusty wooden floor. "Meaning?"

The young guard opens his mouth but his comrade answers for him. "Meaning we're giving you a chance, but if you try anything stupid, we'll kill you."

TWENTY-FOUR

An early morning fog has engulfed the field in a sea of white mist, as if the heavy evening clouds have fallen from the sky. Lucas, Maia, and Miguel stand side by side along the meadow's edge with shovels in hand. Their two armed guards, sipping from their thermoses, quietly chat back and forth with their semi-automatic rifles draped across their backs.

Today is day one.

After they settled into their cabin last night, their guards piled out and dead bolted the door behind them. Hours later, they came back with a contract written on a piece of handmade paper. It was to be read over, signed, and then taken back with the guards.

For the short duration of their stay, Maia, Lucas, and Miguel—"the immigrants"—will be given jobs, which will vary from day to day. The immigrants will be informed of their duties each morning when the guards come for them at five forty-five sharp. Tardiness is grounds for removal. The immigrants are to work said jobs from six a.m. until four p.m. with a thirty-minute break for lunch. The immigrants will each work seventy hours in a one-week period in exchange for new boots, food, and lodging. As previously discussed, the immigrants may be given additional opportunities for work, based on availability, for their requested preserved meat. Should the immigrants cause any disturbance, they will be forcibly removed, forfeiting their items for barter. Should the immigrants cause harm to any property or animal, the act is also grounds for removal. Should the immigrants cause harm to any *person*, the act is grounds for removal or execution, depending on the severity of the crime. The immigrants are not to change location without prior approval. Immigrants must always be accompanied by an armed officer. Immigrants are to remain inside their cabin every evening. Immigrants are not allowed to patronize shops, cafés, the library, or the bar.

"And how do we know you'll provide us with boots and meat after we've done all this work?" Miguel asked.

"You don't," one of the guards said. "But you have food, safety, and shelter, all of which are better than what you'll find *out there*. Give us good work, and you have our word that we'll give you good boots."

Miguel lifted his chin. After years of being on his own, he's not a fan of being a workhorse for the week or being locked up "like an animal," as he had said.

"Miguel, we need this stuff," Lucas whispered. "It's just a short time and will make all the difference on our journey. And Maia's boots are ripping her feet to shreds. We don't have any other option."

"Of course," Miguel said, nodding. "We will get you your boots, Maia."

She stepped forward, facing the line of guards. "If possible, I would like to work extra for socks. Please, tell me what I can do for us each to leave here with a pair of sturdy woolen socks."

The leader turned his back and spoke quietly with the officers. He faced her. "Both your requests for boots and socks involve an intense amount of work by one man. So, every night after dinner, you will go to the village shoemaker with an armed guard, and you will help with whatever he needs for a minimum of three hours."

"And us?" Miguel stepped beside her. "What do we do for the dried meat?"

The guard scratched his chin. "How much do you need?"

"Ten kilos," Lucas said. "I figure each of us can carry three kilos? We have enough room for that, right?" He glanced between Maia and Miguel.

"We'll *make* room," Miguel said.

Another guard shook his head. "Nah, different system here. How many *pounds*?"

Maia, Miguel, and Lucas exchanged clueless glances. Lucas tried to do the quick math in his head. Is a pound a little over double a kilogram? Or is it the other way around? He guessed ... and then added a little more, just in case. "Thirty pounds," he said.

The guard held back a poorly suppressed smile. "You want to work for thirty *pounds* of dried meat?"

Lucas sighed. "I'm not accustomed to your system. Is that a lot or not enough?"

The guard shrugged. "Nah, man. That's perfect."

With that, they each signed the contract. Every night, while Maia is at the shoemaker's, the men will work in the village's food warehouse for their thirty pounds of dried meat ... whatever that means.

"Is that a lot?" Maia whispered as the guards locked the cabin door behind them.

"I have no idea," Lucas grumbled as he climbed onto his bunk. "But clearly, *that guy* isn't going to tell us."

The job on their first day is working in the fields, digging trenches. When Lucas asked what the trenches were for, he was told by an incensed guard to "mind your business and do as you're told."

Maia, Lucas, and Miguel separate across the field and go about their work. Digging, digging, digging, all while their two guards stand by and watch. It's backbreaking work. Despite Miguel being somewhat bitter about the arrangement, he understands. They are outsiders; they can't be trusted. They're desperate for the extra food for when they can't trap or hunt, and Maia can't go another day without new boots.

New Portland is helping them immensely. And the three of them, in return, are helping New Portland.

By doing the jobs no one else wants to do.

After spending the entire morning shoveling, Maia, Lucas, and Miguel have a quick break in the warm winter sun. The guards have left them two cheese and onion sandwiches each, and a small portion of mixed fruit from a jar. Maia peels back the bread and pulls out the cheese. She's never tasted cheese before. Nibbling on the edge, her eyes widen.

Miguel watches her, smiling for the first time since they've arrived. "So good, yes? I'd shovel all day for more of this cheese."

Lucas and Maia respond with grunts and nods, tearing into their sandwiches like savages.

In the afternoon, their assignment is to work on the sewage lines. Some of the village's older pipes need replacing. The three put their heads down and work, hoping by the end of the week, it will all be worth it.

Later that night, after a dinner of rice and beans, they relax on their bunks. Their cabin doesn't have electricity like the rest of the village, so a few lit candles flicker around the room. The temperature has dipped with the sun, so despite their brief break between shifts, they keep a small fire going to help warm their weary bones. Since there is always the possibility of someone watching, they start the fire the old-fashioned way—with a set of flint and steel left on the mantel.

The dead bolt clicks and the front door swings open, banging loudly against the wall. Three guards with flash-lights stand on the other side. One is to accompany Maia, and the other two will take Lucas and Miguel to the factory. But first, they all need to go to the shoemaker's shop on Main Street to get measurements of their feet.

The group walks down the dark country road in silence. Turning onto Main Street, Maia gasps, her hand on her chest.

The street is ... *glowing*.

She blinks back her tears. This has to be a dream. The lamps lining the road are ablaze, a succession of gleaming white orbs. The Christmas lights draped between them are a dazzling display of color. The storefronts are donned with evergreen wreaths, glittering with twinkling white lights.

Her entire life, Maia's had to navigate the darkness. All those years wandering the deserted city streets, transfixed by the useless metal poles, she always wondered what it would be like to see them alight. Never once did she imagine she'd actually see them. Never once.

"Maia," Miguel whispers. "We have to keep moving."

He gently pulls her arm, and she stumbles forward. Her mouth agape, she rejoins the three guards and Lucas, who've stopped to wait for her.

Walking down the center of Main Street, Maia holds Miguel's arm and keeps her head to the sky as they pass beneath the crisscrossing lights. The warm tears coating her cheeks turn icy in the winter air.

Since leaving the shores of New Zealand, Maia has been met with nothing but destruction and decay, the world seemingly crumbling beneath her feet. But *this*? She sighs at the sky. This makes it all worth it.

Approaching the enormous Douglas fir at the end of the road, Maia releases Miguel's arm and quickly wipes her tears. The giant tree is glimmering against the night sky, its multicolored lights reflecting in the ornaments. Maia turns around and walks backward, grinning like a child at Lucas and Miguel.

"I would stay here forever just to see that smile," Lucas says quietly.

"The guard earlier mentioned that they spent years

searching high and low to find all those strands that work," Miguel says, craning his neck to gaze up as they pass. "I thought it was a lot of effort for a few weeks a year, but I have to admit ... this is pretty magnificent."

The guards slow their pace as they approach the shop. A green awning hangs over the large front-facing window with *Main Street Shoes* painted across the glass. Inside the window is a miniature wooden replica of the village. Fluffy white cotton is strewn across the tiny roads, mimicking snow. There's a wooden Christmas tree in the center of the town, painted in colorful bulbs. Maia places her hands against the window, her breath fogging the glass in waves. It looks exactly like New Portland.

The guard knocks on the door.

"Come in!" a muffled voice yells from inside.

When he opens the door, a little bell rings. It's warm inside, unlike their cabin. It's a different sort of heat, a warmth Maia has never experienced before. She pulls off her hat. The building's heat is all-encompassing, like the sun has snuck between its walls.

An old man with a slight hunch shuffles up to greet them. The top of his head is bald, but the rest of his wispy white hair falls across his shoulders, blending with his beard. His bifocals resting on his lumpy red nose are smudged with fingerprints. Maia suppresses her smile. He looks like Father Christmas.

"So! These are our newcomers?" The old man holds out an arthritic hand.

Maia places her hand in his, and he eagerly shakes it.

The guard removes his hat. "These are the immigrants, sir. I'll stay with you and the girl. The other two will go with the guards waiting out front," he says.

"The *immigrants*?" The old man removes his glasses and tucks them into his shirt pocket. "They have names, don't they?"

The guard shrugs.

The old man turns toward Maia. "What is your name, dear?"

"I'm Maia. This is Lucas and Miguel."

They step forward.

"Very pleased to meet you," the old man says, shaking Lucas's and Miguel's hands. "My name is Thomas. And this gentleman." He points to the guard behind them. "His name is Andrew."

The guard nods. Lucas turns toward him, extending his hand. Andrew looks at him, then reluctantly shakes his hand.

"Okay then, let's get to work," Thomas says with a sigh. "Come with me."

They follow Thomas to a bench in the front room with an annoyed-looking Andrew trailing behind. The walls are lined with an assortment of shoes and boots and slippers. A faded, metallic *Merry Christmas!* sign hangs on the wall, next to another sign stating *We trade! Barter to be negotiated prior to sale. Must be council approved.*

"Let's get you fitted. Ladies first." Thomas motions Maia toward the bench.

She takes a seat and slides off each boot, slowly unwrapping her stained and tattered bandages. Andrew grimaces and turns away.

"Let's see the right one first," Thomas says as he pulls up a chair. He slides his bifocals back on top of his nose.

Maia lifts her foot, and Thomas holds it between his hands, shaking his head.

"Oh, Maia," Miguel mutters.

The old man sighs, motioning for her left foot. She leans back, placing it in his hand. There are swollen blisters on the backs of her heels and along her big toes and pinkies. Both of her big toes have lost their nails.

"You've been wearing shoes that are too small." He looks at her over his glasses. "You must be in pain."

She swallows.

The old man looks at Miguel and Lucas. "You'll be headed far north?"

The men nod.

"Well then, you are going to need some serious boots. This is going to take me a few weeks, at least."

"You have one week, sir," Andrew says from the back wall.

The old man peers up at him. "Excuse me?"

"That's all they are allowed to stay," he murmurs.

Thomas holds Maia's feet, turning them from side to side. He clicks his tongue. "Well, better get to work then."

After their fittings, Lucas and Miguel leave with their guards. The third guard, Andrew, keeps his post by the front door.

"No need to stand, young man," Thomas says, and he gazes fondly at Maia. "This girl isn't going to hurt me. Are you?"

"No, sir," she says.

He looks at Andrew. "Sit. Relax. Read a book. There's a stack of them beside the door."

Andrew glances between Maia and the old man, studying them, and he sighs. He slides the gun from his shoulder and props it near the door, then takes a book from the pile and plops into a chair.

"Come with me, dear," Thomas says. "We have a lot of work to do and not much time to do it. In the meantime, let's give you something for those feet." Stroking his beard, he scans the wall of shoes. "Nothing here, no..."

He wanders to the back office, leaving Maia and Andrew alone. She glances over her shoulder at him, and his eyes flicker up from his book.

Thomas comes back with an old pair of tennis shoes and a mismatched pair of socks. "Don't put these on yet —wait until you leave. You'll wear them until we get your new boots. These tennis shoes are a little too big, but will most certainly be a relief compared to what you've been wearing."

Maia sets her socks and shoes by the front door beside Andrew's gun. He stands. She puts her hands in the air and slowly backs away, then turns to follow Thomas.

The cramped room in the back of the shop is filled with boxes of old shoes and piles of leather. The walls have a selection of hanging laces and ropes and string. There are two industrial-sized sewing machines, and an assortment of knives and scissors are strewn about the countertops.

"So," Thomas says as he pulls his chair to his bench. "We've got some time together, you and I. Tell me about yourself."

"What do you want to know?"

"These men with you. You care about them?"

"Very much. They are my family."

"And they treat you well? They are good men?"

"They are," she says with a smile. "Very good men."

"You'll have to excuse the standoffish behavior of the

guards. We've had some bad experiences in the past with taking in strangers. We believe very strongly in community, in taking care of one another. We've set up a peaceful place for ourselves, but unfortunately, it must be protected. It's these men's duty to maintain that. They have a lot of responsibility on their shoulders. You'll forgive them for not trusting you, won't you?"

"Of course, I understand."

"You are wise beyond your years." He takes Maia's hand. "You seem familiar to me. I think maybe I have met you before, in another lifetime. You are good people, you and your men. I could tell from the moment you walked into my shop. Just give the villagers time, they'll warm up to you. And then you won't want to leave."

"Maybe so, but we have to," Maia says.

"We'll see," he says, beaming.

At the end of another long day, Maia, Lucas, and Miguel sit beside their wood-burning stove in their cabin, their door closed and locked. A guard is reading in his well-lit post outside their gate.

"Were they kind to you? The soldiers?" Maia asks the men.

"I wouldn't say they were *kind*, but they were certainly better than our original guards," Lucas says, rubbing his hands in front of the stove. "Had us working inside their food processing plant. Apparently, they've had a late harvest and are behind on a few things. Labor is limited. Miguel and I working there will hopefully allow the workers to take time off to be with their families on Christmas."

"Since it's so cold at night, the guards mentioned the plant is where we'll probably be stationed every evening," Miguel says. "Better than digging trenches, that's for sure."

"And better for the guards patrolling us. They watched us like hawks in there. Did you notice that?" Lucas asks Miguel. "I suppose they don't want us stealing their food."

"I don't blame them," Maia says. "Apparently, they've had some bad experiences in the past."

"I'm sure they have," Lucas says. "At the end of the day, people will do whatever it takes to survive. We are still animals."

"Yes, you are," Maia says absently, mesmerized by the fire.

"We." Lucas corrects her.

She looks up. "Huh?"

"*We* are still animals," he says, a brow lifted.

"Oh." She glances between the men. "Yes, of course. That's what I meant." She waves her hand, and Lucas shoots her a dubious look.

TWENTY-FIVE

I t all happened so slowly. And yet, it didn't take long at all. What even was *it*? A change. Something shifted ... *transpired* ... snuck in without Maia's awareness. Or had it always been there, silently lingering beneath the surface?

Was that *jealousy* Maia felt the night of the Christmas party? Surely not.

Was it?

Prior to that night, one week in New Portland trickled into two. Then two weeks turned into three.

The backbreaking labor New Portland demanded of Maia, Lucas, and Miguel dropped off quickly after that first week in the fields. It seemed to be an initiation; one they thankfully had passed. Miguel and Lucas began befriending their guards, often sharing laughs and stories from their travels while Maia and Andrew trailed quietly behind them. As much as Maia tried to catch Andrew's eye, share a smile, or make small talk, he remained closed off to her.

The guards began to ease from their stations. One guard per person turned into one for all three—usually Andrew. The people of New Portland seemed to soften as well, some even smiled as they passed. Lucas and Miguel were pulled from the fields to help in the factory during the day, preparing and canning food with the other workers, while Maia worked with Thomas, the shoemaker.

The guards stopped coming around after dinner with jobs, so Miguel, Maia, and Lucas have spent their evenings lying around their cabin reading books from Thomas's shop. Every night has become more of the same: Lucas is always the first to fall asleep, while Maia and Miguel, despite their exhaustion, stay up for hours talking. Maia's surprised at how effortlessly she can talk to Miguel. She's never had anyone in her life who she can talk to so openly. Not her grandfather. Not even Lucas.

After their second week in New Portland, they found the door to their cabin was no longer being padlocked at night. The guard outside their fence left his post and has not returned. The three still stick to the rules and remain indoors, but it's nice to know they're being trusted a little more.

Maia has loved her time with Thomas. His shop is so cozy. They've spent weeks together just the two of them, working on the boots and discussing life. He reminds her of Grandpa—his kind laugh and his gentle smile. The sneakers he loaned her have given her wounds a chance to heal. It didn't take long for her feet to feel like new again.

"You know, a few members of council stopped by today, asking about you," Thomas says. Grunting, he picks up a piece of leather from the dusty floor.

"What did they say?" Maia holds out her hands, and he tosses her the scrap. She chucks it into a pile in the corner.

"They wanted to know what I thought of you. They stopped by the food plant, too, and talked to the workers and the guards. They wanted to make sure everything was still running smoothly. They asked about your character and that of the men. It's a good sign, Maia. Tomorrow is Christmas. Did you know that?" He peers up at her over his smudged bifocals.

"I figured it was close." She looks around. "Speaking of guards, I noticed Andrew's no longer here. I haven't seen him since he dropped me off this morning."

"He's been relieved of his babysitting duties. Council finally realized what a waste of time it was." He chuckles and shakes his head, conveniently forgetting that he supported it in the beginning.

She beams at him. "You mean to say…"

"They've decided to trust you. I've also asked them to consider inviting you to the Christmas celebrations tonight."

She looks up at him in surprise. "Really? Do you think they will?"

"I do. These are good people here, Maia. Good people recognize good people."

The bell at the door rings. Thomas and Maia step out from the workshop to find Miguel and Lucas at the doorway with their packs on their backs. Maia's pack is strapped to Lucas's front.

"What are you doing?" she asks, suddenly nervous.

Miguel grins. "They're moving us."

She glances back at Thomas.

He smiles and nods. "Go on," he says.

She grabs her coat and follows the men out the door. Workers have already lined Main Street with small tables, tents, and booths. A massive stage is being assembled next to the village's Christmas tree.

Andrew is waiting for them beside a lamppost wrapped in garland—Maia has since learned the name. No longer in uniform, he is wearing jeans, boots, and a very colorful Christmas sweater.

"*Andrew*?" Maia says. "I barely recognize you." She smiles, and for the first time ever, Andrew actually smiles back.

Maia trails behind the men, watching with amusement as they talk and laugh with Andrew dwarfed between them. This is the first time they've walked these streets like normal citizens. Andrew does not have an assault rifle strapped across his back or a belt with a club or one of those devices—the ones used to communicate with the other guards. Miguel keeps telling Maia the name, but she can never remember. It's a silly name that rhymes. Something like talker talkie? Or a talkie walkie? It's as if a three-year-old named it.

Andrew stops in front of a large, two-story estate just a few blocks from Main Street. Trimmed evergreen hedges line the walkway leading up to its grand entranceway. The porch's white columns are wrapped in garland, and two giant Christmas wreaths hang from the doors.

"It's hard for us to let strangers in," Andrew says. "But I've heard you men have gone above and beyond in your work at the factory. Because of you, the warehouse workers get to be with their families for Christmas. This has not gone unnoticed. Everyone has been remarking about how much they love your company." He sighs. "And so, we would like to offer you this home for your last night here."

Maia, Lucas, and Miguel glance at one another.

"And…" Andrew clears his throat. "We would like for you to join us in our Christmas celebrations tonight. They start in an hour."

"We would love that. Thank you," Miguel says, and he shakes Andrew's hand.

They walk up the immaculate path to the front doors. The home's outside lights emit a warm glow in the early evening light. Andrew unlocks the doors, then stands to the side, motioning for them to enter.

One after the next, they pile inside. A dining room is off to the left of the cathedral entryway and a living room sits to the right, with an enormous Christmas tree beside a fireplace draped in garland.

"This is our Council House," Andrew says. "We use it for parties and guests. Please, make yourself at home. The lights are controlled by switches near the doorways. Make sure everything is switched off before you sleep and before leaving the home. No candles or fires. If you need anything, you know where to find us."

"Thank you, Andrew," Lucas says.

Andrew nods and hands Lucas the keys. "You are free to come and go as you please." He turns to Maia. "Before you head out, Thomas has requested to see you." He turns to leave, but then stops beneath the open doorway, hesitating as the icy evening air tumbles along the floor. "I don't want to say this," he says, facing them, "but I am required by council. Don't let us be wrong about you. The contract still stands should anything change. There are always undercover guards around. This village is surrounded by patrolled walls. There will be nowhere to hide."

"We won't need anywhere to hide," Lucas says. "Nothing will change. You have my word."

"I hope so," Andrew says, and he clicks the door shut behind him.

The three of them turn toward each other, wide-eyed and grinning like children. And then, without a second's hesitation, they race down the hallways, calling to each other from different rooms.

"Come see this!"

"Did you see that?!"

"Wow!"

"This is *amazing*!"

Maia flicks on the room's lights, stepping back from each one in awe. She crouches to the ground, hovering her hand above the vents on the floor with *heat* blasting from every one. She twists the large bathtub's faucet on and back off again, astounded at the steaming hot water pouring out every time.

When the men disappear into other areas of the home, Maia stands alone in the kitchen, listening to the quiet hum of the refrigerator. She opens the door, smiling as its cool air licks her cheeks. The fridge is mostly empty, save for a few items on a small wooden board. There's a selection of cheeses, a small glass bottle of milk, and a jar of preserved cherries. There's a small paper next to the board with *Merry Christmas from the staff at the New Portland Food Processing Plant* written on it. Maia's eyes glaze with tears. She closes the door and leans against it. There in front of her, sitting on the large kitchen table, is a basket of baked goods.

This can't be real.

After insisting repeatedly that she was safe to go alone, Maia walks the few blocks back into town. It is dark, but being so close to Main Street, every other streetlamp is lit. It feels so strange to walk these streets by herself. After weeks of constant supervision by an armed guard, it almost feels uncomfortable—like she's breaking the rules and is about to get caught.

The quiet neighborhood is so peaceful. Maia stops on the sidewalk, watching as a family of four sit around their dining room table having dinner. The man and woman raise their wine glasses while their children dig into supper.

"Like a picture book," Maia whispers.

She thinks of Lucas and Miguel. They could all be really happy here. *Safe*. Living a life Maia has always dreamed about. How are they supposed to leave a place like this and go back into struggle and decay and *bounders*? She sighs and stares up at the sky. Because there is not a *single doubt* in her mind that they must continue on. She—*she* must continue on. There's no reason the men need to go any farther except for her. How could they possibly want to leave after experiencing a life like this?

As Maia enters the small shoe shop, the door's little bell rings.

Thomas greets her with a smile, and he waves his hands excitedly in the air. "Maia! Yes, come in! Sit!"

She perches on the bench in the front room and gazes around. She's really going to miss this place.

Thomas shuffles out with a pair of brand-new boots in hand. "Merry Christmas, Maia," he says proudly, and he hands them to her. "I've just finished the men's boots as well, but I couldn't wait to give these to you."

"Oh, my God." She takes the boots. They are so *beautiful*, and they were made just for her. She slides each one on and ties the laces. Lifting her feet before her, she wiggles her toes beneath the leather. They fit like a dream, and they'll only get better as they wear in. She drops her head in her hands and sobs.

"Oh, Maia, do they not fit?" Thomas sits beside her and gathers her into his arms. "It's okay. Whatever it is, we can fix it."

She looks up at the old man, tears spilling down her cheeks. "No, Thomas, they are *perfect*. Thank you."

———

Later that night, Lucas, Miguel, and Maia head to Main Street for the evening's festivities. The faint sound of thumping music gets louder as they approach, and Maia's face lights up.

"I told you there would be music," Lucas says with a smile.

She grabs his face and kisses him.

Walking down Main Street, there are more people

than Maia has ever seen in her entire life. Food stands line the roads with the most decadent smells wafting through the cool air: cooked meat, baked goods with cinnamon, and fried potatoes curled into spirals and speared on wooden sticks.

Children shove their way through the crowd, giggling and chasing each other. Small firepits have been placed around for additional heat. A large white tent is filled with tables and oil lamps, and there's a stage up front with a band playing songs about Christmas. The people are friendly. A few even introduce themselves.

Andrew approaches and asks if they've ever tried mulled wine. They shrug and shake their heads. Andrew's smile makes his generally somber face nearly unrecognizable. The skin crinkles in lines on either side of his cheeks, reminding Maia of a character from one of her children's books, *How the Grinch Stole Christmas!*

"Come." Andrew leads them to a stand and orders three mulled wines.

The woman behind the counter ladles a deep burgundy liquid into a glass and tops it with a dried orange slice. Maia sips it slowly and her eyes widen. It tastes like heaven.

As they make their way down the street, they cup their cold hands around their hot drinks and watch the night unfold. Miguel and Lucas are on either side of Maia, just like when they travel. She can't hold back her smile.

Perfect. This night is perfect.

They are drawn back to the tent where the band is still playing and stand along the back wall, watching the villagers. An older man with suspenders walks the few steps up to the stage. Raising his hands, he silences the crowd.

"Okay!" he yells, and the microphone screeches. The crowd recoils, and he grabs his belly and chuckles. "This Christmas music has been great, but we've been asked to play a few tunes to shake things up a notch."

The crowd cheers, clapping above their heads.

The man standing beside Maia leans toward her. "You're in for a real treat."

"Why is that?" she asks.

"Have you ever heard the blues?"

She shakes her head.

"It's a traditional style of music our ancestors used to play. Our town loves it!"

Maia lights up and looks back at the stage where three men have gathered. She recognizes their instruments from her magazines. She always looked for musical instruments in the houses she broke into as a youth, but not knowing how to play, they never made much sense to her.

One man holds a guitar, another has a harmonica, and the older gentleman in the middle has the microphone. He props himself on a tall wooden stool as a woman walks along the back of the stage and sits behind a set of drums. When the band begins to play, the music is so loud Maia has to stop herself from covering her ears.

Miguel comes back with another glass of mulled wine for each of them, and they make their way into the crowd. The people are standing shoulder to shoulder, nodding their heads and shifting from foot to foot.

"Lucas!" Maia yells over the music.

"Yes, darling?"

"No one is kicking or throwing their hands into the air!" she says, laughing. She throws her hand above her head in mockery of him.

His smile drops, and he looks around. "Okay, maybe not here, but people *do* dance that way!"

"*Sure* they do!" she says.

He pinches her stomach. "You'll see!" he says with a *tsk*. "So *arrogante*." He shakes his head with a flirtatious grin.

They face forward and tap their feet to the beat. She looks around. Where did Miguel go? She looks for him through the sea of bobbing heads. When she finally spots him, her smile fades.

He's in a dark corner, talking very closely with another woman. Whoever she is, she is *stunning*. Her curly black hair has been beautifully sculpted, resembling a ball around her head. She's wearing large, golden hoop earrings, and her smile is as wide as the sky. Maia stops, suddenly transfixed. She doesn't know what it is that she's feeling, but she doesn't like it.

"Who is *that*?" she asks Lucas.

"Who?" He follows her gaze. "Oh, that's Hannah. We work with her. She and Miguel have a thing for each other."

There's that feeling again—like a stab in the gut. Miguel stands just inches from the woman, gazing down at her with a fondness in his eyes. The woman, *Hannah*, puts her hand on his face. Maia has the urge to run over there and smack it off.

"Hey." Lucas jabs Maia's ribs. "What's up?"

She looks away from Miguel and forces a smile.

"Nothing! Let's get another wine." She pushes her way through the crowd, and Lucas follows.

They get some air outside and grab another drink. What on earth is this feeling? Miguel is her friend, of course she wants him to find someone who makes him happy. But then, why is seeing him with another woman making her so angry? No, it's not anger—is this *jealousy*? She's never had more than one person she's cared about in her life at a time ... until now. Maybe she's just feeling overprotective. Yes, that's it.

She empties her glass.

"Hey, go easy. We've got a long night ahead of us," Lucas says with concern. "Are you okay? One minute you were laughing, and then suddenly you weren't."

"Sorry, it's been a big day. I think I'll get another wine."

"Be careful," Lucas says.

She rolls her eyes. There's that controlling *Lucas* side again. The music inside the tent slows.

"Hey, before you do that." He grabs her hand. "Dance with me."

She smiles. "Do we ... *kick*?" she asks, biting her lip.

He looks down. "No, *slow* dance," he says very seriously, and he leads her back into the tent and finds an opening in the crowd.

She stands across from him. "I don't know what to do," she says, watching the people around them.

He grabs her hands and places them behind his neck, pulling her into him.

"Wow," she says. "If this is slow dancing, then let's do *this* more often."

His eyes are glassy from the wine. "I'd like that."

She sighs, thinking of the dark journey ahead. First jealousy, now guilt. "Me too," she says.

The woman who was playing the drums walks to the front of the stage and takes the microphone. "Okay, family, the tradition continues. We've had a lot of requests for this song. It wouldn't be Christmas if we didn't celebrate the love in our lives, so here's a classic about old friends."

The music begins, and people pair together, dancing in slow circles.

The drummer closes her eyes and sings, "*Should auld acquaintance be forgot...*"

Maia rests her head on Lucas's shoulder, letting him sway her to the music.

"*For auld lang syne, my dear.*"

Maia locks eyes with Miguel across the dance floor, and she lifts her head. He's slow dancing with that other woman, his arms wrapped around her waist ... but there's something about the way he's looking at Maia.

"*For auld lang syne...*"

Butterflies tumble inside her gut as she and Miguel look at one another. So much unspoken in a single gaze. Miguel appears sad. No—something else. There's something else, something ... *more*. She can't look away.

Has he looked at her this way before? She's never noticed ... *Has* she?

"*We'll take the cup 'o kindness yet, for auld lang syne...*"

That woman whispers something in Miguel's ear. Maia swallows hard. He looks down at the woman and smiles, then allows her to lead him outside the tent. He does not look back.

Maia pulls away from Lucas. Without thinking, she

blurts, "We should go. We should grab Miguel and go home."

Lucas looks shocked. He grabs her hands. "You want to go? *Now*? The party's only getting started."

"Yes, but we don't want to lose Miguel, and that house is so nice." She glances around, a panicked fluttering inside her chest.

"Oh, don't worry about Miguel. He's not coming with us."

"*What*?!" she screeches. The people around them stop and look at her. She *knew* it. How could anyone want to leave this place for her? "He's not coming ... He's *staying* here?"

"No!" Lucas starts laughing. She puts her hand on her hip. "No, I meant *tonight*," he says. "I'm pretty sure he's going home with Hannah tonight." He looks around. "Ha! If they haven't already left."

"Yeah," she says bitterly. "They already left."

He tilts his gaze. "Maia, don't worry. He's still coming with us to Leucothea. It's just for the night. Come here."

He wraps her hands around his neck, and she sighs. But then that stabbing gut feeling returns. He's not coming home tonight?

"Why would he give up a night in that beautiful home just to stay with *Hannah*?" she asks, like *allegedly* that's her name.

Lucas puts his hand on her cheek. "*Meu amor,* you have *so much* to learn about men."

She pouts. The wine coursing through her system makes her feel wobbly on her toes.

"Hey, let's finish our dance," Lucas whispers in her ear.

She can hear him, but she's a million miles away. It's clear Miguel has left for the night, but she looks around the tent for him anyway. There's no question she loves him, but she doesn't have *feelings* for him—not in that way. That's ridiculous. Miguel is her friend.

He is just her friend.

TWENTY-SIX

Maia stares up at the ceiling. Eyes dry, head pounding. She hasn't drunk that much alcohol since Grandpa died.

Last night.

That look in Miguel's eyes flashes through her mind over and over again, pounding her memory like a migraine. It wasn't just the way he looked at her ... It was the way she *felt* when they locked eyes across that tent. The way her heart jolted. The way—

Ugh. *STOP.*

She rolls onto her side, looking at Lucas lying peacefully beside her. Lips parted, he is fast asleep. She sweeps a curl from his face. Such a gorgeous human. Guilt clenches at her chest. What *happened* last night?

Nothing. Nothing happened. She was just drunk. She misconstrued her emotions—it happens to people all the time.

Okay, yes, she was jealous. And yes, she cares for Miguel. But she wasn't jealous in *that* way. She's just gotten used to always having him by her side. They've shared a lot of late-night talks, she and Miguel. He taught her how to bo fight. She's slept curled against him almost every evening since they left his cabin. She's known from the moment they met that he was someone special, like she's known him her entire life. It's only natural to want to keep that to herself. She's read books where the characters felt this way about their friends when they've lost them to significant others. Happens all the time ... Right? He's her friend. He is just her friend.

She rolls onto her back, eyes wide at the ceiling. But that *look* they shared. In the light of day, Maia realizes that Miguel has looked at her that way before. More and more, the gaze between them lingers. And the way he smiles at her ... She *loves* that smile.

NO. Stop.

Maia loves Miguel—as a friend. She is *in love* with Lucas. She will always be loyal to Lucas, without a doubt. But this. She closes her eyes. This is too much.

No. It's not too much. It's not—because it's nothing. There's no point lingering on this. Don't ruin everything by confusing the facts.

What are the facts? Maia has two amazing men in her life. One is the love of her life. The other is her best friend. That's all there is. That's all there will *ever* be. She sighs. Grandpa always told her she was too dramatic. She's just tired and hungover and thinking *way* too much. Holding her face in her hands, she shakes her head and pushes Miguel from her mind. Let this be over now.

It was nothing.

Lucas inhales and stretches his hands above his head. "Good morning," he mumbles.

She rolls toward him. "Good morning, my love."

He flips toward her, his face puffy. He's hungover too. Not good on a day like today.

"Are you ready for this?" she asks.

"Not really."

She huffs a laugh. "Me either."

He reaches for her face. "It's our first Christmas together."

Maia holds his palm against her cheek. "It is. The first of many."

"Merry Christmas, Maia."

"Merry Christmas, Lucas."

The two head downstairs.

"Do you think Miguel is back yet?" Maia asks as she turns on the kettle. She eyes the ceiling.

"No." Lucas smirks. "Probably didn't get much sleep last night."

Stabbing gut feeling.

"Well, he better not be late." She raises her voice over the boiling kettle.

"He knows we're leaving today," Lucas says as he grabs a muffin from the basket. He sits at the kitchen table as Maia pours them each a steaming cup of tea and joins him.

Right on cue, the front door opens and clicks shut. A few seconds later, Miguel steps into the kitchen.

"Hey, buddy!" Lucas leans back in his chair with his hands clasped behind his head. "Good night?"

Miguel rubs the back of his neck. He peers at Maia, then looks away. "Yeah ... pretty good," he mumbles.

Lucas grins. "I bet it was—"

"There's hot water in the kettle," Maia says without

looking up. "*Buddy*," she mumbles into her cup. She blows away the steam before taking another sip.

"Thanks, but I'm going to wash up," Miguel replies, and he walks out of the kitchen. "Hey, guys?" he calls from the living room. "Did you see what's under the tree?"

Lucas and Maia slide their chairs from the table and join Miguel in the next room. Beneath the tree, each with a bright red bow, are new boots for Lucas and Miguel. Lying next to them are six pairs of beautiful woolen socks and a large package of dried jerky. Thirteen pounds to be exact—not thirty. The workers at the factory helped them with that one.

"How did these—" Maia kneels before the gifts.

"They must've come while we were sleeping," Lucas says, picking up a boot.

"Like Father Christmas," she whispers with a smile.

After they spend the morning showering and packing up their things, Lucas waits for them at the front door with their packs. Miguel and Maia walk out of their rooms at the same time, meeting in the hallway. An awkward silence hangs in the air between them. Miguel is the first to turn away.

Without thinking, she grabs his arm. "Hey."

He stops and looks at her. She opens her mouth. Closes it again. She can't find the words. What does she say? He forces a smile, then shakes his head and looks away with a sigh. When he looks back at her, a palpable sadness has seeped behind his smile.

She wills him to say something. *Please, say something. Say anything.*

"So," he says. "Did you have a good night last night?"

Maia is shocked—and relieved. He's not going to say anything about what happened between them.

Because it was nothing.

She lets go of his arm, mirroring his forced smile. "I did."

He nods. "That's good. I'm glad."

They stand across from one another in the hallway not speaking a word.

"Guys!" Lucas calls from the doorway downstairs. "Are we doing this?"

Miguel shakes his head and lays his heavy arm across her shoulder. "Come on, *buddy*," he says with a smirk. "Let's go."

She lays her head on his chest and sighs. It was nothing. Thank *God*. She wraps her arm around his waist, and they walk together down the hallway.

"Merry Christmas, Maia," Miguel says softly.

"Merry Christmas, Miguel."

Maia, Lucas, and Miguel head into town. Their packs are all a little heavier, but they have plenty of backup food now. Full bellies. Good boots. Warm feet.

Maia stops by Thomas's shop, but it is dark inside, the front door locked. Her heart sinks. They continue on their way to the gates where they are met by Andrew and a few guards.

"Lucas. Miguel. Maia." Andrew shakes each of their hands. "It has been a pleasure."

"Thank you, again," Maia says.

"You always have a place here," he says. "The guards will hand back your weapons."

The three take back their knives, bow, and staves and then turn to leave.

"Wait!" a voice shouts.

They turn to find Thomas approaching with a bright red Santa hat on his head.

"Thomas!" Maia runs up to him.

"You wouldn't be leaving without saying goodbye now, would you?" Panting, he pats her cheek.

"I stopped by your shop, but you were gone."

"Yes, I had to finish up my gifts for you. Here." He hands them each a small sachet of dried fruit. "It's not Christmas without some sweets."

"You are making it very difficult to leave," Miguel says.

"And your boots? They all fit okay?" Thomas asks the men.

"They're perfect," Lucas says. Stepping forward, he reaches for the old man's hand. "Thank you, sir."

"My pleasure. Thank you for all your hard work, boys. Lots of happy workers these last few weeks. You were a gift to us too."

Maia wraps her arms around the old man, and he hugs her tightly. "I'll miss our conversations," he says quietly as they hug. He grabs her shoulders and whispers, "But I understand you must go. You must follow the pull you feel in your heart, above all else." He winks.

She looks at him, surprised.

They walk to the massive gates and wait as the soldiers push them aside. As they step out onto the forest road, they turn to wave goodbye to their friends, taking one last look at their haven before the gates close. The lock is slid shut with a loud metallic *click*.

They turn to face one another.

"Okay," Miguel sighs, glancing between Maia and Lucas. "Here we go again?"

Lucas shakes his head as he peers down the road. "Yup. We've got pretty much nothing but backroads through forests from here on out. Apparently, the roads are pretty quiet until we hit the mountains in Canada. They're a popular route for people traveling up to Leucothea, so I've been warned about the mobs up there. Let's just enjoy the peace and quiet while we've got it."

Walking down the road, they pass the signs that once warned them to turn back until they reach the street they had originally turned from. They hang a left and continue on, no one speaking a word. Maia glances between Lucas and Miguel on either side of her. Both appear lost in thought, and neither will return her gaze. She faces forward again, the guilt wrapping around her heart like a straitjacket. New Portland was a haven in a dead world. Her entire life, she was told a life like that didn't exist. Is it a mistake to leave? It feels like they've left a guaranteed heaven for a guaranteed hell. Both these men will resent her at some point for this. How could they not?

So, what does this mean? Is this a journey meant for her alone?

The three souls wander down the long mountain road for the rest of the day in complete silence besides the continual *clank* of wooden staves hitting the leaf-littered pavement. Maia listens for the comforting whispers of the trees, but they, too, remain quiet.

Later that night, they set up camp and sit huddled around a fire. It's freezing, not only in temperature but also in temperament. Neither man has said a word all evening.

"Just say it, Lucas." Maia breaks the silence. "I know what you're thinking."

"You don't, actually," he says without looking up.

"Lucas, I *know* you. I'm sure you're probably thinking the same, Miguel?"

"Whoa," he says, hands in the air. "I don't know what this is, but I don't want any part of it."

"I can't take this silence," Maia says, staring at Lucas. "I know you resent me for making us leave."

"I don't," he says, peering up at her.

"Then what's your deal?"

"Nothing," he mumbles, using a stick to poke the fire.

She rolls her eyes, and both she and Miguel look at him. They wait.

"Okay, fine—I'll say it," he says, and he tosses the stick into the flames. "That village back there was perfect. It was *everything* we want for our lives. It was everything *anyone* could *ever* want for their lives. Now here we are, back in the wilderness in the middle of winter, freezing our asses off and risking our lives. And for what? I don't understand."

Maia is speechless. If words could cut.

She glances at Miguel. His eyes flicker to hers before looking away. "So," she says quietly. "You feel the same."

He won't look at her.

"I'm sorry," Lucas says. "I know it's not nice to hear,

but it just doesn't make any sense. It was different when Leucothea was the *only* place of hope for us. It made all the danger and the risk worth it. But now we know better. To leave a haven for the unknown, that's *crazy*. You see that, don't you?"

She stands, a bitter mix of anger and sadness and guilt swirling inside her. All she wants to do is run. She knew it was possible the men might feel this way, but it was too painful to acknowledge. Because then what? She glares into the fire. At the end of the day, this is *her* destiny and hers alone.

She swipes at a runaway tear and turns toward the men. Her eyes bore into Lucas. "Did you see me start the fire tonight?" she asks.

He meets her gaze. "I did."

She glares down at him. "Did you understand *that*?"

He looks stunned.

She lifts her brow, prodding him for an answer.

"No," he says, looking down. "I didn't."

"I suppose I shouldn't expect either of you to understand. That village back there?" She swallows hard, struggling to continue. "It was perfect—it was magical! I would give anything to stay there! To live in a gorgeous home with electricity and running water, are you kidding me?! I could listen to music *every day*. We would have a community. I've never experienced anything like that before. It was a dream!" She glances over her shoulder at Miguel, her eyes glassy. "But I can't. *You* can. We aren't that far— you can still turn back." She cuts her gaze to Lucas and lifts her chin, a layer of ice forming around her heart. "*Both* of you."

He looks up at her in surprise.

"I won't stop you," she says. "But I cannot—I *will not* go back. Whatever's happening to me, who I am ... My destiny has always been north. I thought..." She shakes her head, and she says quietly, "I thought you knew that."

A log shifts in the fire, sending sparks into the air.

"Maia," Miguel says. "We're here. We're in this together."

She looks at him over her shoulder.

"Hey," Lucas says, and she looks back at him. He reaches out to her. Reluctantly, she takes his hand. "You have me, Maia," he says. "You always will."

TWENTY-SEVEN

The next day, the icy rains begin.

Relentless and cold, the heavy drops pound the earth in endless sheets. Since the temperatures hover just above freezing, getting soaked is too serious a liability. So, Maia, Lucas, and Miguel decide to set up camp and wait it out.

They spend the entire day in silence, huddled beneath their tarp tied between the trees. They try to keep the fire going with their limited amount of dry wood, but its blaze fails to bring warmth.

Maia feels a little lonelier today. What once felt bound now feels torn. As hard as she tries, she can't shake it. The words cannot be unsaid, the heartbreak unfelt.

They don't want to be here.

"Hey." Lucas grabs her hand, breaking her daze. "Can we forget about last night? Please?"

She glares at the fire.

"Maia," Miguel says. "We aren't going anywhere. We are with you, every step of the way."

"Are you?" She rips her hand away. "It doesn't feel like it."

"We are in this together," Miguel says. "*Please*, Maia. We are sorry. Can we move on?"

She would love nothing more than to forget about last night. She sighs, glancing at the sulking brothers on either side of her.

"Please, darling." Lucas holds out his hand.

Yes, move on. What's done is done. What's been said was said. Dwelling on it won't change anything.

"Okay," she finally says.

But Lucas's hand remains empty.

The rain doesn't let up for days. In a way, it's a relief, a chance to just *be* without trying to get somewhere. They set up traps in the woods and take turns using the poncho to hunt with the bow. Miguel forages for mushrooms. It's a beautiful perk of the rain. They can rest their feet, enjoy the peace and quiet, nap, and sometimes feast like kings.

The forced break has also been good for them after their fight about New Portland. After a few days, the memory of the evening fades, and Maia lets it go.

When the rain clears, they decide to stay put a little longer to let their things dry. Lucas announces that he's going to head down to a nearby stream to try his luck at fishing. Miguel and Maia sit together on a log by the fire, sipping their mugs of hot water.

"What will you two get up to?" Lucas asks as he preps his daypack.

"Well." Maia eyes Miguel. "I could use some more bo training? I feel a bit rusty."

"Sure thing," Miguel says.

"Okay," Lucas says. He leans down to kiss Maia, but instead of pulling away when he normally would, he lingers. He kisses her, then kisses her again. Miguel shifts uncomfortably beside them. "Good luck," Lucas whispers and he grabs his pack. He glances back at Miguel and adds, "To the both of you."

Miguel scoffs. "Not a chance."

Maia rolls her eyes with a smile.

Miguel stands. "Shall we? I'll get our staves."

Maia and Miguel walk to the cracked and weed-devoured highway, then stand across from one another with their bo in hand.

They bow, and with the crossing of their staves in the air, they begin their routine.

After a few minutes, Miguel backs away and lowers his staff. "Okay—*again*, you are not breathing."

She tips back her head and growls, "*Why* do I keep doing that? Am I holding my breath? I don't even realize I'm doing it."

He laughs at her.

"Miguel, we are each other's backup. You can't have your backup doing a piss-poor job at fighting. *Help* me!"

He steps to stand beside her. "Okay, keep your stance like this. You are doing it like this."

She mimics him. "Okay."

"Now, as you move your staff, breathe out forcefully, like this."

She tries to follow his lead.

He snorts, suppressing his laugh. "Maybe you should just stick to magic."

She shoves him. "*Not* funny!"

"Okay, okay. I will show you." He sets his bo on the ground and steps behind her, wrapping his arms around her. He places his hands over hers. She swallows.

He speaks softly in her ear. "Close your eyes."

She closes them.

"You must become acutely aware of your surroundings," he says. "You must become *one* with your staff. You are separate from it and you are clumsy. Grip it like this, and then move *with* it, as if it is a part of you." He draws her against him, and her heart begins to pound. As he gently moves her staff, their bodies sway together. "Just breathe and strike. Breathe and strike."

They sway, and she loses herself to the motion. Breathing in, they strike.

Breathe out.

Breathe in—*strike*. Out.

His arms wrap even tighter around her, his heart beating wildly against her back. Is he nervous? Is *she*? She swallows again, trying to will her heart to calm. Maybe they shouldn't be touching this close ... Maybe she should move away. But she doesn't. She keeps her eyes closed, turning her head toward him until her nose grazes his.

She should move. But how is this any different from every night when they sleep ... her body curved against his, her nose nestled in his back. She inhales, the same way she does before she falls asleep at night. He smells like pine needles and sea breezes. He smells like ... *home*.

She opens her eyes, meeting his gaze. They've stopped moving, but he has not let her go. Their noses are touching, his breath hot on her lips.

"Okay!" She ducks out from his arms and backs up along the road, pulling a strand of hair from her mouth. "I think I got it," she says. Her laugh is high-pitched and nervous.

"Right. Okay." He puts his hands on his hips and glances around. "I think we are done for the day, yes?"

"Yup. We're done."

Later that night, Miguel insists on sleeping separately.

"You're *joking*," Lucas says, his breath a cloud.

"No, I've been getting too hot lately." He shrugs, and Lucas and Maia look at him like he's lost it. "Just for tonight. You'll be warm enough without me, yes?" he says to Maia.

She sucks in her lips, nodding. She needs to talk to him. Tell him it was innocent and not to worry. They are clearly very close, but he is beating himself up unnecessarily. And now it will be a miserable sleep for them both.

In the dead of night, Miguel's sleeping bag shivers next to hers. She reaches for him, then pulls back. If only she could talk to him. What happened on that road didn't mean anything.

It didn't.

The next morning is clear, crisp, and freezing. With their things now dry, they pack up camp and head down the narrow forest road. The mountains in the distance grow taller each day. Lucas points out to them, calling a few of the more obvious ones by their names. Mount St. Helens. Mount Rainier.

The trees are whispering again. Maia can now make out a few words. *Moss. Youth. Water. Ant.* The words pop from a jumble of mostly indistinguishable whispers. The trees seem to be speaking amongst themselves, and the more she listens, the more she can decipher.

"This sure is beautiful," Miguel says with a sigh.

She glances at him, and he mouths *I'm sorry*.

She closes her eyes and curtly shakes her head. When she looks at him, his smile is tender, and he nods. That was their "talk," and for now, it will have to be enough.

"Yes, very beautiful," Lucas says. "*Anything* is beautiful after the barren deserts of California."

"Or the flooded streets of LA," Maia adds.

"Hear, hear!" Miguel shouts, lifting his bo into the air.

Maia lifts hers and they cross their staves, smacking them midair like a *cheers*.

The three share a laugh, bantering back and forth until the road slopes downward, leading to a cliff overlooking a group of islands. A sign stands next to a small gravel lot. Maia wipes away the dirt.

Seattle Lookout.

They wander to the edge, peering across the half-submerged skyscrapers and small slivers of land jutting from the ocean. So much devastation, yet it all looks so peaceful. Maia thinks back to the newspapers she burned in New Zealand.

World Mourns as Ocean Claims Another Coastal City.

They were all just names back then. Faraway places in strange lands she would never see. And now, here she stands.

"So, this is Seattle," Miguel says quietly.

"Do you see in the middle there?" Lucas points. "That building sticking out of the ocean looks like a UFO stuck on top of a tower."

"It does," Maia says.

They spend another minute or two at the lookout without saying a word. A moment of silence to mourn what looked like another spectacular city.

"Oh, look!" Maia says, pointing to the sky. "I've never seen one of those before. What bird is that?"

They look at the giant bird soaring high above their heads. Its brown wings span at least six feet across, its head crowned in snow-white feathers.

"Bald eagle," Miguel says, shielding his eyes. "It was this land's national bird."

"Ah, yes." Lucas nods. "Land of the free."

After another moment of silence, they turn away one by one to continue down the long and winding road.

TWENTY-EIGHT

There's a hairbrush lying in the middle of the road.

Maia steps over it, hardly giving it another thought. They've come across a few random items lately, strewn along the path: a cooked and picked-over animal bone, a child's shoe, a hairbrush—all signs of human life on this foggy, abandoned road.

Lucas keeps reminding them to enjoy the solitude, as it won't last. He's fairly certain they must be bordering Canada. *Any day now*. There are many roads leading through Canada, but the closer they get to Leucothea, which apparently sits high along the new western coast of Alaska, the fewer roads there are. Lucas was warned by Mario that the road to Leucothea is littered with gangs.

They approach a small bridge. Miguel walks ahead of them and steps to the railing.

"Water?" Lucas asks.

Miguel nods.

"Thank God," Maia grumbles. "Let's find a place to set up camp. I'm exhausted."

They cross over the bridge, each peering down with relief into the crystal blue waters. A water source is a definite stop for the night.

They continue a little farther down the road. While a water source is a must, camping *next* to one is a recipe for disaster. Any person in the area will also be drawn to it, and people can't be trusted.

Maia glances at Miguel. What used to be met with an immediate smile is now met with avoidance. He's been distant. Despite their "talk" the other week, he's cold. He barely looks at her. When she snuggles against him at night, his body stiffens, and he shifts ever so slightly away. She needs to talk to him, but she hasn't had the opportunity.

"Lucas." Miguel breaks the silence. "I think that's an old motel back there between the trees."

They look to where Miguel points. A one-story dilapidated building stands off the side of the road, covered in forest debris. Its small, weed-infested parking lot is separated from the road by a thick line of trees.

They slowly walk up to it. The motel is basic: a tiny office building attached to a dozen small rooms.

"Think it'll work?" Miguel looks over his shoulder at Lucas.

Lucas glances between the road and the motel. "Well, it's not hard to spot. It's right off the main road."

"Lucas," Maia says. "That river is less than a kilometer away, and I *need* to bathe."

He looks at her, then eyes the motel. He nods and

pulls out his knife. "Okay, let's start with the escape route and go from there."

"You two head around back and check," Miguel says quietly. "I'll keep watch up here."

Lucas and Maia slowly creep around the back of the motel, checking the windows. The first rule when settling into any building: it must have an escape route. Some small motels don't have windows in the back, or at least none large enough for Miguel to crawl through. Should anyone break in the front door, they'd be trapped.

The back of the building is lined with sliding glass doors with small cement platforms separated by trellises. Lucas and Maia smile at one another. They walk to the front of the building where Miguel is still standing, holding his bo. With his broad stature, down jacket, and dreadlocks spilling from beneath his woolen cap, he looks like a man you do not want to mess with.

When he turns toward them, he holds Maia in his gaze.

"Good?" he finally asks.

"Yup. Let's start the sweep," Lucas says beside her.

They start with the office building. The door is still locked, which is a good sign. If anyone was staked out in these parts, they'd have broken down this door already. Lucas and Maia peer inside the front window. The room is mummified and covered in dust—completely untouched.

They continue along the row of doors, most of which are locked with curtains open—not a single sign of life. The fourth door is ajar. Lucas pushes against it, shoving piles of leaves across the entrance's tiled floor. They peek inside. An orange cat is on the torn-up bed with a small litter of kittens crawling around her.

"Dinner," Miguel whispers.

"Miguel, *no*." Maia looks back at him. "Please, no—I can't."

His eyes widen. "*Maia!*" He gestures toward the cat, now hissing with her back hunched. "That's a guaranteed source of food!"

She crosses her arms. Horrified, he looks at Lucas with his mouth open. Lucas shakes his head. He knows this is a fight they won't win.

"We've got the river anyway, Brother," he says.

Lucas walks past the cat, still making a scene, and heads toward the bathroom. The bathtub inside is cheap plastic, so no rust, but is filled with dust and dirt and leaves. The small window above it has been shattered. He steps back out. Stopping next to the sliding glass doors, he peers into the backyard. "This could be perfect, but let's check the other rooms."

Most rooms are locked and untouched. A few doors are open, clearly used once upon a time by other travelers passing through. They decide to go with the very last room—it has the easiest escape route and is sans one hysterical cat.

Maia sits on the bed, and a plume of dust explodes. "This is going to be so great," she says, coughing and swatting.

Both men smile.

"Okay." She rubs her hands together. "How do we want to do this?" All she can think about is a hot bath.

"It would be great to find at least one more bucket to save us some trips to the river," Lucas says. "Surely this motel will have them. Might even be able to swap out your old guy for something better?" he says to Miguel.

"No way," Miguel says. "That's my lucky bucket. Trapped more vermin than I could possibly count."

Lucas lifts his hands. "Up to you. Anyway, it's small. We should try to find something bigger. I bet they'll have some in the office building. Stay here, Maia."

He and Miguel leave the room, and she gazes around. Like a time capsule, everything looks untouched. She slides open the bedside drawer to a dusty bible inside. She flips it open, reading a high-lighted passage.

"Blessed are the meek, for they shall inherit the earth," she says. "Lucky us." She sighs and sets the bible aside, suddenly distracted by her hazy reflection in the mirror. She steps closer and swipes her fingers across the thick film of dust.

She *does* look different. She noticed it a little back in New Portland, but she must be changing by the day. Her hair is a deeper red. There are spiraled curls mixing in with her auburn waves. Has her face matured? She sweeps her fingers across her cheeks. Her freckles ... there are fewer of them now.

She's starting to look like the woman from her dreams.

The men see her every day, and even they have noticed it. It must have something to do with her powers. She knows her appearance changes when she uses them. Maybe the more she uses them, the more she changes— *permanently*.

A loud bang crashes, and Maia runs to the door. The men have broken into the office. Miguel is searching inside as Lucas stands guard. His face is stern, and he grips his knife at his side.

Always be ready, he's repeatedly told them. *We can't risk a single moment being unprepared.*

Miguel steps out with two plastic buckets, both with handles still attached.

Perfect.

They wander down to the river. Miguel assembles his fishing pole while Maia starts a fire and places a pot of water on top. Now that they're closer to Canada, they've agreed to always stick together, so she might as well heat the water while they wait for Miguel to catch dinner.

By the time they have three hot buckets of water, they also have a few fish. They head back to the motel. Miguel guts the fish, and Lucas keeps watch out the front window while Maia takes a bucket into the bathroom. As she washes herself, she thinks back to when Lucas left her a bucket of hot water in the bowels of his ship. So much has changed since then. Their love feels different now. Maybe it's just more comfortable ... but they seem to have lost the spark they once had. Although, in their defense, this journey has been nothing short of exhausting, leaving little room for romance.

And now, they have Miguel.

Miguel. The distance growing between him and Maia feels like torture. This has gone on long enough. She decides to take the opportunity to talk to him when Lucas is bathing.

When she steps out from her bath, Miguel has gutted and prepped the fish.

"Okay, Miguel, you're up." Lucas nods toward the bathroom. "Maia, can you get another fire started out back? We'll want some solid embers to cook the fish. I'll stay out front and keep watch while Miguel cleans up."

After starting the fire, Maia wanders through the tall grasses to the pine trees at the edge of the yard. Gazing up, she places her hand against the bark, comforted by the humming of life just beneath the surface.

From the corner of her eye, she notices a delicate green branch shifting toward her. She turns toward it with her hand held out, watching in awe as it slowly grazes its needles against her finger.

"Maia?"

She whips around. Lucas is standing at the open sliding glass door. "You're getting really good at that," he says with a smile.

She turns toward the branch, now back in its original position. "But I didn't do anything," she whispers, peering up at the tree.

Its cryptic whispers wash over her in waves.

Miguel is finished, so Lucas heads inside to bathe next. Maia feeds a few more logs on the fire, then peers back at the motel, her heart pounding. Now's her chance.

She slides open the glass door and walks inside. The bathroom door is shut. She can see Miguel through the open front door, sitting on the curb outside their room. When she steps outside, he stands and backs away.

"Hey," he says awkwardly.

She puts her hand on her hip. "Miguel."

He shrugs. "What?"

"We need to talk." She grabs his hand and leads him across the parking lot. As they walk, his fingers wrap around hers, and she looks down at their hands, wondering when the lines between them began to blur. How did they get here? Is this all her fault?

Out on the road, she lets go and holds her head, lost for words. "I miss you," she blurts out, dropping her hands to her sides.

He peers down at her with a tilted gaze. "What do you mean?"

"Oh, don't give me that," she snaps. "You're distant. Cold."

He looks away, shaking his head.

"We didn't do anything wrong," she whispers. "It meant nothing, okay? *Nothing*." Her tone is cold, and he winces at her words. She closes her eyes. She didn't mean for it to come out like that.

"Nothing," he says, peering down at her with narrowed eyes.

"Can we go back to normal now?" she pleads, her voice breaking. "I feel like you're punishing me. For what, I don't know, but can I please have my friend back?"

He looks away with his brow deeply creased, seemingly waging a war inside himself.

"I need you," she whispers, tears surfacing. She reaches for him, then pulls back, holding her hand against her chest.

He looks at her hand. "I'm here," he says after a while. "I'm sorry I've been distant. I won't do it anymore."

"Don't be sorry," she whispers. "Just ... *come back*."

They stare at each other for a long time on the desolate mountain road. This man. Whatever it is that she's feeling, she's never experienced anything like it before. It's overwhelming. She loves Lucas, but something is happening with Miguel. It feels like a force beyond them, and it only seems to grow with each passing day. He looks at her the way Lucas looks at her but with a deep sadness behind his eyes.

She releases her breath. Gazing up at him, she suddenly becomes keenly aware of what it is that she's feeling.

"Guys?"

They turn to see Lucas standing at their motel door. As they wander back through the parking lot, he eyes the two of them with his arms crossed.

"We ... thought we heard people coming," Miguel says as they approach.

Lucas lifts a brow. "And?"

Miguel and Maia look at one another.

"It was nothing," she says.

"Nothing," he repeats quietly.

TWENTY-NINE

Maia walks through the woods with her handmade bow strapped across her back and three dead squirrels hanging from her hand. Miguel is hunched beside a tree in the distance, searching its base for mushrooms. Twigs snap beneath Maia's boots as she approaches, and Miguel sits up, flashing her an awkward smile.

"Hey," she says, and she continues past him.

There's no point anymore trying to make conversation. It's been over a week since she pleaded with him outside that depressing motel parking lot, and things have gone from bad to worse. She wants nothing more than to move past whatever this is that has grown between them, but it all feels ... *stuck*.

It's blatantly obvious that Lucas has noticed the awkwardness between Maia and Miguel, but true to form, he hasn't said a word. Maia is relieved. If Lucas were to ask her what happened, she would have no idea what to say.

"Wait," Miguel says. "Please."

She stops, but she doesn't turn around. Miguel catches up with her and puts his arm across her shoulder. She used to get so annoyed with him whenever he'd drape his heavy arm across her. She'd playfully push him away ... tell him he was weighing her down. What she wouldn't give to have those days back.

She looks down at her boots and slides out from beneath him, continuing on her way.

"Maia, I'm sorry."

She freezes. Closing her eyes, she fights the urge to sob. So many feelings shoved down inside her gut. She turns around. "For what?" she asks, her voice broken.

"For everything," he says. "This is all my fault, and I'm sorry. I'm ready for this to be done. I *need* for this to be done. We're going to be okay. Right?" He steps toward her. "Please tell me we're going to be okay."

She looks down at her feet, swallowing her ache. When she looks up at him, a worried crease has divided his brow.

"Of course, we're okay." She steps toward him. "You're my friend. I *lov*—"

He stiffens and she turns away, her cheeks flushed with heat. "You're my best friend," she says quickly. "We are okay because we *have* to be okay. Do you understand what I'm saying?"

"I do." He takes another step, and she does the same.

"I need you, Miguel. *Compreendo*?"

He smiles—a real smile. Finally. "*Compreendo* ... Buddy."

She turns to walk, hoping he'll follow. He does.

"You know, I wasn't saying that to be nice," she says as he joins her.

"Oh, *I know*."

She bites her lip. Busted.

"But now," he says, and he puts his arm back across her shoulder. "Now, it will stick forever. You are my buddy."

She shakes her head, beaming up at him. This feels right—normal. Thank God. "So, we're okay."

"We're okay."

She stops and turns toward him. "You promise this time, Miguel? *Promise* me that we are okay and I can have you back, and that this is finally over."

He sighs as he gazes down at her, and he places his hand on his heart. "You have my word."

Maia drops her pack to the ground and joins Lucas and Miguel, now standing beneath the colossal sign.

Welcome to Canada.

"It's hand painted. Think it's legit?" Miguel asks, staring up at the sign.

"I mean..." Lucas hesitates. "I feel like we passed Seattle ages ago. I swear it's been at least a few days that we've been hiking through Canada, but what do I know? My maps are old, and it takes so long on foot."

"We're on the correct path, though—right?" Maia turns toward Lucas.

"Definitely. We're just on the backroads. Which is why we really need to stop and discuss our next steps."

A bald eagle soars above them, and Maia smiles.

They've made it to Canada. They've made it up the coast of America through bounders and harsh desert days and bitter winter nights. Now budding flowers pop from the sides of the roads, reminding them that spring is near—a new season. A new boundary crossed. The days are getting longer. The sun has a little more heat to it, rising a little higher into the sky each day. The air is still cold, but its bite has dulled. More and more, they seem to keep their hats tucked inside their bags.

They find a small park on the side of the road, and Lucas pulls out his tattered paper map and lays it across a picnic table.

"I believe we are somewhere around here." He points at the map. "We've taken the backroads as much as possible to this point, which is why there've been so few signs. Plus, the coastline has completely changed since this map was printed, and everything became so *digitalized*." He swats at a relentless black fly. "Anyway, we need to try to stick around this route." His finger traces up a highlighted red line. "The other route leads to a flooded city called Vancouver, which is apparently inundated with bounders."

A shiver runs down Maia's spine.

"Plus, Mario said they do business with pirates— another good reason to steer clear."

Miguel stands back with a smug look on his face. "What, you don't feel like a family reunion, Brother?"

Lucas eyes him. "There was more than just our ship out there." He looks back at the map.

"Okay, so we'll follow this road until when?" Maia asks.

"We only have a few options," Lucas says. "There's a vast collection of mountains and sounds all along here." His hand motions along the western ridge of British Columbia. "The major route to the west is closer to the sea and half flooded—but not everywhere. Like the western coast of America, there will be goat tracks around the roads that have fallen into the sea." He stands back, looking at his faded map with his hand on his head. "That route will certainly prove to be more challenging, *but* because it's a tougher trek, it will have fewer mobs. But there will also be fewer places to run. Some of those goat tracks are single-file along the cliffs. So, if we are surrounded, we'll be trapped."

"Okay ... *Or*?" Miguel says.

"Or we take this slightly *longer* route to the east. The roads are more open and protected from the sea. I think it will give us a better chance at survival..." He shakes his head, hesitating.

"But?" Maia asks.

"But ... more mobs." Lucas looks at Miguel.

"I'd rather take the eastern route," Maia says. "No matter which way we take, we risk confrontation. At least this way, we have more room and a better visual of what's around the corner."

"I agree," Lucas says.

They both look at Miguel.

"Okay," Miguel says. "And then what?"

"The road will cut through the old Yukon Territory until we arrive at the Alaskan Highway," Lucas says. He bites his lip, and he glances between Maia and Miguel.

"What?" Maia asks.

"This is where it gets particularly problematic. There

are established mobs along those parts that have made a life for themselves robbing travelers."

Miguel sighs. "I don't know if I can handle another ambush."

Lucas looks at him. "It's the only way, Brother."

"Those bounders were ruthless. You don't … you don't understand." Miguel rubs the stubble on his face.

"Is there any other way?" Maia asks Lucas.

He leans over the map, scrutinizing the lines and notes from Jake and Mario. "We can cut even farther over this way." He moves his finger along the lines tracing east. "But it will add a significant amount of time to our travels and doesn't guarantee that we will avoid an ambush. The closer we get to Leucothea…"

"Yeah," Maia and Miguel say in unison.

This is part of it. They knew this from the beginning. Stay away from cities. Take the backroads whenever possible. The closer they get to Leucothea, the higher the risk of *others*. Others who prey on weary travelers passing through. Travelers with food. Supplies. Weapons. The mobs take it all. Some may take your life, but most apparently don't bother with the fight. After robbing you of your supplies, time and the harsh reality of nature will take care of you quickly.

"Okay, I agree with Maia," Miguel finally says. "Let's do the eastern route."

Lucas folds up his map and places it inside his pack. "I think we should stay quiet when traveling again."

"Agreed. Whispers and hand signals until camp," Maia says.

They continue on their way, hiking past another

abandoned ghost town. The windows of the modest homes have been boarded up, and fallen powerlines hang across the street. The day is gray. Rain spits across them in hazy waves—just enough to make everything damp, but not enough to stop and set up camp, especially in a place as open as this.

They pass what appears to be an old gas station. A swollen traveler is propped against a lamppost in the parking lot. His pack has been cut open, and a few leftover contents spill out across the weeds. Flies swarm the traveler's body, and maggots spill from his eyes. Maia covers her mouth as they pass.

Eventually, the trees overtake the buildings and the road narrows again, with vast mountain ranges sprawling across the horizon. They walk all day in silence until they can walk no farther.

As darkness falls, they wander off the road as deep into the woods as they can until they feel their fire will be safe from view. Maia trips on something in the twilight and a branch swings across to catch her. She smiles, gripping the limb like the hand of an old friend.

They sweep the area of debris to set up their tent. They no longer need to sleep huddled together to stay warm, which is probably best considering the blurred lines Maia and Miguel have crossed.

As Maia starts a fire, Miguel comes back from setting up his trusty bucket trap. "We left it a bit late. Hopefully by morning we'll have something to eat," he says. "How are we doing with the dried meat from New Portland?"

"Gone," Lucas says, tying his long hair off his face. The band snaps.

"Time for another cut?" Maia asks.

"*Por favor.*"

She pulls out their utility knife from her pack and flicks out the small scissors. Thankfully, with Lucas's curls, she can give him a decent trim without it looking too bad. She has cut her and her grandfather's hair her entire life, so she knows her way around scissors. But Lucas's heavy head of curls is much different from her thick waves and her grandfather's wispy, pin-straight hair.

They sit around the fire as Maia wipes the last of the fallen curls from Lucas's shoulders.

"Thank you, darling." He tilts his head toward her, and she leans down to kiss him.

Her eyes flicker to Miguel's. He quickly looks down at his hands, tightly gripping one inside the other.

"Shall I work on your dreads?" she asks him. "They're getting a little overgrown."

He gazes up at her. "If you're offering."

She wanders over and stands behind him, finding each piece and twisting the loose hair near his scalp.

"They were my wife's idea, the dreads," he says into the silence.

Maia stops. All these days traveling together, Miguel has not brought up his family since the overpass outside of LA. Lucas watches him with a tender gaze, waiting for him to continue.

"She always had a thing for them," Miguel says. "So, of course, you want to be as attractive as possible for the woman you love. But now ... now I can't bring myself to cut them."

"You do have a full head of them," Maia says as she continues working her way around his scalp.

"My eldest daughter, Ana, she was my little shadow," Miguel continues. "Wanted to do everything I did. She asked for dreadlocks one day. My wife wouldn't have anything to do with it—she always loved my daughter's curls. Both my daughters had hair like us, Lucas. Thick and curly. They were so gorgeous." His voice breaks.

Maia can see his hands from where she stands. Highlighted in the firelight, he is gripping one inside the other. They are trembling.

"I wish I could have met them. I'm sorry I wasn't there," Lucas says.

"Yes, well. This doesn't have anything to do with you." A sting of bitterness taints Miguel's voice. "Not *everything* important in my life has to involve you."

Maia stops. Lucas's face is steeped in sadness. There's still so much unspoken between these brothers. How much she wishes they would talk.

"Sorry," Miguel says quietly.

"How old were they?" Maia asks.

"Ana was seven. The youngest, Miciela, she was only two. She came after a long line of failed pregnancies. She was our little miracle baby." His voice trails off, and a long silence ensues.

Lucas's eyes are glassy as he gazes across the fire at his brother. Maia's grateful she can't see Miguel's face. How it would crush her. She wraps her arms across his broad shoulders and leans her head against his back. He holds her wrists against his chest and sighs.

A wolf howls in the distance and all three straighten, glancing around the dense forest. The fire snaps, sending an explosion of sparks into the air. Another wolf, this one much closer, howls in response. Eerie and long, it sounds like a cry of anguish. The first one echoes its howl, and they continue back and forth, like haunting wails deep inside the darkness.

THIRTY

A few more days have passed as Lucas, Maia, and Miguel trek deeper into Canada's wilderness. The air stays cool the farther in they go, and the misty rain coats them in a chilling layer of damp. Lucas has no idea exactly where they are, but as long as the compass points north, that's all that matters. Every step makes a difference.

The trees' whispers seem to be getting louder along this stretch of gravel road. With the lack of conversation, Maia has had nothing but time to listen. More often than not, the whispers are indistinguishable—until now.

Stop.

Maia glances at the men on either side of her. Miguel and Lucas are both focused on the road ahead. She lifts her bo, straining to hear the trees' whispers over the crunching of boots and the grinding of Miguel's staff against the gravel.

Danger. Stop.

She grabs Lucas's arm. "What?"

He frowns.

"Did you say something?" she whispers.

He shakes his head with a baffled look on his face.

She glances at Miguel, still lost in his own world. She waves her hand to grab his attention. He peers down at her.

"Did you say something?" she whispers.

He shakes his head.

She slows her pace and glances up at the trees. Their whispers surround her.

Stop. STOP. Stop stop stop.

DANGER.

She freezes, her heart pounding. Lucas and Miguel look at her, their expressions puzzled.

"Stop," Maia says. "Danger. Stop."

The men swap a glance. The hairs on the back of her neck lift as the whispers pummel her in waves.

Danger. Danger. DANGER. Stop danger stop danger danger stop stop danger danger.

She drops her bo and covers her ears, turning in the street. The whispers intensify. Her eyesight becomes ultra-focused and her hands fall to her sides as a raven soars down the road, communicating to her without words the situation that lies ahead.

A mob of men is standing just around the steep curvature of the road—a blind spot. There are ten, no—thirteen of them. There are more lurking in the woods. Five. No—six. There are *ten* men hiding in the woods with weapons of every caliber in their hands. The men nod at one another and begin walking toward them. Maia peers through the thickly shrouded bush. A man ducks behind a tree, clicking Morse code on a device.

Three.

He's communicating that there are only three of them. Lucas turns toward her and grabs her arm. His lips are moving, but she can't hear him over the trees. He shakes her arm, then peers over her shoulder. His mouth drops open.

She looks behind her to see a single man walking down the center of the road from where they just came. He has a machine gun in his hand. She squints—it's empty. How does she know this? Another man steps out from the tree line to join him, and another from the other side.

They are surrounded. She, Lucas, and Miguel must've passed right by these men as they hid in the woods, watching them like a predator does their prey.

The trees all at once become silent.

"It's happening," Maia says.

"We need to run!" Lucas pulls at her arm.

"We can't. There are more around the corner," she says in defeat, swiping her bo from the road.

"What? How do you—"

"Just trust me."

She peers into the woods. There's only one man hiding alongside them. The forest is thickly packed, but there's an old factory a few acres back where they can hide.

No, these men will know that building well. They'll want them to run there so they can trap them inside. She glances to the other side of the road—nothing but trees. The mob from around the bend turns the corner.

"*Merda*," Miguel whispers.

"This way," Maia says, pointing toward the empty woods to their left.

"No use running!" the man with the machine gun yells. "Just drop your things, and we'll let you live."

"Run!" Maia screams.

They race into the trees.

"You won't get far!" the man yells from the road. He starts to laugh.

The forest is nearly impenetrable. Weaving their way through the crowded pines, the tangled branches catch and tear at their packs, snapping, snagging, and dragging across their skin. Panicked, Maia cries out. At this point, the mob will quickly catch up with them. With every step they take, they collide with something.

This is why the mob would have chosen this patch of land to ambush travelers. There is nowhere to go. The last time Maia felt this trapped, she jumped from the rails of a ship into an ocean of trash. But now, there is nowhere to hide. They continue pushing their way through, colliding into an endless gridlock of branches and trees, stumbling over thick layers of debris blanketing the forest floor.

She stops, leaning against a tree and gasping for breath. Her head falls against the bark. Its whispers soothe her like a soft melody, reminding her that she's surrounded by family. She lifts her head.

She's surrounded by *an army*.

She peers over her shoulder at the mob of men calmly weaving their way between the trees. They eyeball her from a distance with wicked smiles on their faces.

No, she will not run. She is not the same woman she was back on that ship. She turns to face them and slides her bag from her shoulders, dumping it to the ground beside her staff.

"Maia!" Lucas shouts from behind. He yanks at her arm.

She turns toward him. "Go, Lucas. *Run*."

He backs up, a look of recognition crossing his face as she morphs before him.

"It's okay," she says.

He nods, backing up until he slams into Miguel, now protesting and reaching for Maia.

Miguel's mouth drops open. "Maia, your *eyes*..."

Maia's eyes have always been closed when she starts their fires. Miguel shakes his head in amazement, and she smiles at him as Lucas pulls at his arm.

"You're *magnificent*," he says.

"Brother!" Lucas yells. "Focus!"

Miguel stumbles backward, tripping over his feet until finally turning away.

Maia turns toward the approaching mob. Her temper flaring, she glares at them with a clenched jaw, her hands trembling in fists at her sides. A dozen men snake their way through the trees until they surround her. One man motions for a few others to go around and continue after Lucas and Miguel. Two step to the right of her, another to the left.

Reaching her hands to the sky, she clutches the air and yanks down. *Hard*.

The mob stares at her, confused. A few of them chuckle until a loud crack blasts through the air as a mammoth tree behind her fractures across its base. The men gaze up as the ancient pine wavers for a moment, then groans as it plummets to the earth, crushing three screaming men against the forest floor. They are silenced as blood pours from their mouths.

The others back up, a look of horror on their faces. Maia turns on a heel and whips her hands across her body. Another tree bends to her command, slamming into two more men and crushing them to death. She turns to face the leader, a smile stretching across her face.

"Run!" he screams, backing up. "Abort the mission!" His voice screeches. "*Witch*! Turn *back*!"

The men race back through the tangled forest toward the road. Maia slowly stalks behind them, thrilled as the trees bend to clear a path. She starts to run. A tree shifts toward the ground and she races along the top. The sheer weight of the bent tree causes it to rupture down its center, and it breaks in half with a resounding *crack*, sending it crashing onto the road before the leader. He cowers into a ball as the wood shatters like a bomb.

Maia walks along the remnants of the tree and jumps onto the gravel before him. His mob of men now runs screaming down the road. He staggers to his feet and quivers before her, urine soaking his pants.

She laughs, *tsking* him. The breeze blows her red curls from her shoulders.

He points his shaking machine gun at her head. "Witch! I'll shoot you dead!"

"Oh, come on," she sneers. She pushes the barrel from her face with the tip of her finger. "You and I both know that gun isn't loaded."

He drops it to the ground. "Something is seriously wrong with you—you're a *monster*. We won't forget this. We'll find you."

"No, you won't," she replies dryly.

"Yes! Yes, we will. We will find you, and we will kill you. *All* of you," he says, shaking his finger at her.

She rolls her eyes. "No. You *won't*." She lifts her hand in the air and clicks her fingers.

The man cowers back. Nothing happens. He peers up at the trees from behind his hands. "*Ha*! It didn't work!"

"Just wait," she says, examining her nails.

Without making a sound, a large gray wolf jumps over the fallen tree, slamming into the man. Another wolf jumps over—and another, until a half dozen of them are tearing into the leader. Maia picks his machine gun off the gravel, scrutinizing it, then lets it hang by her side as she walks down the middle of the road, completely unfazed as the man screams in agony behind her.

Miguel and Lucas step out from the trees, their eyes wide and mouths agape.

Maia's demeanor breaks, and she drops the leader's gun. It clanks against the gravel as she slowly turns to the ghastly scene unfolding behind her. The man is now silent, and the wolves, one by one, head back into the woods. Their mouths are bloody and they keep their heads low, snapping and growling at one another.

One in particular continues eating. The *alpha*. He glares at Maia from his feast, and Maia glares back, refusing to break contact. *She* is the alpha now. His mouth pulls back into rumpled layers along his nose, revealing a row of blood-stained teeth. Then he drags the man's life-less body from the road.

THIRTY-ONE

Bits of gravel roll from Maia's feet as she stumbles along the empty road toward Miguel. Lucas is wandering behind him, erratically checking over his shoulder. He scans the forest for men lurking in the bushes.

"Oh my *God*," Miguel gasps.

"What *was* that, Maia?!" Lucas yells, running up to join them.

She stops to peer back at the trail of blood smeared across the road, then faces the men. They stand across from one another in the middle of the street. She tries to hold back a laugh but fails. She snorts, covering her mouth. A grin sneaks across Miguel's face, and he lifts his hands in the air, clapping slowly.

Lucas grabs her shoulders. "Maia! How did you—what..." He shakes his head. "Did you do that? Of course you did that. Did you *do* that? Smashing those trees?!"

"And you ran up that other tree!" Miguel says. "And

your hair! Your eyes—oh my God, your *eyes*! Have you ever seen anything—" He looks at Lucas with his hands on his head.

"Oh yes," Lucas says. "I've seen it."

"That was *unbelievable*!" Miguel yells.

She pulls her auburn hair off her face, twisting it into a bun. "I just felt ... I don't know, *angry*. And powerful. And suddenly, I just ... knew."

"Knew what?" Lucas asks.

She looks up at him with a devious grin. "That I could take them."

He smiles, shaking his head.

"Maia," Miguel says quietly. "You saved our lives back there."

"Oh! *Back there* ... my pack, my bo—I left everything by a tree," she gasps.

"I'll get them. Stay here." Lucas sprints down the road, leaving Maia and Miguel alone.

"Maia, that was..." He blows out a breath. "I will never forget that all the days of my life. I cannot believe this is real. You are just..." He stops himself.

"What?" She grabs his arm.

"You're exquisite."

Lucas approaches, and Maia and Miguel step away from each other. Lucas lifts her pack and she slings her arms through its straps, clicking the buckle around her waist. He hands Maia her staff, shaking his head.

"What?" She takes her bo.

He glances at Miguel. "I'm not sure you're going to need it."

The men grin at Maia, and she clutches the wood

with both hands. "After all that training, I'm *using* this," she says.

"So." Lucas nods down the road. "All clear?"

She huffs a laugh. "Oh yes, definitely clear."

They continue on. Maia pauses, stealing one last glance at the thick trail of blood smeared across the road.

Another dead body.

The alpha wolf steps back onto the gravel. They lock eyes, and Maia knows. He is her ally, but he is not her friend. She nods, and the wolf turns away, disappearing into the trees.

Maia sprints to catch up with Lucas and Miguel, who are now walking down the road with their arms draped over each other's shoulders.

"Simply incredible," the men say, and they head around the road's vacant bend.

Maia awakens in the middle of the night to the distant howling of wolves. She turns toward Lucas, his breathing slow. She looks at Miguel, sleeping soundly on his back. The outlines of their bodies flicker in the fire's soft light outside their tent.

She sits up. That fire was put out when they tucked in for the night—she watched Lucas do it. She exhales, her breath in clouds from the freezing night air, and crawls out from her sleeping bag and unzips the tent. The thin nylon fabric curls as she pulls on the tag, revealing a thick layer of snow outside.

This doesn't make any sense. She sinks her hand into the snow, but she doesn't feel a thing.

This is a dream.

She stands and steps into the snow. The ghostly image of herself glares at her from the middle of the fire, her red hair drifting around her face.

Maia's hands curl into fists at her sides. "Why won't you leave me *alone!*" she screeches.

The spirit says nothing.

She marches up to it, indignant. "*You.*" She lunges but slices through the apparition like air, plummeting into a mound of snow. She screams into the ground and stumbles to her feet. The image faces her, bright red flames lapping up her gown.

"What do you *want*?!" Maia screams. "I'm not running anymore! I accept *all* that I am!"

"*Do* you," the image says.

Maia flinches. The woman from her dreams has never spoken. Not once. Maia reaches out to touch it.

"You accept all that you are? The good and the bad?" the woman speaks again.

Maia pulls back her hand. "I do," she says quietly, her voice trembling.

"If you did, you would see that what you consider to be evil is not actually evil. It is your *thinking* that makes it so."

The sounds of the forest disappear. The crickets and the owls and the howling wolves fade into nothing until the only thing Maia can hear is the intense crackling of fire. She covers her ears, and the fire ignites at her feet.

"*Witch!*"

Maia turns to find the leader she just killed standing before her. His throat is torn open, the skin on his neck hanging loose to the side. Crimson blood pours down his shirt.

"Burn," he says. "Burn, witch. *BURN*."

Lucas steps out from behind him, and Maia gasps. Blood lines the corners of his mouth and he holds out his heart, torn from his chest. "You said you loved me," he says, his voice cold as ice. "But you are a liar. Burn, witch. *BURN*."

"NO! I'm not a liar! I *do* love you!"

"And me?" Miguel steps out from behind Lucas. He is also holding his dripping heart before him.

Struggling to breathe, Maia gasps as tears flow down her cheeks. "I ... I—"

"Maia."

She turns to face the spirit.

"It doesn't *look* like you accept all that you are," the reflection says, crossing her arms.

Maia turns toward Lucas and Miguel, who glare at her while displaying their wounds. "I don't..." she stammers.

The men begin to chant, "Burn, witch. *BURN*."

"No! *Stop*!" She covers her ears as they chant, and she turns to her reflection. "The love I have for these men is different! I can't make *sense* of it!"

"I can," the leader says, stepping forward. "There's something wrong with you. You are a *monster*."

The wolves slowly step from the woods and into the flickering light.

Maia looks down to find she has replaced her image. The fire at her feet is icy hot, burning up her legs, but she can't move. She screams with all her might as the men step forward, chanting, "Burn, witch. *BURN*."

The fire works its way up her gown, devouring her whole as the wolves overtake the men, surrounding her and baring their bloodstained teeth.

Maia awakens, gasping and drenched in sweat.

Lucas reaches for her, carefully guiding her back to her pillow. He wipes her brow. "Are you having nightmares again?"

She struggles to catch her breath.

"I thought they disappeared," he whispers.

"These ... these are..." She swallows hard. "These are *different*."

He sits up. "What do you mean?"

How is she supposed to answer that? Agitated, she snaps. "I don't know. I'm not ... I don't ... I need some air."

"Maia?" Miguel twists in his sleeping bag beside her. "You okay?"

"Just ... *give* me a minute." She unzips their tent and steps outside. Peeling her damp shirt from her belly, she flicks it in and out as she looks up at the blanket of stars glittering between the pines.

She doesn't know why she's being so snappy. She just feels ... *irritated*. Why? *Why* these silly dreams again? She thought she was done with this.

A twig snaps in the distance and she pivots. She's not alone. It's the same feeling she had when stepping onto the shores of LA. She glances between the trees. It's so dark. She can barely see her hand in front of her face.

She spots him, the outline of his body stalking

between the pines. He lifts his nose, gathering her scent, and through the black of night, his eyes meet hers.

After all this time, her tiger is still with her.

"Go home," she whispers as loud as she can. "*Please*! It's not safe for you here."

Another wolf unleashes a long and sullen howl across the wilderness. The tiger sprints away.

THIRTY-TWO

Maia tosses and turns in her nylon sleeping bag. The fabric rustling against itself is loud —annoying. She sighs and flips again.

So tired.

An intense, early morning sun has seeped inside their little tent, filling it with a heat and light Maia cannot escape. Did the sun even set last night? She groans in frustration, pulling her blankets high above her head. She flips again, curling into a ball beneath the covers.

How long has she been sleeping? It feels like five minutes. She rips the blankets away and looks around. Both the men's sleeping bags are empty. She shimmies out of her bed and crawls to the entrance of their tent, sliding the zipper open.

Wavering and groggy, she steps outside, yawning and stretching her hands above her head. She smiles as a chorus of birds and buzzing insects surrounds her. Wildflowers are everywhere. Spring has officially sprung.

Miguel is kneeling beside the firepit, trying to ignite a

fire but to no avail. He glances over his shoulder. "Hey, Maia, can you?"

She lifts her palm to the sky, and flames burst from the kindling.

"*Magnífico*," he mutters.

"Could you please make me some hot water?" she asks, rubbing her eyes.

"I've never seen anyone drink as much hot water as you," he says, shaking his head. He grabs a pot from their pile of cooking supplies next to the pit.

"It's the next best thing since there's no tea," she says bitterly. "Where's Lucas?"

"Checking the traps. Here's hoping we have food today." He leans back on his heels, looking up at her with narrowed eyes.

"What?" She yawns.

"You don't think ... could you—"

"I hope you're not asking what I think you're asking."

"What?"

"You want me to use my powers to kill an animal?"

He shrugs. "Why not?"

"Because those animals are also *me*."

"But you eat meat, yes? You hunt every day."

"Yes," she says, hesitating. "I *hunt* them, fair and square. Seems ... I don't know—*wrong* to trick them into coming to me just so I can kill them."

"We need to eat, Maia."

"Hey, we're not starving yet," she snaps. "This is a new concept for me. Just let me wrap my brain around that one, okay?"

He puts his hands in the air. "Okay, okay. Thought it couldn't hurt to ask. Guess I was wrong."

She crouches down beside him and lays her head on his shoulder. "I'm sorry. I don't mean to be crabby. I just ... how short have our evenings become? I'm so tired."

"*Short.*"

"How short?"

"I would say it's dark for maybe a few hours? We really need to figure out a new routine with sleeping. We must be bordering the Arctic and spring is well upon us, so our evening hours are about to get significantly shorter —and *fast*. I give us a few more weeks, and the sun won't set at all."

She lifts her head. "Really?!"

"You are way too excited about this, Maia. It can actually be challenging on the ... how do you say ... the *rhythms* of our body. It will be hard to know when to be asleep and when to be awake. It will be light outside all of the time. For *months*."

She can hear him, but she's no longer listening. "That is *so cool*," she says, her eyes glazing over as she watches steam gather along her little pot of water.

Lucas returns to the camp, holding up some small creature Maia's never seen before—like a giant brown rat with an elongated body. "Breakfast is served," he proudly exclaims. Then he studies the foreign animal, still needing to be prepped and stripped. He shrugs with a goofy smile. "Sort of."

After wandering for days on end along the forest road, Maia, Lucas, and Miguel approach another lookout. The three stand along the cliff, gazing across a world of mountains sprawling before them.

Maia steps forward, focusing on one in particular. "Is that?" She tents her brow, squinting against the sun.

Lucas steps beside her, a large grin on his face. "Snow."

Miguel joins them, and they stand in silence, gawking at the snow-dusted mountain in the distance. Maia turns to face the men, glancing between them with a smile.

Miguel smirks. "What are you up to, little bird?"

"Guys, *look* where we are. *Look* at that!" she says, pointing behind her. "We're in Canada!"

Lucas smiles. "We've been in Canada for quite some time."

"Yes, but look at this *backdrop*! Look where we are! We're *making* it!"

"*Shhh*," Miguel says, glancing behind them.

"Screw 'em," she says, dismissing him with a wave of her hand.

He laughs.

"Don't get too cocky," Lucas mumbles.

She turns to admire the small patch of snow on the mountaintop. "I'm just so *happy*. Have either of you ever seen snow before?"

Lucas shakes his head.

"Never," Miguel says. "You?"

"Only in my dreams," she replies quietly.

They continue down the path. The entire time, Maia is smiling. The trees have not ceased whispering, and a large pack of wolves is now following them from deep within the woods. She can't see them, but she knows they're there. They are not her friends, but they are her allies. They are there should she need them.

She also knows her tiger is out there somewhere, following her journey. He's alone, which makes her incredibly nervous. Why he keeps his distance, she can't figure out, but this comes as no surprise. None of the answers she's ever sought have come when asked.

They end their very long day camped out in a small field off the side of the road. Since it's probably pretty late, they decide to skip setting up a tent and sleep under the open skies instead.

Lucas is curled up in his sleeping bag beside the fire. He peers up at Maia, sitting cross-legged on top of hers. "You should get some sleep," he says, battling his heavy eyelids. "Won't be long before the sun is up."

"I will—don't you worry about me. I'm going to watch the sunset first," she says.

"You know it's probably close to midnight." Miguel slides into his bag on the other side of hers.

"So?" She shrugs.

He looks at her incredulously. "*So.*" He pokes her ribs. "*You* are the one who is crabby in the mornings. Always wanting your hot water like a *little princess*." He pulls his face into a grimace in mockery of her.

"What?!" She smacks his arm.

"You *are* pretty particular about your hot water," Lucas mumbles into his sleeping bag.

Miguel laughs.

"Oh my God," she says, and she shakes her head. "I'm surrounded by Brazilians."

"You should be so lucky," Lucas says.

She smiles. "Well, I'm not complaining."

He looks at her, brow lifted. She pretends not to notice. She sighs and rests her elbows on her knees, watching as the fiery orange sun slowly disappears behind the majestic rocky peaks.

Later that evening, Maia lies on her back gazing up at the stars. Despite being from the Southern Hemisphere, she's familiar with these northern constellations, having observed them every night in her dreams. At least when she's awake, she can look up at them in peace. Once she falls asleep, however, a terrifying world awaits, and she'll have to confront herself again. Every night it's the same.

The fire has worked its way down to embers. She hovers her hand above the pit and lifts the flames like stringed puppets. She places another log on the fire.

Miguel twists in his sleeping bag. Smiling groggily, he stretches his hands above his head. "Can't sleep?" he mumbles.

She rests her head in her hands. "No, I've got a few things on my mind." She watches Lucas as he sleeps, the fire casting shadows across his face.

"What's up?" Miguel props himself on his elbow.

She gazes at him and sighs. "It's nothing."

"Maia, you can talk to me."

She looks at her friend beside her, feeling torn. "I'm not sure I can," she responds quietly, and she shifts her gaze back to the fire.

He sits up. "Oh, come on, *buddy*. Late-night conversations are what we do best, no?"

Her eyes flicker to his, and he smiles, dimple showing.

She shakes her head, looking up at the sky. "I keep thinking about New Zealand ... my grandfather. It wasn't that long ago when I left, but I was such a different person then."

"How so?"

"Feels silly saying it now."

"Try me."

She sighs. "I thought I could change the world."

"And now?"

"I don't think..." She looks down at her hands. "I don't think I'm as great as I thought I was."

Miguel doesn't respond. When she looks at him, his eyes narrow. "What do you mean?" he asks.

She pokes at the fire with a stick, shifting a log. "My grandfather used to warn me that every person has the potential to do great things—earth-shattering things— both good and evil." She hesitates. "He told me a day may come when I may do things I'm not proud of ... terrible things. Of course, I never believed him. But now there's blood on my hands, and I fear there may be more. No—I *know* there will be more. When I'm the most powerful, there's a darkness that comes out of me, one that doesn't think twice about destruction or ending a life. It doesn't even *occur* to me to care." She drops her head in her hands. "I feel like I'm constantly battling two opposing sides of myself, and I'm *exhausted*."

She looks at Miguel through the blur of her tears. She turns away and wipes her eyes. "My grandfather warned me to never allow the world to harden me, but I'm finding it difficult ... *not* to."

Miguel sighs. "Well, you *are* Mother Nature, yes? They've always said Mother Nature could be cruel."

She peers up at him. "Do you think I'm cruel?"

He shakes his head. His eyes cut to Lucas and then back to her. "I think you are the most beautiful human I have ever met."

Her voice barely escapes a whisper. "But I'm not *human*."

He tilts his head. "You are to me."

She looks away, holding her breath against her tears.

"I'm sorry, Maia," he says. "I've been so distracted by my own demons, I had no idea you were suffering."

"Demons?" She inhales, grateful for the change of subject. "Like what?"

He stares at the fire. "Just ... thoughts that won't go away."

"Thoughts? *Like...*"

When he looks at her, an undeniable look of anguish crosses his face. No words are needed to know what he's thinking. "Like, thoughts I shouldn't be having," he says quietly.

They gaze at one another for a long while in the flickering firelight. There is nothing left to say. Despite all their talks and promises, the harsh reality of the matter continues to burn between them—with or without acknowledgment. It is not *nothing*.

"I'm going to bed," he says with a sigh.

She nods.

He turns away from her and curls up beneath his sleeping bag. She glances at Lucas, sleeping soundly. Is it possible to love two men at the same time? Was it not that long ago that she believed—no, she *knew*—that Lucas was the love of her life? Yet, she had never been with a man before. Was she wrong?

And what about her nightmares? So much shame she has carried her entire life, always fighting against who she is, dragging her guilt like a ball and chain. And now her dreams, which have never led her astray, are reminding her with such tenacity that what she considers to be evil isn't actually evil. It's her *beliefs* that are causing her grief.

So, which is which? And where has her mother been all this time? She used to be so diligent in Maia's dreams, always holding her hand to guide her. But now? *Nothing*.

On top of the uncertainty, Maia has a terrible, nagging feeling that she is walking a rapidly unraveling tightrope. A tightrope between two brothers. A tightrope between two worlds: that of a human and that of a significantly powerful being.

She is *so* tired. What is madness? Repeating the same behavior over and over and expecting different results.

Fighting against *what is*.

THIRTY-THREE

Drip. Splatter. Splat. Drip. Drip.

D A cruel and unremitting spring rain has shrouded the trails in a merciless gloom, leaving Maia, Miguel, and Lucas trapped inside their tiny tent for three days in a row. Time has dragged on in a monotonous blur, one moment fading into the next. The only change is when the sporadic drops of water colliding into their tent turn into a torrential downpour. Back, forth, and back again, the horrible weather switches as if a toddler were in control of a faucet in the sky.

So, they stay put. They catch up on their sleep. Play games. Tell stories. They've gotten into a few fights, made up, then fought again. And now, here they lie, side by side in silence. Everything spoken. Everything unspoken. Maia between two brothers.

She crawls to the end of her sleeping bag and unzips the doorway of their tent to peer outside. "Absolutely miserable," she mumbles and falls onto her back, sighing dramatically. "I really don't know how much more of this I can take."

Miguel sits up and glances between Lucas and Maia with a grin. "Well then, I have a surprise for you," he says.

Maia crosses her arms. "Please don't say corn."

Lucas props on his elbows. "What are you thinking?"

"It's not what I'm *thinking*. It's what I *have*. Maia?" Miguel looks at her, raising his eyebrows.

She stares at him. "What's *up*, Miguel?"

"Look in your bag. Inside zipper."

She sits up. "Why *my* bag?"

"You have the dry bag. I didn't want this getting wet. I have it tucked in an old plastic bag, but you can never be too careful."

"What do you have *tucked*?" She crawls to her pack and drags it toward her. She digs inside, ripping open all the zippers.

"No, not there," Miguel says, peering over her shoulder. "Not there either."

She reaches inside another pocket. "I'm a little disturbed by how well you know my pack," she mumbles.

"Don't worry, I know the rules. 'Never search inside a woman's bag.' I put it in there before we left New Portland. It was a gift from Hannah."

Maia rolls her eyes. "Ugh. *Hannah*."

Lucas sits up. "What is your *deal* with that woman?!"

Her cheeks flush. "No deal. I don't have a deal."

He eyes her. "Sure sounds like a deal—"

"*There*." Miguel points at a small zip on the inside of the pack. "Inside that pocket."

She quickly opens the pocket and pulls out a faded plastic bag, hoping whatever's inside will save her and

Lucas from another fight—there seem to be more of them these days. She sets it in her lap and peels it open, revealing a large joint inside.

"Oh, my *God*," she says, her eyes wide.

"Weed," Lucas says. "We've been stuck in here for days, and *now* you tell us?"

"I was saving it," Miguel says with a shrug.

Maia holds the fat joint before her. Without hesitating, she closes her eyes, focusing on the paper until smoke curls at the end. She smiles, handing it to Miguel.

"Ladies first," he says gently. The way he's looking at her ... If he didn't know she was jealous before, he definitely knows now.

Mortified, she averts her eyes. She sucks in a long, slow drag, then exhales a heavy stream of smoke. "Oh, it's been way too long." Coughing, she hands it to Miguel.

After a few rounds, they lie on their sleeping bags, giggling like children.

"*Shhh*, listen," Maia says, sitting up. "Do you hear that?"

"What, are the *trees* talking to you again?" Miguel asks. A rogue grin.

"Yeah, what are they saying *now*?" Lucas says.

"I should have never told you guys about that. Those trees *saved* you!" She punches the laughing men on either side of her. "And they'll probably save you again." She cups her hand around her mouth. "Don't listen to them!" she yells.

"*Shhh*!" Miguel clasps his hand over her mouth, tackling her. His nose touching hers, he quickly backs away. "The mobs will hear you."

"*Eh*, I'm not afraid," she says, crossing her legs. She looks up at the fallen leaves on the outside of their tent.

"You seriously better stop testing the gods," Lucas snaps.

"There are no gods," she says, rolling her eyes. "It's just us. We're *allll* alone."

Lucas sits up and unzips the tent doorway. "Seriously though." He looks up at the sky. "I know we're a little stoned, but the weather has cleared. Our stuff is soaked, but I think we should get a move on."

"I'm all for it," Maia says, rolling onto her elbow. "I'm sick of this tent and these stinky boys. Get me out of here."

Miguel sniffs under his arms. "I think I smell pretty good."

She shakes her head with a smile.

They quickly pack up camp, wet gear and all, desperate to take advantage of the clear weather.

Walking down the middle of the road, they've barely begun their journey when they approach a large semi-truck tipped on its side, blockading the street.

They slow their pace.

"Looks like a trap," Miguel says quietly.

"Agreed," Lucas says.

"If there *were* people down here, wouldn't you think they'd have found us by now?" Maia asks. "We were only a kilometer down the road."

"Not necessarily," Miguel says. "Some of these mobs are pretty lazy. They often just sit and wait for people to pass."

Right on cue, a man with a large black pirate hat crawls on top of the semi. He stands tall with his hands on his hips. One eye is missing. Gouged out, it's become a skinned-over hole in his skull.

"Halt!" he yells with his hand out.

"You're missing your patch, mate," Miguel mutters under his breath.

Maia slaps her hand over her mouth, suppressing a laugh.

"If you want to pass, a tax must be paid!" the man says. "Leave your packs, and we'll let you through."

"You're dreaming!" Maia says.

"Am I now? You have no *idea* who you're dealing with," the man counters.

"Go on, then!" Maia shouts, flipping open her palm, and Miguel hands her the joint. "Tell us who we're dealing with!"

"We're the Pirates of British Columbia."

"Don't you need to be on the water to be pirates?" Lucas deadpans.

Miguel snorts, and Maia laughs in her hand.

"Fine, laugh." The man picks up a machine gun from the top of the semi, lifting it high on display.

Maia squints.

"Is it loaded?" Lucas whispers.

"I'm … not sure. I can't—I can't focus."

"Shit. We're screwed," Miguel says. "She's stoned."

Maia bursts into laughter, and Miguel joins her, doubling over in hysterics.

"How is this *funny*?!" Lucas whispers.

"Okay, come on out!" the man on the truck yells.

Four men walk out from the left of the large truck, while another six step from the right. The smiles drop from Maia's and Miguel's faces, and they clear their throats. One of the men elbows another, whispering something about there being a woman.

"Bloody hell," Maia says.

Lucas looks at her, panicked. "What do we do?"

She surveys the mammoth pine trees lining the road.

"Hold on," she whispers, nodding at the trees. Lucas and Miguel look at her, confused. "Guys!" she snaps. "*Go.* Hold on," she whispers again.

Lucas grabs her pack, and she hands him her staff. Both the men back up and rush to the side of the road. Miguel crouches beside a tree, and Lucas does the same. They wrap their arms around the trunks.

"What in the *hell*? Those trees ain't gonna save you!" the leader yells from the semi. "We've got some tree huggers, guys!"

His mob of men point and laugh, whispering among themselves.

"Ha! *HAHAHAAA!*" Maia laughs skyward.

The men gawk at her. Some of them start to chuckle again, pointing at the crazy redhead in the middle of the road.

"Well, this should be easy. She's completely lost it," the leader says.

Maia flashes him a coy smile, placing the joint between her lips. She relights the end and inhales. As the smoke streams from her mouth, the winds pick up. She nods at Miguel and Lucas, and they clutch the tree's mossy trunks.

She slowly lifts her hand to the sky, and the barreling winds howl through the trees, knocking the groaning pines together. The men standing in the street brace themselves against the sudden blast of air.

She lifts her hand higher and the gusts build in intensity. She winds back her arm and slams it forward, sending a gale-force blast of air down the street, knocking the men off their feet. They tumble down the road and slam into the truck. Holding their heads, they moan, struggling through the wind to climb back to their feet.

Maia places the joint between her lips and holds her hands before her, walking toward them down the center of the street. The blast of air pushes the semitruck back, back, back, the pirate on top screaming as the metal sparks against the pavement.

Delighted, Maia begins to skip. She whirls around and smashes her hands into the air, slamming a barrage of wind into the semi. The truck flips upside down on top of the pirate, killing him instantly. The other men climb to their feet, screaming and scattering into the trees.

Smiling, Maia pulls the joint from her lips and holds it above her head. She releases her grip. It flies through the air and tumbles down the road, landing on the truck's fuel tank. A minuscule amount of petrol is still inside the large, cracked reservoir. She doesn't need much. She squints, focusing on the joint against the tank. Her heart is pounding as she uses the last of her strength to build heat around the joint. A small flame ignites.

She ducks, and the semitruck explodes, sending a mushroom of smoke into the sky. The men run for the hills while others, engulfed in flames, scream in terror and race between the trees. Maia stumbles back, exhausted and lightheaded, a bounty of red curls hanging across her face.

Lucas races across the road, catching her as she buckles. "You okay?" he whispers.

"Fine." She smiles, her head wobbling.

Miguel grabs her pack and staff and joins them in the middle of the road. "Shall we?" He looks at them with a goofy grin.

"Let's," Lucas says.

They cut around the blazing truck with a large pool of blood seeping from beneath.

"That's some pretty good weed, Brother," Lucas says, repositioning his hold on Maia as she leans against him.

"Waste of our joint, if you ask me," she mumbles.

They chuckle, continuing down the winding road with the rugged Canadian mountains towering high above them.

THIRTY-FOUR

"What is *up* with you lately?!" Lucas clutches Maia's shoulders.

She rolls her eyes and breaks free from his grasp. "Go away, Lucas."

He stares at her in shock, and she glares back at him.

They are unraveling.

There's no denying Lucas has become more distant lately, but then again, so has Maia. She can't even remember what they are arguing about anymore; she only knows they've been fighting a lot. Like ... *a lot*. This journey has been long. And hard. And tedious. Day after day, it's just them against the elements. Bounders and mobs. Thirst and hunger. An almost unending Arctic sun burning deep into the sky. Their boots are wearing thin. Their tempers are wearing thin—or is it just Maia's?

The days are so long, the evenings so brief, and now no darker than twilight. They're sleep-deprived and exhausted. The little sleep Maia does manage to get is consumed by her nightmares, beckoning her to confront the one thing she fears the most.

Herself.

"I don't know why you are so snappy lately, but you are driving me *crazy*!" Lucas growls through gritted teeth. He storms away, mumbling in Portuguese.

They are down by a crystal-blue river, somewhere deep within the old Yukon Territory. Surely, they must be getting close to Alaska, but it's hard to tell. The map Lucas carries is for major highways, not the unmarked backroads they've been taking.

It's a cloudy day but warm. Miguel is once again staying out of Maia and Lucas's fight, fishing by himself along the river. His pole is propped between the rocks, the line cast out and dragging along the currents. Two large fish are lying by his side, dinner for tonight—or today. It's hard to tell anymore.

Lucas storms off for the tree line.

"Lucas!" Miguel stands. "We don't split up!"

Lucas continues on without hesitating, marching into the dense forest. Miguel glances at Maia, and she drops to the ground with her head in her hands. She glares at the shoreline, resentful. Her world is unraveling. The more powerful she becomes, the more powerless she feels.

Small stones shift behind her as Miguel approaches, and he plops beside her with a sigh. Holding her head, she peers up at him.

"You okay?" he asks.

"What do you think?" she mumbles.

There's a long silence.

"Is there anything I can do?" he asks.

She huffs, gazing across the river as a small bird pecks

between the rocks. "This is probably all my fault. *Again*. I don't know why I'm being so ... snappy, but I don't blame Lucas for losing his temper." Her eyes brim with tears.

"Maia." Miguel studies her face. "Don't do that. Lucas is no saint. He is equally to blame for all your fighting—if not more so."

"Why do you say that?"

"Just ... *observations*," he says. "I think you are too hard on yourself. You're going through a lot of changes."

She looks up at him, a tear escaping. "What if I don't like these changes?" She swipes her cheek and looks away. "I can see it. Every day, I can see it."

"Can you not control it? You have free will, yes?"

"That's what they say. But this feels ... *beyond* me."

"Well, if it makes any difference, I still think you are magnificent," he says quietly beside her.

She gazes up at him, and the breeze tousles her streaked red and auburn hair over her eyes. Miguel wraps a red tendril between his fingertips and pulls it down. He releases it, and they watch as it slowly curls back up again. He tucks the piece behind her ear, then runs his fingers through her hair and pulls it off her shoulders, exposing her eyes. He cups her face, his thumb caressing her cheek. "That's better."

She loses herself in his eyes. If love is such a good thing, then why does it cause such pain? Because it is like her, a world of good wrapped in a world of bad.

Maia is in love with Miguel. She has been for a while, although this is the first time she's been brave enough to admit it to herself. Acknowledging her feelings should be such a beautiful thing, but instead, it only brings her pain. She and Miguel can never be—she is with Lucas.

The fact that she has fallen for Lucas's brother only solidifies the fact that she is a monster.

A smile tugs at Miguel's lips and he leans in, his forehead meeting hers. He closes his eyes.

"Miguel," she whispers. She should pull away, but she can't. Being close to him feels like the most natural thing in the world. He opens his pleading eyes and she stares at him, slowly shaking her head. "Please..." she breathes. "*Don't.*"

His hand slides down her neck to her shoulder, then drops to the stones. He leans away, running a hand down his face. "I'm sorry, Maia. *Terrible.*" He shakes his head. "I don't know what came over me."

Unraveling. Unraveling. Maia's world is unraveling. But life around her continues on. The two sit along the shore in silence as the creek babbles over boulders and the birds sing their songs, completely unfazed that Maia's world is crumbling around her.

Maia awakens after another nightmare. The same reflection. The same burning fire. The same snow that she cannot feel.

The woods rustle outside their tent, followed by growling. The pack of wolves has returned. Maia listens with wide eyes as the men sleep soundly beside her. There's more growling—the wolves are threatened by something. A feline hiss.

Her tiger.

She crawls out of her sleeping bag and unzips the door, quietly sliding outside. The wolves continue to growl, countered by an immediate feline roar. Chills run up Maia's spine. The menacing sounds are enough to make anyone freeze in their tracks, but she pushes forward. Straining her eyes against the gloom, she searches between the trees for movement. She can't see anything, but she can hear it.

Following the sounds through the early morning twilight, Maia discovers the large pack of wolves a few minutes' walk from the tent. They've surrounded the single tiger. The sound of his growling is nothing short of terrifying. His large size dwarfs theirs, but he's far outnumbered. He keeps his head to the ground with his ears pinned back, and he bares his teeth, his tail flickering.

Her heart is pounding as she cautiously approaches the angry horde. The wolves turn toward her and back up with their heads to the ground, baring their teeth. The trees' whispers grow louder.

Monster. Monster. MONSTER.

A wolf lunges at Maia but doesn't follow through. She glares at him, clenching her fists. "NO!" She snaps her fingers. "Get back!"

The wolf obligingly backs away. The skin along his snout is rumpled, revealing a row of teeth so white they glow against the darkness.

Maia approaches the majestic tiger. He keeps his head to the ground, gazing up at her like a cub would their mother. She crouches down and holds out her trembling hand, allowing him to gather her scent.

"It's okay," she whispers.

He steps toward her, his cold nose meeting her finger. She reaches for him, gasping as he finally allows her to run her hand through his thick fur. The large pack of wolves pace in a circle around them, growling and nipping at the air.

The tiger has a small wound on his shoulder, most likely from a wolf. Her fingers graze against it, and he growls. These wolves would never stand for this tiger in their territory. It will only be a matter of time before they chase him out or end him.

"You can't be here," she whispers, inching closer to him.

His wet nose grazes hers.

"This is too dangerous," she whispers. "I can't protect you. You *have* to go home."

The enormous cat burrows his head into her shoulder, knocking her onto her hands. The wolves' growling intensifies.

"No," she says to the tiger, her heart aching. He'll die out here if he keeps this up. She stands and says as sternly as she can, "You *must* leave. Now. And don't come back."

She snaps her fingers and points away. The large cat gazes up at her, then around at the menacing pack of wolves. The trees continue to whisper.

Monster. Monster. Monster.

The tiger backs away, and the circle of wolves create an opening, nipping at the air around him. The tiger runs off between the trees, leaving Maia surrounded by wolves.

She closes her eyes and tilts back her head, and another layer of ice hardens around her heart. "Am I a monster?" she whispers to the trees. She listens.

Mother.

They were never whispering *monster*; they were whispering *Mother*.

Mother. Mother. Mother.

She falls to her knees. She can't go back inside that tent, back inside that tiny nylon hell where her unraveling life awaits. Maybe it would be best if she were alone.

When she opens her eyes, the wolves have disappeared. She turns her gaze skyward and gasps, her eyes wide and unbelieving.

The sky is blanketed in undulating waves of green.

The northern lights.

She falls onto her back with tears streaming down her face. And this is where she stays, lying in awe with her mouth agape as bright green ribbons roll across the sky and the whispers of the trees wash over her.

Mother.

Mother.

Mother.

THIRTY-FIVE

Maia and the men decide to pack up camp as early as possible and head to the river to have another meal. Miguel has found a good spot for fishing, and they need to take advantage before hitting the road again.

The three walk in silence along the deserted road toward the creek, dragging all their hurts and worries and frustrations like shackled weights behind them. How did they get here? How is it that, in this dangerous and deserted land, the one thing hurting them most is each other? Or is this all Maia's fault? She glances at the men on either side of her. They both appear frustrated, concentrating. Unhappy.

Definitely Maia's fault.

She plops down beside the creek as the men take turns fishing and hunting. She should help, but she needs to pull herself together.

Okay. This isn't a horrible situation—it's not. She's just going through a lot of changes; her mother warned her that she would. Her mother also cautioned Maia to guard against her temper, that it will strengthen as her powers grow.

So, that's what she'll do. She'll continue to work with the light within. She doesn't have to cave into the darkness. She has free will. The first thing she'll do is cut herself off from Miguel. Harden her heart. It's for the best. Friends—they are good friends. She'll no longer allow herself to think differently.

And Lucas? Once they settle in Leucothea, things will be better. They'll have more time together alone. She glances at him walking along the shore. Memories of him on their island in the Great Pacific Garbage Patch come back to her. The two of them laughing under stormy skies branched with lightning, collecting water in the rain. Their first kiss under the tarp. Building a raft out of the world's refuse. Talking beneath the stars. So many memories they hold.

Her eyes cut to Miguel, now watching her from the corner of his eye. She sighs and looks away. She really wishes she could talk to someone right now—her grandfather, her mum. Anyone to help her make sense of all this.

No. She doesn't need to make sense of *anything*. What she needs to do is harden up. She inhales and stretches her hands above her head, and a few birds fly across the sky.

Okay, this is okay. She rolls her neck. She can work with this. She is powerful—this is good. She has saved their lives now on repeated occasions—also good. She and Lucas have hit a rough patch, but this trip is really hard. Trying. This is fine. They'll pull through this.

Miguel is her friend and she'll be strong enough for the both of them. The next time they're alone, she'll tell him that she loves him as a friend, and that he *must stop* what he is doing. Always gazing down at her with those gorgeous brown eyes and telling her how *magnífico* she is.

A new anger burns within.

Miguel.

She glares at him as he watches her over his shoulder. *Why* is he making everything so complicated?! This is actually all *his* fault. Here she is, blaming all this tension on herself when it's him. She takes a steadying breath, then peers back at the creek. This is fine. They'll be fine. Everything is fine.

Lucas wanders over to her. "Miguel forgot my knife at camp. I have to go back and get it. Actually, I *swear* Miguel said he got it, but I'm not going to argue with him. It's not far, so you guys just stay here. I'll be right back."

She stares at the creek and nods.

"Hey." He sweeps her hair off her shoulders, and she looks up at him. "My God." He steps back. "Just when I think you can't get any more beautiful." He shakes his head, smiling.

It's so good to see him smile. He never smiles anymore.

He crouches down beside her. "I'm sorry things have been so tough lately. I know you have a heavy burden on your shoulders, and we are all sleep-deprived and exhausted. I don't mean to fight with you."

She turns toward him. "I'm sorry too, Lucas. I'm *so* sorry. What I've been going through is no excuse for the way I have been acting. I'm trying to fix it."

"You don't need to fix anything. You are perfect

exactly as you are." He kisses her tenderly and stands. "I'll be back soon. I swear Miguel said … never mind."

"Hey." She grabs his hand. "I love you."

"I love *you*, Maia. With all my heart. You know that, don't you?"

"I do."

She watches him walk to the tree line and disappear into the forest, and then she glares at Miguel, securing his fishing rod between the rocks. Okay, this ends *now*.

She stands and marches toward him, taken aback when he seems to be walking toward her with just as much fury.

"We need to talk!" she yells as they approach one another.

"Yes, we do! I can't do this anymore!" He looks as angry as she feels.

She slows. "What? What are you—"

"I can't … I can't keep *watching* you with my brother and pretending—" He hesitates, and the anger on his face melts into sorrow. "And pretending that I'm not in love with you."

"*Love*…" She lets the word slip from her lips. "You mean, like a friend, right?"

He steps closer, his face inches from hers. "What do *you* think?"

Rage boils within. "YOU!" She pushes his chest, but he is like stone. She pounds on him, but he is solid, motionless. "This is all *your* fault!" she screams in his face, a red-hot fury seeping into her cheeks. "You're supposed to be my friend! And now you are ruining *everything*!"

He doesn't move, his eyes glassy. Finally, he breaks.

He turns away with his hands at his head, then he rounds on her. "You think I wanted *any* of this?!" he screams. "I finally get my brother back in my life, the *one thing* I've wanted since I was a boy, and then *you* happen!"

"Right." She nods, crossing her arms. "Right, so this is *my* fault."

He holds her face. "Choose." His voice breaks at the word.

She shoves him. "*What*?!"

"Me or him."

"You *must* be joking. You know I'm in love with Lucas. You *know* this!" she yells, cursing the tears streaming down her face.

"No," Miguel says, his voice now sullen. "You are confused. You *love* Lucas. But you are not *in love* with him."

"How *dare* you!"

"And you know what?" he says. "I'm sorry, but he's not in love with you either. You've been through a lot together, and you care deeply for each other—no one is denying that. But you're not in love. He knows it. I know it. *You* are the only one who doesn't seem to know the difference."

"*Stop* it! What are you doing? How *dare* you judge me!"

"I'm not judging you, Maia. I love you. I'm in love with you. And I know you're in love with me too."

She drops her hands to her sides as she sobs. "What do you mean, 'he knows it'? What does he know?"

Miguel sighs. "Maia, Lucas is a selfish prick. We both are. The only difference is that I'm honest enough to admit it. He sees that you're in love with me, but he's not going to say anything. How could he? And risk losing you? He'd be crazy to do such a thing. But he sees it. I promise you, he sees it."

She drops her head in her hands. This isn't happening. This *can't* be happening. What did Miguel just say? He loves her. Lucas doesn't? She doesn't. But she *does*. This isn't happening.

Miguel's breath is sawing out of him as he stands before her, vulnerable. Waiting. "I know you love me," he says quietly, his eyes pleading. "I *know* you feel this too."

Finally, she decides to say it, and another layer wraps around her heart. It has to be said. This *has* to end—no good can come from this.

"You are mistaken." She lifts her chin. "I don't love you."

His mouth drops open.

She shakes her head and says it again, her voice trembling, "I'm not in love with you, Miguel."

He glares at her with tears in his eyes. "I don't believe you." He grabs her face and kisses her.

Despite herself, she kisses him back. She throws her arms around him, her heart *aching*, and he lifts her from the stones. They were always meant to find each other, she and Miguel. She can't begin to understand why, but she knew it from the moment they met. The moment he stepped around the corner at his cabin, something inside her knew. She's hated herself for it, but she's yearned for him. Every day. Longed for this moment. Right now. This single flashing instant where their worlds have collided together and fallen apart—

A knife clanks against the stones.

"*Maia*?"

Miguel and Maia separate to find Lucas standing before them.

That look on his face. Lucas has looked at Maia in a million different ways in a million different places. From the basement of a pirate ship to a disintegrating raft in the middle of the ocean. The flood zones of LA. Slow dancing in a tent beneath the Christmas lights.

Never. Never has he looked at her like this.

His horrified demeanor breaks into anger, and he screams, charging after Miguel. He slams into him and they roll against the stones. Lucas climbs on top of Miguel and swings hard, pummeling his fist into his mouth.

Maia screams with her hands at her head. "Stop! *Please!*"

Lucas rolls away and climbs to his feet. "*Bastardo!*"

Miguel stands, panting. He glares at Lucas but says nothing.

"Lucas, please—" Maia starts.

"*You.*" He throws his finger in her face. "I will *never* forgive you!" He shoulders past her, then stops and turns around. "No, I'm not leaving. This is *your* fault!" He points at Miguel. "*You* leave!"

Miguel stands before Maia, wiping the blood from his lip and swallowing hard. His eyes plead for an answer.

She can only stare at him, too terrified to speak. There are no words that will fix this. No matter what she says, she will lose everything.

He nods, looking at his feet. "Fine," he says quietly. "You've made your choice." He walks toward their packs along the trees.

"Miguel?!" she cries out. "What are you doing?"

He picks up his pack and turns toward them. The heart-wrenching look on his face steals the breath from her lungs. "Exactly what Lucas did to me all those years ago." His cold eyes cut to Lucas. "*Leaving*." He walks into the forest.

"Miguel!" Maia screeches. "Please don't do this!"

He disappears from sight.

She turns to Lucas, clutching for his hand. He swipes it away.

"How long?" he says, his voice clipped.

"What? No! This is the first time. He just kissed me now—nothing has happened!"

"*Nothing*? Nothing has happened?! I just came back to the river to find my brother kissing my girlfriend! And that wasn't just a kiss—you were kissing him *back*! You were kissing him ... like the way you kiss ... you were..." He glares at her, tears falling down his cheeks. "That was not *nothing*."

She can't catch her breath. Her world is spinning, falling apart. This isn't happening. This is just a dream. This isn't happening.

"You know what?" Lucas says. "I was wrong about you. You *are* a monster." He walks away and grabs his pack, leaving her bag alone beside the trees.

"Lucas, please ... don't—"

He disappears into the forest.

She tips her head back, unleashing an agonizing wail as the relentless Arctic sun burns deep into the sky.

THIRTY-SIX

"*Y*ou *are my sunshine...*"

Maia lies on the pebbled shore singing softly to herself, waiting for Miguel and Lucas to come back. Surely, they're coming back. Those men are her world. They can't *not* come back.

"*...my only sunshine.*"

Never separate was the rule. Under no conditions do they separate.

Birds flutter against the bright blue sky, and a furry bumblebee buzzes around Maia's head.

"*You'll never know, dear...*"

It lands on her nose before flying off again.

"*... how much I love you.*"

Is she dreaming? Somebody wake her from this nightmare.

"*Please don't take ... my sunshine ... away.*"

Another tear tumbles down her cheek. There's rustling in the woods. She sits up. The trees continue to whisper *Mother*. Or is it *monster*?

I was wrong about you. You are *a monster.*

So tired, but she cannot find refuge in sleep. Is it daytime? Or is it night? There's no way of telling anymore. The days have become one. Long. Unending. Nightmare.

More movement in the woods. Maybe it's her tiger? She crawls across the pebbles, hands slapping over one another through the grassy weeds and flittering bugs. More rustling. Is it her tiger? *Please* let it be him.

She stands and shields her eyes, peering into the woods. A gray wolf steps out—the old alpha—and her heart sinks. His pale yellow eyes gaze at her, and he tilts his head.

"Go *away!*" She grabs a stone and chucks it at his feet. He flinches. She picks up another stone, and another, hurling them at the wolf until he backs up and disappears into the forest.

She stands alone along the shore, breathing hard, and her temper surges. She grabs a handful of stones, clenching them in her fists, and screams. Hundreds of birds burst from the trees, and the ground quakes, clinking the shoreline's pebbles together. She gasps, long and desperate, and falls to her knees with one final jolt from the earth.

The birds are a distant cloud on the horizon.

She opens her fists to small clumps of grit cutting into her palms. She flips them over, the red sand falling to the earth, and she knows.

Lucas and Miguel aren't coming back.

Maybe it's for the best. Lucas called her a monster, a fate she once considered worse than death. And yet, her heart still beats. He promised he would never run, but he left. Not that she didn't deserve it. Maia told Miguel she didn't love him—a bald-faced lie. She *purposely* tried to hurt him, desperately clawing for control over their rapidly deteriorating situation.

And now, she is alone. The ache inside her heart is nothing short of excruciating.

She climbs to her feet and grabs her bag and staff, then wanders down the road with her pack of wolves trailing in the woods behind her. Maybe Miguel and Lucas are back at their old camp, waiting for her. Maybe they can fix this. Maybe Lucas didn't mean what he said. Maybe she can tell Miguel *she* didn't mean what she said.

Maybe she could wake up from this nightmare.

Lucas's bracelet has been discarded across the road. Sniffling, she picks it up and uses her other hand and teeth to tie it to her wrist. Lucas will want this back when he calms down.

When she arrives back at their old camp, the morning fire is still smoldering. The fish Miguel caught are strewn along the dirt. They had come back here—or at least Miguel had.

For the first time in a long time, the trees are completely silent. She sits on the same stump she sat on this morning. It seems like only moments ago they were all here together. The men were packing in silence while Maia sipped her hot water, pretending it was tea. Pretending she didn't notice the side glances from Miguel. Pretending that she and Lucas were fine. Pretending she wasn't succumbing to her temper, just like her mother had warned her against.

She glares at the spot where their tent once stood. The woods where she told her tiger to *go away*, surrounded by a pack of wolves. So much has happened here. So many terrible memories.

Keep moving—this has been their motto from the beginning. Maybe she'll find the men up the road somewhere. She lifts her pack from the ground and throws it across her back, stumbling from the weight. Then she picks up her staff and continues on her way.

She wanders down the empty, winding road in a daze. No map. No compass. No men. The sun isn't going to set for God-only-knows-how-long. It will just hover along the horizon ... up and down, up and down. Like torture, the worst day of her life will never end.

This is for the best. Maybe she *should* be alone. Now she can't hurt anyone but herself. She scans the road for any signs of Miguel or Lucas. Have they wandered this way already? Are they still headed north? Is *she* still headed north?

The wolves have stepped onto the road and now follow in a line behind her. There are at least a dozen of them. They aren't kind, but neither is she.

A skinny old man steps onto the street, holding a large machete. Maia rolls her eyes. She's not in the mood.

"Okay, missy. Just stop there."

She keeps walking.

He smiles, amused. "Not one for rules, are you?"

She keeps walking.

The smile fades from his face as he peers behind her. "Are *those*?"

"Wolves," she says dryly.

The wolves growl and reveal their teeth.

"Now, now. Just leave this one be," Maia mutters as they walk past the man, holding out his trembling knife.

Maia and her pack continue down the road. She glances over her shoulder. A few men have joined the old man. They now slowly stalk behind her. She lifts her arm above her head and points her finger to the sky. With a single flick of her wrist, she motions it down. A loud crack booms through the air, and a massive tree crashes across the road, dividing the men from Maia and her wolves. The men run screaming into the woods, and she laughs for the first time in days.

Okay then, let's have some fun.

She flicks her finger as she walks, and the trees fall one after another behind her, exploding across the road. The wolves frighten and run away, their howls echoing across the wilderness. Their calls sound mournful—drawn-out cries into the unremitting summer sky. It's fitting, really. Their wails of agony are like the anthem of grief inside Maia's heart. She flicks her finger, felling another tree. The gentle giant collides with the cement, sending bark and wood tumbling across the road.

The entire path behind her becomes a mess of broken trees, their insides hollowed out like guts, left to die useless deaths. She doesn't understand why she's doing this, but she doesn't try. Maybe the pain she's creating will drown out the ache she feels inside. Her heart has fractured to pieces like the fallen trees behind her, scattered across this long winding road to the Old Arctic Circle.

This is what happens when you follow your heart.

Let this be a warning to you.

325

THIRTY-SEVEN

A high-pitched whine beseeches Maia from the other side of her closed lids. She grumbles, swatting the air. A sniffing nose grazes her hair, now draped like a curtain over her face. She lifts her head and opens her eyes.

She's propped against a tree. Grimacing, she rubs her neck, and the whimpering wolf wanders away. It spins in a circle before plopping down in the dirt.

Rubbing her eyes, it takes her a minute to recall how she got here. After leaving their camp and causing a world of destruction, Maia trudged along the winding road for hours until she couldn't take another step. Then she stumbled off the road and fell against a pine. She didn't bother with her sleeping bag or even taking off her pack. She just slid down the side of a massive tree and closed her eyes.

How long has she been passed out? There's no way of knowing. It could have been hours or it could have been days—although she highly doubts that. Losing the basic signs of night and day can make a person go mad. She pushes the thought from her mind.

Glancing around at the large pack of wolves around her, she smiles. They're actually quite magnificent creatures. A few are curled up to each other, another is licking its paw. One buries its nose into a pile of leaves, hot on a scent. None seem to care much about her.

She leans forward, stretching out her cramped legs from beneath her. The old alpha lifts his head from the ground, watching her.

"I'm not naming you," she says aloud.

He cocks his head.

"Learned that lesson the hard way," she mumbles, distracted by her nails. She must've started biting them again yesterday in her daze.

She leans her head against the tree, watching the leaves flicker in the lazy summer breeze. She's so *exhausted*. It feels as if she's been through a war, and all things considered, she has.

She holds her head in her hands as the events of the previous day come flooding back to her. Miguel stood before her with tears in his eyes and proclaimed his love for her. He had such conviction in his belief that she and Lucas loved each other, but they weren't *in love*. Her aching heart wrenches. There's truth to what he said—although it isn't the full reality of the situation.

No matter how strongly she feels for Miguel, she knows the love between her and Lucas extends far beyond friendship. She didn't realize how different her love was for Lucas until she met Miguel, but she still loves him. Lucas is no doubt a part of her, the fabric of his heart woven deeply with hers. He has saved her, over and over again. And she's saved him. He held her head while she died and came back to life. The things they've lived through, the memories they hold. Living without Lucas feels as wrong as loving Miguel feels right.

From the moment Maia realized her feelings for Miguel, she knew they could never be, which is why she denied them for so long. To act on her love for him would be the ultimate betrayal against Lucas, and she would lose him forever. Yes, she allowed Miguel to kiss her. And yes, she kissed him back—she couldn't *not* kiss him back. But she fought against it every step of the way.

She lifts her chin. She doesn't know if she could have done something differently, but she does know she did everything she could to keep the peace. She never wanted anyone to get hurt. Whatever that is, it certainly isn't the behavior of a malicious person. Lucas called her a monster, but he was wrong. She is not a monster.

For the first time in a long time, Maia feels a brief respite of peace. Now, this journey will be only her, alone in the world. This will be better. She won't have Lucas's disapproving glances or Miguel's heartbreaking pleas to love him. She no longer has to carry the bone-aching shame while balancing a tightrope between brothers.

Another layer of ice thickens around her heart. Grandpa had warned her. He told her to never allow this life to harden her, but it's so much easier this way. She has found freedom in her brokenness.

The old alpha wanders up with a dead squirrel in his mouth, and he drops it at her feet.

"Thanks, bud," she says, and she gathers the lifeless creature in her hands.

With everyone splitting up so quickly, she's lost most

of her supplies. She's starving, but she's pretty sure Lucas has the bow. She no longer has a tent or any kitchen supplies. No pan, which means no more hot water. Because, of course. She smiles, thinking of Miguel when he would mock her about her precious hot water.

Ache. Ache. Ache. She shakes him from her mind.

Thankfully, she still has her large utility knife, which will work just fine for most of her needs. She'll just have to pray that whatever water sources she comes across from now on will be clean enough to drink without boiling.

She gathers some kindling and makes a fire. After prepping and cooking the meat, she scarfs it down while the wolves drool around her. Then she unravels her sleeping bag and lays her pack to one side—a makeshift fill-in for Lucas. She drags a large log across the dirt to the other side: Miguel. Now when she goes to sleep, both men will be there, still lying beside her. And for a little while, at least, she can pretend that she hasn't lost everything.

She takes one last look around at her pathetic little camp. Just a single sleeping bag and a pack of clothes off the side of the road in the middle of nowhere. The wolves never stick around for long, so it will only be a matter of time before she's alone again, most likely while she's asleep.

She doesn't care. Zipping the bag around her head, she closes out as much of the light as possible.

And she sleeps for days.

When Maia awakens, the wolves are gone.

She climbs out of her bag and plops next to the barren firepit. For a moment, she can nearly see Miguel kneeling next to it. She smiles. In her hazy daydream, he glances up at her and winks as he heats up her little pot of water. Lucas is standing beside her. She reaches for him, and both men disappear.

This morning, despite her deep ache, Maia has reached a new level of acceptance of her life. In fact, she's nearly content with it. Like a battle wound, her pain is a reminder that she was once surrounded by two men who loved her, and who she loved in return. And for a little while at least, she was happy, just Maia and her little family out in the world.

Now, she'll continue her journey to Leucothea. This ordeal has only strengthened her resolve, and God have mercy on anyone who stands in her way. She didn't come this far and lose this much to give up now.

She'll move on, but she will never let go. Every step she takes, she will look for Lucas and Miguel. For the rest of her life, she will search for them around the bend of every road, across the vast expanse of every forest clearing, and in every boot print left in the dirt. She will never let go, but she will keep moving.

She stands and gathers her things. "I am not a monster," she says alone in the woods.

And so, she walks. Day in and day out, one foot in front of the other, all while the sun hovers up and down along the horizon, never once sinking into it. Every day, she walks until she can go no farther, and then she wanders off the road to camp for the ... day.

Maia's hunger has reached unbearable levels. So far, finding water hasn't been much of an issue, and the wolves have been pretty good at bringing her food, but she hasn't seen the pack in days. She has no bow, no fishing pole, no buckets for traps. Her stomach is caving in on itself, her hunger near maddening.

She takes a steadying breath, willing her anxious heart to calm. She can't do this. She can't—she *won't*. She sighs again, and she knows. She has no other option. She *must* do this.

She crouches on the ground and places her open palms on the dirt. And then, she waits.

A ground squirrel pops his head from behind a tree in the distance. Obeying her silent command, he scuttles along the forest floor, drawn toward her open palms. As he sniffs the tip of her fingers, she marvels at how different he looks from the tree squirrels she has grown accustomed to. His ears are so small they're nearly nonexistent. His tail is half the size of the southern squirrels.

She holds back her tears as he climbs onto her hand, trusting her with his life. She sits back on her knees and draws the small creature closer, stroking the top of his head. His little paws wrap around her finger and he stretches his body closer, staring up at her with his black almond eyes. His little nose grazes hers as he breathes in the scent of his sweet mother.

A sob escapes her lips, and she tightens her grip around him. "*Thank you*," she whispers, and she kisses him. She grabs his head and turns away, his whiskers tickling her palm. With a swift twist, his life ends so that hers may continue.

After making a fire, she devours the meat that will now sustain her, listening to the crackling wood and the screeching insects. The fire's flames flicker and twist, its smoke bathing her in clouds.

She is not a monster.

THIRTY-EIGHT

Wandering down the road in a daze, Maia spots a manmade barrier ahead: trees stacked across cars. A few men are patrolling the wall, shuffling their feet as they cross back and forth. Another mob.

She stops short and tips back her head with a grand sigh of annoyance. She just wants to get *through* this already and get to Leucothea. She hasn't slept in she doesn't know how long. She doesn't have the energy to fight or use her powers—she barely has the energy to walk. She glances to either side of her; she'll have to take a shortcut.

She stumbles off the road into the densely shrouded woods. So tired. And hungry. *Is* she hungry? How long has it been since she ate that squirrel? And *where* are her *wolves*?

She pushes forward, banging into tree after tree with her head down, lost in a stupor. A nagging feeling keeps tugging at her gut. Something feels off. Maybe she's going the wrong way. She pivots. Which way is the road? A nervous prickle rolls up her spine. Maybe she should turn back. Which way is *back*?

The whispers of the trees shift from incoherent murmurings into precise words.

Stop. Danger.

How did she get so turned around? Irritated, she covers her ears as the trees' whispering surrounds her. *Danger. Mother. Danger.*

Her pack is so heavy, the weight pulling at her shoulders. Her neck muscles burn. Just keep moving. She pushes forward.

Stop. Danger. STOP DANGER.

"*Shhh!*" Maia swats at the air. She gazes down at her empty hands. Where is her staff?! She turns around. How long has she been walking without it? Her beloved bo, the *one thing* she had from Miguel. *Gone.* She wraps her arms around her concave gut and folds over, moaning softly.

Ache. Ache. Ache.

"*Dammit!*" she screams at the ground.

Danger. Mother. Danger. Danger. Stop.

She lurches forward, covering her ears. Wait, this is where she just came from. No, go to the left. She turns on a heel, and twigs snap beneath her feet. A broken tree branch digs into her arm as she passes, and she cries out, punching the tree as if it hurt her on purpose.

She pushes forward. No, this is wrong too.

Danger. Danger.

"*Stop!*" she yells at the trees. "I don't know where to go!"

A twig cracks in the distance, and Maia's head snaps toward the sound. Something smells different—she's being followed. By the wolves? She sticks her nose in the air, sniffing the scent like an animal. Her brow creases. No, not the wolves.

She stumbles forward, clutching the tree trunks as she passes, focused and resolute. This is fine, she just got a little turned around. She's been following her gut from the beginning. She'll find her way again.

She enters a small clearing with an immense stone structure towering beside the trees. She steps next to it. It looks like a mammoth person.

Stacked on top of the massive base are two rocky rectangles forming the legs. On top of them lies an enormous boulder forming the body. Propped on top of that is a long slate slab forming the arms. A square boulder sits at the very top as the head.

She drops her pack to her feet, standing in awe before the colossal structure. She runs her hand along the cold slate. This ... this was put here on purpose.

This is a warning.

She glances over her shoulder. She's read about these. They used to be erected by the natives of the Arctic.

Danger. Danger. DangerDangerDangerDanger.

She peers around, an animal-like instinct kicking in. Someone is lurking—she can feel his eyes on her. Maybe she can break all the trees at once and run for her life? She's never felled more than one tree at a time. Can she do more?

She steps into the middle of the clearing with the stone structure towering ominously behind her. Her heart racing, she scans the trees for whoever's lurking behind them.

A piercing sound cuts through the air, and she cries out. Something *bit* her. She glances down at her leg and panic sets in. A small dart with a colorful array of feathers is embedded in her thigh. She wraps her hand around it and yanks it from her skin.

She limps forward, gasping through gritted teeth. Okay, where are you?

Movement within the forest catches her eye, and a man steps out from behind a tree. Maia freezes. He has long black hair, and his dark eyes are cold as ice. He lifts a long wooden tube and places the end against his mouth.

She reaches out. "*NO!*"

His cheeks puff and he blows.

Maia twists as another dart pierces her shoulder. "*Ahh!*" Horrified, she rips it out and throws it to the ground. "Please! I come in ... *peace...*"

These darts have drugs on them.

Her world begins to blur. She tries to summon the strength to break a tree, or ... or ... Her eyes flutter, battling the drugs coursing through her veins. Men and women begin to show themselves. One by one, they step out from behind the trees. There are so many.

Maia stumbles forward, the muscles of her legs prickling, and a fiery temper swells within. She lifts her heavy hands to gather the wind, and another dart pierces her stomach.

She screams and charges. Darts fly, and she loses feeling in her feet, tripping over herself and tumbling to the dirt. She flips onto her back, and a man peers into her fading vision.

"Miguel?" she whispers.

Another man peers over. And another. They glare down at her as they shake their heads, speaking to one another in a language she cannot understand. She knows they're strangers, but all she can see is Lucas and Miguel. She reaches out with a trembling hand. One of the men lifts something high above her head and smashes it into her.

Maia awakens to a throbbing headache, her mouth bone dry. She lifts her heavy head from the cement, and it wobbles like a newborn. Groaning, she scrunches her eyes open and closed as her vision slowly trickles back. Where is she?

She gazes around the small brick room. There's a single window with bars over it and a large metal door on the other side of the room with a narrow rectangular opening at the top. She squints at the light pouring through the slot. Another set of black eyes peer back at her. The opening slides shut.

Shivering uncontrollably, Maia curls into a ball on the cold and dusty floor. Her muscles along her shoulder ache. Same with her thigh, her back, her stomach. And then the memories come back to her—all the sites where she was shot. She rolls onto her back, crying in agony. With the last of her strength, she lifts to her feet, but her legs give out and she stumbles into the wall, collapsing back to the floor. Wrapping her arms around herself, she rocks back and forth as a wave of nausea swims about her gut.

"No," she says, swallowing. It's coming. Her stomach clenches. She crawls on all fours, her hands slapping against the cement as she drags herself toward the door. "Get me out of here!" she screams.

She vomits until she passes out.

Maia awakens to the sound of her room's large metal door opening. It bangs loudly against the wall, and a flood of light pours over her. Three men enter the room.

"No, *please*—" she mumbles as they pick her up by her arms.

One of the men drops her to the ground and wipes his hands on his pants, yelling something in a foreign tongue. Maia is covered in vomit.

Serves him right.

They pile out of the room, slamming the door behind them as Maia lies shivering on the floor. A few minutes later, the door swings open again. She lifts her head to the men charging back into the room with buckets. She backs up on her hands and feet as they douse her with water. They come in and out of the room, drenching her again and again as she trembles and screams in the corner. Then they lift her by her shoulders and drag her out of the room.

They haul her through the halls of the small building, then out into the light. She fumbles to gain her footing, but the drugs are still heavy in her system. Everything is mumbled, jumbled, blurry. She tries to lift her knees but her legs are too weak, the men moving too fast.

As they lug her alongside the building, she catches

sight of herself in the windows. Her sunken face is smeared with dirt. Her clothing is soaked and covered in vomit. There are twigs in her knotted hair and black circles beneath her eyes.

She looks like a bounder.

Lucas's voice rings through her memory. *You never know the stories people belong to ... the battles they've faced.*

The men drag her to a large outdoor tent where a small group of people have gathered, sitting in rows of white chairs. A long table sits before them, with a dozen seated men and women facing the crowd. The men haul Maia down the center aisle toward the table.

The people turn and stand to gawk at her. They whisper and cover their mouths. They look horrified, shaking their heads and grimacing. The men release her, and she collapses like a bag of bones to the ground. Her head is so burdensome, she cannot find the strength to lift it.

The man sitting at the center of the table looks down his nose at her. He carries an air of authority, and he points at her, speaking to the men beside her in a foreign language. His tone is harsh. He's clearly annoyed—that she understands. She tries to focus on the ground beneath her, swallowing the bile rising up her throat. This ground is not spinning. This ground is not spinning.

The leader before her stands, this time speaking in English. "Who are you? DO YOU SPEAK ENGLISH?"

She presses her cheek to the dirt. "I ... am Maia," she mumbles between breaths. "Please ... let me go."

"You were wandering our grounds, incoherent and talking to yourself. You are a danger to our society."

"I'm not. I swear I'm not. Please ... let me go," she says to the ground.

"I'm sorry, but I cannot do that. You are not of right mind. You are a danger. You know where we are."

"I swear—"

"Your word means *nothing*!" He slams his fist against the table. "The last person we released came back and slaughtered my daughter in the middle of the night! You were talking to yourself in our woods, screaming into the air at *nothing*! You are a liability! You leave me no choice!"

"No, please—" She lifts her wobbling head.

"You will be executed."

"*What*?!" She struggles to lift herself.

"It will be swift and humane." He looks at the men, motioning his hand. "Take her away. Put her out of her misery."

"NO!" she screeches.

"Oh, and make sure there're no children around this time? Martha's granddaughter had nightmares for months, and *I* had to hear about it."

Maia fumbles to her knees. Her body is like lead, clumsy and wavering. The men yank her arms and lift her from the ground. She finds enough feeling in her feet to stand and she pushes against them, sending her tumbling backward into the chairs. The villagers scatter in a panic, falling over themselves and racing between the seats.

"*Why* is she not in cuffs? This day keeps getting better and better." The leader drops his head in his hands.

The men tackle her between an aisle. Shoving the chairs aside, they climb on top of her and twist her arms behind her back, cuffing her wrists in cold metal.

"*Please*, don't do this!" she cries into the ground.

The men grunt as they pick her up, and she hangs between them with her legs dragging behind her. Lifting her teetering head, she greets the horrified eyes of the villagers, staring at her with their hands on their mouths. There's so much judgment behind their glares. Fear.

So, this is how it ends.

THIRTY-NINE

The two men holding Maia clutch her arms as they converse back and forth, pulling apart her cuffed hands behind her back. She clenches her jaw, breathing through the pain as the metal cuts her wrists. They drag her to the far side of the jail she'd awakened in earlier. Another two men sweep the area—probably making sure they can execute her without being seen—while her guards haul her to the back wall of the jail.

Pushing her against the brick, they shout in her face with words she doesn't understand. They point at her feet and kick her knees to keep her upright, but she keeps buckling to the ground. They finally agree to leave her crouching in the dirt.

They back away, speaking back and forth as one of them loads his gun. Maia tries to summon the last of her strength to break a tree. Or harness the wind. Call the wolves? But she can't even stand, let alone use her powers to fight. She is shattered, a shell of the woman she once was.

She closes her eyes, trying to rein in her focus. Is there anything she can do? She racks her brain for something to save her, but there's nothing. She has no one.

When she opens her eyes, a vision of Lucas and Miguel appears. They stand side by side behind the guards.

Hello, little bird.

She smiles, a tear tumbling down her cheek. For a while, at least, everything was perfect.

One of the guards steps before her, and she looks up at him with broken eyes. His gaze softens, and he swallows. The other guard yells at him, his tone irritated and impatient. The guard repositions his stance, and he blows out a breath. He lifts his gun, pointing the trembling end at her head. She watches him, waiting.

Breathing hard, he continues to point his gun. Then he drops his weapon and walks away, shaking his head. The other guard rushes up to him and swipes the gun from his hand. He berates him just inches from his face and then marches up to Maia. Holding her in an icy glare, he rams the cold metal of the barrel against her forehead.

She peers beyond the guard to her vision of Miguel and Lucas standing behind him and prepares herself. *It will be swift. Humane.* She hopes it doesn't hurt.

Something moves behind Miguel. It's the hand of a child, reaching around his leg. Maia squints. The little girl from her dreams peeks her head out from behind his leg.

Maia gasps, and the little girl holds out her hand. "Wait!" the girl shouts with an older woman's voice.

"*Wait*," she says, and she nods at Maia with a knowing smile.

Maia stares at her in shock.

As the guard pulls away, Lucas, Miguel, and the little girl disappear. Maia looks around, confused. An elderly woman gripping a cane is walking up to Maia's guard. The guard, nearly twice the woman's height, bows in respect and begins to speak. The old woman hushes him.

She kneels before Maia so that they are face to face, then she turns and shoos the large guard away as if he were merely a child. Surprisingly, he does as he's told. The old woman's dark brown eyes exude wisdom. Gazing at the pounamu around Maia's neck, she delicately picks it up and inspects it between her fingers. Then her kind eyes flicker to Maia's, and she stares at her for a while.

"What is your name?" the old woman asks.

Maia chokes on her words. "*Mother*," she whispers.

The old woman leans back. Smiling, her eyes become like crescent moons. She leans in real close and whispers, "I thought you might say that." Chuckling, she cups her delicate hand against Maia's cheek.

The woman turns to the guards, saying something in their native tongue. The men swap a glance, confused. She stands and repeats herself. This time, her voice is loud and stern. One of the men runs off while the others rush to Maia's side. They unlock her cuffs and lift her to her feet. She clutches her aching wrists. They push her forward, still holding tightly to her arms. She struggles to put one foot before the other as they lead her away from the jail and back across the grounds.

The old woman hobbles behind them, pointing her

finger and barking out orders. The men argue back, their rebuttals like pleas, but they continue to obey whatever the woman is demanding.

The leader who ordered Maia's execution rushes toward them with a small crowd of people following in his wake. He and the old woman begin to argue. It is clear the elderly woman is speaking stern words to the man as she points her finger repeatedly at Maia.

The leader looks at Maia, his face fraught with concern. Finally, he nods and steps to the side, and the old woman turns to her. Her wide smile causes her skin to gather in rumples, her eyes reduced to gladdened slits.

The men still clutch Maia's arms as they guide her to a small, circular hut surrounded by gardens swarming with butterflies. The old lady opens the door, revealing the most beautiful bedroom Maia has ever seen.

A large bed is in the middle of the back wall, with long white sheets cascading from a circular rod in the ceiling. The small bedside tables on either side are adorned with candles and vases of wildflowers. Large, open windows line the walls, with white curtains flowing in the breeze.

The guards dump Maia to the hardwood floor. Her arms have just enough strength to stop her head from slamming against it. The elderly woman chastises the men and shoos them out.

Within seconds, the room fills with women, young and old. They crowd around Maia with soothing voices, delicately touching her face, her hair, her filthy wet clothing. They point and whisper about her eyes. They inspect her bruises and wounds. Two women place her arms over their shoulders and guide her to the bathroom, where another woman is filling a large bath with buckets of hot water.

Curious children peek in the windows, and the women draw the curtains closed. They smile tenderly at Maia, nodding their heads and whispering unknown words in soft, hushed voices. They take off her muddy boots and peel off her layers of wet clothing.

As they slowly lower her trembling body into the hot bath, she begins to sob. Their soothing voices hush her as she weeps, meeting her gaze with sympathetic tears. They tilt back her head, washing the mud and the debris from her hair. They drape warm cloths over her arms and legs, wiping away the grime from her skin. They lean her forward into their cradling arms and clean the puncture wounds on her back.

Maia peers up through the haze of her tears, meeting the eyes of the elderly woman in the corner. She is speaking to a younger woman who nods as they whisper back and forth.

"Thank you," Maia repeatedly whispers to the women around her.

Shhh is the only response she understands.

Eventually, the women guide her out of the tub and into a soft robe with colorful tribal designs. They comb her wet hair and braid it off her shoulders, then lead her to the large bed in the next room. They feed her a nourishing cup of hot broth, and then one by one, they quietly exit the hut, leaving only Maia and the elderly woman inside.

A guard stands watch at the front door, every so often

glancing over his shoulder with a look of remorse. Maia recognizes him as the same guard who couldn't—*wouldn't*—shoot her.

The old woman is softly humming as she unravels the black blinds down each of the windows. She finishes at the front door, allowing the shade to drop all the way to the floor. The only light now comes from a single candle beside Maia's bed. The elderly woman perches on the bed and takes Maia's hand within hers.

"Why?" Maia manages to breathe.

"Because, Anâna, you are our sweet mother. You've come back to us."

Maia peers up at her, confused. *Anâna?* "What are you talking about?"

"I have had many dreams about you. I've known you were coming for a long time. I didn't recognize you at first because you never showed your face in my visions, but I knew you would be wearing a small jade pendant. You have come from the lands of New Zealand."

"Yes," Maia whispers, her tears saturating the soft cotton of her pillow.

The old woman smiles. "I've told the council of this tribe that you are sacred and to be taken care of with the highest honor." She glances back at the door and then at Maia. "But despite my authority, we still have to compromise. You'll be taken care of, but you'll be guarded. We need everyone to feel safe. So please, just stay in this room and rest. You have gone many days without sleep, I can see it in your eyes. Just rest. I will come back to you in a few days, and then we will chat, okay?" She stands to leave, grabbing her cane.

Maia reaches for her. "Thank you. You saved my life."

"Yes." The old woman cups Maia's face. "I did. And you, in turn, will save ours."

The old woman blows out the candle, blanketing Maia in the sweet relief of darkness.

FORTY

M aia spends the next few days drifting in and out of a dreamless slumber. Curled into herself, she keeps one hand on her chest so that every time she wakes, she knows her broken heart is still beating.

She relishes the darkness. The silence. The absence of bugs and dirt and rain. The only time Maia fully awakens is when a flood of light pulls her from the black void, most often from another woman tiptoeing into her room with a tray of hot food. Every time they come in, Maia is given a small plate of meat, vegetables, and fruit. After countless charred squirrels over an open fire, the explosion of flavors in each of these dishes is enough to bring tears to her eyes. The women will often sit quietly in the back of the room while they wait for her to finish, smiling and nodding to every mumbled and garbled "thank you" Maia can utter.

With no cues of night and day, there's no way of knowing how long Maia's been in here. However, she's noticed the sound of a large bell outside ringing every so often, after which the commotion of the people outside her hut dulls to an eerie silence. Maia can only assume this may be their cue to head in for the "night" for dinner and sleep.

Day after day, the local children faithfully line the blacked-out windows of Maia's hut, trying to get a glimpse of the visitor who caused such a commotion *and* has two armed guards outside.

"My aataa says she's nothing but trouble."

"Well, my grandpa says she carries the soul of the Great Spirit."

"What do you think she's doing in there?"

Maia uncoils herself from the fetal position, stretching wide across her bed. The sharp pains from her wounds have lessened, and the sore on her head from where she was hit no longer throbs. She walks across the dark room, lighting candles as she goes, and heads into the bathroom to bathe with the few buckets of tepid water left for her. Afterward, when she pulls at the small plug at the base of the tub, she smiles. Such a good feeling to drain a bath of clear water.

She slides into some light linen pants and a button-up shirt left freshly washed and folded on a chair. Heartily fed and well-rested, she feels like a new woman.

A large oval mirror hangs above an antique wooden desk with copper handles. She pulls out the chair and takes a seat, gazing into her reflection. She still has a wild mix of auburn waves and red curls, but her freckles are nearly gone. She's never seen her face without freckles, at least not outside her dreams. Her skin is like porcelain, her jawline more pronounced. The few childlike features on her face have nearly disappeared. The dark circles beneath her eyes have also dissipated. She looks healthy and rejuvenated—on the outside. But inside, her heart is still aching.

She nearly died a few days ago, or however long it's been. She stared into the cold end of a loaded gun, and who was there to help her? She has saved Lucas and Miguel on multiple occasions. It was she alone who got them beyond the barricades and the bounders and the mobs. But yet, the moment her life was left dangling on a string, who was there to save her?

A stranger.

She thinks of the young woman from the Northern Tribe back in New Zealand, risking everything to help her when she was trapped under the monstrous shadow of that elder.

Another child's giggle sounds from outside the hut. Maia turns toward the window, still closed behind its heavy black blinds. She sneaks up to the glass, listening to the hushed whispers of the children on the other side. She quickly lifts the curtains, nearly blinding herself from sunlight. The children scream and run away, and Maia covers her smile.

Yes, *light*. She's ready for some sun. Walking from window to window, she rolls up the heavy black blinds, allowing a deluge of light into her small hut. She cracks open one of the windows and breathes in the rich scent of the earth. The guard from her front door races around the cottage, yelling at her in foreign words.

"Whoa!" She lifts her hands. "Fresh air?"

The man shakes his head. "No! No, no!"

"Okay! I'm sorry." She closes the window.

He's not the same guard as before. He looks at her suspiciously, then walks back to the front of the cabin.

She steps from the glass and sighs, gazing around at the artifacts layering the walls. It's like a museum in here. A large white hoop is hung above her bed with woven strings crisscrossing the middle. Maia tilts her head. It looks like a spider's web but with tassels and feathers hanging below it. The walls are lined with portraits of people dressed in colorful outfits with beadwork and feathers. There's a mounted fur headdress and strips of intricately woven beadwork hanging from hooks. A rawhide tunic has the skull of a large horned creature hanging above it.

A piece of driftwood is mounted above the desk, painted in vibrant designs. The tip is wrapped in leather with three gray and black feathers dangling beneath. Maia lifts it from the wall, admiring the paint's fine detail.

"She's a gorgeous piece of work, isn't she?"

Maia turns to find the old woman closing the door behind her. She quickly places the stick back on the wall.

"The children ran up to me like a flock of cackling hens to let me know you were finally up and about. I'm so glad."

Maia turns to her. "I want to thank you again for saving my life the other ... day. How long have I been here?"

"*Mmm* ... I'd say about five days," the old woman says, hobbling over to her.

Maia's cheeks flush. "I'm sorry. I should leave. I'll just gather—"

"Don't be silly. You are our guest. You stay as long as you like."

"Oh, I could never."

"Oh, but you must. Besides, you are not ready."

"Ready?"

"*Mmm-hmm*." The old woman gazes up at her with a closed smile, her skin crinkling around her eyes. She changes the subject. "It was not easy, you know, convincing my men to let you go. You were in quite a state."

Maia looks down at her ravaged fingernails. "Yeah, life hasn't exactly been kind."

"*Mmm*, yes. It does that from time to time. Often, though, what appears to be your worst nightmare can turn out to be your greatest blessing." She reaches up to lift Maia's chin. "Do not be too quick to judge things off first glance, Anâna."

Maia's brow creases. "Anâna?"

"Yes, dear. You told me that was your name." She motions Maia toward the desk chair. "Come. Sit."

"My name is *Maia*," she says as she sits, peering at the old woman through the mirror.

The woman gathers Maia's thick hair behind her and begins to braid. "You told me your name was *Mother*." She peers over Maia's shoulder. "Anâna means mother."

"I told..." Maia smiles as she remembers. "Yes, I did say that, didn't I?"

The woman finishes Maia's braid and places her hands on her shoulders. "All better. Come, let's get some air."

Maia stands. Side by side, she's at least a foot taller than the old woman, who's now linking their arms.

She leads Maia to the front door where she knocks three times against the glass. The guard cracks it open.

"We're going for a walk," the old woman says.

The guard looks at her with wide eyes. He opens his mouth, but she lifts her hand, silencing him. "I'm not asking for permission." She shoves open the door.

He looks unsure, but he steps aside anyway.

Maia pauses on the doorstep, savoring the sun's warmth. The garden around her hut is even more beautiful than she remembers. Whatever they've planted, the butterflies love it. The path from her door splits into many, leading to other modest-sized buildings situated between the towering pines, and there's a grand white tent in the distance.

A small horde of children runs past. A young girl takes one look at Maia and freezes. "*Wow*," she whispers, gawking up at her. The two children behind her run into her back.

"*Shoo shoo*. Go play," the old woman says. The children run off giggling. "And you," she says, turning to the guard following closely behind. "Leave us be."

He responds in their native tongue.

"You tell him he can take it up with me. This is not up for discussion. *Go*." She waves her hand.

Maia and the woman continue down the path. "What you see around you is our equivalent of a downtown." She gazes up at Maia, beaming. "This is where our community buildings are. Our territory stretches for miles—used to be government land, but with no more government, we have simply taken back what was ours."

Maia nods.

The old woman continues. "As you can see, besides the small clearings needed for our buildings, our footprint has been light. This has always been the way of our people. Beyond these buildings, our homes are spaced between the trees. The rest of our territory is practically untouched by man, besides the trails we use for hunting and gathering."

Maia looks down at the old lady. "This is so beautiful." She hesitates, embarrassed. "I'm sorry, I never asked your name."

"Quite all right." She pats Maia's arm, chuckling. "You have come a long way. I have many names, but you may call me Tema. I am this tribe's medicine woman."

"Tribe?"

"Yes, Anâna."

"Are you Inuit?"

"Some are. Our community is made up of various Indigenous Peoples that have come together here in the old Yukon Territory. Those who were once divided, or at the very least separated, have become united in these dark days—there are so few of us left. We have combined our resources and have made a haven for ourselves. Isn't it just *splendid*? We are so proud."

"It is. And it all works out? I mean, combining people from such different backgrounds?"

"Everyone is encouraged to maintain their old traditions and languages according to their ancestry. Although being people of the land, it's been harder on some than others. Some of our land has been swallowed by the sea. Other land along rivers has disappeared as they've risen over their banks and formed new routes. The volatile weather confused the animals and they've changed migrations. Some no longer exist.

"But every person here has come on their own accord. We have a council made up of representatives from every group present. We have libraries and even a small museum to teach the next generations our histories. Most of us work very hard at living as close to our heritages as we can, but certain allowances must be made. We will always teach our children our stories, but we've had to evolve. Life is very different from the life of our ancestors. We now live with a mix of old traditions and new. We are a democracy—we vote on everything. Our language has turned into a combination of English and our old languages." She hesitates with a shrug. "We're still working with some on the English. But we are all brothers and sisters. Now, more than ever, we must unite as one."

"I've been to a place with this similar feel, in America. This seems like a haven."

"Our tribes have not always been a haven for our people. There was a long period in history when our people were stripped of their homes, their culture, and their identities. They were intimately connected to their land, so having it taken away had dark consequences that spread across many generations.

"*But*," she says with a sigh, "those are stories for another day. My father reclaimed these beautiful lands for us many years ago, and we will never allow anyone to take them from us again."

"Of course. You have every right."

"Our tribulations have united us. We must be the heroes of our stories. There will always be a villain to fight." She turns to Maia, studying her eyes. She adds like an afterthought, "You have eyes like our huskies."

Maia hesitates. "Thank you?"

Tema takes no notice. "You are on your way to

Leucothea, I presume?" The way she says Leucothea ... the name is dragged out with bitterness, like something dangerous or vile.

"I am. Do you know anything about it?"

"Oh, I *do*." She shakes her head. "Soon I may tell you about it, but not now. Now we are preparing for our celebrations next week. It is summer solstice," she says with a wide grin.

"What does that mean?" Maia turns to the old woman.

"That means, sweet Anâna, that darkness is coming."

FORTY-ONE

They call it a dreamcatcher.

Maia wavers, standing on her bed and gazing up at the hoop. She runs her fingertips down the weave, then reaches around a feather, softly sweeping it against her palm. A catcher of dreams. She wonders what sort of worlds lie trapped between these strings. Surely, she can't have been the only one staying in this room who's been haunted by their dreams. Although, since arriving here, she has not had a single nightmare. Every evening, when she closes her eyes after the night-time bell rings, her world becomes blissfully silent. Black. As if she's crawled into the gaping hole in her heart while she sleeps.

It's only when she awakens that her nightmares return.

She runs the dreamcatcher's feathers between her fingers. Despite the consuming ache that still gnaws at her heart, there's something inside her that knows she'll be okay. It is a quiet knowing, one easy to ignore when her pain becomes too loud, but it's still there, softly whispering beyond a shadow of a doubt that all will be well.

Three knocks tap against the door. When Maia opens it, she holds her hand against the sunlight.

"Maia! Rise and shine!"

It's Chayanne, a young woman Tema introduced to Maia. After recovering, Maia insisted she contribute to the community's workload. Now Chayanne comes to her hut every morning with a basket of breakfast, which they enjoy together before heading out to work in the greenhouses.

Maia is surprised at how quickly she has integrated with the people of this tribe. They have come to an understanding that despite her horrific introduction, she can be trusted. Of course, the blessing of their shaman has helped greatly in this regard. The guards have left their posts from outside her front door. The tribe's chief, who ordered her execution, has even stopped by for tea and a new introduction. He didn't apologize, which Maia understood. He's a proud man who was only trying to protect his people.

Maia has been invited to dinner every night with a different family, often staying up much too late listening to their stories, backgrounds, and traditions. Every day after lunch, she spends time with the children, learning new games played with balls and sticks. And then, like clockwork, Tema steals her away to walk around the grounds. In the midst of it all, Maia has found herself laughing again.

Chayanne sets her basket of food next to a small table by the windows. This is where they have breakfast—generally an assortment of fruit, fresh bread, and Maia's new favorite: Chayanne's famous eggs cooked in rolled willow bark over a fire.

Maia looks around in a panic. "Did you bring—"

"Don't you worry your pretty little head," Chayanne says with a smile. She pulls a large thermos of tea from the bottom of her bag.

Chayanne is, without a doubt, the most stunning woman Maia has ever seen. Something about her aura exudes a quiet strength. She was the young woman Tema was speaking to in the corner when Maia was first brought into the hut. Maia will never forget her face: proud and graceful, with full lips and striking doe eyes. Her long, silky black hair has become the source of Maia's envy—she can't help touching it. Chayanne has used this to her advantage. Every morning after breakfast, they take turns braiding each other's hair before heading off to work. It's an incredible bonding experience between the women and an old tradition of Chayanne's people.

Maia has met quite a few souls since leaving the shores of New Zealand: from the boat that saved her and Lucas when they were stranded in the Pacific to the community of New Portland and now here. Most of the people have generally been kind, but there have been a few to whom Maia was immediately drawn. What *is* that? It's like her soul recognizes their soul. Thomas in New Portland was one of them. Lucas, of course. Miguel—without a doubt. And now, Chayanne. Sometimes when you meet a person, you just know. What is that?

Soulmates, maybe. Old souls, connected from previous lives.

Chayanne piles some berries on Maia's plate.

"I'm glad I met you," Maia says.

Chayanne laughs. "Don't be. Today we're cleaning out the chicken coops, and that, my friend, is not nearly as nice as the pruning and weeding you've been doing."

Maia smiles. "I'm just happy to help. Your tribe has been very kind to me."

"Well, we truly are the best. You should probably just forget about Leucothea and stay here." She winks.

Maia leans forward. "Speaking of, do you know much about the place? Tema doesn't seem to want to talk about it."

Chayanne stares at her, hesitating. "I do ... but if our shaman doesn't want you to know about it, that's not something I should interfere with."

Maia sits back in her chair. "I suppose."

"Maia..." Chayanne hesitates again, her eyes narrowing.

"What?" she asks.

"I know we haven't known each other long, and please tell me if I'm overstepping, but ... what happened to you? I mean, before this. I know about your life in New Zealand and that you were with others on your way north. But then what happened?"

Maia sets down her tea, battling the ache clawing within.

"I was there when they ordered your execution," Chayanne says. "You were like a skeleton, screaming at nothing. You were filthy. They thought they were doing you a favor."

She looks at Chayanne. Sometimes she wonders the same. "I was with two men," she says after a while. "One was my partner, Lucas." She grimaces saying his name aloud, as if speaking of the dead. "And his brother, Miguel. I loved them both so much. But I betrayed them —both of them. So, they left."

Chayanne stops chewing, watching Maia. She swallows. "Oh, Maia."

"The whole thing was my fault. It was a mess."

Chayanne sets down her fork. "I'm sorry if this isn't my place, but they *left* you? *Alone*? In the middle of the wilderness with mobs of men prepared to attack around every corner?"

Maia looks up at her. "I never thought of it like that."

Chayanne levels her a look. "Maia, no one is perfect. We all go through times when we see a darker side of ourselves that we'd rather not. Doesn't excuse two men who supposedly love you from abandoning you in the middle of nowhere."

Anger surges within. Not so much at Miguel. She told him repeatedly that she didn't love him. Lucas screamed at him to leave. How else could he have responded? He left Maia and Lucas *together*. But Lucas ... Lucas left Maia all alone on that riverbank. He swore he would never run, but he *left*. She knew this before, but she still held it against herself. But Chayanne's right. How *could* he?

She can feel it in her chest, another icy layer hardening around her heart. She finishes the last of her tea. "Okay, I think I'm done talking. Let's go to work."

On their way back from the chicken coops, Maia and Chayanne carry their shovels as they trek past another community hut. A crowd of men and women have gathered in the field beyond the building, calling out like an army. Maia slows.

Chayanne whispers, "It's our defense building. Our people used to have the best warriors in the world. It's our mission to get that back."

"What are they doing?"

"Come on, I'll show you." Chayanne grabs Maia's shovel and places it with hers beside the door. They tiptoe across a massive room filled from floor to ceiling with weapons: guns, bows, blowguns, spears, and staves. Maia stops before the staves, mesmerized.

"Maia." Chayanne is by the back doors, motioning for her to join.

Just outside is a group of men and women forming a circle. The two men in the center lift their bo in the air and begin to fight. Maia walks away from the doors and squeezes through the crowd, drawn to that familiar *snap* of wood as the staves cross. Their moves are so similar, yet so different.

"Pretty amazing, isn't it?" Chayanne whispers.

One of the men is the guard who wouldn't shoot her. He locks eyes with her for a brief moment before turning away to block his opponent's move. Their moves are quick, strong. Maia has only ever been a part of the fighting; she's never been on the sidelines to watch. Her heart *yearns* for it.

Once finished, the guard walks up to Chayanne. "Hey."

"Hey," she says with a smile. "I was just showing Maia your smooth moves."

He looks at Maia, still catching his breath, and he lifts his bo. "You familiar?" he asks.

"Very," she says.

He hands her his staff, and she takes it between her hands. It feels so good to be holding one again.

"Do you mind?" She nods at the empty field behind them.

"Go for it," he says, wiping his brow.

She tries to inconspicuously back away from the crowd to practice spinning. But when she flips the staff in the air and catches it behind her back, she unintentionally commands the crowd's attention.

Another man hands the guard a new bo, and he approaches. "Shall we?" he asks.

She grins, halting her spin with the edge of her hand. "I'd love that."

A new circle forms as they stand across from one another and cross their staves in the air with a *snap*!

They begin. The guard is fast, but so is Maia. Swing, block. *Breathe*. Swing, swing. Block. With every snap, every block, and every swing, Maia finds her confidence slowly seeping back into her system. The quiet drumming in her heart resounds louder with every swing: she's going to be okay. No, she *is* okay. Now.

The fight that started slow and polite quickly becomes competitive, and the crowd around them grows into three, four, five people deep as word spreads about the new girl fighting a soldier.

When they finish, a crowd of men and women surround Maia, shaking her hand and patting her back.

The guard pushes through the people. "You're good. Who taught you how to fight like that?"

She sighs. "An old friend."

"Well, that was great. I'd love to do it again before you leave."

"Me too."

"I'm Shinesho, by the way," he says, extending his hand.

She shakes it. "Maia."

The crowd separates and Tema appears, making her way toward Maia. "It's time for our walk," she says, and she pulls at Maia's arm, stealing her from the crowd.

The two women wander past the field with the teepee —Maia has since learned the name—with a massive pile of wood beside it. This is where the celebrations will take place tomorrow night.

"I've decided that I'll continue on my way after the celebrations," Maia says.

"*Mmm.*" Tema nods, clutching Maia's arm as they walk. "Yes, you will continue your travels. Whether or not you'll go after the celebrations, however," she says, lifting a finger. "That is yet to be seen."

"What do you mean?"

"You are not ready."

Maia balks. "What do you mean? I feel like I'm ready."

Tema is silent beside her.

"Well, if I'm not, how will I know when I am?"

Tema chuckles. "Trust me, Anâna, you'll know." She stops walking and takes a step back, eyeing Maia with concern. "Tell me, now, what is it that still breaks your heart?" She sweeps her hand over Maia. "You carry within you such exquisite beauty, but there's a heavy darkness shrouding your light. It is intense. Suffocating."

Maia looks away, suddenly finding it hard to breathe.

"Darling," the old woman says. "*You* are the one holding that darkness."

Surprised, Maia looks at her.

"It covers you, yes," Tema says gently, "but *you* are keeping it there."

"I can't imagine my life without them," Maia whispers. "I love them so much."

"Ah, yes. Love. Love carries with it all the light and all the darkness in the world. The same person who once filled your heart with joy can be the same one to shatter it."

Maia looks at her through her tears. "How do I make it stop?"

"Make what stop? The shattering? You don't. You must accept it. By accepting it wholly without fighting against it, you can let it go. This is one of the great truths in life. Whatever you resist will persist."

"I don't want to let them go. I *can't*."

"Anâna, the more you fight the darkness, the more *attention* you focus on it, the more it will strengthen. You are brokenhearted and have allowed that darkness to swallow you whole. It is time now to come back to the middle." She links her arm through Maia's, and the two begin to walk.

"All darkness is not bad," Tema continues. "As you can see up here near the Arctic, where all we have is light, you crave the dark. Nighttime has always been portrayed in our stories as evil, but there's so much beauty to be found in darkness. The night is when we restore, when our bodies heal. Balance is always necessary."

A little girl runs up to Tema. She wraps her arms

around the old lady and peers up at Maia. "Are you a god?" she asks.

Maia laughs. "No, I'm Maia."

The girl reaches for her, and Maia kneels down as the child places her hands on her cheeks. "Same thing," she replies.

Maia smiles, and the child runs off.

"These children. The light of my life, I tell you," Tema says, reaching again for Maia's arm.

"You seem hesitant to talk to me about Leucothea," Maia says to Tema. "Why is that?"

The old woman sighs. "Because I know it's imperative that you go there, and I don't want to cloud your vision."

They've made their way back to Maia's hut, stopping outside the front door.

"Why would talking about Leucothea cloud my vision?"

"Come. Sit." Tema hobbles to the two wooden chairs in the hut's garden.

They sit side by side in silence. Maia waits.

"Do you remember on your first day here," Tema says, "I told you I dreamed of you?"

"I remember."

"I hear from Chayanne that you have dreams as well."

She fights the urge to bite her nails. "I *did*."

"Do not be quick to push those away. I believe dreams to be very sacred; they are messages from our souls."

"Oh," Maia says bitterly. "I'm *aware*."

"*My* dreams tell me not to meddle in your quest to Leucothea."

"What does that mean?"

"It means, as much as I want to tell you everything I

know, most of those things are rumors, and I am not to tamper with your fate."

Maia shakes her head, frustrated. "Why would you telling me some rumors tempt my fate?"

Tema reaches for Maia's hand, clasping it between hers. "That, my dear, is not up to us to know."

"Ugh, *enjoy the journey*, right? I am *so sick* of this journey. I just want to be finished already."

"Oh, well. Then you might as well be dead."

Maia laughs.

"*The journey* is the point," Tema says. "It's the best part —it's the *only* part. We all want to be done, to reach this point of completion." She turns toward Maia. "That point of completion? It's an illusion. It simply doesn't exist. As soon as you have the one thing you desire most, your ego will move on to the next. That's its *job*. It doesn't care if you're happy. It just wants you to grow."

Maia slumps, crossing her arms. "That's not exactly what I want to hear."

Tema smiles, satisfied. She gazes across the garden.

"Well, unfortunately," Maia says, "I've heard the name Leucothea a few times now on my travels, and it's never mentioned in a positive light. I'm really starting to worry."

"What are you worried about?"

"That it's not the haven I thought it was."

"*Mmm*. Maybe not." Tema looks up at her with a twinkle in her eye. "Maybe that's the reason you're here."

FORTY-TWO

The big celebration of the summer solstice has arrived.

Maia sits on her bed, twisting Lucas's faded bracelet around her wrist. Through everything that's happened, she's grateful it has somehow remained bound. Made by Miguel and worn by Lucas, it's all she has left of them. Like her koru pounamu from her mother, the bracelet carries a part of each man within its strands. She can only hope, wherever they are, that they are okay. Safe. Her tiger too. Is he still out there, waiting for her in the woods? Will she ever see any of them again?

A few men wearing large feather headdresses pass by her windows. Tonight, after a large feast, the people of this tribe will celebrate the longest day of the year around a raging fire. It's been all the talk since Maia arrived.

After tonight, the days will begin to shorten, and eventually, the sun will sink far enough below the horizon to shroud the land in darkness. Maia hopes she'll be deep into the next leg of her journey by then, but

Tema keeps insisting that she wait until she's "ready." Maia still doesn't know what this means, but she's decided to follow the guidance of this new guardian angel in her life and to trust—for now.

After dinner, the large community gathers in the middle of the field with the late evening sun hanging low in the sky. Maia sits quietly on a chair, watching as men, women, and children stomp dance around a fire to beating drums and chanting men. Tema is sitting in the teepee with its doorway flaps tied back, along with the chief and a few others. All are wearing an assortment of traditional indigenous dress.

Maia catches Tema's eye, and the old shaman smiles at her. She grabs her cane and slowly hobbles across the field. As she takes a seat beside Maia, she leans in and shouts over the drums, "You know, sweet Anâna, when I look at the men and women dancing around the fire, it reminds me of an Inca term for human. Do you know what it means?"

Maia looks at her. "I don't."

Tema beams. "It means animated earth."

Maia gazes back at the dancers. *How fitting.*

"The ego has always made us feel separate," Tema continues, "which can cause us a great deal of pain. But this is another illusion. We are all connected, to our Earth, to each other. I know you've been through a lot, but please do not be so quick to judge. Every person who comes into our lives is there for a reason. We may not understand it at the time, but that doesn't mean it's not deeply significant."

Maia continues watching the dancers and Tema gently grabs her chin, drawing her attention back to her.

"Just remember, child, we are never finished. We are continually evolving entities. Whatever circumstances you are battling with, they begin *here*." She points at Maia's chest.

"With everything?"

Tema smiles. "The laws of the universe are intricate and complex, many of which are beyond our abilities to comprehend. We want to *know* everything. But to understand it would be like explaining a mountaintop to a fish. So, this is where faith comes in. Every person you see here is battling the same thing."

"And what's that?"

"Learning to love what we fear, which, sweet Anâna, is most often ourselves. We are powerful beyond measure, but our mind is like a blindfold. Most people will live their entire lives without ever questioning the lies their ego feeds them. Without ever knowing who they truly are or what they are capable of."

Chayanne approaches with a small wooden bowl in her hands.

"Ah, yes. Finally!" Tema shouts over the drums, happily moving on to the next subject while Maia stares at her with her mouth open. Tema takes the bowl from Chayanne and turns to Maia with a smile. "You are ready. Take this."

Maia accepts the bowl, filled with a sloshing yellow liquid. Tema taps the edge with a nod.

"I don't—" Maia begins.

"Drink this," Tema says. "Drink, and let it set you free."

Maia lifts the bowl. It smells like bananas and ... *mud*. "What is it?" she asks.

"Maia ... *Trust*." Tema taps the dish again. "Drink."

Maia touches the bowl to her lips, eyeing Tema. She sips. "It tastes like fruit," she says after a few gulps. She looks down at the sloshing liquid. "Oh." She grimaces. "And something *bitter*."

Tema smiles. "Yes, the bananas are supposed to help with that." She nods at Chayanne, who takes the bowl.

"Now what?" Maia asks.

"Now, we wait," Tema says, grasping Maia's hands.

Maia's surprised at how quickly she's lulled into a trance. Transfixed by the chanting men and the banging drums, she watches as the men and women shift from foot to foot and the fire's sparks drift into the air. She stares down at the old woman's arthritic hands wrapped around her own, watching with an amused detachment as they disappear.

When she looks up, she's no longer in a vast field but is once again in the forest from her dreams. She gazes around at the familiar Arctic trees, the pines stretching like skyscrapers against a starry night sky.

A scared and younger version of herself now whimpers before her. She looks like she did when she left New Zealand, with freckles and wavy auburn hair. Maia reaches out to her, and the girl cowers back, falling into the thick blanket of snow.

This is exactly like her dreams. Only now, *she* is the terrifying ghost standing in the fire. She looks down. The flames lap up her white dress, but she does not feel the burn.

The girl begins to weep, and she tries to escape, crawling behind two men. Maia gasps.

Miguel and Lucas.

They stare at her, emotionless as she burns before them. She tries to run to them, but her feet remain bound.

"Anâna," Tema's voice whispers beside her.

Maia twists where she stands, but there's no one there.

"You believe that being who you are will make you unlovable, and have therefore held yourself in that fire your entire life by judging your magnificence. You must let that go. You are both a powerful being *and* a human being. You will be strong and you will stumble. You are powerful and vulnerable. Maia, this is who you are. Be who you are with all that you are. Untie yourself from the fears that bind you and set yourself free."

Maia gazes back at the men standing before her. How *much* she misses their faces. Grandpa now stands beside them, and he nods at her with a smile. Her beloved Huck sits panting beside him with his stick at his feet. Beside him stands her mother.

All the love she has lost.

Lined in a row behind them are all the men whose lives she's taken. They do not chant, nor hold their wounds before them. They stand before her in peace, as if in solemn acknowledgment that everything that has occurred was always meant to be.

Maia lifts her chin. Every time she has judged herself, doubted her instincts, or shoved herself in a box, she has reaffirmed the belief that who and what she is was not enough. She's been apologizing for who she is her entire life, seeking approval from everyone but herself. But it would have never been enough, because the only acceptance she ever truly needed was her own.

The cowering reflection of herself stops weeping. She dries the tears from her eyes with the back of her hand and lifts herself to her feet. The small child from Maia's dreams trudges across the snow, pushing between the rows of people until stopping before Maia. She reaches into the fire and takes Maia's hand.

With that, Maia breaks free from the blaze and steps into the snow.

The child leads her to her young reflection, now standing separate from the souls behind her. With a swipe of her thumb, Maia erases the tears coating her cheeks, and then she folds her into her arms. "I love you," she whispers. "Exactly as you are."

The images around her dissipate like the rain, leaving her standing alone in the woods.

"I am not a monster," she says to the darkness. "I will not burn for this."

When she turns around, the fire is gone.

The next morning, Maia awakens in her hut. She peels back the sheets and hangs her feet from the bed. Wiggling her toes, she takes a deep breath and looks around. Everything's the same, yet something has shifted. Something ... significant.

She slides from her bed and places her feet against the hardwood floor, stretching her arms above her head. She peers up at her hands. They feel light, like she's been freed of the heavy shackles she's been carrying her entire life.

She steps to the mirror above the desk and gasps,

taking a step back with her hand on her chest. The last of her auburn waves have disappeared, leaving a full head of red curls. Her few remaining freckles have also vanished. Her blue and green eyes do not glimmer like when she uses her powers, but they are deep and striking.

The change in her appearance has been so gradual for such a long time, this slight shift would be almost imperceptible to most. Yet, it is profoundly significant.

"Well, look at you," Tema says from the doorway.

Maia turns to face her.

"And?" The old woman hobbles up to her.

Maia smiles. "I'm ready."

"Yes." Tema gazes up at her and runs her fingers through her curls. "You certainly are." When she smiles, her skin creases like fans around her eyes. "Come, child. I have something for you."

FORTY-THREE

Tema leads Maia beyond the tribe's defense building and its large open field to a small barn tucked between the trees. Approaching the doors, she stops and turns toward Maia with a childish grin on her face. Maia smiles, thinking of Miguel—the way he'd laugh when she was acting mischievous.

What are you up to, little bird?

That old familiar ache crawls from the depths. She pushes it back down.

Tema presses her back against the large wooden doors, and they swing open with a long and rusted groan, flooding the inside of the dusty building with light. Balancing on blocks in the middle of the room is a small wooden boat, a little larger than a canoe. Its timber frame is tightly bound in leather, with two small benches inside.

"We call it an umiak," Tema says. "Although this one was custom-made for a special person in mind, so it's much smaller than our average boat."

"*Wow*," Maia whispers. She runs her hand along the smooth leather. "It's beautiful."

"It was made with the skin of the caribou. I want you to have it for the final leg of your journey."

Maia turns to her. "Oh, *no*. No, I could never accept a gift like this."

"It's not a gift. You'll be giving us something in return."

Maia tilts her head. "But I don't have anything to give."

"Oh, but you do." Tema hobbles up to a wooden chair in a dark corner of the room. Reaching into a large cloth sack, she pulls out a carbon hunting bow nearly identical to the one stolen from Maia in LA. She holds it before her, the large contraption dwarfing her small stature.

"I don't understand," Maia says with wide eyes. She takes the bow into her arms, fighting the urge to cradle it like a child.

"The elusive caribou. Tomorrow, you will go into the mountains, and you will hunt one for us."

"*What*?"

"Should you have any doubts, just follow the raven. You will return to us when the time is right."

"But how will I know?"

"Maia. *Trust*. You'll know." She places her hand on the small boat. "There's a powerful river that cuts through our land. When you come back, you will take this boat along that river for the final leg of your journey. Its waters empty into a wide bay that leads to the ocean. There you will find your city of Leucothea, sitting high upon the cliff."

"But..." Maia shakes her head. "What if there are no

caribou? What if I can't find anything to bring back to you?"

"Oh, but you will, Anâna. You will."

———

Walking among the trees, every step Maia takes feels weightless. Back in her element, she closes her eyes, brushing her fingers along the mossy trunks as she weaves between the trees. She feels at one with them, sensing their presence like the limbs of her body. Their whispers wash over her like sweet hymns of the Earth.

"Hello, old friends," she whispers.

It wasn't that long ago Maia was pushing her way through these very trees as they chanted repeated warnings of danger. She was lost, in more ways than one. Her world had been split open, torn apart. But now she has been set free, made anew. She was taken in by strangers and given a second chance. She only has to complete this one final mission, and she will be on her way.

The tribe has graciously resupplied her pack, given her new clothing, and refurbished her boots. She now has a solar watch and a handmade eye mask to wear each "night" to ensure a better sleep. Tema said her hunt could take weeks, and that it is imperative that she *trust the journey*—a saying she has admitted disdain for on more than one occasion. But Tema keeps reminding her anyway. Maia cannot control finding the caribou any more than she can control the new direction her life has taken.

Oh yeah, and something about a raven.

Maia walks along the narrow path leading to the west

of the mountains. Every day is the same: wandering up and down trails, searching for hoof marks and scat. She refuses to use her powers to call the caribou to her. If she's going to take a life, it will be a life she is worthy of taking.

That evening she sits down in front of a fire, ripping the feathers from a duck she shot with an arrow. It felt amazing shooting again. A great horned owl lands on a branch above, his yellow eyes like saucers. Maia stops. She's never seen this owl outside her dreams. She can't help but smile. Just like her nightmares, the majestic bird seems to have a permanent scowl across his face.

She wonders if the wolves will come back around now that she's out on her own, or even her tiger. But so far, she remains alone. The last time she sat alone beside a fire in the wilderness, she was carrying the weight of the world, so afraid of who she was. How different she was just a short time ago ... and yet, if she's being completely honest, a small part of her still feels the same. The ache inside her heart still lingers. She still misses Miguel and Lucas so much it hurts.

Letting go is not a process set in stone.

———

The following morning, Maia wakes early and continues on her way. Another day passes, and then another, but she does not give up hope. It feels so natural being out in the wild. She could stay out here forever, caribou or not, but Tema has told her the trip to Leucothea is just a few short weeks along the river. She's come too far to become complacent.

Walking along the trail, Maia catches a new scent in the breeze. New sounds, too, just below the hill where she stands. She crouches in the tall grasses, slowly inching toward the edge.

Just below, in a grassy field surrounded by forest, are a few hundred caribou.

Her eyes widen. Right there—her ticket to Leucothea is *right there*. The low sun streams across the meadow, highlighting clouds of the animals' breath in the cool mountain air. Their antlers are majestic, surprisingly on the heads of both males and females. They do not sound at all how she thought. Their repeated grunts sound more like a hog.

She carefully slides her bow before her and pulls out an arrow.

Something snaps loudly in the distance—a large twig or a branch—and the caribous' heads snap up. They stand frozen, their ears flipping forward and back as they listen for the predator. A wolf, maybe? Maia scans the far edge of the field but can't see anything. She shifts her focus back to the caribou—one in particular standing on the outskirts of the herd—and draws back her string.

There it is again, the same noise from something in the woods. The caribou look back at the sound, their necks stretching long as they rear up on their hind legs. Another twig breaks, and a large black bird lifts in flight, surprising both Maia and the herd. The bird carves chaotic circles into the sky, cawing as it soars.

A raven.

The caribou run. Maia races along the hilltop, following the stampede, and nocks her arrow. This is her chance; if she doesn't shoot now, she'll lose the caribou and a great deal of time. She focuses on a male at the end of the herd.

And then the creature responsible for the commotion steps from the tree line and into the sun.

Maia skids to a stop, squinting across the field. A lone man walks along the brush, his hands at his head as he watches the herd running in the opposite direction. Two water canisters hang at his side. He has tribal tattoos covering his left arm down to his wrist. The tattoos along his right arm stop just below his elbow.

Maia lowers her bow.

The caribou race toward the edge of the field and scatter between the trees. The man turns away, revealing long dreadlocks tied behind his back.

Miguel.

He disappears into the hazy forest.

Without a second's hesitation, she drops her bow and races down the hill. "MIGUEL!" she screams, barreling down the cliff, her arms circling at her sides. She races past a flock of birds, and they lift in flight with a great deal of fuss. "Miguel! *Stop!*" she screams, a wave of panic fluttering within. She's going to lose him—*again*.

Her pack feels like an anchor. She wriggles free of it midstride, and it rolls into the grass. She keeps running, waving her arms and screaming.

Miguel steps out from the trees with his hand at his brow. He squints at her.

She gasps. *Yes.*

He steps forward—he sees her.

YES.

"Maia?!" he shouts.

"*Miguel!*"

He drops his water canisters and races toward her across the field. When she reaches him, she leaps into his arms and wraps herself around him.

"You're alive," he gasps, burying his head in her neck. "Thank God, you're alive."

Panting, she drops her head against his, and they hold each other for a while.

"Are you okay?" he whispers between breaths. He lowers her to the ground. "My *God*, I've missed you."

Lost for words, she gazes up at this rugged man with such a beautiful soul. She felt so strong just moments ago. Now, looking up at him gazing down at her, she feels like she could crumble to pieces all over again.

"I don't know what to say..." He shakes his head. "I can't tell you how worried I've been. I looked everywhere for you. Are you..." He looks her up and down. "Are you okay? Are you hurt—"

"I'm okay," she says.

He grabs her hands. "*Look* at you."

"Look at *you*," she says. His right eye is swollen and purple, there's a small cut on his cheekbone, and his lower lip is busted. "Are you okay? What happened to you?"

"*Lucas*," he says bitterly.

"Oh my God, *Lucas*!" She looks around. "Is he—*where*?"

"We split up. I mean, we're together, but he's out hunting with the bow. I'm supposed to be finding water."

She blinks. "You guys are ... *together*?"

He sighs. "After our fight, it didn't take long for me to realize losing you would be the biggest mistake of my life, so I raced back to the river, but you weren't there. So then

I went back to our camp to wait for you. When neither of you showed up, I decided to make my way north, hoping I'd catch up with you somewhere along the way. I traveled on my own for a long time after that. Eventually, I found Lucas camped by the side of the road. He was in a state. When he told me he left you by the river and you were out in the wilderness on your own, we ... had words."

She narrows her gaze. "*Words*."

"Yes." He shrugs. "With our fists."

"Oh, *Miguel*."

"We're okay now. We aren't the same, but we're okay." He shakes his head. "I just can't believe you're standing here before me. I was starting to believe I'd never see you again."

She gazes down at their hands clasped tightly together. If only they could stay like this forever.

"Maia, I'm so sorry I demanded you choose between us. I just ... I became so *desperate*. I couldn't imagine spending another day not being able to hold you. Not being able to kiss you or call you mine."

"Miguel, before you say anything else, there's something I need to say." She pulls her hands from his grasp.

"Okay." He blows out a breath and takes a step back.

"Living my life without you would leave a *gaping* hole in my heart." She swallows hard and looks up at him through the blur of her tears. "But I can live with that loss. I know this now. *You* taught me that by leaving me. Living my life without Lucas would also cause me a tremendous amount of pain, but I could live with that too. It would be horrible, but I'd be okay."

He stares at her, his face burdened with worry.

"But leaving Lucas for his only brother, the *only* family he has left in this world, no matter how much I..." She chokes on her words, and he looks away. "No matter how I feel about you ... *That* I could not live with. It's just who I am. You must understand, I could never betray him like that."

He won't look at her. His eyes are glassy, and he glares across the field.

"You were wrong about us, Miguel. I do love him."

This makes him look. "I know," he says.

"And he loves me too," she says.

"Look, I didn't say what I said to lie to you. I said it because I know there will *never* be another soul in this world who will ever love you as much as I do—not even him."

She bites her trembling lip.

"You're my soulmate, Maia. I never believed in that stuff before, but now ... now I have never been more sure about anything. I keep racking my brain, trying to understand how two people like us can be brought together but can't *be* together. It's not right. In my heart, I know you're my person. I *know* it. And yet ... somehow it isn't meant to be."

She drops her head in her hands, and every ache she's shoved deep inside her gut cuts through her again.

"Come here." He pulls her into him, wrapping his arms around her. "I don't want to be the cause of any more of your pain. So I'll back down." He rests his cheek on her head, holding her as she cries. "But I will never stop loving you. I will never stop praying that somehow, life will bring you back to me."

She inhales, wrestling an ocean of grief inside her heart. *Back?* Did he just say ... back?

He peers across the field. "I suppose we should grab your things. I'll take you back to our camp, and you can fill me in on your life."

He steps away, and she grabs his hand. "Miguel?"

He hesitates, taking a breath before facing her again.

She looks up into those brown eyes that she loves so fiercely. "I didn't mean it, what I said back at the river," she says. "I do ... I *do*..."

"I know."

Love you. She should say it. She wants to more than anything, but she can't. No good can come from it.

He places his hand on her cheek, and she closes her eyes as he wipes away her tears. He sighs. "I really want to kiss you right now."

"Please ... *don't*," she whispers.

"I won't. But I'll remember that kiss for the rest of my life."

FORTY-FOUR

Back on the road, Maia and Miguel walk side by side. It feels so surreal having him beside her again. She peers up at him, wanting to smile. Wanting to cry. Wanting to touch him but holding back. So many thoughts racing through her mind. She's with Miguel. She's about to be reunited with Lucas. What will happen next?

Miguel said *back.*

He slows, sighing heavily, and nods behind her. "Our camp is just through those trees. I'm..." He sighs again, like he's finding it hard to breathe. "I'm going to let you two talk. I still need to find water."

"Okay." She reaches out to him. He looks at her hand but does not hold it. Wounded, she pulls back and holds it against her chest.

This is torture. She doesn't know how to act around him. He steps forward and slowly unwraps her hand from the trembling bundle at her chest. Closing his eyes, he kisses the tops of her fingers. Then without speaking another word, he turns and walks away.

Maia watches him trek down the road, feeling like her heart's being ripped from her chest. She's losing him all over again. It occurs to her now how she became so destroyed, and a small part of her wishes she would have never picked up that caribou scent. For a brief moment, she had found peace.

She steps into the forest. She doesn't know what awaits her as she walks toward the men's camp, but she knows nothing will ever be the same. Wafts of smoke drift between the trees, and she follows the scent. Approaching their camp, she finds Lucas crouched next to a fire with his back toward her. A few dead rabbits lie in the dirt at his side.

"I found us some critters," he mumbles without turning around.

"That's good," she says.

His head snaps up, and he slowly stands and turns around. Tears fill his eyes. "*Maia?*"

He looks awful. Whatever fury he unleashed on Miguel was met with equal, if not more, lashes upon himself. His hair has grown out, his beard too. Maia remains planted in place, all her sadness and anger and love for this man coursing through her at once.

He rushes up to her and wraps his arms around her, sobbing and speaking Portuguese. She yearns to hold him, but all she can think about are the last words he said to her.

He pulls back, confused. "Maia—"

"I am *not* ... a *monster*," she says.

His eyes widen. "I didn't mean it! I can't believe I said

that—I didn't mean it!" He grabs her shoulders. "I was just so angry ... and *hurt*."

"You *left* me!"

"I came back! I came back for you, but you were gone! I searched for you everywhere—"

"*When*?!" She tears away from him. "When did you come back for me? I sat beside that shore for *ages*. Then I went back to camp and waited there—"

"We must've missed each other somehow ... I don't know how. I walked along the road at first, but coming back, I took the exact same trail we always took."

"I took the road," she says.

"See?! I came back for you, Maia. I could never leave you."

"But you did! You left me! You swore you were done running—we made that promise to each other. Is that the sort of man you are? Still running when things get tough? I nearly died out there, Lucas!"

He wipes the tears from his eyes, but says nothing.

"Yes, Miguel kissed me and I didn't stop him and I'm sorry for that. I am so *sorry,* Lucas! But the harsh reality is I *have* developed feelings for him. *Strong* feelings."

He walks away with his hands on his head.

"But I would have never acted on them! I love you, Lucas. You have to know it would have never gone any further than that kiss."

"I know," he says quietly, staring at the fire. "Miguel told me you fought against it. He told me he was the one who made the first move." He turns toward her, tears coating his cheeks. "He *also* told me how he feels about you. I'm not blind—I know you feel the same. I could see it every time you looked at him." His eyes harden. "Just what am I supposed to do with that?"

She stands before him, silently sobbing. "I don't know," she breathes, and a cavern of silence fills the small space between them.

The anger on his face softens. "You nearly *died*?"

She glares at him, nodding once.

"I will *never* forgive myself for leaving you." He slowly walks toward her. "Down by the river ... I saw red. I was inconsolable. I've never felt anger like that before, seeing you two together. Seeing you kiss..." He closes his eyes, and she holds her hand against her mouth. He looks broken, a ghost of the man she once knew.

"Look, what's done is done," he says. "Miguel and I can get over this. We *will* get over this—we're family. But what I cannot get over is losing you. I saw what was happening between you and Miguel, and I didn't say anything. I didn't stop it. I didn't fight for you. But I'm fighting for you now."

She blinks.

"I love you, Maia, with all my heart. You brought me back to life. And even though it hasn't been an easy life since meeting you, I would still choose it, again and again. Please, give us another chance. I know things have changed. I know you have feelings for Miguel. I know this complicates the hell out of everything. But I can't go down without a fight—I *won't*. You are my life. If you decide to be with him, then there's nothing I can do. But I won't have you choose him because I've stepped aside. I'm not going anywhere," he says quietly. "That is, if you'll have me."

She stares at the ground, remembering the first time

he uttered those same words to her before they made love on their raft.

He sighs, and he takes her hands. "You have a choice. As much as I can't imagine living without you, I also know I could never share my life with someone knowing her heart belonged to someone else."

But her heart *does* belong to someone else. No matter what happens, she will always be torn between brothers. It's not possible to make a decision and not be broken from it. So, she must choose the option that will cause the least amount of heartbreak.

And hope it's the right one.

"Maia, do you remember when we were on that raft in the flood zone of LA? You had just jumped off Jake's ship, and you told me there were two things you knew without a shadow of a doubt. You said the Old Arctic Circle was your destiny. And?"

She looks up at him. "And..."

He waits.

She remembers now—of course she remembers. "And so are *you*," she whispers.

"*Yes*." He wraps his arms around her. "We'll get through this. I know we will. There's nothing we can't do, as long as we're together."

She lays her head on his chest, and they embrace in silence under the thick awning of the trees.

Miguel walks up with his canisters of water, and Lucas and Maia pull away. The anguish on Miguel's face is unmistakable. His eyes meet hers, pleading without words. "Are you two ... *okay*?" he asks.

"We're okay," Lucas says.

Miguel does not look relieved.

Lucas doesn't waste a second. "So what do we do? About the three of us traveling."

"I don't ... I can't—" Miguel stutters.

"Why don't I take you two back to the tribe?" Maia says. "I have a debt to sort, and you need food and sleep ... and a *bath*."

That last comment manages to drag a smile across both the men's faces.

———

While hiking back to the tribe, Miguel, Lucas, and Maia spend the next few days filling each other in on what transpired while they were apart. While it's weird at first, their short time together seems to soften the wounds that plague them. Despite the hurt and betrayal, they seem to be relieved to be back together, wanting so desperately to move on from the dark hole they had fallen into.

But Maia and Lucas still haven't kissed, and Maia and Miguel barely look at one another. Nothing is as it was, and it may never be again.

Letting go is not a process set in stone.

FORTY-FIVE

When Maia, Lucas, and Miguel arrive at the tribe, hardly a word has been spoken between them all day. It's clear the men are exhausted, but they have pushed on in silence.

Maia's not surprised to see Tema waiting for them at the gates. "Is this our welcome committee?" she asks as they approach.

"I knew you were coming," Tema says, and she tilts her gaze. "No caribou?"

Maia looks down. "I let them go."

"Good girl," Tema says, surprising her. The old woman glances behind her at Lucas and Miguel. She leans in and whispers, "But I see you have brought with you a pair of *strapping* young lads."

Maia forces a smile. She nods once, keeping her gaze on her boots.

Tema places her hand on Maia's shoulder. "Anâna?"

Her eyes flicker to Tema's.

"So *distracted*," Tema says, clicking her tongue.

"Remember, child, *why* you are here." She flashes her a knowing smile.

Maia wraps her arms around her. "I've missed you."

"Me too," she whispers, squeezing Maia's shoulders, and then she pushes her way between Lucas and Miguel. She links her arms through theirs and looks up at them with a mischievous grin. "Come, come," she says with a chuckle. "Let's get some food in those bellies." She leads the men, this little gray-haired lady half their height, and Maia follows, smiling despite herself.

Later that night, Lucas and Maia are in her hut, alone for the first time since Christmas. Unsurprisingly, Tema has offered her spare bedroom to Miguel. "An old woman can dream," she whispered to Maia before retiring to bed.

Lucas and Maia are lying on their sides, looking at one another in silence.

"I don't know what to say," she whispers.

"Don't say anything." He pulls her into him and kisses her. She kisses him back, wrapping herself around him as he softly drags his lips down her neck.

Her eyes flicker open. Staring at the dreamcatcher above her bed, she focuses on the crisscrossing weave, trying desperately to ignore the fact that something once familiar in their kiss is no longer there.

The tribe has welcomed Lucas and Miguel with open arms. Of course, this is probably because they came with

Maia. Chayanne has remained distant, often shooting the men a reproachful look from the corner of her eye, but Shinesho has taken a particular liking to Miguel. And Shinesho, Maia has since learned, is the leader of their army. A great warrior. His lineage traces back to a tribe from the Amazon floodplains, back when they were a rainforest.

Watching Shinesho and Miguel together is like watching old friends. They spend most of their days with one another, often walking around sharing stories, practicing bo fighting, and hunting. Shinesho is also teaching Miguel about his blowguns—or so Maia has heard. She refuses to go anywhere near the things.

Some of the tribe's younger women have also noticed Miguel, which is unsurprising. Maia has to force herself to look away as they giggle a little too loud, gazing up at him and nonchalantly touching his arms.

Maia has made her choice. She is loyal to Lucas. She loves him and he loves her. They just need to move forward from this nightmare and they'll be okay. She's not ready to give up on him. She can't—she *won't*. They used to be very happy together. They will be again...

But Maia is always watching Miguel.

She hasn't been able to talk to him with Lucas constantly by her side, but it's been really nice seeing him laugh again. Lucas, too. They say time heals. Every day that passes is a gift. Maybe there's still hope for the three of them. Is it incredibly naïve to hope?

Maia and Lucas sit together on a wooden picnic table beside the defense building's field. Miguel and the children have set up football nets—although some people are calling it soccer. Maia doesn't care. Whatever it's called, they're kicking a black and white ball around the field and trying to get it into the goals.

The tribe's chief is also sitting with them. Lucas has had his back toward Maia the entire afternoon as he and the chief chat away about things Maia finds incredibly boring.

She leans across the table, resting her head on her hands. Lost in a daze, she follows Miguel's every move. He tilts back his head, laughing as the children run in circles around him. He kicks the ball across the field, and the children run screaming after it. Leaning over, he rests his hands on his knees and catches his breath. Maia sighs.

"We'll be right back," Lucas says beside her.

"*Uh-huh*," she says as he and the chief step away. "No worries."

Miguel glances over his shoulder, locking eyes with her across the field. He stands, facing her. His gaze is strong—blatant. *I see you.* Butterflies flutter inside her chest, but she does not look away.

A child runs up, tackling Miguel from behind. He playfully falls to his knees in defeat, and the children surround him, climbing on top of him while giggling and screaming.

This is so adorable, she can't stand to watch. Looking down at the bracelet still tied around her wrist, she fights the urge to rip it off. Lucas says he doesn't want it anymore. Why is she even wearing it?

Because Miguel made it.

Much later that evening, Lucas and Maia are lying in bed with their blackout curtains drawn, their little room lit by flickering candlelight. Maia has her head on his chest, her arms wrapped around him. Lucas has been so strong, allowing his love for her to overrule his jealousy. Although, it is a little concerning how little he's left her side. It's been good for them to spend so much time together, but Maia can't help feeling a little nervous that this will only contribute to his already strong urge to control things.

"I think it's time to move on," she says, propping herself on her elbow.

"I agree. We're so close, and the days are already becoming shorter," Lucas says.

She falls onto her back, looking up at the ceiling. "The tribe has given us a boat, but we can't just take it. I need to go back and hunt a caribou. That was the deal."

"I'll go with you. We need to get away just the two of us anyway. It'll be romantic."

They both laugh.

"Yes, *so* romantic," she deadpans.

"Hey, I have something for you," Lucas says, sitting up. He leans across the bed and reaches for the bedside table drawer. "First, you must close your eyes. *Por favor,* my love."

She sits up and closes her eyes.

"Hold out your hands."

She does as he says, and Lucas places something light and rubbery inside. "Okay, open them," he says.

She opens her eyes and gasps as a bright yellow duck looks up at her. "Oh, *Lucas.*"

"I found it back in LA, to replace the one we lost on

our raft. I've been waiting for the right time to give it to you."

She cups his cheek. "You're sweet."

"I'm always thinking of you."

The yard outside the hut has become blanketed in a soothing chorus of crickets. Maia peels back the sheets and tiptoes across the room to peek behind the curtains. She glances over her shoulder at Lucas, a smile curving.

"What is it?" he asks.

She turns to face him, sighing in relief. "Darkness."

Early the next day, Maia is alone in her hut packing up their things when there's a knock at the door.

Tema peeks her head in. "Anâna?"

"Come in, come in!" she says with a smile.

Tema hobbles in and latches the door closed behind her. Maia continues packing, trying to ignore the serious look Tema has on her face.

"Lucas told me you are preparing to go back out and hunt a caribou," the old woman says.

Maia faces her. "I am. We can't accept your umiak without giving you something in return. I'm happy to do it. I should be back within a couple of weeks."

"That's not necessary. You are ready to go to Leucothea. The men are preparing your umiak. You will leave today."

Another knock at the door.

"Come in!" Maia shouts, and Miguel steps into the room. "But ... Tema," Maia says. "I can't take that boat without giving you something."

JILLIAN WEBSTER

"Ah, my dear," Tema says gently. "You *have*."

Maia narrows her eyes. "I'm confused."

"Am I interrupting something?" Miguel asks. He points a thumb at the door. "I can come back."

Tema flashes Maia a saddened smile and leaves without speaking another word.

"Hey." Maia smiles awkwardly at Miguel, dropping a pair of socks into her pack. "I swear that woman should come with an instruction manual."

He sucks in his lips, sighing heavily through his nose.

She freezes. That's not a good look. "What is it?"

"I hear you're leaving," he says quietly. "I've come to say..." He hesitates, gazing at her with bloodshot eyes. "I'm not coming with you."

"*What*? No—*why*?!"

"I can't. I'm sorry, but I can't. I need to find my own way now."

Tears line her eyes, panic rising within. "Miguel ... please—"

"The tribe has given me an open invitation to stay, so that's what I'll do until I figure out my next steps. I'm ... *happy* here. And I can't ... I can't..." He looks away, frustrated. "I can't go with you."

She looks out the window, biting her lip.

"Please, tell me you understand," he says quietly. "You *must* understand."

She looks back at him, swallowing hard. "I understand," she whispers, quickly wiping a tear.

He stares at her for a long time without speaking, his eyes weary and broken. "I need to move on. You have Lucas, and I'm happy for you."

"No you're not."

"*Of course* I'm not!" he snaps. "But I need to find my own—"

"How am I supposed to live without you?!" she shouts.

He glares at her incredulously. "Don't you *dare*."

She shakes her head, fighting her sobs. "Will I ever ... see you ... again?" she chokes out.

"Lucas is my brother. I'll be in your life forever, Maia. I just need to be in it in a way that also brings *me* peace. And as hard as I try, I cannot find it. Not now—not yet."

She nods, sighing, and dries her cheeks with her hands and then wipes her hands on her shirt ... Looking around, distracting herself, desperate to hold on to her composure. To stop herself from falling to her knees and begging—

"*Please*, Maia," he says. "Please give me your blessing. At least give me that," he pleads.

She feels sick to her stomach. "I understand. It would be wholeheartedly selfish of me to ask you to stay with us knowing you're unhappy. I was foolish to believe it could have been any different." She steps before him, wanting to touch him, to hold him one last time. She reaches for him with a trembling hand.

He flinches. "Please," he says, closing his eyes. "Don't."

She drops her hand to her side and sobs.

"Please don't do that, either." He grabs her hand, pulling her into him and wrapping his arms around her.

She clasps her hands behind his back. She won't let go. Don't ever make her let go. "Promise me you'll visit?" she sobs into his chest. "Miguel? *Swear to me* that I'll see you again."

He pushes away and places his hand on his heart. "I

promise you, Maia. I swear to you with *my life*, you will see me again."

"When? How?"

"Once you're settled in Leucothea. I'll visit you."

"What if you can't find me?" she whispers.

"I'll *find* you. I promise, I'll find you."

"When?"

"What is it now—early autumn? By next winter, just a little over a year from now, you will see me again. I've been told it still snows up here, so just wait for the second year's snowfall, and I'll be there."

"That's a long time, Miguel."

"That's all I have to give."

Maia nods, lost for words. Even if she had them, there would be nothing left to say.

FORTY-SIX

Lucas and Maia step before Tema, the chief, Shinesho, and Chayanne. The tribe's iron gates tower behind them, and their two bloated packs are propped against a tree. The air is crisp, cool. A faint breeze rustles the branches above while pine needles crunch beneath their boots.

Lucas steps forward, shaking the chief's hand. As they speak, Maia glances again behind Shinesho through the gates.

He leans toward her. "He *uh* ... he couldn't make it," he says quietly. "But he said you two already said your goodbyes."

She steps back, nodding quickly as that old familiar ache stabs from within. The faster they can get away from here, the faster she can shove everything back down again. She's gotten really good at that.

Tema hugs Lucas and then turns to face Maia. The old woman places her soft hand on Maia's cheek. "My sweet Anâna. Go forth. You have the blessings of the gods. You will do great things. I look forward to the day I see you again."

Maia hugs the little old lady. "Thank you, Tema, for everything."

She chuckles that same endearing chuckle. "No, Maia, thank *you*," she whispers, her eyes gleaming with tears.

Chayanne steps forward. Maia reaches out and Chayanne throws her arms around her. Maia grunts in surprise, then smiles.

"I'm really going to miss you, friend," Chayanne whispers.

"Come visit?" Maia asks as they pull away.

"Shoot. *You* come visit. We've got the better spot," Chayanne says with a wink. She rubs the side of Maia's arm.

Maia swallows back her tears. "Deal."

A few men bring over Lucas's and Maia's packs and help guide them over their shoulders. They simultaneously click the waist straps closed.

Lucas reaches for her. "Ready?"

She takes his hand. "I am."

Together, four men lift the umiak onto their shoulders, and the small group sets off down the tribe's gravel road leading to the river.

Down by the shore, the men place the boat at the water's edge.

"Okay," Shinesho says, handing Lucas a map. "This is the best guide we have with the river so swollen. We've re-outlined the new route from when this map was printed, but it's been a long time since anyone has taken the entire course to the ocean. There are some rapids, one big one in particular that should be somewhere around this red circle." He points at the map. "But, again, no one has been that far in a really long time. Just tackle it like we've discussed, and you should be okay."

"How long until we arrive at the ocean?" Maia asks.

"Hard to say," Shinesho says, scratching his chin. "Two weeks? Depends on the weather and how much time you take for camping and sleeping. Leucothea is just around the bend from where you come out. You can't miss it. Oh, and darkness will be coming quickly now, so don't waste any time."

"Thank you," Lucas says, shaking Shinesho's hand.

"It's been our pleasure. We hope to see you both again. You're always welcome." He nods at Maia with a smile.

The men hold the boat in place while Lucas sets their packs between the benches. He steps inside, then helps Maia climb in. The boat wobbles as she takes her seat, and the men push them into the middle of the river. Maia picks up her paddle, and Lucas does the same.

"Hey." He turns around with a smile on his face. "Here we are again, back in a boat."

She shakes her head. "Here's hoping it goes smoother than the last few times."

"Let's just say if you decide to jump off this one, you won't have to go far."

She can't help laughing. They sit in silence, sharing smiles as the water's current begins to pull them down the river. Her Brazilian pirate. Things are going to be okay. Things are going to be okay because they *have* to be okay.

"Are you nervous?" he asks.

"A little. You?"

"A little. Oh! I nearly forgot." He reaches into his pocket and pulls out the yellow rubber duck. "We should secure this to the front of our umiak." He smiles. "For good luck—" His eyes cut behind Maia to the shore, and the smile drops from his face. Lifting his hand, he waves once.

Maia turns around. Miguel is stepping into the shoreline, panting. His eyes bore into her, and she fights the urge to stand. He places his hand on his heart and nods a single solemn nod. *I swear to you.* Her chin quivers. His face is the last thing she sees before the current pulls them around the bend.

Gripping the sides of the small boat, she's finding it hard to breathe. When she twists back around again, Lucas is staring at her. Add this to the arsenal of looks he has given her since she's known him. What is plaguing his face? Guilt? Sadness? There's no point explaining what just happened, so she stays quiet. His eyes flicker down, and he turns around, setting the duck beside him on the bench. He plunges his paddle into the water and aggressively heaves the boat forward.

She dips her paddle into the water and pushes against the river. With every stroke she takes, she shoves her ache down into that dark space inside her soul. Keep moving forward—this was the deal from the beginning. There are no other options.

She isn't as excited to get to Leucothea as she once was, but the fact still remains that it is her destiny. She knows this with every fiber of her being. Her nerves tingle at what may await. It was good she thought it was a haven for so long—that belief alone gave her the strength to carry on. What happens next, there's no way of knowing. She can only take this last leg of her journey one day at a time.

Their little umiak cruises down the center of the river. After all this time traveling by foot and watching for bounders and mobs around every bend, this is a beautiful change of scenery. The currents are somewhat fast at this point, leaving little to do but steer and take in their new surroundings.

The forest on either side is dense. A bald eagle perches high up on a branch, and a few deer lap at the river's edge. The animals lift their heads, eyeing Lucas and Maia as they float by.

There's something following them in the woods. Maia catches a streak of orange between the trunks and relief blooms in her chest. After all this time, her tiger is still with her.

Maia and Lucas pull their umiak into a stony bend to set up camp for the night. It's been an incredibly peaceful handful of days on the river, which has been good for them. Lucas drags the boat onto the shore and then lifts their packs out, dropping them beside Maia. She gathers some wood and stacks a pile on the stones, then lifts her hand above the timber. The fire roars to life.

"I've been meaning to ask about that," Lucas says, standing behind her. "Did you ever use your powers around the tribe?"

"No," she says with a sigh. "I'm not sure people would understand."

"But Tema knew?"

She looks at him over her shoulder. "Oh, Tema knew."

They both smile.

"So, we must be getting pretty close. Shall we talk about a plan?" He sits next to her by the fire.

"What do you mean?" she asks.

"Once we get to Leucothea. Surely it can't just be to find a community and settle down. We've had that opportunity a few times now and left."

"I don't know." She leans against a log. "I certainly still want those things, but I won't know why I've been called to Leucothea until I get there."

"I've heard some worrying rumors about the place from the chief," Lucas says, adding more wood to the fire. "Nothing specific, but it doesn't sound promising."

"Yeah, I know," she says. "I've gotten that same impression. Are you still okay going?"

"Where you go, I go."

"But do you *want* to go? Do you still want to be out here with me?"

He gazes up at her. "More than anything."

Darkness falls, and Lucas unrolls their sleeping bags beside the fire while Maia strings the noisemakers she made back at the tribe around their camp. Lucas sits on the ground with his back against the umiak, and she plops down in front of him, leaning between his legs. He wraps his arms around her.

"Do you think we should talk?" she asks.

"What about?"

"You know what about. We haven't really talked about what happened with Miguel."

"I just want to move forward, Maia—move on. Time heals all wounds." He rests his chin on her shoulder. "I have you back in my arms again. Miguel said he'll visit. That's all that matters."

———

The next morning, the skies are still dark. Lucas and Maia sit beside the fire, drinking hot tea and nibbling the last of the caribou jerky gifted by the tribe.

"How close do you think these rapids are?" she asks with a yawn.

"I assume by our map that we must be approaching them soon. Maybe today? We'll definitely want daylight to navigate them."

"And we'll be in them for a while?"

"No, but they're apparently quite treacherous," he says.

She sips her tea. "What about getting out and carrying the boat around?"

"Could do." He nods. "But the land around there is dense and unruly. Without a machete or a rope to haul the boat up and down cliffs, it will add a significant amount of time to our trip. Plus, we're so close to Leucothea, we risk running into mobs."

"*Ugh*, no," she says. "Let's just take our chances on the river."

"Agreed."

With the sun lingering just below the horizon, Lucas and Maia put out their fire and gather up their things, placing them inside the boat. Lucas ties the packs to the inside benches and wraps a few precious supplies and their first aid kit in dry bags the tribe gave them.

They stand next to their little umiak, holding hands.

"Are you ready?" she asks.

"We can tackle anything, the two of us. I know this without a doubt. Just take it one step at a time, yes?" he says.

She nods.

"We'll take the rapids in small bits," he says. "Every time there's a calm area along the shore, we'll aim our umiak for that so we can take a breath and make a plan for the next part."

"Right, an eddy. I remember," she says.

"You'll be in front, so you'll be in the best position to look for the *V* formed between the white waves, where the water is darkest," he says. "It'll be the deepest part of the river to try to aim the umiak."

"Got it."

Together they drag their umiak to the water's edge. Maia steps inside, shuffling to the front bench as the boat rocks from side to side. Lucas pushes them out a little farther and climbs in.

Their boat is grabbed by the currents and begins cruising down the river. The tension is high. Glancing around, they try to pick up clues as to when the rapids may start.

When they turn around another bend, they no longer have to guess.

FORTY-SEVEN

Up ahead, the river has expanded from another two rivers feeding into it. The once placid blue waters are now white and angry, with small waterfalls coursing over fallen trees and clusters of boulders.

Lucas and Maia's little umiak rocks back and forth, gathering speed.

"This is it!" he yells from behind.

Her heart is pounding, and water splashes across her face. She presses her knees together and pushes her feet against the sides of the boat to steady herself.

"Maia!" Lucas shouts. "Eddy! To the right!"

She sees it. Together, they paddle across the rapids to the calm patch of water. Their boat spins behind a large boulder, and Lucas grabs a tree branch to hold them in place.

"Remember, don't worry about the entire course!" Lucas shouts. "We just need to cross the river in patches.

Look." He points across the surging waters. "Just paddle like crazy until we get to that other eddy."

Maia blows out a breath. "Okay!"

"*Vamos!*"

They plunge their paddles into the water, and the umiak heaves forward. The currents slam into them, carrying them much quicker than Maia anticipated. The front of their umiak strikes a boulder and the boat swings to the side, spinning them backward down the rapids. They cruise past the eddy.

"Turn around!" Lucas shouts. He heaves his paddle into the water, and their boat swings around.

Up ahead, a mammoth pine tree has fallen across the river.

"Maia! Paddle to the left!"

She looks to the left. A small eddy swirls in a cove beside the tree, but with the rate their boat is cruising down the rapids, they'll never make it. She has to do something. The large trunk is dead—no longer rooted to the earth. She'll have no power over it. She chucks her paddle behind her.

"Maia?! What are you doing?"

She slides off her seat to the bottom of the boat and hooks her feet beneath the bench. They're coming up fast; she doesn't have much time. Holding her trembling hands before her, she focuses on the water surging around the tree. She cries out, commanding the river to heave against it, slowly pushing it out of the river. A wall of water forms beneath it.

"Maia!" Lucas screams. "What's happening?!"

"*Duck!*" she screams. "Lucas! Duck down!" She falls onto her back, using all her strength to hold the tree above them as their boat skims beneath, soaking them in the wall of water. Her hands drop behind her and the tree crashes down, pushing their umiak on a wave.

"*Ahh*!" Lucas screams behind her. "Oh my God, *Maia*!"

She lies on her back, laughing at the sky.

"It's not over!" he shouts.

Lightheaded, she grabs the sides of the umiak and sits up. It takes a moment for her to gather her bearings. Lucas grunts behind her as he steers the boat against the rapids, and they soar down a small waterfall. The tip of the umiak crashes into the water, sending a wave of white across them. Maia shakes her head from the assault, searching the boat for her paddle. Water has filled half their umiak, but their bags remain tied. She grabs her paddle and crawls to her seat.

"Oh ... *God*," she gasps.

The river ahead has vanished beyond a heavy cloud of mist.

"Waterfall!" Lucas screams.

Within seconds, the tip of their umiak hurdles over the edge, and the river disappears beneath them. Maia reaches for the boat, but it slips from her grasp and she falls through the air, slamming into the water below. The surging river twists her body beneath the water like a rag doll.

Breaking the white surface, she gasps. "Lucas!" The water smashes into her, and she wipes her hair from her eyes. "*Lucas*!" She spots him swimming toward their overturned boat, and she paddles toward him.

He grabs hold of the umiak. "Maia!" he shouts, looking around.

"Behind you!" she says.

He glances over his shoulder and sighs in relief as she swims up beside him. They hold tight onto the upside-down boat and rest their heads against it, looking at one another in shock as the river carries them away from the rapids and into calmer waters.

She dips her head beneath the water to survey the damage. The boat's still intact, but they've lost a pack. She comes up for air, looking around in a panic.

"What is it?" he asks.

"We lost a pack."

He lays his head on the boat again, saying nothing.

"There's a beach ahead," she says. "Let's get out and dry off."

Each grabbing a side, they grunt as they heave the umiak out of the river, then collapse onto their stomachs in the sand. Panting and soaking wet, they catch their breath, staring at one another not speaking a word. The air is cold, but with the shock of it all, Maia doesn't feel a thing.

Lucas grins. His chuckle grows louder until he rolls onto his back, laughing so hard he can't breathe.

"What on earth, Lucas."

"We made it! Maia, we *made it*!" He throws his fists to the sky. "That was the worst part!"

"We lost a pack."

"But we still have our boat! And we're *alive*. Thanks to you!" He leans on his side and reaches for her. "I knew you could do it."

She smiles. "Thank you for believing in me."

"I've always believed in you, Maia. Always."

"I know you have." She rolls herself upward and glances at the boat. "We lost our rubber duck … *again*."

"Yes, I think we're done with those," he mumbles. "Nothing but trouble."

She laughs. "Probably should get a fire start—"

That's when she sees it. A pool of red has spread in the sand around Lucas's right calf. His pant leg is torn and soaked in blood.

"Oh my God, Lucas," she breathes.

"*Mmm*?"

"You're hurt."

"What?" He flips onto his back, gazing up at his hands, and he sits up. "No, I'm—" He sucks in a breath. "*Merda*."

He peels back his tattered pant leg, revealing an open gash on his calf—his skin and muscle torn down to the bone. The adrenaline from the rapids must've numbed his pain.

"*Meu Deus*," he whispers.

"Oh, Lucas." She covers her mouth.

He looks at her, his eyes wide in alarm. "Do we have our first aid kit? Is that in the pack we still have?"

She gazes at him, defeated, and shakes her head.

"This is bad. This is *really* bad," he says, his voice shaking.

She slides closer to him, tenderly touching the peeling skin. He flinches. He's going to bleed out. They're so close to Leucothea, and he's going to bleed out.

"Fix it, Maia. Can't you fix it?"

She looks up at him in shock. "*How*?! How am I supposed to fix this?"

"You just lifted a massive tree from the river! Surely you can fix this!"

"I told you, I can only—"

"Dammit!" he yells at the sky, and he drops his head in his hands.

"Okay, listen—we can do something about this. Do I need to make a tourniquet or something?" She looks around for their one remaining pack.

"I don't think so. Just apply pressure. A *lot* of pressure."

She races to their umiak and flips it over, quickly untying their pack from inside. Then she drags the bag over and tears it open, pulling out a wet T-shirt and a roll of duct tape. There's one bottle of pre-boiled water inside. She unscrews the lid and slowly pours it over his gaping wound, picking out a few small stones embedded in his skin. He lies on his back, gritting his teeth.

She gathers his wound together, her trembling hands slick with blood. It's not a clean cut—there are pieces of his skin missing, torn away. She wraps the shirt around his leg and rips off a strip of duct tape with her teeth, wrapping it around the makeshift bandage. She sits back on her heels. The blood doesn't take long to soak through.

He props himself on his elbows, watching her apply pressure to his leg. His eyes soften. "Wouldn't that be something," he says quietly. "We're this close, and I—"

"Don't you say it," she snaps.

Holding his leg, she drops her head to his thigh. Can she heal him? She has powers over the Earth ... Are humans not also part of the Earth? She focuses on his wound, trying to conjure up the power to heal his leg, but she knows this is beyond her. She holds on to his bleeding calf and prays—pleads—with everything she has. *Don't die on me, Lucas. Please, live through this.*

Please.

FORTY-EIGHT

Lucas is asleep by the fire. His bleeding seems to be under control at the moment, but it doesn't last long when he stands. Maia has decided to let him rest for the night, which is also giving their things a chance to dry. As soon as they have a little light, she'll get him into the umiak.

And that's where they'll stay until they reach Leucothea.

She stares at the fire. She isn't sure what time it is; her watch was in the pack they lost, and the days have become so short. The original plan was to camp in the evenings versus paddling a boat down a strange river in the dark, but now they no longer have a choice. After tonight, Maia will have to allow their umiak to drift along the currents while they sleep, and hope with all that she is that Shinesho's map is correct and they're close.

She bites her nails and glances at Lucas, his face highlighted by the glow of the fire. He doesn't look good. He's lost a lot of blood, and she didn't have the right supplies to sufficiently clean his wound. She's afraid to check it, remembering something about giving a severe laceration enough time for the blood to clot. If she removes the wrapping too soon, she may encourage it to bleed again. But what if it's getting infected?

If it's infected, then there's nothing she can do. But if it's okay, removing the bandage too soon could kill him. Right?

She drops her head in her hands. This journey. *My God*. This journey has taken every last piece of her. And now, if it takes Lucas too...

The next morning, Maia helps Lucas limp to the umiak. He curls up on the floor between the benches, and she elevates his leg. She's emptied out their remaining pack of anything she could find to layer below him to keep him as comfortable as possible.

"Just hang on," she says as she pushes the boat out into the water. "We're nearly there." She hoists herself onboard and grabs a paddle, guiding them down the serenely quiet river. It's dawn, giving her just enough light to make out the water's edge. The risk of paddling down a river in the gloom is nothing compared to the risk of losing Lucas, whose life now hangs on a thread.

Days have passed—how many, Maia can't be sure.

She's lost her appetite, but she still takes brief breaks to fish and feed Lucas, who now wants nothing to do with the food. The color of his skin continues to fade, and now, patches of a strange rash have formed along his face and neck. She feeds him water, pleading with him to drink, but even this has been a time-consuming endeavor that she can no longer afford. She needs to paddle. She needs to spend every waking moment of daylight moving their boat as quickly as possible to where the river meets the sea. Every minute that passes is another minute Lucas inches closer to death.

He's spent the bulk of the last few days curled up in a ball, clenching his teeth and shivering—at times violently so—from a dangerously high fever. After all this time. All the risks they've taken breaking into abandoned homes, wading through flooded shopping malls, and living on an island of trash. One of their biggest concerns has always been avoiding an injury ... A cut. A single cut can kill.

And after all that, a *river* may be the cause of Lucas's undoing.

She keeps her focus on the tasks at hand: paddle, and pretend. Pretending is the only thing stopping her from giving up and crawling in a ball beside him. She pretends that everything's going to be okay. She pretends the raw blisters on her palms aren't so excruciating that she feels sick most of the day. She pretends she doesn't wish that Miguel was here with them. She pretends she doesn't notice the new smell wafting every so often from Lucas's leg.

It feels like she's back in her cabin again, high in the mountains of New Zealand, sitting beside her grandfather and pleading with him to stay alive. Her whispers to Lucas are exactly the same:

"You're doing great."

"I'm right here."

"Just a little more sleep, and you'll be okay."

"Please be okay."

"*Please don't leave me.*"

Darkness falls, and Maia lies beside him in the boat.

"Dear God," she pleads as her exhaustion pulls her to sleep. "The last time I uttered these words, you didn't seem to care much to listen to me. I've never asked you for much, but please, I'm *begging* you ... if you're up there, give Lucas the strength to live through this. *Please.*"

She wraps her arms around him and lays her head on his chest, falling fast asleep to the beating of his heart and the gentle rocking of their drifting umiak.

"Maia?"

She awakens to Lucas shifting beside her. A hint of light has crept back into the sky. Time to paddle.

"I'm here," she says, sitting up.

He opens his eyes, searching for her in the clouds.

"I'm right here, Lucas," she says softly, laying her hand on his chest.

His eyes focus on hers and he smiles, his teeth chattering. "I'm s-s-so cold," he says.

"I know. I have everything we own on you. It's just the fever. Hang on. We're *so close.*" Her voice cracks.

"Maia. If ... I don't make it—"

"*Stop.* You're going to make it. You're strong. Just a little while longer, and we'll get you all taken care of. Good as new." She winks, swallowing back her tears.

He smiles. His skin is like ash, the whites of his eyes drained into a deadened yellow. She grabs the cloth from the floor of the boat, fallen from his head overnight, and dips it into the river. She rings it out and places it back on his head. He moans.

"I know it's cold, but it will help with the fever." She leans down and kisses his cheek. His skin is hot on her lips. She turns away and softly peels back the layers of clothing covering him, revealing his calf. She carefully unravels the tape around his bandage and lifts the crusted brown layers of cloth. Strings of pus drape between the shirt and his wound, and there's a swollen halo of red around the gash. Bright red lines trace out across his skin.

The infection has entered his bloodstream.

She delicately lays the cloth back over his leg, swallowing the bile rising up her throat.

"How ... does it look?" Lucas's raspy voice sounds behind her.

She wipes the tears from her eyes and glances at him over her shoulder, forcing a smile. "It looks good."

He looks away. "Liar."

"Lucas." She lies down beside him. "Just ... *hold on*, okay? You can do this."

"I want to thank you again," he gasps between breaths, "for saving me back on that pirate ship. You *saved* me. I was dead inside ... But then I met you, and I found love in a dark world. Things were really incredible for a while. Don't you think things were really incredible for a while?"

She lifts herself up, holding her breath against her tears, and she nods.

"What I wouldn't give to be back in our home base in LA," he says. "Just for a night. Just the two of us, lying next to that fire, listening to the rain..." His breathing is rapid, and the smile drops from his face. "I didn't deserve you."

"Stop, Lucas. *Please.*"

He lifts his hand. "Just ... let me get this out." Grunting, he repositions himself. "I said I didn't have anything left to say, but I lied. I do have something to say, and once again, you won't like it."

She waits.

"I knew from the beginning," he says.

"Knew ... what?"

"You. *Miguel.*"

She looks away.

"I saw it growing between you two ... every day. The more I saw, the angrier I became ... and I projected that anger onto you. I'm sorry for that, Maia. It's just ... the way you looked at him..."

She glances back at him, and he smiles the saddest smile she has ever seen. He whispers, "You never looked at me that way."

"Please, *stop*—"

"I was s-s-selfish." He shivers. "I love you, Maia. I just ... couldn't imagine ... living my life without you. So I fought to keep you as my own even though I knew that maybe ... maybe you would have been happier ... with ... my brother."

"*Lucas...*" She starts to protest, but his words have ripped the breath from her lungs. She clutches her chest.

"I am *so* sorry," he gasps. "A bigger man would have loved you better ... s-s-stepped aside ... placed your happiness above his own ... But I'm not a bigger man. You always believed me to be better than I actually was."

"Okay, *stop* talking about yourself in the past tense, Lucas. You're not dead."

"Not yet," he says, panting. "But if we don't get ... to Leucothea soon ... I will be."

She climbs onto the bench and grabs her paddle. "Well, then I won't stop paddling until we get there." She glares at him from the corner of her eye. "We'll fight about this later."

"Just don't let them put me in the ground, Maia. Burn my body—"

"*Lucas*! I swear to God, if you don't stop talking, I will kill you myself."

He chuckles, then begins to cough. He coughs so hard his lips turn blue, and then he lays his head back, his body shivering in short, aggressive spurts. "Maia?"

She looks down at him, and he raises a trembling finger to his eye. He drags it down to his chest, rising and falling with his rapid breath.

"I love you too, Lucas," she says. "I always have." She looks ahead, paddling with everything she has.

After a few more hours of daylight, darkness falls, and Maia has to put down her paddle and allow the river to guide them. She crawls beside Lucas and lays her head on his chest, waiting for the moment it doesn't rise again. His heartbeat, the one she knows so well from all those nights lying beside him ... She can barely hear it now.

Maia awakens to a strange clattering cutting through the darkness. *Noise?* It's a loud noise—an unnatural noise. She lifts her head, straining to see. There's something out there. She can hear it, but she can't see a thing.

She fumbles around their little boat, now rocking side to side, and searches for the flashlight. When she finds it, she flicks it on, scanning the narrow beam across the water. They're no longer on a river. It looks like they've floated into the ocean.

The night sky to the right of them is lit behind the hills, the clouds reflecting a bright hazy light from something on the other side. Something *massive*. There's another loud and repeated clanking of metal—undeniably new and strange sounds. They're unmistakable.

"Lucas," Maia whispers, shaking him. "*Lucas!*"

"*Mmm.*" A soft moan escapes his lips.

She exhales relief. "Lucas, we're here! Lucas? We're *here...*" Her voice breaks, and she fumbles around for her paddle. When she finds it, she paddles in a panic toward the other side of the cliff. Panting, heaving, paddling with all her might, she can't get the umiak to move fast enough. "Hold on, Lucas. *Just hold on.*"

After what feels like a lifetime, the umiak turns around the bend, and Maia gasps, dropping the paddle in her lap.

A vast city of lights rises up before her. The skyscrapers are endless across the expanse, one after the next, towering high into the night sky. Their lights glitter against the water, like a carpet of stars has been dragged into the sea. Antennas Maia has only ever seen sticking out of the ocean now pierce into the clouds, their red tips flashing like the beacons that once guided her below the sea.

Tilting back her head, she begins to sob.

Two massive brick columns stand on either side of the bridge before her, supporting an immense metal blockade stretching across the river's entry into the city. An alarm bell begins to ring, echoing loudly against the night. The lights on top of each column flash, and search-lights flicker on. They scan across the water until they reach the umiak, each one landing on her.

She crawls beside Lucas and lifts him by his shoulders. His head flops against her chest.

"We've made it," she whispers. "Lucas? We're here..." She shakes him, but his head is heavy against her. "*Lucas*?!"

More lights flood across them, and the alarm bells continue to ring. It's overwhelming, but she does not look away. Sobbing so hard she can't breathe, she holds Lucas against her and lifts her hand to the sky, reaching for a light so bright that it burns.

ACKNOWLEDGMENTS

This novel was a force to be reckoned with.

It took me three years to write the first book of this trilogy, *The Weight of a Thousand Oceans*—four to publish. Since it was the first piece of fiction I had ever written, I reached out to a few people for advice and help.

This novel, however, had a life of its own. I wrote almost the entire thing in a week. It took me a year to polish and publish *The Burn of a Thousand Suns*, and most of that time, it was just me and my computer. However, there were a few souls that I turned to, and to them I'd like to give my most heartfelt gratitude.

To my husband, Rich, for your unending love, support, and listening ear. For believing in this. For believing in me. You are my best friend and the love of my life; I can't imagine doing this adventure called life with anyone else.

To my father, Phil, and stepmother, Bonnie, for your constant support and love.

To the Packmans: Elizabeth, to whom this novel is dedicated, for your enduring friendship and support. For our daily talks and your honest input and advice. For believing in me, challenging me, and loving me. And to Jesse, for believing in me so much that you bought more copies than anyone I know. You two are the family I've made, and I am so lucky to have you in my life.

To Amanda Hughes at Haint Blue Publishing, for being my friend, my confidant, and the best editor in the world. Once again, the thought, detail, and attention you put into my manuscript blew me away. And your comments are gold.

To my fantastic team of beta readers: Caroline Ansley, Barbara Semenick-Watt, Elizabeth Packman, and MJ Carstarphen. Your dedication and input made *Suns* a better story, and for that, I thank you.

And, last but not least, to my cover designer, Murphy Rae, for another spectacular cover.

BIBLIOGRAPHY

The following materials were useful to me in writing this book:

Banerjee, S. *Arctic Voices: Resistance at the Tipping Point* (Illustrated ed.). Seven Stories Press, 2013.

Brannen, P. *The Ends of the World: Volcanic Apocalypses, Lethal Oceans, and Our Quest to Understand Earth's Past Mass Extinctions* (Reprint ed.). Ecco, 2018.

Carroll, S. *The Big Picture: On the Origins of Life, Meaning, and the Universe Itself* (Illustrated ed.). Dutton, 2017.

Cozzens, P. *The Earth Is Weeping: The Epic Story of the Indian Wars for the American West* (Illustrated ed.). Vintage, 2017.

Lewis, Jon E. *A Brief Guide to Native American Myths and Legends*. Running Press Book Publishers, Updated edition 2013.

McLaughlin, Kelly. "N.Y. Sea to the Islands of Seattle: Maps show what major U.S. cities would look like if world's glaciers melted." *Daily Mail Australia.* February 9, 2015. https://www.dailymail.co.uk/news/article-2945078/U-S-maps-major-cities-look-like-submerged-hundreds-feet-water.html

Orange, T. *There There* (Reprint ed.). Vintage, 2019.

Spence, L., & Lewis, J. E. *Native American Myths and Legends*. Amsterdam University Press, 2013.

Wainwright, J., & Mann, G. *Climate Leviathan: A Political Theory of Our Planetary Future* (Reprint ed.). Verso, 2020.

Wallace-Wells, D. *The Uninhabitable Earth: Life After Warming* (Reprint ed.). Tim Duggan Books, 2020.

"What the World Would Look Like if All the Ice Melted." *National Geographic.* September 2013. Accessed online https://www.nationalgeographic.co.uk/environment-and-conservation/2017/11/what-world-would-look-if-all-ice-melted

ABOUT THE AUTHOR

Jillian Webster is a writer of dark, compelling fiction with a fantastical twist. Originally from Michigan, Jillian traveled to New Zealand on a "six-month adventure" with nothing but a backpack and a dream ... and never left. She now lives in a charming little home by the sea, tucked in a bay of rolling green hills speckled with sheep (and the occasional goat).

You can find her most days with her head in the clouds and her fingers on a keyboard. When not writing, she enjoys yoga, cooking, and hiking in the pristine New Zealand bush with her husband and their dog.

The Forgotten Ones is Jillian's debut fiction trilogy.

Stay connected: jillianwebster.com